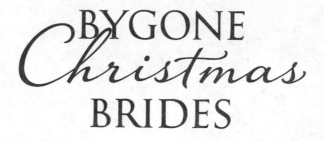

BYGONE *Christmas* BRIDES

Six Stories of Old-Fashioned Christmas Romance

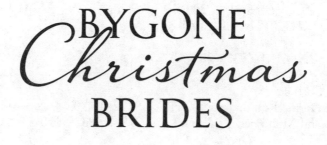

BYGONE *Christmas* BRIDES

Ginny Aiken, Carla Gade,
Pamela Griffin, Tamela Hancock Murray,
Jill Stengl, Gina Welborn

BARBOUR BOOKS

An Imprint of Barbour Publishing, Inc.

Lost and Found ©2006 by Ginny Aiken
'Tis the Season ©2013 by Carla Olson Gade
I Saw Three Ships ©2006 by Pamela Griffin
Colleen of Erin ©2006 by Tamela Hancock Murray
A Right, Proper Christmas ©2006 by Jill Stengl
Mercy Mild ©2013 by Gina Welborn

Print ISBN 978-1-68322-289-7

eBook Editions:
Adobe Digital Edition (.epub) 978-1-68322-291-0
Kindle and MobiPocket Edition (.prc) 978-1-68322-290-3

All scripture quotations are taken from the King James Version of the Bible.

Published by Barbour Books, an imprint of Barbour Publishing, Inc., P.O. Box 719, Uhrichsville, OH 44683, www.barbourbooks.com

Our mission is to publish and distribute inspirational products offering exceptional value and biblical encouragement to the masses.

ecpa Member of the
Evangelical Christian
Publishers Association

Printed in the United States of America.

Contents

Lost and Found by Ginny Aiken. 7

'Tis the Season by Carla Gade. 69

I Saw Three Ships by Pamela Griffin. 135

Colleen of Erin by Tamela Hancock Murray 201

A Right, Proper Christmas by Jill Stengl 267

Mercy Mild by Gina Welborn 333

Lost and Found

by Ginny Aiken

Prologue

"I f I might be so presumptuous, sir," Joseph, Mervyn Gwynne's some-time secretary said, "begging pardon, of course. It is sheer folly to permit a daughter to evade her duty."

Mervyn sighed. Why did Joseph pick the worst moments to discuss ticklish matters? This latest episode of gout was his most debilitating yet, and he had no interest in mental calisthenics.

"I've told you more times than I can be bothered to count," he replied, "that Rhiannon is not evading her duty. She is in Cardiff to help my dear sister with those three hooligans Deirdre is raising."

"Humph!"

The snort didn't bode well for Mervyn's current misery. Joseph was nothing if not tenacious.

"The girl belongs at your side, sir. I'm certain Miss Deirdre—er—Mrs. Wylie can avail herself of the aid of any disadvantaged young woman from Cardiff. I'm certain many of those can be found there. Of course, Mrs. Wylie could always tame the little beasts herself."

"She's in the family way again, Joseph. And my sister has always been delicate. She needs help, and Rhiannon loves the little ones—who are not beasts, as you well know. They're merely healthy youngsters, who, by the way, dearly love Rhiannon as well."

"Everyone loves Rhiannon, if I might say so myself." Joseph's squared jaw resembled a rock cliff. "But Cardiff, sir! The girl has likely lost every sense of who she truly is and from where she comes. I fear life in the big city has led her to put on all kinds of airs and affectations."

Mervyn tried to ease his left side but winced at the jab of pain. He shook his head. "She was still the sweet, spirited young woman I've always known the last time I visited."

"But that was nearly a year ago now. You couldn't join the family this past Easter, could you?"

"You're right. We had trouble at the mine at that time, and I could not leave. The last time I saw Rhiannon was, indeed, last Christmas."

"And we're now in the month of October. Our Lord's birth is almost upon us again. The girl should be here with you."

"Enough, Joseph!" Mervyn slid down his pillows to lie flat on the bed. "I'm in misery and don't wish to discuss this any further. I see no reason to drag my daughter back here where the mine and the accidents that happen too often filled her with fear all those years ago."

"She must face reality. She's no longer a child, and life is fraught with dangers—"

"I said enough, man. I intend to spend Christmas in Cardiff with her, as usual."

Joseph humphed again. "Should this curse of gout allow you."

"If the good Lord sees fit for me to travel."

Mercifully, Joseph didn't counter Mervyn's sentiment. The stubborn man left the room, and Mervyn turned to prayer. After a good long while of communion with his heavenly Father, he slept again.

⁂

A fortnight after Joseph's harangue on Rhiannon's supposed duties, Mervyn, in a mite less pain, thought the matter put to rest. He'd been making progress with his recovery, the mine had been running smoothly, and all seemed as normal as his life ever became. But he'd conveniently forgotten Joseph's unpredictability.

After the man regaled Mervyn with the latest details of that day's affairs at the mine, had him sign those documents that required his signature, and listened to Mervyn's directions regarding other matters of importance, he paused in the doorway to the room.

"Yes, Joseph?" Mervyn inquired.

"Ahem!"

Yes, he'd suspected trouble lay ahead. The throat clearing now confirmed the suspicion.

"I'm afraid I have bad news."

"No surprise there, my man."

Joseph frowned but didn't comment. "Since the most acute phase of your malady has passed, and we've seen to all urgent mine matters,

I fear I must leave for an inexact length of time—but I should be back for Christmas."

Mervyn raised an eyebrow at the implied length of Joseph's absence. "I do wish you'd come up with an exact length of time the next time you must leave. To vary the routine, you understand."

Joseph's frown deepened, and Mervyn fought to stifle a laugh.

"Well, you see, sir," the secretary said with extraordinary dignity, "it's about an emergency. How can a man ever gauge how long it might take to attend to one? Surely you do understand."

"This is hardly your first such emergency, my man. I've grown accustomed to your comings and goings."

The secretary wrung his hands. "But it truly is a matter of urgency, sir. I have a duty there, but I assure you, I would never think to shirk my duty to you, either. Still, I must indeed see to this situation."

Joseph's agitation, as always, was sincere.

Mervyn sighed and realized how often he did so around Joseph. The man seemed to invite much sighing and required great forbearance. "I do understand. I've never known you to be anything but responsible, and I suppose you do have a private life of some sort. I cannot imagine you to be any less responsible there."

"So may I have the time?"

"What good would it do me to deny you?"

Joseph's gray eyes widened. "Oh dear, Mr. Mervyn. You surely don't mean you've changed your mind and have decided to keep me here, do you?"

"Of course not. I've yet to deny a needy soul. And if you aren't the epitome of one—at least at this moment—then I don't know what one is."

"Thank you, Mr. Mervyn. I do thank you from the bottom of my heart."

In a whirl of paper and brown flannel, Joseph fled the room. Mervyn laughed out loud. Joseph's pattern of behavior was so regular, or perhaps it was more that Joseph and his doings were so regularly irregular, that Mervyn couldn't fault the man this time. He did, however, wonder.

What did Joseph do while he took off to see to one of his "emergencies"? He sighed—again. He doubted he would ever know.

Chapter 1

T hat's a lovely portrait, Miss Meggie-moo," Rhiannon told her little cousin. "Now, how would you like to tell me who is in it?"

The strawberry-blond child nodded and smiled. "This one's Mama"—she pointed at one stick-and-blob figure with a great deal of plum stuff smeared over it—"and this one's Papa"—this one had gray instead of the plum—"and these are we."

The "we" wore splotches of various shades over their irregular physiques, but they all shared one characteristic. None could be recognized in any way. But that might be expected when the artist was a whopping five years of age.

"You are one very talented miss," Rhiannon declared.

Meggie beamed.

Rhiannon gave the girl a one-armed hug. Gwynneth, Meggie's younger sister, lay sprawled over Rhiannon's other arm, her expression angelic despite her earlier bout of fretfulness. It seemed the baby was in the miserable process of cutting teeth, and nothing short of absolute exhaustion appeared to help soothe her.

"Are you gonna hold 'er like that all day?" demanded Dafydd, the fiery, carrot-orange-haired three-year-old. "I wanna build a fortress."

"It seems to me, young man, that time has come for your afternoon nap."

"Nooooooo. . ."

The boy ran toward the nursery door, but Meggie tackled him around the ankles and the two tumbled to the floor in a wild tangle of arms, legs, and giggles.

Rhiannon laughed. Without rousing the sleeping eighteen-month-old, she stood and took the baby to her crib. She tucked a whisper-soft wool blanket around the sturdy body, ran a finger over the silky cheek, and hurried back to the free-for-all in the other room.

She clapped her hands, but the two continued in their puppylike play. A smile curved her lips. The little scamps had stolen her heart the moment she'd laid eyes on them at birth. She'd always wished for younger siblings, but the Lord hadn't blessed her parents with any other children.

And then, when she turned sixteen, her mother died of influenza. Papa had been inconsolable and Rhiannon couldn't stem her own tears, much less help him. Her father had, of course, been in no condition to care for a young lady, especially since he bore all the burden of running his mine.

Just three months before Mama went to meet her Lord in heaven, Auntie Deirdre had married. Everyone expected her and Uncle Owen to have children immediately, so it was decided that Rhiannon should live with the newlyweds as they awaited the blessed arrivals. That way, she'd be ready to help her aunt, whose health had always been considered delicate, at the appropriate time.

But the Lord didn't see fit to bless her aunt and uncle with children for another three years. During that time, Rhiannon became educated, and she and her young aunt had become the dearest of friends, almost inseparable. Then the stream of rambunctious little cousins flowed forth. Rhiannon loved every single moment she spent with the children.

But enough was enough. "Come along, you two. It's time for a nice, long nap now. Go on—to bed with you both. Cousin Rhiannon has loads to do this afternoon."

The usual grumbles followed, but Rhiannon remained firm. After a few more minutes of the expected wheedling, the children marched off to their beds. Rhiannon ran downstairs, hoping Auntie Deirdre felt well enough to have tea downstairs instead of up in bed.

She found her father's much-younger sister in the parlor, a tufted footstool under her swollen ankles.

"I'm so glad to see you here!" Rhiannon hugged the lovely blond. "Is today a better day for you?"

"The nausea isn't as fierce as it's been," Deirdre said, relief in her voice. "But these ankles—I now know quite well how a sausage feels."

"Oh, Auntie, I'm so sorry for all this."

Deirdre smiled. "Just think of the blessing at the end of my time.

13

That is all I'll let myself consider."

"And rich blessings your little ones are, too." The pillow under Deirdre's right arm seemed flat, so Rhiannon reached down to adjust it. "That pillow doesn't look very comfortable," she said. "Let me fluff it up for you."

Deirdre smiled, Rhiannon fluffed, and the two women discussed details of the meals for the following week.

A short while later, Mrs. Llewellyn, the Wylies' housekeeper, came into the pleasant room. " 'Fraid I must interrupt. We've a stranger at the door, here to see Miss Rhiannon, he says."

Rhiannon frowned. "A stranger? A *man*? Me?"

The dour housekeeper nodded.

"Goodness!" Deirdre exclaimed. "Who could it be?"

Mrs. Llewellyn shrugged. "Won't know if you don't go see."

Many times over the years, Rhiannon had longed to have a private chat with the sometimes insolent woman. But because the housekeeper did run the house so smoothly, she'd refrained from speaking out about the unpleasant attitude. Today, with Deirdre so beset by the troubles of pregnancy, she was again sorely tempted. She bit her tongue, however, and waited until Mrs. Llewellyn returned to her kingdom in the kitchen.

Deirdre tried to rise.

"Oh no, you don't, my dear," Rhiannon chided. "Don't even give it a thought. I'll take care of this matter myself. And it shouldn't take long. I can't imagine what anyone would want with me."

"Be careful, Rhiannon. You never know who might concoct an odd ruse with which to distract you. He may have evil motives, you know."

"I understand, Auntie, but I also know the Lord goes with me wherever I go. He'll fight my battle for me."

"If you wish, you can show the gentleman here into the parlor. There's always safety in numbers."

"If I feel the need, I surely will."

In the entry, the closed front door surprised her. Mrs. Llewellyn's blatant disdain of Rhiannon's caller made her chuckle—laughing was better than letting irritation rule. The woman did have a way about her, one Rhiannon didn't understand, much less appreciate, but she preferred to view matters in a humorous light whenever possible.

She opened the heavy wooden door. "Joseph!"

Her father's—exactly what *was* Joseph? Her father's secretary? Valet? Manservant? What did Joseph do?

Oh, it didn't matter, did it? "What—"

"Hello, Miss Rhiannon."

"What are you doing here in Cardiff?"

"Ahem!" He yanked off his hat and twirled the plain brown head topper in his hands by the brim. "I—ah—had business here. How are you, miss?"

Rhiannon knew all too well about Joseph's tendency to come and go—mostly go—as he wished. He sometimes left Papa in a bind at the mine office.

"I'm fine, as you can see for yourself." She couldn't get him to meet her gaze, and so she feared the worst. "Is—is Papa well? Oh, please tell me he's not—not. . ."

"Goodness, Miss Rhiannon! Don't even entertain such a notion. Your papa is. . .as well as can be expected."

"Joseph! Speak and tell me the truth. I beg you. You've never been one for half answers and vague ramblings. Don't start now. What is wrong with Papa?"

"Well. . .Mr. Mervyn *is* beset by another episode of gout, miss. He is in. . .*some* pain. Gout is a painfully miserable condition."

"Oh dear. I'm afraid I don't know much about it, Joseph. I do know Papa has these spells every so often. Is it serious?"

"Well, miss, the pain does fell him. He must take to bed since he becomes quite incapacitated by the disease."

"Incapacitated!" Rhiannon's pulse pounded in her temples. "Why didn't you send for me? Why didn't you fetch me sooner?"

Again Joseph averted his gaze. "You must know what an unassuming man your dear papa is. He would never wish to impose on you—"

"How can you say that? Papa would never impose on me. I'd consider it an honor and would love to care for him."

A strange, satisfied smile burst onto his face. "As I told him you would at each of the previous occasions. But he feels that to alert you to his medical woes would only trouble you with his misfortune. And, of course, he always mentions your fear of the mine as a reason to leave you be."

Guilt brought tears to Rhiannon's eyes. "Does he think I'd be so selfish as to put my fear before him?" A sob rose to her throat. "Oh, Joseph. Please tell me this isn't so."

For a moment, distress seemed to flit over Joseph's nondescript features. Then the slender man squared his bony shoulders and met her gaze. "He entertains no such notion, Miss Rhiannon. Still, I knew you'd want to know just how the man is faring. After all, you've always been a good Christian girl, and the dear Lord does call children to honor their parents."

"Oh, I do, I do, Joseph." She dabbed at her eyes with her lace hanky then squared her own shoulders. "My mind is made up. Even though Auntie Deirdre is in a bit of a difficult time, she does have Uncle Owen. Oh, and Mrs. Llewellyn, too, in spite of her temperament. Papa has no one."

"Ahem!" Joseph tipped his chin upward. "He does have me, miss."

"Of course, Joseph. But it's just not the same thing. I'm his daughter, and you—you're his—his. . ."

"Precisely!" He tugged his lapels straight. "So what is your plan, Miss Rhiannon?"

"Goodness, Joseph! I have scarcely learned the news, and you want me to have a plan ready-made?" She shook her head. "Aside from going to his side, I'm not sure what I'll do. I suppose I'll figure it out as I go."

He didn't seem satisfied, but Rhiannon couldn't do a thing about that. Right now, she had packing to do, a delicate aunt to upset with the news about her brother, sweet children to sadden at the departure of their adult playmate, and her own comfortable routine to disrupt.

But it was all for a worthwhile cause. Papa needed her. Even if he still lived near the mouth of that murderous hole in the ground. She would have to trust God to keep underground accidents at bay. She could never bear to witness the grief and turmoil the families of the miners suffered with each loss.

And there was—

But no, she couldn't think about *him*.

Why did God have to let tragedies happen? They touched so much. Even the heart and hopes of a young girl—the young girl she'd been when she vowed never to return to the village. Tragedy touched even the choices she made later in life.

She feared it always would.

Chapter 2

Rhiannon didn't know quite what to think when she walked out of Papa's room. She'd arrived only a scant fifteen minutes earlier and had rushed to see him. She'd expected to find him wan and racked by the pain. Instead, she'd seen the same Papa she always saw, a robust, hearty man, rosy-cheeked and cheerful, if indeed sore from the gout.

He, in turn, had been stunned to see her. Happy, yes, but stunned nonetheless. She never liked to think the worst of others, but she had to wonder if Joseph had lied to her about Papa's condition. He wasn't in agony, much less on his deathbed, as Joseph's vague hints and evasiveness had suggested.

Rhiannon had found his behavior odd for the usually straightforward if not blunt man, and in light of Papa's real condition, she found it outright bizarre.

She leaned against the bedroom door. The house was familiar, and she felt as though she'd wrapped a warm, comfortable blanket around her. But the village. . .

Arriving had brought back memories she'd tried hard to suppress. But she hadn't been able to do so. They'd come at her with a life all their own. As she'd ridden in the carriage, she'd tried not to look out at the cottages that filled the village. Many of them sheltered miner families, and too many of those families had lost loved ones in the mine.

That accursed hole in the ground.

Her stomach roiled just at the thought. The sound of the widows' wails, the sobs of the orphans it created, rang in her heart. How could anyone with any sense go down there? How could any woman tie herself to a man who did that kind of work day after day after day? How could anyone live with the risk?

Over all the normal sounds inside the family home, and despite its thick walls, she could still hear the pumping of the machines that made the colliery work. They emitted a relentless pulsation, and it felt to her the beats counted out the number of men whose lives it had taken, those men whose lives it had yet to take.

It wasn't loud, but rather hushed, like death itself.

"Well, hello there!"

The deep male voice startled her back from her somber thoughts. Rhiannon looked up and couldn't prevent a gasp. "Tre–Trefor?"

"Indeed. And you must be my little friend Rhiannon, all grown up."

The light in his warm brown eyes reflected more than memories of the young girl who'd tagged along behind him. She suspected her own eyes were full of appreciation for her champion and hero. He seemed to like what he saw.

To her dismay, she liked what she could see, as well. Tall and broad-shouldered, Trefor resembled the youth she remembered in the clean-cut lines of his attractive features, the curve of his smile, and the confident way he carried himself. The former, however, had been a boy. This was a man.

"Cat nab your tongue, then?" he asked, humor in his words.

"Silence surely is unusual for me, don't you think?"

"There is a truth, indeed."

His gaze never left her face, and Rhiannon felt her cheeks go hot. Her fair skin would reveal every hint of her discomfort. But there was nothing she could do about it.

Before she could respond, Trefor asked, "What would be bringing you back? I understood you'd vowed, back when you were all of sixteen, that you'd never be setting foot in the village again."

Rhiannon shrugged. "Circumstances change. Papa is ill. I felt the need to be at his side."

Trefor looked puzzled. "But this isn't his first spell of gout. And you've never troubled yourself to return before."

Her blush turned fiery. "And just who made you judge of my choices, Trefor Davies?"

"Not judging, I am. Just repeating what I've heard."

She still sensed the sting of judgment. "And what is it to you if I come or go? My father does understand me."

"We're all after understanding your fears, and everyone respects the dangers in the mine, but we cannot comprehend why you'd be leaving your father and your home. It's not as if you've ever needed to deal with the mine itself."

"Does compassion count for nothing with you? I've seen too many women and children torn to shreds by the pain of their loss. My own mother never forgot the loss of her father and brother. I cannot bear to see more of that."

Trefor's expression changed, but Rhiannon couldn't quite read what it revealed. Then he asked, "What is making this spell of gout so much different from the others? Why did you rush to your father's side this time when you didn't before?"

"No one ever bothered to let me know before. Joseph showed up at my auntie Deirdre's home—surprised me, to tell you true—told me Papa was ailing, and so here I am."

"So here you are. And will you be staying this time?"

Rhiannon couldn't contain the shudder. "Only so long as it takes for Papa to be back on his feet. Auntie Deirdre needs me in Cardiff. Her newest babe is due to arrive just after Christmas."

Trefor's lips pressed tight. "I see."

Rhiannon felt like stamping her foot, but she was no longer the young girl who'd followed him and fought against being dismissed by him and his friends. "I doubt you do see, but it's not for you to see, is it?"

He seemed ready to object but then changed his mind. "Will you be spending the Christmas holidays here at home, or will you be running away to Cardiff again?"

"Will you close down the colliery?"

"That is not what my job would be calling me to do. It's only your father who can be making that decision. But I heartily hope not."

"Why ever not? Do you want more men to die?"

Anger flared in his eyes. "Of course not, Rhiannon. But the men make a good wage in the mine. It's decent, honorable work that feeds and supports all those families. What would you be having them do if the mine were closed?"

She couldn't answer, so she chose the coward's way, and she knew she did just that. She changed the topic. "What brings you here today?"

He gave her a wry smile. "The mine. I'm after having my daily meeting with your father."

Rhiannon's stomach lurched. "So you really are a miner."

"And proud of it, Rhiannon. Don't you be forgetting that."

She really wished he'd chosen a different line of work. The interest she'd seen in his gaze matched the interest she felt. Not to mention that it brought back to life all the girlish feelings of adolescent love she'd once held for him.

She shook her head to dislodge the troublesome thoughts. "Ah—what do you do for Papa?"

"I'm his superintendent."

The groan slipped past her lips. "So you're responsible for the well-being and safety of the men."

He again shrugged. "I'm told I do a good job."

"I don't doubt it. But you're in and out of that pit."

"Daily."

"I see." The chat had gone on long enough. At least for her it had. "Well, Mr. Davies, it's been interesting to meet you again."

"Rhiannon?" he said in a soft voice. "Don't be forgetting the most important thing."

"What would that be?"

"The Lord goes with us into the mine, just as He goes with us to chapel on Sunday mornings."

"Then why would He leave anyone to die in the pit?"

He shook his head, a sad look on his face, nodded farewell, and then went into Papa's room.

A pity. Such a splendid man wasted and in danger deep in a hole in the earth.

⚜

What was it about that prickly redhead that still had a hold on him? Trefor shook his head. He'd been unable—or perhaps more truthfully, unwilling—to shoo her away when they were younger; and now, all these years later, he'd let her under his skin, let her rile him.

"Well?" Mervyn Gwynne asked. "Will you stay standing there like a statue, man?"

Trefor shook his head. " 'Tis sorry I am, sir. If you'll forgive me, I can be telling you about today's work."

Trefor gave his employer a clear, concise listing of the day's accomplishments and the mine's output. As usual, Mervyn complimented him on a job well done, and Trefor thanked the older man. Then, as he was about to open the door to leave, Mervyn called his name.

"Yes, sir?"

"I heard you speaking to my daughter as you came in. I do remember you always had a soft spot in your heart for my little girl, how you let her shadow you when boys your age would have sent her packing instead. What do you think of how Rhiannon has grown?"

A pang of alarm shot through Trefor. What could he tell his employer about the man's daughter? That she had always been an appealing child and had become the loveliest woman Trefor had ever seen? That he'd always had Rhiannon's memory tucked in the farthest corner of his mind? That on one or two absolutely mad occasions, he'd dared think of dangerous possibilities?

Of course not. So he blurted out, "She's certainly bigger."

Mervyn laughed. "I hardly think Rhiannon would see that as flattering."

Trefor was glad for the lowered lighting in the room. He didn't want Mervyn to see the mortification on his face. "That isn't what I was meaning, sir. But she is no longer a child."

Mervyn's eyes danced. "And she's a fine young Christian woman, well educated, gifted in the care of children, and helps run my sister's home like a fine-tuned clock. A true gem for any wise man."

Why did Trefor feel like a hound at the rear of a hunt? He edged closer to the door. "Sure I am that she is."

"Only a fool would let her go."

"Ah—certainly."

"I'm glad you're no fool, man. You do an excellent job for me. I'm proud to call you friend."

That was enough. "Heading home I should be, sir. I've practice tonight."

"For the *eisteddfod*, right?" When Trefor nodded, the door knob in his hand, Mervyn went on. "Good, good. It shall be a pleasure to hear you sing, then."

Not even the nervousness that beset Trefor each time he stood in front of an adjudicator during the traditional competition could rival the flurries of agitation he felt right then. He gave Mervyn a final nod in farewell, pulled the door shut, and left.

What did Rhiannon's return have to do with him?

More to the point, why would Mervyn ask the questions he had?

If Trefor didn't know better, he'd be thinking the older man had something in mind. Something that was never meant to be.

⁂

Mervyn dropped back onto his pillows. He chuckled. Pity Margot hadn't lived to see the results of his nudging. She would have had herself a good laugh, too.

That girl of theirs—she'd yet to bother herself with finding a man she would love and cherish and who would care for her. She wasn't so young anymore.

And Trefor Davies? A better man Mervyn didn't know.

"That was splendid, sir," Joseph said as he extricated himself from within the bowels of Mervyn's large wardrobe. "The boy isn't totally dense, and he should know to take the lead from here."

"Oh, Trefor Davies is anything but dense, and he knows perfectly well what my questions meant. I just have to wonder if perhaps my nudging won't make him react in the opposite way than we want."

Joseph tugged down his coat sleeves. "I shouldn't give it much thought, sir. It's inevitable. Anyone with eyes can see they're each other's perfect match. They might perhaps lack a certain vision, a large enough measure of discernment. The Lord surely blesses those who seek discernment. One can only hope these two find it as they mature. Goodness knows they're ripe enough already."

Mervyn shot his secretary a pointed look. "You speak of them as though they were apples hanging from a tree."

"One can see them as fruit, sir, sown by the Lord, tended by Trefor's parents, you, your sadly mourned wife, and your dear sister. I'd say they're now ready for the picking, if one might be so bold to say."

"Picking?"

"Of course. Picking as in picking a mate, as in picking one who will answer a call, as in picking one who will carry on a legacy of faith and tradition."

Sometimes Joseph's way of speaking left Mervyn dizzy. This line of thought threatened to do just that. "I don't quite see what Trefor and Rhiannon have to do with answering calls and carrying on legacies. I just want my daughter married, and I'm wanting me a fistful of grandchildren."

"Oh, you shall have them, sir. You shall. In due time."

Then the maddening fellow opened the door and headed out.

"Joseph!" Mervyn called. "What are you up to now?"

Joseph glanced back and, to Mervyn's eternal shock, gave him an impish wink.

Winking? Impish? *Joseph?*

"I'm off to see about some reaping," the secretary then said.

Mervyn dropped back onto his pillows, his thoughts in the usual swirl Joseph left in his wake.

When would he ever learn? It was always best to let Joseph just leave. He knew he really shouldn't try to extract answers from the bewildering man.

Joseph was Joseph, unpredictable, mysterious, and quite exasperating. But all too often, he also happened to make a great deal of sense.

Even when Mervyn couldn't quite discern it.

Chapter 3

Two days after her initial meeting with Trefor, Rhiannon lingered too long over tea in Papa's room. Trefor arrived as she was gathering Papa's plate and silverware.

He seemed as surprised to see her there as she was to be caught unaware by his entrance.

"I can return later," he told Papa.

"Nonsense, my man, nonsense. After all, you and Rhiannon are great friends from long ago. What could be more pleasant than to chat among friends?"

"Oh, but I wouldn't want to interrupt business," she said. "I'll be back in a while with that book you wanted."

"What's the hurry, Rhiannon?" Papa asked, his cheer a mite overdone. "Have a seat, both of you. It's grand to pause for a moment of rest at the end of a long day, Trefor."

Rhiannon perched at the foot of the bed, the tray at her side on top of the wool blanket. Trefor took the large armchair where Papa liked to sit and read.

Looks were exchanged.

The silence grew thick and uncomfortable.

"Ahem!"

Everyone turned to the door.

Joseph smiled. "A tea party, I see."

Trefor snorted.

Rhiannon gaped.

Out of the corner of her eye, she saw Papa's face turn ruddy, and then he coughed.

Joseph seemed oblivious to everyone's response. "Just exactly what Miss Rhiannon should be up to on a regular basis. If only a wise man would step up and make her his honorable wife."

Her mortification knew no bounds. "Joseph!"

"Would you agree with my dear sister, Deirdre, and me," Papa said to Trefor, "that with all her accomplishments and her beauty, Rhiannon should have gentlemen queued up to seek her hand in holy matrimony?"

She turned to that traitor. "Papa!"

Trefor squirmed in the large chair.

Joseph marched into the center of the room. "And although you and your lovely lady wife weren't blessed with a large brood," he said to Mervyn, "I'm certain Miss Rhiannon will make a fine breeder."

Rhiannon wailed and rose; the silver and china clinked.

Mervyn chuckled. "If you have any doubts, just take look at Deirdre, will you? She'll be having her fourth in a few months."

Fire in her belly, Rhiannon glared. "How could you both be so horrid to me? Have you no shame? You've certainly shamed me in front of Trefor."

She ran from the room, slammed the door, and somehow made her way to the library, a sheet of tears blurring her vision. How could she ever forgive Papa and that—that ratty secretary or valet or whatever Joseph was?

Auntie Deirdre, Uncle Owen, and Papa had made no secret how they felt about Rhiannon's unwed state. She knew they wished to see her "settled" in a home of her own. Trouble was, none of Owen's friends had ever sparked the slightest twinkle of interest in her.

In fact, no man she'd ever met had managed to dim Trefor's memory. To her current regret.

She collapsed into the plump settee in the far corner of the library. One thing was certain: she could never face Trefor again. Not after the disastrous encounter in the room of that meddling matchmaker father of hers.

Rhiannon sniffled into her linen handkerchief. What a dreadful situation. But at least it proved one thing. She didn't belong back here in the village. Papa seemed more than well on the road to recovery. They certainly didn't need her. First thing in the morning, she'd call that rat Joseph and have him ready the carriage for her.

She simply had to return to Cardiff.

"Oh!"

Rhiannon sat up at the soft cry. "Who's there?"

"Are you well, Miss Rhiannon?" asked Ceridwen, the new maid. "I'm after the book I—ah—well, you see, it's that I'm fond of reading, and I found a book here—"

"Help yourself," Rhiannon said. "I'm a great reader, too."

"But you weren't here for reading, were you now?"

She sighed. "No. I had to compose myself."

"It's surprised I am to find you like this. What is the matter?"

Rhiannon didn't think she could make the village girl understand. But she felt the need to talk, to let her feelings out. "I don't belong here, Ceridwen—"

"Everyone calls me Ceri, Miss Gwynne."

"And everyone calls me Rhiannon, Ceri. Please do."

"That I couldn't be doing, miss. Miss Rhiannon—will that do?"

"It'll be fine." She took a deep breath. "Papa and Joseph and Auntie Deirdre have this notion that I need to marry, and soon. It troubles them to think I might be unhappy as a spinster. But I'm not unhappy, not as unhappy as I'd be if—"

Ceri's blue eyes narrowed. "If what?"

"If I married the wrong man just for the sake of wedding."

"Would you be having a 'right' man you'd rather marry?"

Rhiannon couldn't stop the blush. "Not really."

"Ah—it sounds like you've been struggling with yourself."

"No, not me. It's just that his life isn't one I can live." Rhiannon knew she shouldn't speak so openly, but at the moment she couldn't help herself. Ceri seemed interested, and she also seemed perceptive. "Are you married?"

Ceri nodded. "Only six months."

"Who's your husband?"

"Phillip Roberts," she said, stars in her eyes. "He's a fine man, and a good worker at the mine."

"Oh." Rhiannon didn't know what more to say.

The silence grew.

Ceri frowned. "Do you know him? Are you disliking him? I assure you, Phil is a hard worker and kind and decent."

"Oh, Ceri, I don't know your Phil, and I'm certain he's all you say he is. It's just that—well, you see—he's a miner."

The blue eyes opened wide. "Ah, I see. And you are fearing the mine, then."

"An unreasonable fear," Trefor said from the door. "But I am understanding it. And also why you left your father's room."

"You must see now why I don't belong here. The mine is bad enough. But then Papa. . ." She shook her head. "And we can't forget that—that troublemaker Joseph. Goodness! He's as dreadful as Papa."

Trefor winced. "Heavy-handed they were."

Rhiannon squared her shoulders. "You'd best run, Trefor. You might find yourself hog-tied and wed if you don't. Those two are a frightening force."

Alarm looked comical on Trefor's face, but Rhiannon was in no mood for humor. She headed for the door. "You can come or you can go as you please, Trefor Davies. It's your business what work you do and how often you meet with my father. As for me, I'll be leaving first thing in the morning. Papa is well enough, and Auntie Deirdre and the children do, indeed, need me. I refuse to stay here until the next mine disaster comes about."

"But, Miss Rhiannon!"

She stopped and glanced at the young woman. "But what?"

"What about our dear Lord? Are you forgetting Him? He's our Protector, our Guide, our Father who loves us and who'll never leave us or forsake us!"

"He's forsaken those who go into the depths of that pit." She drew a deep breath. "Call me weak, if you must. But I cannot see spending the rest of my life worried over what I'll find at the pithead, remembering what my mother went through when her father and brother died down there. I could never bring a child into a life like that, one where the Lord could forget that child's father inside the ground."

Trefor made a noise deep in his throat. "I can see that your mind is made up. You'll not be listening to reason. Good evening, Miss Gwynne. It's been—interesting, meeting up with you yet again."

Rhiannon blinked. He'd tossed the words she'd spoken back at her. *Hmm. . .*

"Back home to my Phillip I'll be heading, Miss Rhiannon," Ceri murmured. Then, before she left the room, she added, "Right your father and auntie might be, worried about you. I'm not liking the mine any more than you, but I'd rather be living with faith in God and at my Phil's side than all alone but for that cold, cold fear."

Ceri's words pierced deep. Rhiannon was alone; she'd felt that way even in the midst of the bustle at Auntie Deirdre's very full home, no matter how much she loved her aunt and the children, no matter how much they loved her. Was she ready to face an empty future?

And why should Trefor care so much how she felt about the mine? Did he—could he possibly be in with Papa and Joseph in their tiresome meddling? Could the interest she thought she'd seen in his eyes have meant something?

Surely not.

And had Ceri meant to say that Rhiannon's faith was lacking? True, she couldn't trust that the mine wouldn't explode, cave in, and kill more men. How could she trust the God who'd let that happen so many times before?

⁂

"He wasn't any happier than she was, was he?" Mervyn mused.

Joseph shook his head. "Perhaps we did push her a bit far."

"But they're stubborn and blind." Mervyn felt another cough build up in his chest. "Please fetch me some fresh water, Joseph. I've been fighting a wretched tickle in my throat all day."

The secretary left the room, and Mervyn tried to get comfortable. He was more than tired of his bed. He'd been feeling fairly well of late, but once Rhiannon arrived, he'd realized that the only way to keep her in the village was to continue his recovery at a slower pace than it truly called for.

He was heartily sick of pillows and blankets and the boredom of his room. He wanted to return to his office, return to his men.

But he had a duty to see his daughter settled, and he wouldn't let up until that day came to pass.

Joseph walked in and set a pitcher of cool water on the small chest at the right side of Mervyn's bed. "Here you are."

"Thank you." He took a deep drink then met his friend and secretary's gaze. "Do you think we went too far?"

"You know as well as I do that the good Lord has a plan for His children."

"Of course I know that. And as far as that daughter of mine and my superintendent are concerned, that future is one full of the love and joy that come with a family."

"I couldn't agree with you more."

Mervyn's cough lasted longer this time than the last. "I'm afraid I've come down with some silly new—thing. And just when we're making progress with Rhiannon and Trefor."

"It's just as well that you're abed and stay there, sir."

Mervyn smiled. "I like the way you think, Joseph. Oh, indeed, there will be love and joy for Trefor and Rhiannon. And the grandbabies will be for me to spoil."

Joseph nodded sagely. "And we'll trust the Father to deal with Miss Rhiannon's extraordinary fear—"

"Unreasonable fear, you mean."

Joseph shrugged. "In either case, we'll have to trust the Father to heal her fear of the mine."

"The only thing that keeps our lovely future at bay."

Chapter 4

Trefor wished Rhiannon hadn't come back. During the time she'd been gone, he'd worked to persuade himself that his feelings for her years ago had been only those of a childhood friend. But at the back of his mind, one detail always remained. Rhiannon, at sixteen, had been the same age some village girls were when they married or even bore children.

And he'd been working in the mine for a while by then; at eighteen he'd done the work of a man, just like any other miner.

Still, he'd tried. And he'd almost succeeded. Until he saw her in the hall the other day. Then he'd known he'd always have strong feelings for Rhiannon Gwynne, and it didn't matter how much effort he put in to change that fact.

His feelings had nothing to do with her natural beauty. The silky, golden-red curls and green eyes were wonderful to look at, as were the delicate face and her feminine figure, but what most caught his eye was the vibrant energy that seemed to surround her. She made him think of a magnet. He was the helpless bit of steel.

He feared he wouldn't be able to resist her appeal if she stayed much longer. And losing his heart to her would be a terrible mistake.

She hadn't overcome her fear of the mine.

He still was a miner.

How could those two facts ever be reconciled?

As always when a problem seemed too great, Trefor turned to God for strength, wisdom, and guidance. He fell to his knees and prayed.

And not just once.

He prayed often and would continue to pray until the good Lord saw fit to give him the answers to the questions he'd asked today.

When Rhiannon went to bid her father good-bye early the next day, she carried with her a certain amount of fear. She didn't want to see the disappointment on her father's face when he realized she wouldn't stay. She also didn't want to discuss her fear of the mine.

But what met her when she entered the room sparked fear much greater than what she'd brought with her. Papa was ill. Much more so than when she'd first arrived.

Papa's eyes watered, his cheeks burned red, his breath wheezed, and when he tried to speak, a fit of coughing cut off the words before they even began.

The fever, the rough breaths, and the misery he obviously felt took Rhiannon back a number of years. Yes, she'd been young then, but nothing would make her forget her mother's fight against a particularly virulent case of the influenza. In a short time, Mama had lost her fight.

Papa couldn't die; he just couldn't.

Of course, she wouldn't even think again of a return to Cardiff, at least not until Papa was back on his feet. Auntie Deirdre would make out well enough with the help of her housekeeper and husband, and surely the three of them would find a young woman to take Rhiannon's place.

She, on the other hand, couldn't leave Papa's care in the hands of the unpredictable and mysterious Joseph. What did he know of nursing? Would he even know to call a doctor to see to Papa's care?

She doubted he would. So she simply had to stay.

She'd deal with her feelings—for the mine, as well as those for the mine superintendent—once she had her father back on the road to health.

"Joseph!" she called out the door. "Please come to Papa's room. I need your help."

Not only did Joseph run in, but Ceri also appeared, her fair skin flushed, her blond hair bouncing in its knot atop her head. Mrs. Devane, the Gwynnes' longtime housekeeper, followed, hampered by her generous girth and advancing age.

"What is wrong?" Joseph asked as he came to a stop.

"Papa's ill—again!"

"Oh dear!" Ceri cried. "What would you be needing for him, miss? How can I be helping you?"

"Goodness gracious!" Mrs. Devane clucked. "Mr. Mervyn, I was warning you the other day. That walk you were taking to that office of yours downstairs didn't do you much good."

Rhiannon frowned. "I thought he'd been abed for weeks."

"He had," the plump lady said. "Needing his papers, he was saying. As if a paper would be doing him any good."

Papa pushed himself up on one elbow. "All of you," he said, his voice a croak, "take your blathering somewhere else! Can't a man get a minute's rest here?"

Another series of coughs punctuated his peevish words. Then he fell back onto the pillows, rolled over, and closed his eyes. "I need to feel useful," he added with a shiver, as if chilled.

Rhiannon gestured the others from the room. "You'll be far more useful if you take the time to truly get well." She tucked the blanket around his shoulders. "I'll come back with some tea and toast in a bit. Rest now."

She dropped a kiss on his head then left the room. The others had waited for her in the hall. Although she'd never dealt with anything more serious than the occasional nursery upset tummy and sniffles and scrapes, Rhiannon knew she had to act.

"Joseph, I need you to fetch Papa's doctor. I don't think old Dr. Gruffud is still available, is he?"

"No, but his son, young Dr. Gruffud, would be happy to come. He's been treating your papa's gout."

"Then please go fetch him." To the two women, she said, "We'll be needing plenty of plain food, easy for him to eat. I should think his throat hurts from all those coughs."

Mrs. Devane nodded, lines drawn by worry on her brow. "Not liking the looks of him, Miss Rhiannon."

"I'm not, either. Reminds me of—"

"Of your dear mama, all those years ago."

Rhiannon nodded. Her eyes burned with tears that threatened to spill. But she couldn't let them. She had Papa to think of. His health had to come before anything else.

She turned to the young maid. "Could you perhaps heat a stone for his feet, Ceri? Please watch that you wrap it well. We don't want to burn him."

"There is good, Miss Rhiannon. He will surely be sweating out the illness then."

Rhiannon only nodded. If only influenza were a matter of sweating out a bit of a cold. It was a serious disease, one that had killed, even those who had been healthy and well before it struck its nasty blow, and the gout had weakened Papa.

She wrote a brief note to her aunt, alerting her of Rhiannon's uncertain return date. Joseph took the envelope with him when he went after Dr. Gruffud.

The wait for their arrival proved more difficult than Rhiannon would have thought. She found refuge in Papa's office with a good book and warm blanket, since the weather had turned colder overnight.

The doctor's diagnosis didn't surprise her. Papa did, indeed, have influenza. Everyone in the household was at risk. They could all come down with the dread disease, but Papa would still need care. Rhiannon knew it wouldn't be easy, but she promised the doctor she would do her best.

Papa had fallen asleep by the time the doctor left. Rhiannon returned to the office, but this time, the book did nothing to hold her attention. Although she tried to pray, her fears and the memories of Mama stole any vestige of peace she might have found. As the sun was setting, Ceri came into the room and lit a fire in the broad hearth.

"You surely will be catching the influenza if you put off caring for yourself," she chided Rhiannon. "Much good you'll be doing your papa then."

"Thank you, Ceri. You're right. The room is chilly, even though I hadn't noticed. I wrapped myself in my wool blanket and spent hours trying to pray."

A wise pair of blue eyes assessed her. "Thinking yourself sick is silly, right?"

She sighed. "You're right. But I feel the Lord's left me. I don't think He hears me pray."

Ceri hurried to Rhiannon's side. "Having to help you with that, me."

The young woman took Rhiannon's icy hand and, in a soft voice, led them in a loving conversation with their Lord.

The opening door interrupted their prayers.

"Sorry," Trefor said. "I didn't realize anyone was here."

Rhiannon turned aside and wiped her tears with a quick flick of her hand. She didn't want him to see her weep.

"Did you come to see my father?" she asked, wrapping herself in her pink blanket again.

"Wanting to talk to him about the mine like every other day," he said.

Before Rhiannon could stop her, Ceri slipped out the door. She sighed. Perhaps this encounter with her childhood hero would go better than the last one had. "Papa's taken ill again, Trefor. We had young Dr. Gruffud out here earlier. He said it was the influenza."

Trefor shook his head. "Not good—"

"Don't do that!" she cried. "Don't you be counting him for dead, Trefor Davies! I'm here, and I'm going to make sure he recovers."

Something lit his expression, and to Rhiannon it looked like admiration. *Oh my!*

"Good for you," he said. "But now I must be seeing him about the mine."

She crossed her blanket-covered arms as her anger began to rise. "Did you not hear what I just told you? Papa is ill. You are not taking into that room the worries and troubles of that miserable mine. How do you expect him to heal if you fill his head with all that?"

"That miserable mine, as you call it, is feeding a whole village full of families. It cannot just go idle, waiting for your papa to get well."

Rhiannon recognized the truth of Trefor's words. But she couldn't let him trouble her ailing father. "Very well. Because of those families, the mine must run. But I don't much care how it goes about it."

His red cheekbones said she'd piqued his temper. "You would be caring if it meant the next meal on your children's table."

"Then if you're so passionate about the murderous thing, run it yourself. Surely as Papa's superintendent, you know what must be done. Go ahead. Do it. Just don't be troubling Papa while he's abed."

He looked ready to argue but then seemed to think better of his initial impulse. "I still need information, and since it isn't mine to do as I wish, I can't be doing just anything I think of on my own. Decisions must be made—"

"You are an honorable man, Trefor," she said in a calmer voice. "I understand you don't want to overstep your bounds, but Papa—Papa could die if he doesn't get the rest he needs. I saw Mama die of this cursed disease. I'll do whatever I must to see that he doesn't do so, as well."

Trefor remained an unmovable wall.

Rhiannon took a deep breath. "Fine. If you're unwilling to make the decisions yourself, then have patience with me. I'll use whatever sense the Lord gave me and make those decisions until Papa can do so for himself again. I'll take all the responsibility myself."

The alarm on Trefor's face solidified her decision. "I know what you're thinking," she said. "You think I'm not capable of running the mine. But you're wrong."

Had she really said those words? Was she out of her mind? "Well, if you'll just give me a chance to understand what it takes to keep it running, I'll show you I can. With your experience in that hideous black hole and my common sense, I'm certain we'll do as well as Papa and you have done."

Had Rhiannon been an innocent bystander, and Trefor reacting to someone else's words, she surely would have found his increased horror humorous. But since it was directed at her and her earnest efforts, it only served to spur her along.

"I find your response insulting," she said on her way to the door. "And it's certainly far from humorous—should it be your feeble attempt at humor. And now, if you'll excuse me, I have a great deal I still must do."

She left the room, head high, shoulders firm, spine straight. Her exit would have been dignified and majestic had she not been swaddled in the silly pink blanket from her bed.

Instead of dignified, however, she only managed to look absurd. All those masses of thick, warm fabric got tangled around her ankles, so rather than glide away with grace, she lurched and staggered down the hall.

A male chuckle followed in her wake.

Chapter 5

Her intentions had been good. The results, however, weren't.
Trefor hadn't wanted to take over the mine operations, but when Rhiannon decided she would make the decisions he didn't dare make and her ailing father couldn't, he'd known he was in for a rough time.

He'd had no idea how rough.

To his every question, she'd replied, "What do you think?"

When he reminded her she'd agreed to decide, she'd said, "Very well. If you don't have any ideas, then you'll just have to shut down the mine. That's my decision."

In the end, she'd had her way—of sorts. He'd taken over the day-to-day running of her father's mine and made each and every decision needed. But Trefor had also won one minor victory. He'd made her listen to each one of his decisions, to every last trouble he'd encountered. His conscience had demanded that at least one Gwynne knew the workings of the mine.

Not that she'd cared. She'd focused all her attention on her father's health. And Trefor had been unable to fault her for that. He understood her love for Mervyn.

To Trefor's relief, Mervyn did begin to recover from his bout of influenza. As serious a disease as it was, it appeared the man would beat it. But not soon enough for Trefor. Especially since Mervyn wanted nothing to do with the business that, up until now, had meant more to him than anything but his daughter.

Now he wanted Trefor to run the colliery. Trefor couldn't understand the man's reasoning.

"Of course you can do it, my man," Mervyn insisted each time Trefor hesitated to take action without the older man's input. "You did quite well while I couldn't even raise my head. Besides, it's the perfect time for a younger man to take the reins. I'm getting old. All I want now is time to spend with Rhiannon and those grandchildren she'd better hurry and give me."

That bothered him more than just about anything else. Each time Mervyn mentioned grandchildren, Trefor felt walls close around him. Had he let his most private dreams and wishes show?

On the rare occasion Trefor had allowed himself to dream, he'd thought of a future with Rhiannon at his side. He'd also dreamed of children—red-haired little ones with green eyes and charming smiles.

But reality hadn't changed. Nothing more than friendship could exist between them. The woman Rhiannon had become would never accept the love of a man like Trefor, a miner through and through. As much as she loved her father, and despite Mervyn's love for his mine, she would never consider a future at the side of the man who'd worked hard with Mervyn to implement many improvements in the mine.

Trefor would never leave his village; he belonged here. He was certain Rhiannon accepted that as fact. Just as he accepted that, at some point in the coming days, she would leave. Rhiannon didn't belong here.

The sooner Mervyn recovered, the sooner the sweet temptation of Rhiannon's presence would be gone. The longer she stayed, the more Trefor feared falling in love.

Or perhaps he'd already done that a number of years ago. The feelings he'd believed nothing more than the foolishness of an adolescent lad seemed to have returned a thousandfold the day she came home.

But he couldn't let himself love Rhiannon. Not the way a man should love his wife, not with that forever kind of love. So he continued to seek God in prayer; he asked for the Lord's help time after time after time. He couldn't fight his love for the beautiful Rhiannon on his own. And that was a battle he had to win before she left the village again.

Otherwise, she'd leave his heart the true victim of her father's ill health.

⚜

If she had to face Trefor Davies one more time, she would surely go mad. Rhiannon could scarcely turn around in her own home without running into the man. Even though Papa was well on the way to a full recovery, he still couldn't return to work. He tired too easily, and a nagging cough lingered.

Not that Rhiannon wanted him to deal with the mine again.

While everything about the colliery repelled her, she knew some of her ideas had merit. But she'd wanted Trefor to make the decisions. She'd seen a spark of—was it ambition? Desire perhaps? Whatever it might be, she'd seen it in his eyes. And since Papa had repeated more times than she cared to count how little he was ready to do about the mine just yet, she'd wanted Trefor to have the opportunity to see how capable he could be.

She couldn't let herself love him, but she could give him a future that might keep him out of the mine. If he were to run the business aboveground, then perhaps the woman he eventually married wouldn't have to fear that hole in the ground as much as Rhiannon did.

She wished. . .

But no. Rhiannon couldn't stay. No matter what. The memories of her mother's suffering after the loss of her father and brother would never go away. But she could leave Trefor with a better future than the one her mother's loved ones had.

She only wished Papa's normally robust health would hurry up and return. She had to get back to Cardiff as soon as she could. Just as she'd feared, she could no longer deny her renewed feelings for the diligent, capable man Trefor had become.

And she feared that when she left, she'd be leaving her heart behind.

⁂

November took what felt like forever to end. Rhiannon hadn't expected to still be in the village when December arrived, but there she was, Papa still weak from his battle with influenza and unable, or perhaps unwilling, to return to work even now. Had his recent serious illness shown him how fragile life could be? Had that influenced his view of working the mine?

She didn't know, but she wished he'd take a step into the future, no matter what that future held.

The weather had turned bitter. Rhiannon wrapped her wool shawl tighter around her and looked out the office window at the mountains, their tops white with the snow that fell fresh all too often these days. The sun had set hours ago, and the moon now hung in the dark sky.

If she looked just to the right of the house and toward the far end of the valley, she could see the pile of rubble near the mouth of the mine. Snow might fall and cover it, but each day men went into the earth, dug for hours, brought out the good with the bad, and added more waste to yesterday's lot. The heap served to remind her of those who risked their lives underground, even when they'd left for the day and now took their rest in the safety of their homes.

Trefor...

Even though he still ran the colliery these days, Rhiannon knew he had gone inside on any number of occasions.

"Why?" she'd asked.

"Making sure the new uprights were put in right, I was."

The chill of fear pierced her to the bone. "You went in, not knowing if the uprights supporting the mine's roof were right? You knew there was a chance they might fail and the roof cave, but you still went in?"

"You'd be wanting me to send my men in without making sure they'd be safe? What kind of man would you be thinking me?"

"A sane one."

"A coward."

"Of course not. Just a reasonable man."

"How could the men I send underground be respecting me if they knew I wouldn't do the same?"

She had no argument then. She knew he was right, but her fear remained. She had turned and left the room. He'd gone into her father's room, where they'd spent a long while engrossed in the business she... she hated.

There. She'd admitted it. She hated her father's mine. The place where the man she loved worked.

And she'd also admitted the truth of her feelings. She loved Trefor Davies. Heaven help her, since she could no longer help herself.

No matter what happened, today, tomorrow, next year—her heart would never be the same.

⚜

"Do you think we pushed too hard?" Mervyn asked Joseph after a distracted Trefor left his room. "I've been more than ready to leave this dreary room for days—no, weeks. And nothing. They still argue at every chance. Didn't you hear them before he came in here tonight?"

Joseph nodded. "Can't say for certain. But I have thought of something. I should perhaps leave for a while. That way Miss Rhiannon will be forced to do the office work she's tried to make Mr. Trefor do. She'd learn more about the colliery, of how you both work to improve the conditions and the safety of your men. Knowledge might help ease some of her fears."

Mervyn laughed. "Now there's your most inventive excuse to disappear as of yet, my man."

Joseph's expression grew even more serious. "But, Mr. Mervyn, it's the absolute truth. If she begins to work at his side—really work with him, not just shift all the work onto him—she'll see that while the colliery does have its risks, it isn't quite the man-killer she believes it to be. Besides, Mr. Trefor is a man of great faith. Perhaps he'll help her find hers again."

"It's too late now, Joseph. Perhaps you should have thought of that a week or two ago." Mervyn shook his head. "No. It's past time for me to leave this bed. Our plan is never going to work."

"Have patience," Joseph argued. "Just a little longer."

"I think you're mad, but I'll give you a few more days."

"Remember, Mr. Mervyn"—a twinkle appeared in Joseph's eyes—"there's nothing more romantic than Christmastime and all the lovely festivities that surround our celebration of the Lord's birth."

Mervyn laughed. "You are right there. Now if only we could get them to enjoy those festivities together. . . ."

⚜

"You must go in my place," Papa argued.

"But I know nothing of the local eisteddfod," Rhiannon wailed.

"You don't need to know much. You only need ears to listen and then enjoy. Besides, ours is more of a *cymanfa ganu*, a singing of hymns, than a true eisteddfod competition, where all sorts of poems and dances and songs are performed."

"But you said I needed to judge. I don't know enough about these hymns to be a fair judge—"

"You'd only be an honorary adjudicator," he cut in with a wave. "The real ones will carry the burden of deciding the winner of the singing festival."

Eventually, and with great misgivings, Rhiannon agreed to take Papa's place. And that's how she happened to be at the chapel two weeks before Christmas, seated just in front of the altar with the rest of the adjudicators.

To her surprise, she enjoyed every minute of the competition, the singing more than the few poems some had wanted to recite. Fortunately for her, her judging talents, meager as they were, would be needed only to decide the winner of the singers.

But just when she'd begun to relax, a new competitor took his place. Trefor waited until he was given the signal to start.

In Welsh rather than English, as was required at the event, his rich tenor voice flowed over Rhiannon in a way that differed from all that had come before. His song of praise rose and fell, and his love for God showed in the reverence on his face, the deep emotion in his voice.

To her dismay, Rhiannon had to acknowledge yet another trait that appealed to her. Trefor was hardworking, honest, brave—and now devout, as well. She wished she had the depth of faith he revealed with his hymn of praise. Maybe then she wouldn't feel the need to leave the village; maybe then she'd have the courage to see if what she'd thought she saw in his eyes that first day back was real.

A knot formed in her throat, and tears burned in her eyes. She loved the Lord. But did she dare. . . ? Could she really trust God? Could she leave her fears with Him and step forward into. . .*what*? What could God possibly have in store for her?

Deep inside, without making a sound, she prayed, *Father in heaven, I confess the boundaries I've put on my faith. I've let fear and cowardice rule. But I don't know how to change. How to have the kind of faith courage requires. I can't do it myself, but if You're the God of all, the King of kings, surely You can show me how—how to trust.*

Applause broke into her prayer. Her heart swelled with pride at the admiration everyone expressed for the man she loved. How she wished she were worthy of him.

But this wasn't the time to think that kind of thought. It was time to judge. And while Rhiannon tried to remain impartial, the one performer who deserved to win was—

"Mr. Trefor Davies!"

The chief adjudicator wore a broad smile as he congratulated the winner. Rhiannon's could be no less broad and bright. That night, images of Trefor filled her dreams, his voice again raised in earnest worship of his Lord.

The next day, Rhiannon spent the better part of the morning with Ceri. The two women cut, tied, and then hung bunches of mistletoe and branches of holly throughout the house. The scents and sights of the approaching holiday served to cheer Rhiannon in a way nothing else had as of yet.

"More mistletoe, Miss Rhiannon?" Ceri asked, a twinkle in her eyes.

"I'd say we've hung plenty all over the house."

"A kiss, you'll be after."

Despite all her efforts, Rhiannon blushed. "Not at all. Auntie Deirdre always fills her house with pretty greens, and I think Papa will appreciate the color when he finally comes down."

"Mmm..."

"I do mean it, Ceri. I can't wait for Papa to join me at the table again. And I want the house to feel as joyful and festive as possible."

A mischievous smile curved the maid's lips. "I'm after believing you."

Rhiannon didn't believe herself, either, but she let the matter go. At least until later when she ran into Trefor as he walked out of Papa's room.

"Good evening, Rhiannon," he said.

"And to you." Then she added, "You were wonderful at the eisteddfod. I was glad to see you win."

"I do my singing for the Lord," he said. "Glad others enjoy it, me."

"I certainly did."

They fell silent just for a moment, but then, to Rhiannon's surprise, Trefor smiled. "You'll be owing me a congratulating kiss, then."

"What?"

He pointed upward. She looked, and there, directly over their heads, hung a bunch of the greenery she and Ceri had spread all through the house. She stared, unable to think of a thing to say.

Then Trefor took matters into his own hands. She didn't have to say a word. He placed a hand on her shoulder, curved a palm against her cheek, and pressed his lips against hers.

In that one brief, tender moment, Rhiannon felt all her girlhood dreams come true. The man she loved took the time to gift her with her first kiss.

Chapter 6

Every time she thought back to that kiss, Rhiannon wanted to run and hide. Which is precisely what she did the moment Trefor pulled away.

How could she have behaved in such a silly, girlish way?

Even now, her cheeks burned at the memory of her cowardly response. Well, it wasn't her response to his kiss that had been cowardly. No, she'd enjoyed every second of that warm, tender caress.

The way she ran when Trefor whispered the most amazing words in her ear was cowardly.

"I've always loved you," he'd said.

She'd burst into tears and headed right for her bed. No amount of Ceri's cajoling had budged her. Mealtime came and went. Papa's request to join him also went unheeded. And Rhiannon did nothing but berate herself.

She'd been a fool to stay this long. She should have insisted Papa go with her to Cardiff for further medical care the moment his fever broke and he was able to travel. Now she faced a greater heartache than even she could have imagined.

Because now she knew. She knew what could be. If only. . .

But no. Nothing had changed. Trefor was still the superintendent of the mine. And she still felt the same abhorrent horror for the dangerous black hole. Who knew when it might unleash its murderous appetite again?

But now her fondest wishes were at arm's reach—for another woman perhaps. Another woman might be willing to risk the deadly possibilities in exchange for the joy of Trefor's love.

But how could she live if, after she shared in the beauty of that love, the lethal pit one day took her husband away? How could she face their children, should the Lord see fit to bless them that way?

She couldn't. Surely she'd go mad with the pain.

So she did the only thing she could. She began to pack her bags and prepared to make her escape as soon as Joseph saw fit to return.

Oh yes. That maddening man had done it again. He'd up and left one day. He'd murmured dire pronouncements of "emergencies" and "duties" and all sorts of other things. But they hadn't meant a thing to Rhiannon.

Nothing but yet another delay. Papa couldn't take on Joseph's duties in the office—whatever they might be—as well as the bit of his own work he'd started to do—at least, he'd insisted he couldn't. Rhiannon, her father had said, simply had to stay and help. There was far too much work for Trefor alone. He played on her pity, and although she felt quite certain he wasn't nearly as weak as he'd said, she had no way to prove her suspicion.

She wouldn't put it past Papa and Joseph to orchestrate the disappearance as just another way to throw her, again and again, in Trefor's path.

Which is precisely what happened one especially awful day.

"Rhiannon, dear," Papa said. "Please hand this to Trefor."

The three were in the office, a room she'd always thought of as huge. Now its walls felt far too tight around them for her comfort. She glared at the gleeful matchmaker.

"I'm sure Trefor can walk around and get it himself," she answered.

Trefor's jaw turned rock hard. "I'll be after making myself scarce, Miss Rhiannon."

"Nonsense, my boy!" Papa boomed his response with the overdone jolliness he'd adopted of late. "You're busy with those figures, and it's no trouble for Rhiannon to bring these sheets to you. Wouldn't want you to be losing track of your sums."

He stood. "I won't be forcing myself where I'm not wanted."

Something in his gaze shamed her. He'd been honest with his words of love. She, in turn, had been cowardly behind her silence—and hurtful with her evasiveness ever since.

She'd hurt the man she loved. She'd put her fears before his feelings, and this was the result. "Trefor. . ."

But he was gone.

And Papa wasn't pleased. "I hope you're satisfied," he said. "You've been more than rude to the most decent young man I know. And one who once was your dearest friend. I don't know what has happened to you, Rhiannon. Maybe Joseph was right after all. Maybe sending you to Cardiff did lead you to put on these airs and attitudes I don't admire."

Her father's words only served to make her guilt worse. But what could she say? That she loved Trefor but refused to let him know? That her fear mattered more to her than the feelings they shared? That she still felt she could never be the wife Trefor needed or he the husband she did?

No. It was better by far that Papa thought her haughty and mean. Someday she hoped she could change his mind, someday when the pain she felt now had eased to a dull ache, when she'd walked away from the love she'd dreamed of all her life.

"I'm sorry you see me like that." She left the room.

The time had come to leave for good.

But life had a way of turning her plans to nothing more than wishes. The next morning, as she sat down to a breakfast of toasted bread and tea, Joseph reappeared. But he didn't come alone.

"*Y Nadolig* is nearly here!" he exclaimed, his thin face wreathed in a wide smile. "I couldn't think of a happier way to celebrate Christmas than for the family to be complete."

He stepped aside. Uncle Owen and Auntie Deirdre, her arms stretched over her huge middle to hold baby Gwynneth close, walked in, wearing equally wide smiles. Meggie and Dafydd tumbled in behind them, their cries of greeting welcome and sweet.

Tears filled Rhiannon's eyes. "I've missed you!"

She slipped from the chair, dropped to her knees, and opened her arms wide. Meggie rushed into the hug and giggled, while Dafydd scrubbed the spot where Rhiannon smacked his cheek with a kiss.

"Ugh!" he said.

"You'll be changing that tune soon enough, my boy," Uncle Owen said. "Before you know it, you'll be looking for the mistletoe instead of letting chance catch you beneath a bunch."

Her uncle's words reminded Rhiannon of that other, more significant kiss. And the plans she'd so diligently made. Plans she could no longer carry out. Her relatives' presence in the family home made it impossible to return to theirs.

"Why—what made you come?" She turned to her aunt. "Isn't it dangerous to travel so close to your time?"

Auntie Deirdre smiled. "I don't feel any better or any worse whether I'm here or in my bed back home. So when Joseph came to deliver Mervyn's invitation, I couldn't resist. I wanted to be home by y Nadolig."

"But what if the baby comes too soon?"

"Then it comes," her aunt said. "I'm sure the Lord knows what He's about. He's been bringing babies into the world for much longer than I care to think."

An uneasy feeling started in Rhiannon's gut. "And how long do you plan to stay?"

Uncle Owen smiled yet again. "That is my surprise. I've closed the mill and given my people a holiday. We won't reopen until after Twelfth Night."

January twelfth! Rhiannon thought she'd go mad if she had to stay this close to Trefor for that long. But she couldn't let anyone know.

"I see," was all she said. When she thought she could speak without revealing her distress, she asked, "Does Papa know you're here?"

"Joseph says he's been expecting us and can't contain his anticipation," Uncle Owen said. "But we haven't been up to see him yet."

At his words, Joseph made a peculiar sound. Rhiannon slanted him a look and had to stifle a laugh. She'd be willing to venture a guess that Papa's unpredictable secretary had fabricated a tale of suggestion and hint worthy of Mr. Dickens for her relatives' sake. Papa likely knew nothing of the "invitation" Joseph had delivered.

"Ahem!" The secretary tugged on his lapels. "I'll be on my way to see if Mr. Mervyn is dressed and ready for guests."

Rhiannon chuckled. "Make sure you do *ready* him, Joseph. And do so with care. Shock so soon after his illnesses could be a dangerous thing."

She didn't specify to whom the shock might prove a danger.

Brown eyes narrowed and lips pressed down tightly. Joseph nodded then disappeared.

"That man!" she murmured.

"Oh dear," Auntie Deirdre said. "Do you think Joseph would do all this without Mervyn's knowledge?"

"I wouldn't put it past him." Rhiannon gestured toward the table. "Come on in. Join me. Mrs. Devane always has plenty of fresh bread, eggs—whatever you might want. And remind me to give Joseph a generous gift. I'm so happy to see all of you I'm about ready to give him a kiss."

"Lucky man, him," Trefor said from the door to the dining room.

Uncle Owen barked a laugh.

Dafydd repeated his earlier "Ugh!"

Rhiannon gasped, and her cheeks burned.

Meggie giggled and ran to Rhiannon's side.

Auntie Deirdre then cried, "Trefor Davies! Just look at how you've grown!"

"Thinking you have as well, Mrs. Wylie," he replied.

Deirdre patted her middle and laughed. "Can't be hiding it much longer, can I?"

His cheeks reddened, and Rhiannon knew she'd never seen a more appealing man.

"Not meaning that, me."

"But it's true," Owen said and held out a hand. "Owen Wylie, and Mr. Trefor Davies is. . . ?"

Trefor gave the hand a firm shake. "Mr. Gwynne's superintendent at the mine."

Owen's gray eyes flashed to Rhiannon and back. "I see. Good to meet you, I'm sure."

Trefor's jaw tightened, and he glanced at Rhiannon then gave a brief nod. "Having to head to the mine, me. A pleasure."

He left.

Rhiannon's shame returned, but before she, too, could make her escape, her aunt caught her eye. "So that's how things are."

She shook her head, tears too close to the edge. "I don't know what you mean—"

"I'm sure that you do," Auntie Deirdre said. "But you'll tell me all when you're ready and not a minute before."

Her room offered a welcome escape. Rhiannon took refuge there and didn't come out until Ceri brought a message from her father. He wanted Rhiannon to join the rest of the family around his bed.

She donned her cheeriest smile and opened the door. "Here I am," she said. "What did you—"

The rumble of a train cut off her words. Then the ground shook as it rolled along the tracks. Rhiannon froze.

No train ran at that time of day.

Ceri's wail rose up from the kitchen. Doors opened and slammed shut. The chapel bells rang out a wild alarm.

Her father leaped from the bed, yanked on the thick wool robe draped over the foot of the bed, and rummaged for his sturdy work boots. "The mine!" he cried.

They all knew what the sound meant.

Rhiannon heard the echo of an earlier rumble, felt the earth's quake of years ago; she saw the grief on her mother's face and the wooden caskets holding her grandfather's and uncle's remains.

Her temples pounded with her pulse.

Pain squeezed her heart.

Her breath failed.

Nausea rose.

But it wasn't what she saw, heard, remembered, or felt that kept her immobile and chilled. It was the last words Trefor had uttered that scared her the most.

"Having to head to the mine, me."

She began to shake. At first, shudders ran through her. Then her hands shook. Her knees felt weak, she went lightheaded, and her teeth chattered. Had it not been for the gentle hand that reached out and clasped her elbow, Rhiannon would have fallen to the floor.

"He's more than the mine superintendent, isn't he?" Auntie Deirdre asked.

Rhiannon couldn't answer. She felt herself led, and when something firm caught her behind her thighs, she sat. The tears began to fall, and only then did she realize her aunt had guided her to Papa's bed.

For long, silent moments—silent in the room, since outside the chapel bells continued to sound their alarm—she cried, fear ruling her every thought, hampering her every breath. And then the bells, too, fell silent.

Rhiannon realized the room had emptied but for her and Auntie Deirdre. "Where did they all go?"

"Mrs. Devane took the little ones. Joseph asked her when he, Owen, and Mervyn left for the mine."

Rhiannon moaned. "That soulless pit—"

"It may be soulless, but you aren't, and neither am I." She reached out her hand. "Let's pray."

Her first impulse was to refuse her aunt, but then, from the deepest corner of Rhiannon's mind, the image of Trefor singing at the eisteddfod gained strength. As did the contrast between his faith and hers—or rather, her lack of faith.

Because she now knew that her fear was nothing more than a lack of faith. She'd prayed for greater faith, for the Lord's help there. But now this happened. Would what faith she had be enough? Would the Lord hear the prayers of a woman like her? Did she have strong enough faith?

Rhiannon didn't know. The one thing she knew was that her faith was strong enough to try.

She reached out, took her aunt's hand, and bowed her head.

Chapter 7

S oon, however, prayer wasn't enough. Rhiannon felt the gnawing need to go to the colliery and see the devastation herself. True, whatever accident had taken place had done so deep beneath the surface of the earth. But the real devastation took place in the lives of those left to pick up the pieces aboveground.

What a terrible cloud to mar the joy of the upcoming Christmas.

She hurried to her room, rummaged through one of her two packed valises for a heavy wool cape with a hood, threw it on, and then ran outside. On the way to the pithead, she noticed other women and children, quiet and frightened, exiting cottages and hurrying down the road.

The frigid wind bit at her face and seeped under the edges of her cape. She pulled the heavy fabric closer but knew nothing would take away the cold she felt deep in her heart. A prayer for Trefor bubbled up to her lips. She prayed he hadn't been inside, that all the men had already left before the explosion or cave-in, but she feared her hope was in vain. It was too early in the afternoon for all work to have ended before the explosion, and somehow she knew that Trefor was inside that shaft.

She started to run but found it hard to stay upright. Patches of dirty snow hid slick ice. Her smooth shoes weren't adequate to negotiate the frigid, winter-rough surface.

What had gone wrong? Many times she'd sat in while Papa and Trefor discussed all the safety improvements they'd made, all those they planned to implement. She knew how careful they were with each and every aspect of the mine, the equipment, and especially the lives of the workers. It seemed to her they thought through every precaution and implemented it as soon as feasible.

She hurried past the chapel, sparing no more than a glance for the two elderly deacons who stood in the doorway, deep frowns on their brows. She approached the mine, her steps slowing the closer she came to the cluster of sheds. A large group had gathered outside the wooden structure that covered the entrance. Whispered conversations sped back and forth, the sound almost as sharp as the rush of the bitter wind.

Rhiannon spotted a familiar figure to the left of the slag pile, filthy with dirt and coal dust. "Papa!"

Everyone turned. She'd cried out her dismay, while no one else dared speak out loud. Still, she couldn't believe her father had gone inside the killer pit.

She hurried to his side. "Why did you—"

"Go home, child," he said. "This is no place for you."

"Are the men inside? How many? Was it an explosion? Or did a roof cave in? What happened?"

"Rhiannon, please. Go home." He wiped a shaking hand down his worried face. "We don't know much yet. Yes, there are men inside, but we don't know how many, much less what actually happened. Let us do our work, and you'll know as soon as we do."

When he wouldn't meet her gaze, she knew. "He's in there, isn't he?"

Papa's shoulders sagged. In a shaky voice, he said, "Trefor went in after his men. I tried to stop him, but he wouldn't be held back. After a bit, I couldn't continue. All that time I spent in bed has weakened me more than I thought."

The regret in his face hit her hard, but not as hard as the truth. "They're not coming out, are they?"

A woman not two feet away gasped then glared. She turned on Rhiannon, a hand raised as if to strike her. Papa caught the woman, who crumpled in his arms and sobbed.

Over the head of the terrified woman—a miner's wife—he met his daughter's gaze.

"Go home," he repeated.

This time she obeyed. As though she wore a sign proclaiming her a foul thing, those who'd gathered to wait parted, unwilling to risk even a brush with her skirts. The whispers resumed, this time angry and hot, turned against her.

Tears blurred Rhiannon's vision, but despite the sudden blindness, she knew what she had to do. She couldn't bear it; the man she loved would surely die in the ruined shaft. She could not—would not—stay until they brought out his body, crushed and broken, from the murderous hole in the earth.

Rhiannon gathered the fullness of her gown in her hands and ran home. There, she gave thanks for the foresight that had kept her from unpacking her bags. She called Joseph, who, unhappy but ever the respectful retainer, helped her drag her luggage to the carriage house.

There, he fell on his knees, shrouded by the shadows inside. She'd never witnessed her father's secretary's prayers, but she was doing so now. She noticed the tears in his eyes.

He glanced up when she called his name.

"I have to leave," she said. "Now." She gestured toward the door. "My bags are there. Please, *please* help me go. Hitch the horses for me. I'll have one of the station hands return the carriage once I catch the train."

"Where will you go?"

"To Cardiff. I'm sure Mrs. Llewellyn, Auntie Deirdre's housekeeper, will let me in. I just—just can't stay here. I don't belong. I never should have come back."

"Nonsense!" he said, his voice reminiscent of Papa's at his best. "Your father needed you. He was ill and you helped him. Surely you know how much he loves you. He needs you here. You mustn't leave."

"You don't understand. The colliery"—she spat out the foul word—"is everything here. And I can't bear even the thought of it anymore. It's a killer; it respects nothing and no one, and I can't watch it kill—"

"Mr. Trefor."

The floodgates opened, and while she'd cried on her way back from the mine, that had been nothing compared to the grief and misery that racked her now. "He's down there. He went after his men. . . ."

Joseph closed his eyes. A wince of pain shot through his face. "I'm so sorry, miss."

"So am I." She took a deep breath. "Surely you must see now that I have to go. Please don't try to stop me. The train's due in about a half hour, and I intend to leave on it."

"I can't change your mind, can I?" he asked in a tired voice.

"No."

"At least let me drive you there. You're too overwrought to handle Mr. Mervyn's lively pair, and the roads are covered with snow and ice."

She shrugged. As long as she reached the station in time to catch that train to Cardiff, what did it matter who held the reins?

Moments later, her bags secured, they took off, and Rhiannon turned for a last look at the village that had both given her life and taken her love. Now that she was leaving again, she would never return.

Rhiannon lost herself in her memories—thoughts of her childhood, those happy days before her grandfather and uncle died, before Mama died, too. She thought of the many times she'd followed Trefor, how she'd dogged his footsteps, wanting to be near him at all times.

His friends had teased him; he'd defended her. True, he'd only seen her as an irritating pest, but his kindness toward her had never failed. Trefor had always been warmhearted, generous, honorable, decent, and true. And those qualities were the ones that made him follow his men that day.

Yes, she loved him, but she didn't have the courage to stay. She didn't want to see his dead body. And even if he survived, she doubted he'd come out whole. Many of the village's residents had lost limbs inside that mine. She didn't have the courage to see him maimed.

She asked the Lord's forgiveness for her weakness, for her cowardice, for her secret departure. She hadn't even left a note to explain herself. She'd only thought to go, to put as much distance between herself and the mine as she possibly could.

The carriage gave a sudden lurch to the right. "Whoa!" her father's secretary-cum-driver yelled.

"Joseph?" she called. "Are the horses. . . ?"

"Everything's fine, Miss Rhiannon."

The vehicle continued to clatter over the rough surface. She bounced on the hard seat. "Are you sure?"

"Not to worry. One of the carriage wheels must have hit some ice."

One of the horses gave a sharp neigh then, and the carriage took another lurch. Joseph muttered just low enough for her not to catch what he'd said. Then, louder, he added, "Just sit back, miss. We'll be at the station any minute now—"

This time, the carriage went left while the horses went right. A hideous shriek rent the air. The vehicle heaved and shuddered over to its side. Too fast for her to react, Rhiannon's world tumbled away. Top and bottom traded places; she flew through the air; her arms and legs hit the seat, the floor; finally, something struck her head.

Everything went black.

❧

Trefor prayed as he and one of his men dug through the rubble that blocked the passage through to the newest part of the mine. "Besides Rhys Morgan," he said as he drove his shovel deep again, its metal edge scraping against stone and dirt, "any other men missing?"

"Two," Lloyd Maddox said. "Ewan Kimball and Dylan Keith."

He prayed for the men, that his and Lloyd's efforts achieved results before Ewan, Dylan, and Rhys died from the gas—*if* they hadn't already died from injuries in the initial collapse.

They dug for hours, through thick mud and rock. They sweated; rocks scratched and scraped them; they bruised knees, foreheads, elbows, and ribs. Determination carried them forward, their lamp a symbol of the hope they carried in their hearts.

Through every second of toil, the memory of Rhiannon's fears played in Trefor's mind. He hadn't been inside the shaft at the time of the accident, but he knew too well how often rescuers were trapped by subsequent collapses. He'd told Rhiannon he trusted God, and he did. He had to each time he entered the mine.

But Trefor knew, in a corner of his heart, that he also valued the knowledge of his skill and strength. He prided himself in his ability to work the mine and survive. That, and the ease with which he could lead the men safely through completion of a day's work.

Had he been prideful? Had he called it faith when his successful toil deep within the ground had been a matter of self-centered pride?

He and Lloyd had heard a number of frightening creaks since they'd reached the blockage of fallen rock, broken wood, and as always, the ever-present mud. The wooden supports for the mine roof over their heads might not hold up; in fact, they probably wouldn't hold up much longer. If the initial collapse had weakened other areas and something tested them again, he and Lloyd could end up just as trapped as the other men.

Had Rhiannon's fears of the mine been more realistic than his simple faith? Would today's accident claim three—five—lives? Would he ever see Rhiannon again?

Unwilling to give in to fear, clinging to faith in his Lord, and determined to save his men, Trefor persevered. He worked through the exhaustion in his every bone, through the damp coolness of the earth, through the pain in his ragged hands.

When he thought he couldn't go on for one more inch, another loud creak rang out overhead. But instead of retreat, the threat served only to strengthen his faith. If it were the Lord's will, all five of them would get out alive. He wouldn't doubt the Lord.

Seconds later, he broke through the blocking mess. On the other side, three injured but still-breathing men met him with gratitude in their eyes.

"Thank You, Father," he breathed.

And the roof cried out again. Everything around them shook. Rhys Morgan waved toward his two bleeding companions. "Crawling I'll be," he said. "Help them, or we'll all be dying in here."

"It's lost we are without You, Father," Trefor cried. "Help us now!"

Inch by miserable inch, the three men worked to ease the way out for the two more injured miners. Then the worst came to pass. To their rear, over the spot where they'd just been, the roof crashed down again.

Their lamp fell and went out. Rocks flew down around them. The earth bucked and rolled. Dust surrounded them and fouled their air. But Trefor refused to doubt his God, the God who'd brought him to the trapped men in time.

"Just a bit farther we need to go, Lord!"

He didn't know how exactly they did it, but an eternity later, Trefor spotted the flicker of a far-off lamp. "Help!" he cried. "It's help we're needing now. They're still alive."

And help they had. A flurry of activity relieved him and Lloyd of their precious burdens. Hands reached out to support even them. Blankets swathed them. Crystal-clear water soothed their parched throats. The praises of the villagers rose toward heaven.

Trefor wept. "Thank You, Father."

If he were never to have Rhiannon's love, at least he now knew that this was where he belonged. Sinful pride would have no place in his life. He knew that by the grace of God, and only by that grace, he had reached his men. The Lord hadn't abandoned him in his moment of need; Trefor had placed his faith right where it belonged when he'd trusted the almighty Father. That faith would see him through even the heartbreak he knew was to come.

After a new mine accident, there'd be no question about Rhiannon's feelings. She'd only be leaving the village sooner, if she hadn't already left.

❧

"Lord?" Joseph asked as he tried to hurry over the icy road. "This wasn't how it was supposed to come out. Why? Why did it have to end this way?"

But no answer was forthcoming this time.

And he couldn't stop to wait for the answer that would come. Rhiannon had been hurt when the horses spooked, fled, and the carriage overturned.

He regretted his stick-thin build. Were he a larger, stronger man, Joseph felt certain he would have been able to carry Rhiannon to safety. As it was, he had to hurry back to the village to fetch help.

It didn't help that he'd twisted his ankle in the accident.

Tears had filled his eyes when he saw the gash on Rhiannon's forehead. She hadn't responded to his many pleas, even though he could see she still breathed. Unable to help her himself, he'd protected her from the wind and made her comfortable with the robes and blankets in the carriage, then began the hobble back home.

Who would help them, he didn't know. With that dreadful accident at the mine, everyone in the village was sure to be at the pithead, waiting for any news.

"Don't abandon me now, Lord! I know I'm not utterly blameless here, but for Rhiannon's sake, lead me to help."

❧

As soon as he saw his men in caring hands, Trefor knew he still had one more thing to do. "Coming back I'll be," he told Mervyn. "This won't be taking long."

The Lord's blessed mercy toward the miners gave Trefor the strength to hurry to the Gwynne home. He wanted Rhiannon to see him, dirty, scraped, and bruised but still alive. She had to see that mine accidents weren't always fatal, that the Lord had seen and would continue to see him through.

He pounded on the heavy wooden door.

Mrs. Devane answered. "Who'd be knocking down our door—Mr. Davies!"

His breath came out in a ragged burst. "Rhiannon! Where is she?"

The plump lady gave him a look of distress. She wrung her hands and shook her head. "Gone. Wanting to play with her, the children were, but when we went to her room, we found all her things gone."

If he hadn't leaned against the doorframe, Trefor feared he would have dropped to the ground like one of those chunks of stone in the mine. "Too late," he said in a rough voice. Although he knew the answer, he had to ask. "Will she be back soon?"

Mrs. Devane shrugged. "I couldn't be saying. I didn't see her, and I haven't seen a note, a letter—nothing."

Despair filled him—but not for long. The clock in the Gwynnes' entry vestibule clanged out five chimes. He realized that, while he'd thought days if not weeks had passed as he dug his way through the mine debris, it had been only a few brief hours. There was a chance he could reach the five-fifteen train before it left. That is, if she'd planned to return to Cardiff on that train. "Returning to Cardiff, is she?"

Again, Mrs. Devane shook her head. "I wouldn't be knowing, Mr. Davies. I didn't see her. . ."

He didn't wait for her to finish her response. He hurried down, again avoiding the ice and snow that had turned the road into a treacherous mess. If Rhiannon hadn't yet left, Trefor meant to see her one more time. "Father? Giving me one more miracle, would You be, please?"

Head down against the bitter wind, Trefor hurried the short way down the road to young Dr. Gruffud's home. He knew the man would be there, tending to the injured miners, since that was where he kept his medical supplies. Trefor had made sure Lloyd understood that the men needed the physician's expert care, that they had to be transported to the doctor's place.

Old Dr. Gruffud answered the door. His rheumatism had bent him double, but the man's eyes remained as sharp as they'd ever been.

"How would I be helping you?" he asked in his gravelly voice.

"Your horse!" Trefor said. "Could I borrow it for a while?"

Seconds passed as the elderly doctor studied Trefor. Something in his expression, or perhaps it was just the filth and blood on his face, must have led him to respond to the urgency in Trefor's plea.

"Go on. But don't be bringing him back all sweated and leaving him to dry all night."

"I would never do that, and I'll be thanking you proper when I return."

Moments later, Trefor guided the gentle animal down the road, cautious to lead the beast's steps away from the patches of ice. With every pace, he breathed another prayer, a chain of pleas for Rhiannon's understanding, for her willingness to believe, to trust the Lord, even in this other matter between them.

Trefor meant to press her, to make her admit her feelings for him. Somehow he knew her fear for his life had made her flee. And her fear wouldn't have been so sharp had she not felt for him as he felt for her.

He hoped.

"Trefor!"

The weak voice sounded familiar. He looked down and, to his shock, saw Joseph on the roadside, cold, disheveled, his steps uneven and unsteady.

"What's happened?" he asked as he made to dismount.

"No!" the secretary cried. "Don't stop. Miss Rhiannon is hurt up ahead. The horses slid on the ice—we were on our way to catch the train. Hurry! She must not be out in the cold any longer. She's been there too long already as it is."

Before Joseph had finished his disjointed explanation, Trefor had urged Dr. Gruffud's horse back up to his previous pace. This time, however, hope spurred his ride.

Moments later, he reached the overturned carriage. He found Rhiannon, chilled, pale, weak, and unconscious but still alive. He'd never seen a lovelier sight. With infinite tenderness, he gathered up in his arms the woman he loved, the one he believed God meant for him to wed. With Rhiannon's head pressed against his heart, he led the horse toward the village.

When he reached Joseph, the canny secretary took advantage of Trefor's reluctance to release the injured woman, clambered onto the steed, and led them all the way back.

As they reached Dr. Gruffud's home, Rhiannon's eyelids fluttered open for a second or so. He didn't think she'd registered much, not even that he held her in such an intimate, compromising embrace. She sighed then breathed a word.

His heart took flight on the wings of that breath.

"Trefor," she said.

Epilogue

I n the following days, Rhiannon recovered her health, and her cheeks once again glowed with the soft color of summer roses. Trefor had left her side only to visit his injured men. He hadn't dared stay away any longer than that; he had to make sure she didn't try to bolt again.

"You must be trusting me some."

He smiled. The local lilt had returned to her speech, something she'd obviously worked to lose while in Cardiff. But what she asked of him was no laughing matter.

He shrugged. "And how should I be doing that? While I went after my men, escaping you were. How can I be trusting you again?"

"Should I remind you what you said before?" When he sent her a questioning look, she continued, "It's not me you should be trusting, but rather God. You said you trusted Him to bring you out of that shaft collapse. You want me to trust, but you should be trusting Him to show me how to live with that fear."

He arched a brow. "Seeing that truth, are you now?"

Rhiannon, lovely in a pale green dress that played up the shade of her eyes and the red lights in her hair, made a helpless gesture with her slender hand. "I'll never trust the mine, Trefor. Lying I'd be if I said otherwise. But you did come out alive."

"At this time of year," he said, "surely you'll be seeing how God sent us His Son to set us free. That freedom is also from the fear of falling mine walls. Trapping you, that fear is."

"It's not that easy, Trefor. I'm trying—"

"Trying alone. The Father will be giving you the strength to break the bond of fear—if you let Him. Keeping us apart, that fear is, too."

Rhiannon reached out and touched his hand. The warmth of her gentle caress reached deep into Trefor's heart. Before he could react, she spoke.

"I asked the Father for more faith, and His answer was the mine collapse. I don't know how I can trust."

"Trusting Him, I am when I go into the mine, and look!" He gestured to himself. "He's brought me out in one piece all the time."

"But—"

"But you ran in fear. And far away from the collapsed mineshaft is where you were hurt."

"Oh, but that wasn't much. Not like what happens in mine collapses."

"Yes. More could happen in the mine. But breaking a neck in a carriage accident is no small thing. Caring for you, the Father was, too. Just like He cared for us in the mine, for me."

Her eyes opened a bit wider. "He did, didn't He? Protected us both."

"Of course, and He'll be doing it always. For the life He's given us."

She thought a moment. "I do know His love is constant and certain. I don't see how else we both would have come through mostly unhurt."

She ran a finger over a knuckle that still bore a scrape from digging through the fallen rock. Then she laced her fingers around his. Trefor felt the need to hold her in his arms, to bring her close, but he didn't dare. They'd come so far, and he didn't want to scare her off again.

In a quiet voice, she asked, "A gift from Him, this is, no?"

He squeezed her hand but didn't respond.

She continued. "Away from Him, we're lost, in the dark, a dark as deep as that mine of yours. But with the Lord's help, we can come through—no, He can bring us through."

Trefor sent up a quick prayer and took the chance. He slipped an arm around her shoulders. Rhiannon didn't pull away, but rather leaned closer to him.

He pressed a kiss onto her temple. "Wanting faith, you were. Sounds like the Father showed you the way to that faith. Drawing you closer to Him."

Her green eyes glowed with so much love that his heart took flight. "He's drawing me closer to you, too."

"Thanking Him, I am," he said in a voice that shook just a bit. "I'd be saying, too, His lost lamb has now been found."

"And staying where He's brought me, right here at your side."

And stay she did.

Days later, in the deepest, darkest hours of Christmas Day, just before the sun began its rise, the singing of hymns and carols during the traditional *Plygain* service finally drew to a close. That's when Rhiannon and Trefor made public their troth and announced to the village their intention to wed.

The sun rose and brought light to the village. The chapel bells rang to celebrate the birth of Christ. And in heaven, angels rejoiced that another lost lamb was led back to the fold of faith.

Welsh Rarebit

4 slices whole-wheat bread,
  toasted
4 slices Canadian-style bacon,
  warmed
4 slices ripe tomato
1½ cups shredded sharp
  cheddar cheese

¾ cup whole milk
½ teaspoon of mustard
  powder
1 teaspoon Worcestershire
  sauce
Dash ground red pepper
1 beaten egg

Place a slice of toast on each of four plates. Top each with Canadian-style bacon and a tomato slice. Set aside. For cheese sauce, in heavy saucepan stir together cheese, milk, mustard, Worcestershire sauce, and red pepper. Cook over low heat, stirring constantly, until cheese melts. Slowly stir about half the hot cheese sauce into beaten egg; return mix to saucepan. Cook and stir over low heat until cheese sauce is thick and bubbly. To serve, spoon sauce over toast. Makes 4 servings.

Ginny Aiken, a former newspaper reporter, lives in Pennsylvania with her engineer husband and their three younger sons—their oldest son got married and flew the coop. Born in Havana, Cuba, raised in Valencia and Caracas, Venezuela, she discovered books early and wrote her first novel at age fifteen while she trained with the Ballets de Caracas, later known as the Venezuelan National Ballet. She burned that tome when she turned a "mature" sixteen. Stints as a reporter, a paralegal, a choreographer, a language teacher, and even a retail salesperson followed. Her life as a wife, a mother of four boys, and the herder of their numerous and assorted friends, brought her back to books and writing in search of her sanity. She's now the author of twenty-five published works, a frequent speaker at Christian women's and writer's workshops, but Ginny has yet to catch up with that elusive sanity.

'Tis the Season

by Carla Gade

Dedication

In remembrance of my Dad, Kenneth Olson, the first man I kissed under the mistletoe. With precious Christmas memories—especially Christmas lights and pickled herring.

Christmas is a season for kindling the fire for hospitality in the hall, the genial flame of charity in the heart.
WASHINGTON IRVING

Chapter 1

"Slow there, boys. Whoa, Hippocrates. Whoa, Galen!"

Annaliese Braun arched back as she drew in the reins with a firm grip. Spooked by a high-pitched whistle, the pair of riled horses continued their unsteady trot. The conveyance shook and the horses lurched ahead. The carriage shuddered beneath her as she tried to maintain control and pull the horses to a stop.

"Easy fellas," Annaliese called out to them, peering at the packed dirt road before her. The carriage felt askew. She leaned over and beheld the large wheel wobbling at her side, looking up in time to see a large branch strewn across the mountain road. The team shifted and with a jolt, angled back. The rear wheels slid into the wide gulch at the side of the road. Wet with leaves from last night's storm, the slippery descent tipped the carriage at a precarious angle on the uneven terrain. The carriage rocked from side to side, back and forth, as the horses wrestled to gain footing.

I must stop the horses! Annaliese moved to the edge of the footboard of her father's red landau. As she felt for the tread, her cotton pelisse caught on the side lantern. She steadied the toe of her ankleboot on the small step and tugged at her long cloak. As she struggled to free herself, the horses bucked and knocked her onto the damp ground where she landed in a most unladylike fashion. Hippocrates and Galen shuffled about as they dug their hooves into the rocky, leafstrewn slope.

She looked up at the carriage looming over her, trying to find her voice. The harnesses released and the wheels rolled forward—toward her legs beneath the coach. Annaliese pushed against the ground trying to move, when strong arms grabbed her by the shoulders, hoisting her from harm's way.

She landed with her back against a warm, thumping, masculine chest, facing the bent knees of buckskin breeches tucked into knee boots. "The horses!" she screeched out. "I am all right, please get them!"

"You are sure?" he asked, with a slight guttural intonation.

"Please, hurry!" *Schnell!*

The man sprang to his feet and climbed up the shallow embankment to the road, running after the confused horses. He took hold of Galen's harness and yanked back. *"Ho. . . halte,"* he called out, working his way in front of the team, bringing them to a stop. Hippocrates tossed his head and blew out reverberating snorts.

The man led the horses to a small glade off the side of the road, drawing the faltering carriage behind them.

Annaliese was taking deep breaths, trying to regain her senses, when the handsome rescuer squatted down in front of her, taking deep breaths of his own. His green eyes, brightened by his ruddy face, gazed at her intently. "Miss Braun, it is good to finally make your acquaintance," he said, a subtle inflection of Dutch upon his tongue.

Annaliese blinked. It really was he, and she was not dreaming after all. The man she'd longed to meet, had continued to avoid all summer, took her by the hands and gently pulled her to her feet. She rose, finding herself in such proximity to him that there was nothing else she could say but, "Why, Mr. Yost, how do you do?"

"Stephan, if you please, miss," the Heath House resident carpenter said, taking a few steps back from her. "It is what I am accustomed to." His eyes roamed the top of her head with curiosity. "To answer your question, I believe I fare better than you this day."

From the corner of her eye, Annaliese noted her plaid chin ribbon dangling somewhere in the vicinity of her temple. She winced. "I must be quite a sight." She lifted her hands and felt the disheveled state of her bonnet.

A crooked grin rose above Stephan's cleft chin.

Annaliese withdrew her bonnet of braided straw and gathered taffeta, and her thick plait plopped onto her shoulder. She often wove her unruly locks into a neat coif surrounding the crown of her head, but the pins from the back must have come undone, as had her pride.

She released a deep sigh as she glanced down at the hat, turning it about in her hands. The back was crushed and fall leaves were plastered to it. "Perhaps I should begin a new fashion and leave them." A nervous laugh escaped her lips and she began to pluck the leaves from amongst the small plumes and other trimmings. "I should have thought of it before the resort guests went back to their grand homes in the cities. They could have shared the latest fall headdress with their elegant friends." Enough of her nervous chatter. What did he know of fashion, with his rugged apparel befitting a tradesman?

Stephan nodded, muffling a laugh, and turned to look at the horses.

As he did so, Annaliese pulled off her soggy chamois driving gloves and discreetly felt the back of her pelisse, finding that the damp ground had saturated the fabric.

"If you are all right, Miss Braun, we should see to the horses and your carriage."

"Yes, of course."

Stephan took long strides up the incline and turned to her, extending his hand. She placed her ungloved hand in his firm grip and he carefully helped her to the road. Then the handsome Dutchman motioned for her to walk ahead of him.

"You may go ahead, thank you." She fanned her warm face with her gloves in the absence of her fan. Who would have ever expected to need a fan on a morning outing in the country in late October? She followed Stephan to the roadside patch where her geldings nosed through wet leaves and nibbled on the spiky grass. Careful to keep her backside away from Stephan's view, she worked her way around the team and wagged her finger at them. "Hippocrates and Galen. You have been most naughty today. There shall be no carrots for you."

Stephan's eyebrows lifted. "Hippocrates and Galen?"

"My father named them after the ancient physicians," she answered. Stephan issued a slow nod.

Annaliese raised her brow and shrugged. Did he understand the logic or simply find their names peculiar?

He cocked his head. "Now tell me, Miss Braun, how did your intelligent horses deposit you and your carriage into that gulch?"

Annaliese swallowed. *Gulch?* It was a gulch all right, and she had fallen straight in. Stephan Yost may have rescued her, but her heart was in the precarious position of rebelling against her plans for the future.

❧

Stephan gazed at the woman before him, her light brown braid framing her brow and flowing rebelliously onto her shoulder, and her long, rumpled, military-style coat dampened by her fall. Yet never had he met anyone so *mooi*—beautiful—in his life. He had admired her from afar, capturing an occasional glimpse of her at the resort. But their paths seldom crossed, he being busy with his first season at Heath House, building and making repairs, and other ventures. She, well, he wasn't sure exactly what she did besides facilitate activities for the rusticators. When he first learned that she was the daughter of the resort's doctor, he was tempted to injure himself so that, by chance, if she assisted her father with his patients, he might gain the chance to meet her. He kept his ears tuned to the chatter of the guests and soon discovered that Dr. Helmut Braun was an esteemed and wealthy physician from New York. The doctor's daughter would never consider associating with an itinerant carpenter.

"It all happened so fast," she said, snapping him back to the present. "The horses spooked and took off, and as they went faster the carriage began to shake. It felt like the wheel started coming undone, and then they almost ran over that downed tree." She pointed at the huge branch nearby. "Then down in the gulch they went. I suppose I really should not blame them. They were as scared as I." She pouted at her dun and bay and caressed their faces. "Isn't that right, Galen? You, too, Hippocrates."

Stephan walked over to the loosened carriage wheel. He knelt and ran his hand along the spokes as he inspected it. "I think I can fix this and get you on the road again. Do you have a toolbox with spare linchpins?"

"We do," she said.

He angled his head toward the downed branch. "First I will clear that from the road."

"*Gut*, we would not want anyone else running into it."

Stephan stood and stretched. "*Gut*, you say. Your German word sounds much like *goed* in my Dutch."

"Yes, it does sound similar. You must find it helpful, being here amongst so many Germans in this area, especially down the mountain in the German Valley."

He nodded. "*Ja.*"

"Ja," she said, donning a little smirk that made her cheeks color.

A chuckle rose in his throat. "Will your hooved physicians be all right for a minute while I see to the downed branch?" He patted Hippocrates on the neck, or was that Galen?

"They shall be fine, so long as they are not spooked again. They are normally docile creatures." Miss Braun patted their necks.

Stephan turned and strode toward the road.

"Let me help you," she called, then hastened her steps beside his longer strides.

Though he knew her slim figure would provide no strength for the task, he did not object to her offer. Her company pleased him. Stephan released a cheerful whistle to an old Dutch folk song, but Miss Braun reached up and clamped her palm over his mouth.

He pivoted toward her, staring at her, not knowing what to make of the gesture. Slowly, he lifted her palm and puckered his lips, about to tease her with another whistle. Perhaps it was some sort of game.

Miss Braun peered up at him with a look of desperation and planted her soft lips over his. He met her wide-eyed gaze of deep azure, trying to gauge when to pull back from this most pleasurable meeting. She withdrew and slipped her hand over his mouth again then placed her finger to her lips. "Shhh... You'll scare the horses." She slowly released her hand and winced, her cheeks flushing with color.

"I see," he whispered, nodding. "You do not want me to whistle."

"No." Her lips rounded as she formed the word and she drew in a little breath.

"Then you shall have to employ me to that end." Stephan leaned down and pressed his mouth over hers, enjoying her sweet taste. When she did not resist him, he placed his arm around her shoulders and drew her closer. Her palm rested against his chest and he breathed in deeply. His calloused hand found its way to the nape of her neck and he worked his fingertips into her soft hair. He thought he could hear her sigh, when she quickly pivoted to a sharp sound piercing the air.

He spun toward the loud whistle. A barefoot lad in breeches and a too-small coat stood by the road's edge and placed his fingers in his mouth, about to whistle again. Stephan held up his hand. "Quiet! You'll scare the horses." He looked over his shoulder, seeing Miss Braun hurrying to the horses' side as they became restless. At least they were now tied and the carriage's brake locked in place.

Stephan jogged toward the youth, who was now bent over, hands pressed to his knees, trying to catch his breath. "What is it, lad?"

"*Ich habe gejagt—*"

"Speak English, boy."

"I have been chasing after Dr. Braun," the boy said, with his German accent. "I saw his red carriage *und* whistled, but he hurried on." Ah, so that was what all this whistling was about. The boy must have spooked Miss Braun's horses.

"Sorry, but Dr. Braun is not here. Miss Braun was driving his carriage." Stephan pointed to where she stood holding onto the horses' reins under the shelter of some trees.

The lad looked up at him, his eyes pleading. "But I must see Dr. Braun. *Mein onkel ist krank.*"

Miss Braun came forward and Stephan and the boy walked toward her. "Your uncle is sick? Who is he?"

The boy's eyes moistened. "Mein onkel ist Herr Rolof Schroeder."

Miss Braun pressed her fingers onto the child's shoulders. "*Sprechen sie auf Englisch, bitte.* Where is your uncle now?"

"He is at his mill on the West Springtown Road. *Wo ist*—Where is the doctor?" the boy asked.

"He is at Heath House." Miss Braun glanced at Stephan, worry tensing across her face.

Stephan gripped his jaw. "It won't take long for me to fix the wheel. Annaliese, get the toolbox, please, and make sure the horses' harnesses are secure. Come quickly, lad, and help me move the branch from the road."

"*Danke,*" the boy said with a relieved sigh.

"I beg pardon, miss," Stephan said with a grimace, eyeing Miss Braun apologetically. "I believe I called you by your given name in error."

Miss Braun moistened her lower lip. "You may call me Annaliese. If you promise not to call my horses Herr Hippocrates and Herr Galen."

"I shall be sure not to do that. Besides, I intended to call them *Dokter* Hippocrates and *Dokter* Galen." Stephan chuckled.

The youngster grinned and peered up to the tree branches looming overhead. Stephan and Annaliese followed the lad's gaze to the nest of mistletoe wrapped around the branch of the black gum tree. "*Ist sie ihre liebchen*—your sweetheart?" the lad asked looking from Stephan to Annaliese.

The pair spun toward the boy, each protesting in turn.

"*Nee!*" Stephan grunted.

Annaliese hiked her chin. "*Nein!*"

Chapter 2

How could she. . .why did she. . . ? Yet, with her eyes fixated on Stephan's lips, the only solution that had come to mind was to kiss the man to keep him from whistling, lest her horses become frightened once more. And now, Annaliese found herself perplexed by the feelings the kiss had stirred within her. The first humiliating kiss had been unsettling enough, but the one he had stolen from her—that she had allowed him to take—had positively altered her.

Although Annaliese had admired the resort carpenter from afar from the moment he arrived at Heath House, she had suppressed her attraction to him, just as she had the fellows who had shown interest in her through the years. Although she had enjoyed a few brief summer romances, she had long resolved that her contentment in life would come from caring for her father into his old age. Papa had given her so much since her mother died, sacrificing even his own chance at romantic love, or so she thought, for her sake. Love, after all, was not all about romance, it was a greater joy, and calling. Then why had it pricked her heart that Mr. Stephan Yost, the one man she had secreted an attraction for, had not seemed to take notice of her—until now? And here she was rescued by him, kissed by him, and about to travel down Schooley's Mountain with him on an act of mercy.

Annaliese closed her eyes and breathed in the fresh scent of the tree-lined road. The end of the season at Schooley's Mountain's famous resort had arrived. She'd come down the mountain to deliver some clothing that had been left behind by summer residents to the old stone church. Each year the reverend and his wife were happy to accept the resort's donation and distribute the garments to those in need. Mr. Heath and a worker had loaded the carriage, and she assured them that she was more than capable of making the delivery on her own. Others would be available to unload the items, and it was merely a few miles of travel. Although it had rained the night before, evidenced by the carpet of freshly fallen autumn leaves, the day was brimming with promise. As she had driven past a clearing coming down Schooley's Mountain Road, a grand view of the pastoral Musconetcong Valley opened up before her, and the sun was breaking through the clouded morn.

Now Hippocrates and Galen were ready to go, with another mission ahead—to come to the aid of Herr Schroeder. It appeared that Stephan was almost finished making the wheel repair. The millwright's worried nephew paced about, every now and then hovering over Stephan's shoulder to assess his progress.

Annaliese called to the lad. "Would you like to give the horses some carrots?"

"Ja," he said and came around to where she stood in front of her team.

She unfolded a cloth that she'd wrapped pieces of carrot in and handed them to the boy. *"Vas ist der namen?"*

He took the carrots and offered each horse a nibble. He patted their faces and smiled up at Annaliese. She glanced at his worn clothing. His breeches were patched at the knees and his vest had a torn pocket. He appeared clean, though his hair was a bit mussed. Then it occurred to her that she shouldn't be making hasty judgments, as she surely was an unkempt spectacle in her own right.

"I am Rory Schroeder. You needn't speak to me in German. I only speak that way when I am upset, like my uncle does." The anxious boy looked back at Stephan.

Stephan rose, wiping his hands on a rag. "Well, Rory Schroeder, we are ready to be on our way." He extended his hand toward the lad. "I'm Stephan Yost, a carpenter from up the hill at Heath House. You have met Miss Braun."

"Yes sir," Rory said, glancing up at her.

"If you take that small toolbox and put it away where Miss Braun tells you, I will take one last look at the carriage and we will go see to your uncle's health," Stephan said.

Annaliese led Rory to the boot at the rear of the landau. After putting the toolbox away, she looked over the edge of the conveyance, at cartons of clothing on the seats and floor. Her mouth twisted as she tried to think of where two extra passengers would fit.

"I can make some room for us," Stephan said.

"Would you, please?" she asked.

"Ja. I can drive if you wish."

"I would appreciate that. I thought perhaps you could take Rory and me to his uncle's, as it is along the way, and then you might go to Heath House to fetch my father. That is, if you can. I have already imposed on you enough this morning." She thought of his rescuing her from being run over by the carriage, his repairing the wheel, his indulging her with kisses. . . .

"That is no problem for me, and I am happy to help." He opened the door of the open-topped landau and shifted the cartons of clothing around, making room for the boy in the seat behind the driver's platform. "Climb in, Rory."

Stephan handed Annaliese up to the driver's seat. To his credit kept his eyes upon her face and not the back of her damp pelisse. He then settled in beside her. She turned to Rory and said, "I am praying for your uncle as he waits for us to get to him. I am not a doctor, but I can perhaps lend him some comfort until my father arrives."

"Tell me, Rory, what were you doing so far up the mountain road?" Stephan called back over his shoulder, as he drove the carriage out onto the road.

The boy kneeled and leaned on the back of his seat, facing the front. "Uncle Rolof sent me to the mineral spring to get some healing waters. He has sent me every day, but he is getting worse. I was praying to God when I saw the doctor's carriage up ahead and then it turned onto the post road."

Annaliese tilted her head toward Stephan. "It was a divine thing how this all turned out, though I dare say, I hadn't thought so when my carriage went off the road."

He glanced at her and nodded. "Divine." He looked back toward the road ahead, and she noticed the corner of his mouth curve.

She clasped her hands in her lap and drew them in toward her abdomen, releasing a little sigh. *And all because of a whistle.*

"It is a good thing I whistled," Rory said.

"I guess you have never heard, then, that it is unlucky to whistle in a wind," Annaliese called back to Rory.

"It was not windy. I've never had bad luck with it, though some call whistling the devil's music," the lad said, tugging his floppy hat over his ears. "Can you whistle, Miss Braun?"

Annaliese grimaced. "I don't know, but I shan't risk scaring the horses again."

"I heard that if a girl whistles she will grow a mustache," Stephan called back to the boy.

Rory let out a hearty laugh. "What else have you heard, Mr. Yost? Do you know any stories?"

"Hmm. Let's see. . . I once read about a man who met a strange person in a ravine—" Stephan cast a sidelong grin at Annaliese. "The man was a Dutch colonist of old New York and was traveling through the Catskill Mountains. The stranger asked the man to carry a keg to his village for him. After the man arrived and had a feast, he fell into a stupor and slept for twenty years. When he awoke everything had changed—his wife was dead, his daughter married, and America was an independent country."

"That must have happened before the American Revolution!" Rory said.

Annaliese and Stephan chuckled at the boy's naivete.

"That was the story of Rip Van Winkle by Geoffrey Crayon," Stephan told the boy.

"Mr. Crayon is a good friend of my family, from our hometown in New York." Annaliese turned back to Rory. "I shall tell you a *geheimnis*—a secret. The author is really Esquire Washington Irving, but he goes by another name for his publications in *The Sketch Book*."

"Why does he use another name, Miss Braun? Isn't that lying?" Rory asked.

Annaliese wrinkled her brow. "I think it is like this, Rory. My horses are named Hippocrates and Galen, but my father calls them '*die docktoren*,' and Mr. Yost has also called them the *docktors*."

"Some people call my uncle Herr Schroeder and some call him Mr. Schroeder. But I call him Onkel Rolof." Rory shrugged and turned around in his seat, seemingly satisfied with her answer.

Stephan cocked his head in her direction and smirked.

Annaliese smiled back, until his gaze fell to her lips. She lowered her lashes and cupped her hand on her cheek, sliding it over to conceal her mouth. She dared glance at Stephan again and saw the crinkles at the corner of his eye. The stubble on his face below the profile of his high cheekbone glinted in the dappled morning sun. His dark blond hair hung past his neckcloth, which was peeking out above the collar of his brown frock coat of worsted-wool. Not a fashionable man, but keenly attractive, no less. Handsome, witty, benevolent, hardworking, gallant. . . By all means, Stephan Yost was the perfect catch—if she were looking.

—as he was, when he caught her staring at him, and grinned.

⁂

Stephan snapped the reins as he ascended the mountain, and Hippocrates and Galen responded in turn. They were making good speed, though he was careful not to exhaust them, as they had a return trip to make to Schroeder's Mill. The "docktors" were a good team of horses, when they were not subjected to the sound of a whistle. But he was glad of that. In fact, he was rather fond of whistling, or rather, of *not* whistling.

Stephan turned the carriage between the stone pillars marking the entrance to Heath House. He drove down the wide trail lined with colorful maples and junipers, and slowed the team as he neared the clearing of the rustic resort. He scanned the semicircle of cottages with the main hotel at its apex. Hopefully, he'd find Dr. Braun at his own cottage, where he served his summer patients. Stephan drove the landau up to the unpainted clapboard cottage and pulled on the brake. He peered down at the troublesome wheel that, for the moment, appeared stable.

Ephraim Marsh, longtime manager and new owner of the resort, came out of the modest building followed by his father-in-law, Joseph Heath, the former owner of Heath House. Mr. Marsh leaned against the porch rail and grinned. "You look like a dandy driving that fancy carriage, Yost. Say, is everything all right? Where is Miss Braun?"

The front door swung shut behind Dr. Braun as he followed the men out to the porch. Stephan remained in the driver's seat, relieved to see them all. "Dr. Braun, you are needed at once. Rolof Schroeder has taken ill, and your daughter is at the mill ministering to him until you can come."

"I shall get my bag," the doctor said, and entered his cottage again.

"How did you learn of this?" Mr. Marsh asked.

"His young nephew saw Miss Braun driving the doctor's carriage and stopped her," Stephan said.

Mr. Heath cocked his head back. "All the way down the mountain?"

"She had not gotten that far." Stephan looked over his shoulder to the cartons of clothing remaining in the carriage. "Before she arrived at the stone church, the carriage went off the road—on the turnpike between Springtown and German Valley. I discovered her as I was coming back up the mountain from Swackhammer's forge, where I had gone for a repair this morning."

Dr. Braun returned and looked up at Stephan in alarm. "Was Annaliese harmed?"

"Nee." Stephan shook his head. "The carriage had a loose wheel, which I repaired."

"Danke, danke," the doctor said, and exhaled. He climbed up beside Stephan. "You may continue to drive, as you know the way to Herr Schroeder's."

Stephan looked over at Mr. Marsh. "I shall make up my work later." He hoped his employer would understand.

Mr. Marsh nodded and handed him a bottle of water from the spring, from the resort's ample supply. "Go now. See to Schroeder. When you are through, assist Miss Braun with the delivery to the church to be sure the carriage remains stable."

"*Dank u.*" Stephan gulped some water and set the bottle by his side. He wheeled the carriage around and headed back toward Schooley's Mountain Road. "Come on, boys, you have a patient to see."

Annaliese's father looked straight ahead, observing his team of horses. "I see you've become acquainted with *meine* docktoren, ja?"

"Ja." Stephan chuckled. "Hippocrates, Galen, and I have come to know each other well today."

The physician turned toward Stephan. "Und my Annaliese?"

"Ja, and your daughter." Stephan tightened his grip on the reins.

"I had never met her until today, sir, although I had seen her around the resort."

"Mmm-hmm," Dr. Braun murmured, staring at Stephan with lifted brow. "You are the quiet one. I see you about busy repairing this, building that. How did you find your first season at Heath House?"

Stephan turned onto the main road. "I have enjoyed being here. It is not as pretentious as Saratoga Springs. Though I did recognize some of the guests from Saratoga."

"Ja, some folks are inclined to taking the waters in various locales. It is addicting to some," Dr. Braun said.

Stephan narrowed his eyes, looking at the doctor. "Addicting? Like. . .opium or laudanum? I wasn't aware minerals had those kind of qualities."

"Nein, nothing like that. Addicting in the mind, that is," Dr. Braun said. "Although there are health benefits to the mineral waters, I tend to think it is the fresh outdoor air that does our visitors the most good. I know it has served my daughter and me well for some twelve years now."

"You have been coming here for that long?" Stephan asked.

"Ah, yes," the doctor said. "Annaliese was only a girl of twelve when I first came to be Heath House's physician. I was a recent widower, and it seemed like a wise choice to leave my practice in the city for the summer so that my daughter could enjoy the outdoors whilst I treated patients."

"And has she liked it?" Stephan asked.

"Meine *fräulein* ist not made for the city. At the end of each season I nearly have to surgically extract her from *der* mountain in order to get her back to Manhattan." Dr. Braun chortled. "Und you, Stephan? Do you prefer the mountain air to the city?"

"I do," Stephan said, as the docktors trotted along. "It is more pleasant to work in the country than in the city. I have worked in many places, and I like it here. Yet now that the resort season has ended, I have a limited amount of work to do off-season. I might scout around to see if there is a need for a carpenter in the area."

Dr. Braun crossed his arms, hiking his chin. "May I ask you this, Stephan Yost, have you experience building houses?"

Chapter 3

Annaliese enjoyed the magnificent fall foliage as Stephan drove the carriage down the mountain at a pleasant pace. She sat sideways so she might participate in the conversation with him and Papa. Stephan had cleared the seat for her when Herr Schroeder agreed to accept a donation of clothing for his great-nephew. While her father saw to his patient and she remained near to administer assistance, Stephan had helped Rory sort through the crates to find garments to fit him. The boy entered the stone house with clothes piled high in his arms, Stephan following only as far as the door, where he left a pair of boots for the lad. Annaliese had invited him in, but Stephan insisted on staying with the docktors.

"I am so glad to know that Herr Schroeder will be well again soon," Annaliese said. "It was kind of his neighbor to promise to look in on him and be sure he does not drink too much water from the mineral spring."

Stephan looked at Papa. "I thought the mineral waters restored good health to folks and that is why they are so admired."

Annaliese worried her lip, afraid that the answer Stephan was going to receive was more than he was anticipating.

"Only in moderation," Papa said. "I encounter the same problem with long-term visitors at the resort. When they overindulge in consuming the water from der mineral spring they become prone to a stricture of the digestive system and occasionally develop an intestinal infection. Left untreated, the consequences can be dire."

Stephan scratched the back of his head, clearing his throat.

Papa continued. "The chalybeate mineral springs are beneficial for Herr Schroeder's condition of nephritis—the inflammation of his kidneys—but only in limited measure."

Stephan nodded. "Ben Franklin said, 'Do everything in moderation, including moderation.'"

"Der Good Book also cautions us, 'All things are lawful. . . but all things are not expedient.'"

Annaliese groaned. "Oh, Papa, only you could find scripture to apply to this malady."

"You do know, liebchen, there is a wealth of medical wisdom found in God's Word." Papa patted his leg to the rhythm of the horses. "My remedy for Herr Schroeder came directly from the Bible. 'Drink no longer water, but use a little wine for thy stomach's sake and thine often infirmities.' Und eat more sauerkraut."

"I did not know sauerkraut was in the Bible." Stephan chuckled. "But I might refrain from telling Mr. Marsh your remedy."

"For der sauerkraut?" Papa asked. "Only if he requires it."

"Nee, the part about not drinking the water," Stephan said.

How Annaliese would love to see Stephan's facial expressions.

Papa waved his hand in the air. "Eh, he knows my ways. Mr. Marsh also knows I encourage his guests to take the mineral baths at the spring house. *Vergebe mich*, I should not have said that in mixed company." He angled back toward Annaliese. "Your *vater* ist getting *zu alt*."

Annaliese squeezed Papa's shoulder. At four and twenty, if anyone was getting old it was she, at least from the vantage point of her employer's new bride, Levinia Heath Marsh. Her friend, still aglow in her recent state of matrimony, had teased Annaliese throughout the summer each time an eligible patron of Heath House took notice of her. But Annaliese dismissed each suggestion. Many of those gentlemen were visitors who hailed from the elite society of Philadelphia, New York City, or Baltimore. They would surely dismiss her once they discovered that she had no intent of discontinuing her summer routine at Schooley's Mountain. How could she ever leave her father's side when she was all he had?

"What about your parents, Stephan?" Papa asked.

The question piqued Annaliese's interest, and she anticipated hearing the quiet Dutchman's reply. Stephan had simply appeared at the resort at the beginning of summer—a lone carpenter whom no one seemed to know and who kept to himself, busy at his trade. Word got out at last that the reserved worker had been employed at other famous resorts, yet Levinia had once inferred that his references were far more impressive than that.

"My parents are in the old country. I immigrated with my cousin Hans a few years before the War of 1812. We enlisted, but he–he did not survive. I have been on my own since." Stephan snapped the reins.

"Und you decided to stay in America though you have no family here now," Papa said, more of a statement than a question.

"Ja." Stephan said no more.

"Will you return to Heath House for another season?" Papa asked.

Stephan shrugged his shoulders and released an unintelligible grunt.

An awkward pause hovered over them as the conversation came to an abrupt halt. As they rumbled past the crooks and turns in the road toward German Valley, Annaliese became drowsy. She hadn't realized she had succumbed to her fatigue until her eyes sprang open at the sound of the *clop, clop, clop* of the horses' hooves beneath her as they crossed Neitzer's wooden bridge over the Raritan River. Annaliese patted her cheeks and took in a deep breath. The carriage stopped at the tollgate and Papa paid the two-cent fee before turning onto Fairview Avenue. They had arrived at the old stone church.

⤞✽⤝

Stephan's attention remained unduly long upon Annaliese's pleasing face as he settled her to the ground, having helped her from the carriage. The gentle pressure of her hands upon his shoulders when she leaned on him for support reminded him that he could never allow a woman to count on him again.

Annaliese's clear blue eyes held his gaze as she put her hands by her side. She cleared her throat and glanced down at his hands, still holding her waist. "Thank you, Stephan."

Stephan groaned inside. Every thought, every action in her presence was out of plumb since they'd kissed that morning. He removed his hands and stepped aside. "You are welcome, Miss Braun."

"Miss Braun?" Her cheeks colored and she cast her gaze at the pebbled ground. Her eyes flitted up again. Did he detect a hurt look from beneath the gentle curl of her long lashes?

"Annaliese," her father called from the door of the church.

"Reverend Hendricks has asked us all to take the noon meal with him and Mrs. Hendricks."

"That sounds delightful, Papa." Annaliese tilted her chin at Stephan as she faced him. "I know you have already spent much of your day coming to our aid, but if you would care to remain for the meal, we shall be happy to release you of your obligation to us."

"Miss Braun. . .Annaliese. . .I consider you no obligation." He swallowed. "It will be a pleasure to stay for the meal, as it is my pleasure to serve you." He dipped his head, inclining a slight bow.

She offered a shy smile. Where was the impetuous young woman who had silenced him in the glade beneath the mistletoe? The mystery of Annaliese Braun only incited him to want to discover more about her.

Stephan reached into the landau and grabbed a crate of clothing.

"Here, I will take that." The pastor of the Union Church held out his arms.

Stephan passed the crate to the sturdy-looking man. "Thank you, sir."

"Reverend Hendricks, this is Stephan Yost, from up at Heath House," Dr. Braun said by way of introduction.

The reverend nodded, as did Stephan in kind.

"I will gather those loose items after you men take care of the crates," Annaliese said.

"Hand me one, Stephan," said Dr. Braun. Stephan handed a crate off to him and the two older men went into the church.

Stephan left the largest crate for himself, piled high with all sorts of garments. "I will be back to help you with that," he said, as he picked the crate up and looked at her over his shoulder.

Annaliese went to the carriage and leaned in. "There's not much left. I think I can handle it myself," she called. "I will be right along. Thank you."

Stephan entered the stone building and Reverend Hendricks led him to an alcove where the clothing was to be stored.

"It was benevolent of Mr. Marsh to donate clothing, once again, for those in need. He does so at the end of each season," the reverend said.

"Ja, it is a generous deed," Stephan said. "Do you need me to shift some of those crates around?"

"Yes, please," Reverend Hendricks said. "Perhaps I can find a spare box for the loose items still in the carriage. What are they, shoes and umbrellas?"

"I believe so." Stephan looked toward the hallway. What was keeping Annaliese? "Where is Dr. Braun? Did he go outside to help his daughter?"

"No, I sent him across to the house to let Mrs. Hendricks know that company had arrived." The minister held up a fancy rose-colored gown and grinned. "I am not sure this will be useful to the town folks, but, eh, we never know. Perhaps some young maiden can use it for her wedding."

A twinge of foreboding pricked at Stephan. "I am going to see what is keeping Annaliese."

The minister nodded. "Good, and then you and Annaliese can join us at the house. 'Tis directly across the way. She will show you."

Stephan stepped through the large door of the church, and his gaze immediately fell to the sight of a growling dog baring its teeth at Annaliese. She stood by the open carriage door, fraught with terror. Her eyes darted to Stephan and he slowly nodded to reassure her. His heart pounded as he searched about to see if there was something he could use to ward off the animal. He could whistle, distract the dog, but he feared that the already agitated horses would bolt. There, a shovel. He eased along the facade of the building and retrieved the tool, which was leaning against the front wall. He then scooped up some pebbles.

The dog's ears pointed up, his haunches rose, and he snarled at Annaliese. Stephan inched toward the animal and, coming around the side, he tossed the pebbles at it. The dog jerked around and barked fiercely.

Stephan gripped the wooden handle of the shovel with both fists, holding it across his chest. He crept toward the dog, trying to get between it and Annaliese. He pushed the shovel toward the animal. "Get! Get out of here!"

The dog lunged at him.

Annaliese screamed. "Stephan!"

A loud whistle pierced the air as Reverend Hendricks came at the dog with a whip and snapped it against the ground. "Down, Luther! Down!"

The dog went whimpering to his master, who leashed him at once. But Hippocrates and Galen hurtled forward, catching Annaliese's coat and gown in the carriage door and knocking her down. The horses stormed down the road in a fury.

Reverend Hendricks restrained his barking dog and Dr. Braun hurried over to Annaliese. Stephan dashed to her side.

"I am well, Papa," Annaliese said as she observed the damage to her calico day gown. She peered up at Stephan. "Are you all right, Stephan?"

Stephan gazed down at her. "Ja, I am fine." He shook his head, marveling that she thought nothing of herself. His head pivoted in the direction the horses had taken.

Dr. Braun followed his gaze, his palm clamped to his forehead. "*Mein vagon!* Die docktoren!"

Annaliese's eyes became moist as she looked at Stephan. "The horses—"

Stephan tossed his coat over the fence and turned to her father. "I will bring your horses and carriage back to you." And Annaliese.

"Schnell, bitte!" Dr. Braun cried out as Stephan jogged down the road.

Luther barked in the distance.

❦

Annaliese still trembled inside. This day had been one painful, dreadful, or humiliating ordeal after the other. First, the carriage accident, then the kissing incident, Rory's ailing uncle, the dog attack, and now the missing horses and carriage. . .and Stephan. Shouldn't he have returned by now? Perhaps she should go after him. Nein, Papa would never allow it.

"You look very lovely, dear. I thought that gown might fit you well," Mrs. Hendricks said, looking at the rose-hued silk gauze gown she had found for Annaliese lying atop one of the boxes of the donated clothing. "I will do my best to repair the tears on your own gown and pelisse, but it might require some creative handiwork."

"I appreciate your help, Mrs. Hendricks. You have been most kind," Annaliese said.

The robust woman smoothed her apron. "Why don't you have a seat? I am sure Stephan shall return soon, and then we shall eat. I have prepared a fine stew."

Standing at the window, Papa turned around and announced, "He is back. With the horses."

"God be praised," Reverend Hendricks said, while his wife gazed heavenward, uttering a silent prayer. "My neighbor's son is waiting for him and will help him secure the conveyance and the horses."

"Das ist gut. Danke." Papa exhaled deeply.

Annaliese paced, waiting for Stephan to enter the Hendricks' parsonage. She wished to run outside to see how he fared. How the horses were. If the carriage was all right.

Apparently sensing her apprehension, Papa placed his hand on her arm, staying her. "I will go see."

She resumed her pacing but paused when the door opened behind her. She spun around and saw Stephan at the doorway, with Papa behind him.

Stephan took in a deep breath and stepped over the threshold into the keeping room. *"Hallo!"* His gaze traveled over her, lingering overlong.

Annaliese blushed and offered a demure smile. Oh, if he could see how handsome he looked with his bright eyes glistening, his face colored from exertion.

He raked back his wind-whipped hair and grinned. "You needn't have dressed for the occasion, Miss Braun. Yet, I do say, you look rather fetching in your new gown."

Mrs. Hendricks came to Annaliese's side. "She does look lovely. 'Twas a blessing to find a spare gown with the donated garments, even if it is befitting a ball or a wedding."

"Ja, indeed," Stephan said with a nod. "Though I do not think your carriage is as fortuitous. I explained to your father that the brake is in need of repair."

"Jacob Day, the carriage-maker, should be able to take care of that for you," Reverend Hendricks said. "Though I fear I am responsible, since Luther frightened your team."

Papa waved his hand dismissively. "Annaliese already had a minor accident with the carriage this morning. It could have been damaged then."

"Though we must be sure to let folks know not to whistle around the horses, as it frightens them," Annaliese said to Reverend Hendricks.

"How will you keep them from doing that?" Mrs. Hendricks asked. "Why, anyone could whistle at any given moment."

Stephan put his fist to his mouth and cleared his throat as he cast a stealthy glance Annaliese's way.

Oh, that she could disappear.

"Herr Schroeder's nephew, Rory, whistled while trying to get Annaliese's attention earlier today and frightened the horses, resulting in the accident," Papa said.

"What was so urgent?" Reverend Hendricks asked. "Is Herr Schroeder still unwell?"

"Ja, but I suspect he will recover soon," Annaliese's father said.

"That is good to hear," Mrs. Hendricks said. "The lad would become an orphan if he lost his uncle."

"Hasn't he any parents?" Annaliese asked.

Mrs. Hendricks shook her head. "Herr Schroeder has raised his great nephew since the boy's grandfather died in the war."

"Rolof's late sister's husband," the reverend said. "Rolof's wife passed away from the influenza a few years ago and he has cared for Rory alone ever since."

"You speak of his grandparents," Papa said. "I assume they raised their grandson until Rolof became his guardian."

"Yes. Luisa Krause, the boy's sweet mother, died shortly after the birth and—" Mrs. Hendricks hesitated and looked at her husband.

"'Tis a shame, the boy never had a father." Reverend Hendricks tightened his lips. "He has taken on his uncle's surname."

The stool Stephan was leaning on suddenly pushed away from him, scraping against the floor, garnering everyone's brief attention. His face grew flustered as he settled the stool.

Papa looked down, shaking his head at the reverend's statement. "That is unfortunate."

Mrs. Hendricks clucked her tongue.

"How old is Rory?" Annaliese asked.

"I would say he is about ten or so," Mrs. Hendricks said.

Stephan's gaze shifted in her direction and she noticed the muscles in his jaw stiffen. Did he not care for the lad? But how could he not? The boy was affable, polite, and even funny.

Reverend Hendricks moved toward the chair at the head of the long table. "Please be seated everyone, and we can continue our conversation over our meal. We shall enjoy the *hasenpfeffer* that my wife has made for our dinner."

"Hasenpfeffer?" Stephan asked.

"Sour rabbit stew," Mrs. Hendricks said cheerfully. "With potatoes and fresh rye bread."

"*Wonderbar!* Annaliese's *mutter* used to make that for me." Papa looked from Mrs. Hendricks to Annaliese as they were seated. "Something gut for the day's troubles."

With the day not yet over, Annaliese could not help but wonder what else this day would bring.

Chapter 4

Stephan entered the parsonage with water dripping off his slouch hat and the caped shoulders of the oilcloth coat that he'd borrowed from the reverend. "The docktors and the landau are secured in the barn for the night."

"I did not realize we were expecting another rainstorm," Reverend Hendricks said. "Snow will be upon us before you know it."

"Oh dear, not yet. 'Tis only October. There remains a late harvest still for many to tend to." Mrs. Hendricks took Stephan's wet garments and hung them to dry.

Reverend Hendricks placed his hand on Stephan's back. "Come join us by the hearth, young man, where you can warm yourself."

Stephan sat on a Windsor chair by the large fireplace, facing Annaliese and Dr. Braun, who were seated in the settle, but he doubted anything would remove the chill he had after finding the headstone with Luisa's name on it out in the church-side graveyard. As he stood there in the pouring rain, a torrent of tears streamed down his face. Luisa, the young woman he had once loved—he'd found her at last, but there was no way to redeem the past. She was gone.

Stephan stared into the fireplace as Mrs. Hendricks poked the timbers in the hearth.

"This is a pleasant surprise, to have overnight guests at the parsonage," she said, as several sparks flew up.

"'Tis kind of you to accommodate us on such short notice." Annaliese glanced at her father apologetically, as he dozed against the high-backed settle. "Papa missed his afternoon nap."

Dr. Braun's eyes sprang open. "Who ist napping?"

Annaliese's face filled with mirth and she patted her father on the arm.

Stephan observed the warmth that passed between father and daughter. How he missed his own parents in Holland, though he trusted they were in his eldest brother's good hands. At times he wondered if it might have been best for him to return home after Hans had died, but by then he'd been offered employment by a comrade in New York, and he hadn't looked back.

"Stephan, I understand you are the new carpenter at Heath House," Reverend Hendricks said.

Stephan shifted in his chair. "Ja. It is a good resort, for its rustic charm. Mr. Marsh manages it very well." *Why must people ask so many questions?* Not that he had anything to hide. Not really. Not for certain.

"Folks have been resorting to Schooley's Mountain since the end of the last century. George Washington even stayed at Heath House," said Reverend Hendricks.

"Mr. Marsh preserves the room that the president slept in at the Alpha, the resort's oldest building." Stephan noted Annaliese, sipping her tea, looked like a fine society lady. "Is that correct, Annaliese?"

Annaliese nodded. "The furnishings are just as they were while he visited there, from what I understand."

"It is reported he wrote in his diary that he was not fond of traveling up the mountain in those years before Schooley's Mountain Road became part of the Washington Turnpike," the reverend said. "He called Dutch Valley to Schooley's Mountain a 'hazardous and round about thoroughfare.'"

"Dutch Valley?" Stephan asked.

"The name of this area before it became known as the German Valley," Reverend Hendricks said. "You have not visited my church before. Do you attend elsewhere?"

"I do," Stephan said. "I attend the stone church at Pleasant Grove, on top of the mountain by Heath House."

The reverend steepled his hands beneath his chin. "Ah. Many of the employees of the Heath House and Belmont Hall resorts attend there, whilst much of the German community come here."

"As do Annaliese and I," Dr. Braun interjected.

"Thank you," Stephan said, glancing up as Mrs. Hendricks handed him a tankard of coffee. He turned again toward the reverend, who sat in an upholstered wing chair. "Has your church been here long, sir?"

"Ah, yes. The original church was an old log cabin built in the 1740s.

For a long time it was the only outpost for pastors traveling abroad. Folks walked miles, many barefoot, to hear the sermons preached here," Reverend Hendricks said. "They used to heat the building by an eight-foot-square charcoal pit in the center of the building. It nearly smoked the parishioners out each Sabbath, as there was no chimney."

"And the pastor?" Stephan asked.

"He endured it. Reverend Henry Muhlenberg was a hearty and ambitious sort." The reverend folded his hands in his lap. "He was the patriarch of the Lutherans in America."

"He could speak eight languages," Annaliese added.

"Indeed he could, Annaliese, and that gave rise to the hundreds of congregations that he oversaw throughout New Jersey, Pennsylvania, and many other regions. He also had a few sons who became clergy, one of whom became a general in the War for Independence. And his namesake was also a pastor here and is responsible for having built this stone church in 1774."

Mrs. Hendricks, in a nearby chair, looked up from her stitching and clucked her tongue. "You needn't give him the entire church history, dear."

"I find it interesting and like hearing about the buildings," Stephan reassured her. "Your church is a unique structure, as churches go, with its sloping room and no steeple."

The pastor held his palms up. "Nor does it have a chimney, like the log church."

Stephan clasped his hands behind his head and stretched as he observed Mrs. Hendricks rise from her sewing and stoop by a low cupboard of the paneled wall to retrieve a log. He quickly rose. "Here, allow me to do that."

"Thank you, Stephan," she said, glancing toward the window. "The rain might have slowed, but I would like to keep the chill from setting in."

Stephan followed her gaze toward the window. If the rain stopped entirely he might make it back on his own, although it was growing dark—too dark for traveling. "I hope Mr. Marsh has concluded that we had a delay due to the rainstorm."

"I am sure of it," Dr. Braun said. "He knew our destination, and that we would have to remain here if the weather became inclement."

Annaliese smiled at Mrs. Hendricks and set her cup on the side table. "Our fine hostess would never have allowed us to return under such formidable circumstances."

"Thank you, dear. Now perhaps you can help me set the table for our light supper," the minister's wife said.

Annaliese rose from her seat. "I was just now going to offer." She walked across the wide span of the hearth, pausing in front of the log stack. She bent over and retrieved a paper from the floor.

His letter. It must have fallen from his waistcoat pocket. Stephan stood abruptly. "I believe that may be my letter from the Schooley Mount post this morning." He'd hardly had the time to contemplate a response. But now. . .

Annaliese held the folded paper with the broken wax seal. She turned it over, glancing down at the addresses. "Yes, it is addressed to Mr. Stephan Yost." Her eyes widened. "From. . .*Count de Survilliers*, Joseph Bonaparte!"

Annaliese handed Stephan his letter. "Please forgive me, Stephan. I was astounded to behold such a missive, in my very hands."

Stephan nodded as he accepted the letter and slid it into an interior pocket of his waistcoat. "My former employer."

Annaliese tilted her head with curiosity. "Joseph Bonaparte? Napoleon's brother? The former king of Spain?"

Stephan smiled. "I was not a member of his royal court, if that is what you were thinking."

"I thought you worked up at Saratoga Springs?" Papa asked Stephan, although that was news to her.

"I met Mr. Bonaparte at Saratoga. When he saw my carpentry work and learned that I had also worked on the Sans Souci Hotel, he contracted me to work for him. He employed me for the winter at Point Breeze, his estate in Bordentown. It is an impressive property overlooking the Delaware River." Stephan looked at Mrs. Hendricks. She was listening attentively with the others, who were now gathered around him. "I apologize if I am keeping you from your work, Mrs. Hendricks."

"I find this utterly fascinating. Do go on, please," she said.

Annaliese wondered, had Mrs. Hendricks just insisted that he share more? What little Annaliese was learning of Stephan, he did not seem overly forthcoming regarding his private affairs. Perhaps that would change in time, with her, as they got to know each other. She was hoping, after all, for. . .a friendship.

Stephan rubbed the back of his neck and drew in a deep breath. "The estate burned to the ground this past January—"

"Oh, yes. We heard about that, did we not, dear?" Mrs. Hendricks inquired of her husband.

"I understand that the neighbors were able to save some of his valuable belongings," the reverend said.

"He was most grateful for their coming to his aid. He immediately set about rebuilding on his property by converting his brick stables into a new mansion. Mr. Bonaparte contracted me to remain until its completion in June."

"And that is when you arrived at Heath House," Annaliese said, glancing at the floor. She would not want him to think she had been observing him since he had arrived in Schooley's Mountain, although she had certainly taken notice of him.

"Ja. He provided me with an excellent reference for Mr. Marsh when I expressed my desire for employment at Heath House. He informed me that he was fond of Schooley's Mountain and had almost built his estate by Budd's Pond."

Mrs. Hendricks gasped. "Truly? Could you imagine that?"

"I have heard that he has visited the spring," Papa said. "Perhaps he will resort to the new Belmont Hall sometime, in keeping with his finer tastes."

Annaliese perched her chin upon her fist, glancing up at the beamed ceiling. "I hear that Belmont Hall is exquisite, but I must say that I shall always prefer the rustic charm of our little cottage at Heath House." She hooked her arm around her father's elbow. "In fact, I wish we could live here all year round."

Papa craned his neck toward her and proffered a grin. "Perhaps you shall receive that wish someday, my Annaliese."

She widened her eyes. "Might you consider it, Papa?"

Her father's palms turned upward and he glanced at Stephan, but for an instant. "Eh, we shall see."

The carpenter's brow drew into a subtle arch before his eyes darted toward hers. "You might ask Mr. Marsh to install a larger woodstove in your cottage, although it would take a bit of work to ready the abode for winter's use."

"'Tis a lovely idea. Although Mr. Marsh would never allow it. The resort will close up completely until spring preparations." Annaliese cast her gaze away.

"Maybe someday you will remove here for good, Dr. Braun," Reverend Hendricks said. "Perhaps when you retire."

"We would love to have you a part of the community year round." Mrs. Hendricks looked from Papa to Annaliese with a smile. She then turned to Stephan. "What about you, Stephan? Where do you go in the winter months, other than to the grand estate of Mr. Bonaparte?"

Stephan widened his stance, clasping his hands behind his back. "That is yet to be determined. The letter from Bonaparte. . . His resident carpenter has been dismissed and he desires that I return for permanent employment."

"Do you mean to say that if you take the position we will not see you again at Schooley's Mountain?" Reverend Hendricks inquired.

"That is the count's request," Stephan said, his mouth pulling taut.

Mrs. Hendricks sighed, and sighed again. Her gaze flitted toward Annaliese and back again to Stephan. "You be sure to take the matter to the Lord, won't you, Stephan?" she said, smoothing her hand over her mobcap.

Stephan gave the reverend's wife a nod and looked down at the floorboards. Annaliese lowered her head but felt his gaze on her. She looked up, their glances caught, ever so briefly, and a torrent of emotion saturated her with loss, regret, and could-have-beens.

"Come now, Annaliese. Let us prepare the table. It is time to sup," Mrs. Hendricks said. "You men can retreat to the parlor."

As Mrs. Hendricks went to the kitchen, Annaliese gathered the creamware plates from the hutch and set them around the table. The pattering of the rain, falling heavily on the rooftop, harkened to her long-dormant thoughts of discovering love. If ever that were to be, surely she could love someone like Stephan Yost.

Annaliese turned around to retrieve the bowls and collided with Stephan. She drew in a little breath and was about to say she was sorry, but the words would not form.

Stephan steadied her by his firm grip upon her forearm. As he looked deeply into her eyes, the pressure of his hold lightened. His hand trailed over her wrist and his fingers twirled around hers, sending warm shivers through her. His eyes darkened, and he seemed to breathe in her scent.

And then he released her.

Chapter 5

Stephan stood in the frosted yard of the Union Church's cemetery. Speckled with red and gray slate grave markers, some in flowing German script, Stephan stared at the only one that mattered:

IN MEMORY OF

LUISA

BELOVED DAUGHTER OF

HEINRICH AND FREIDA KRAUSE

1792~1810

AGE 18

Stephan slammed his clenched fist against his thigh. *Nee!* She was too young. Her name should not be inscribed upon a tombstone at all. She should have never carried his child. He should have never left her. She should be alive.

Stephan groaned beneath his breath, "Oh, God. How can You forgive me?" He closed his eyes tightly, and his temples pulsed. He pivoted around and swooshed the air from his lungs into the cold morning air.

"Stephan."

The small cloud of condensation hung in the air between him and Reverend Hendricks. "Luther and I returned from our morning walk and saw you out here." The minister looked down at the headstone. "Did you. . .know her?"

Stephan swallowed the lump in his throat. "I knew her."

Reverend Hendricks shoved his hands into the pockets of his black frock coat, eyeing Stephan with concern. "Did you. . .love her?"

"Not enough." Stephan rubbed his temples.

"You are Rory's father."

"I believe I am."

Moments passed until Dr. Braun's call broke through the silence. "*Guten morgen*, Reverend Hendricks, Stephan. We are ready to depart when you are."

Stephan looked up and saw the doctor on the path in front of the church. "Good morning, doctor. The horses are harnessed to the carriage so we can leave now, if you wish." Stephan looked back at the reverend. He hesitated, not knowing what more could be said.

Reverend Hendricks nodded in understanding. "Perhaps we can continue this conversation another time."

"Perhaps."

Stephan stuffed his hands in his coat pockets and strode toward Dr. Braun, looking down at the crunchy earth beneath his boots as he went. He took a deep breath and glanced up as Annaliese ambled toward her father, looking as crisp as the morning. A bittersweet chill rustled over his skin at the sight of her.

"Good morning, gentlemen," she said, smiling. She glanced about and took in a deep breath of the fresh morning air. "There is something about the air after it has rained. It is like all things are cleansed, made new again."

Stephan could feel his brow lift slightly, affected by Annaliese's optimism. *If that were only true, many things would be different.*

"Each day is a gift," Reverend Hendricks said. " 'It is of the Lord's mercies that we are not consumed, because his compassions fail not. They are new every morning: great is thy faithfulness.' "

"Amen," said Dr. Braun. " 'Tis gut medicine."

" 'Amen.' The word is the same in English, German, and Dutch," Reverend Hendricks said.

"I know we say 'amen' in agreement, but what does the word mean exactly, Reverend Hendricks?" Annaliese asked.

Reverend Hendricks inclined his head toward Annaliese and then glanced around the group as he spoke. "The original Greek word means 'so be it.' " As the reverend spoke the last words, his gaze rested on Stephan.

So be it.

Stephan brought the carriage around, and he and Annaliese and Dr. Braun said their farewells to Reverend and Mrs. Hendricks, thanking them for their hospitality. Onward they went, through the tollgate, over the bridge, and up the turnpike road to Schooley's Mountain. Annaliese sat with a blanket over her lap on the driver's seat next to

Stephan, while Dr. Braun sat in the back of the carriage.

"How kind it was of the reverend and his wife," Annaliese said, "to allow us to stay with them overnight. Mrs. Hendricks was even able to repair the tears on the seams of my coat and on my gown. I do say, Papa, it would be nice to have a large home someday, with plenty of room for guests and little wanderers, like Rory Schroeder."

"Do you not like our apartment in Manhattan?" Dr. Braun asked.

"Oh yes, Papa, it is a beautiful place, but you know how I feel about the city." Annaliese angled toward Stephan. "We live in an impressive building, in the Dutch style, in fact. But our apartment is rather supercilious for my taste. I prefer a more homelike atmosphere."

"I know your taste is not the same as your mutter," her father said.

"I fear, Papa, we have allowed our home to become somewhat of a museum to her memory," Annaliese said.

"You may decorate *die* apartment any way you desire, mein liebchen."

"There is only so much that can be done with ten-foot arched windows, Papa. And the ornate marble fireplaces." Annaliese tapped Stephan's sleeve. "Do you know that our ceilings are fourteen feet in height?"

"That sounds like Bonaparte's mansion," Stephan said. "I take it you would not be comfortable there, either."

"Not at all. Too much pretense." Annaliese curved her shoulder and grinned. "Although I would not mind visiting Point Breeze someday, just to take it in. It must be grand. I do not see why Mr. Bonaparte would ever need to go to a resort when he owns such a place."

"One thousand acres," Stephan said.

"He should have moved here and bought all of Schooley's Mountain," she said. "I would have."

"Would you settle for a little piece of it, Annaliese?" Dr. Braun called from the back.

Annaliese spun around. "I would!"

"Then, Stephan, you may stop up ahead, as I asked you to earlier," the doctor said.

Stephan snapped the reins and they continued up the steep dirt road. He turned the carriage onto a cleared path and parked in front of a large, newly shingled house.

Annaliese looked curiously from her father to Stephan and back again. "Papa, what are we doing here? Does anyone live here yet? I have seen the house being built but did not realize it was yet finished."

"It is not finished," Stephan said, before jumping down from the carriage and securing it. He took a rope and tied the horses to a black gum tree.

Dr. Braun stepped down, onto the soggy leaves littering the drive. "Annaliese, the ground is too *vet*. You shall have to remain in the carriage." He winked at Stephan and turned back to his daughter. "You will have to keep the docktors company."

"Papa! Don't be ridiculous!" Annaliese protested from her perch, readying to get down.

Stephan chuckled and eyed Annaliese's father. "If I may?"

Dr. Braun nodded.

Stephan swooped Annaliese into his arms and carried her up the front steps of the house. He leaned down for the door handle, released the latch, and gently kicked the door open.

"Oh!" Annaliese sighed.

Dr. Braun cleared his throat behind them and Stephan set her down on the unfinished oak flooring.

Annaliese spun around, facing her father. "Papa, it is beautiful! Who owns it?"

"Why, you do, liebchen," Dr. Braun said, taking her hands in his. "Do you like it?"

"Oh, yes, yes. Am I dreaming?" she asked.

"The previous owner decided to move to the shore and took the builder with him. So I have bought it for you. . .if you agree to spare a room for your dear alt vater in his retirement. I have asked Stephan if he might finish the interior so we can move here by Christmas."

Annaliese's eyes glistened as she looked from her father to Stephan. He placed his hand over the missive from Bonaparte and knew at once he must decline the generous offer. He might not be able to give Annaliese his heart, but he at least could give her a home.

❧❧❧

The fresh scent of new wood and plaster filled Annaliese's senses as she wandered from room to room in the fine, two-story house. She could hardly believe that this charming dwelling would soon be her home. She made her way from the dining room back to the double parlor where Papa and Stephan engaged in conversation about the house. "In time for Christmas, you said, Papa?"

"Ja, I have an interested buyer for our apartment in Manhattan. His stipulation is that his family be allowed to move in by Christmastime," her father said. "So what do you think? Shall I agree to his terms?"

"A home for Christmas? Yes!" Annaliese twirled around and nearly bumped into Stephan.

The corners of his eyes crinkled as he gazed at her. "You are pleased with your new home, ja?"

"I am. And have you agreed to finish it for us?" she asked.

Stephan grinned. "I try to finish what I start."

Annaliese looked up at him, narrowing her eyes. "What do you mean?"

Stephan leaned his palm against the door frame. "I worked on the house this summer, during my hours off from Heath House."

"No wonder I hardly saw you around the resort."

"Stephan, you are a very industrious man," Papa said. "Now we shall have to find you a place to stay once Heath House locks up for the winter."

Annaliese tilted her head. "Perhaps the Hendricks would allow you to stay with them."

"Well, if it would be all right with you, Dr. Braun, I could reside here while I work on the house. Perhaps Mr. Marsh would allow me to borrow a cot."

"You will freeze," Annaliese protested.

"The fireplaces are in working order," Stephan said. "As long as you don't mind me christening them."

Papa walked over to the hearth. "You would need to light them anyway so you have some warmth while you work. It sounds like a fine solution to me."

"Then it is settled. You have yourself a home." Annaliese joined Papa near the fireplace.

"Until Christmas," Stephan said.

"Und vat will you do after that?" Papa asked him.

Stephan shrugged. "I have not yet decided."

Annaliese ran her hand over the frame surrounding the opening of the fireplace. She thought of the request Stephan received from Joseph Bonaparte, the good Bonaparte, as Americans called him. Would he accept the invitation of permanent employment in Bordentown? That was so far away, in southern New Jersey. She might never see him again.

Stephan walked toward her. "What type of mantel do you envision, Annaliese?"

The deep timbre of his voice brought her out of her contemplations. "Oh. . .I do like the look of carved wood. Nothing overly ornate though."

"No beasts or dragons?" he asked.

"Heavens, no!" She giggled.

Stephan angled his jaw. "Cherubs, perhaps?"

"Can you really carve all those things?" she asked.

"Woodwork is my specialty," Stephan said. "May I suggest some dentil molding with some botanical carvings, and fluted columns on each side? A medium stain of oak, possibly?"

Papa chuckled. "Ha! You know my daughter quite *vell*!"

Annaliese beamed. "Your suggestions sound perfect to me." She floated toward the large bay window at the front of the house. "Could the window and door trim match?"

"Ja. And the balustrade and railing for the stairway as well." Stephan smiled broadly. He seemed to take joy in his work, and in pleasing her. Or was that her imagination?

Annaliese looked up the stairwell. "Is it safe to go upstairs? I would like to see the bed chambers."

Stephan gazed upward, past the hard oak treads. "It is safe. But the walls remain unplastered. There are only the partitions there now."

"I would like to look around," Annaliese said. "Which room will be mine?"

"Any one of your choosing, dear," Papa said as he opened the front door. "Stephan, you go up with her. I vill check on the docktors. We do not want them running off again."

Annaliese climbed the first tread and looked back at her father. "Hippocrates and Galen will need to become accustomed to this location as their new home." She clamped down on her lower lip, widening her eyes. "I did not notice a barn. Is there a stable for them?"

Stephan joined her at the bottom of the stairs. "There is a shed behind the house, ample enough for a temporary shelter for the horses and the carriage. But I can build a barn, come spring."

Annaliese noticed the muscle in his jaw twitched. Perhaps Stephan's statement was premature, unless he had hopes of returning to Heath House next year. Or was something else on his mind? On any account, she must discourage it. This talented man had a great future in store for him, and she was certain that it did not include a spinster like herself.

Chapter 6

Bracing his elbow on his knee, Stephan leaned over and swung his hammer into the warped frame of lattice on the rear of the spring house. The enclosure guarded the reservoir of healing waters that streamed into the upper-level basin and the lower-level bathhouse for those who wished to take the cure. With November nigh upon them, he busied himself with end-of-season tasks, including the maintenance of the mineral springs. He climbed up on top of the low roof, with the aid of some nearby boulders, and went to work securing several loosened shingles. He tossed a small fallen branch onto the ground.

"Hey, what are you doing up there? You almost hit me!"

Stephan peered over the edge and saw young Rory Schroeder standing with his arms crossed over his chest and a scowl on his face. Stephan wiped the perspiration from his brow with the back of his hand. He hadn't counted on seeing the boy quite so soon. "Sorry, son." Stephan groaned inside. Why had he called him that?

"Mr. Yost! It's you! Are you all right? You don't look so well," Rory called up to him. "Here, let me come up and help." He bounded up the huge rocks before Stephan could protest.

Stephan grabbed Rory by the shoulders as the lad steadied his footing on the low-pitched roof. "How did you do that so fast, boy?"

"I always climb up here," Rory said. "Let me show you where I sit." He planted himself down, back against the wall of the upper part of the building.

Stephan lowered himself down beside him, knees bent and boots holding him secure. He looked at Rory. The boy sat leaning forward, with his arms crossed over his knees. "What do you see out there?" Stephan asked.

"It is not so much what I see, but what sees me." Rory angled his head, looking up at Stephan. "It's the water coming down the mountain in that trough. They call it healing waters."

"That they do," Stephan said. "You are a deep thinker for a kid."

Rory stared at the water coming down the hill. "That's what Uncle Rolof says. He does not like to listen to my prattle."

"How is your uncle?" Stephan asked.

"He is feeling better, but he was mighty sick." Rory looked at Stephan. "Do you know him? I told him that you drove us to the mill the other day to help, and he said you had a familiar-sounding name."

"I reckon there are many Yosts in this region. I hear there are many in Pennsylvania and New York as well," Stephan said.

"Are they all relatives of yours?" the lad asked.

Stephan chuckled. "Nee, I have no relatives in America." *Except one.*

"Nee? What does that mean? Wait, let me guess." Rory scrunched his face, looking up. "Hmm. . .it means 'no.' Am I right?"

Stephan smiled and nodded his head. "You are right. Now you know a word in Dutch."

Rory scratched his head. "How do you say 'yes'?"

"Ja." Stephan's gaze settled on the boy's blond hair, so much like his, and large brown eyes, like his mother's.

"That is German," said Rory.

Stephan nodded. "It is. But it is the same in Dutch."

"Dutch. . . Is that where you are from?"

"I am from Holland. Dutch is the language spoken there."

Rory tossed a little twig off the roof. "I would like to go to Holland someday. And Germany."

"It is very far from here," Stephan said. "It took me six weeks by ship over the Atlantic Ocean."

Rory's eyes widened. "I have never seen the ocean before. Are there sea monsters?"

Stephan laughed and pointed to the stream of water. "About as many as there are swimming down that trough. But I will tell you this. Do you know who Napoleon Bonaparte is?"

"He was that evil emperor from France. We learned about him in school," Rory said.

Stephan cocked his head. Of course the boy went to school. Stephan had noticed a few log school buildings in the area. So why did it surprise him? Rory was a very bright boy. His boy.

Stephan pulled in a deep breath. "Napoleon's brother, Joseph, the good Bonaparte, as Americans call him, lives in southern New Jersey. I used to work at his estate, and I helped build his new mansion."

"He does? You did?" Rory's eyes got even bigger.

Stephan nodded. "Ja, the Bonapartes are no longer allowed in France. The story goes that Joseph Bonaparte was out hunting in the Pine Barrens one winter day when he came across tracks in the snow that looked like a two-footed donkey. He followed them and heard a great hissing sound and a fearsome creature suddenly appeared. It had the head of a horse and legs like a bird, and great wings." Stephan held out his arms. "Then suddenly it flew away."

Rory stared at Stephan with his mouth open. "Is that one of those tales made up by Miss Braun's friend? The one who wrote about Rip Van Winkle?"

Stephan laughed. "Nee, that creature is called the New Jersey Devil. But that account might have been made up by Mr. Bonaparte."

Rory narrowed his eyes. "You don't think that creature knows its way to Schooley's Mountain, do you?"

"If there were such a creature, I do not think he could find his way here. He most likely has a distaste for the mineral water. Too much iron in it," Stephan said.

Rory frowned. "It would probably make him too heavy to fly."

"Ja," Stephan said with a nod.

"I like the water. But Uncle Rolof will not allow me to go to the cataract down the road by myself. He says it is too dangerous for me. So that is why I come here. I like the sound of the water flowing down the wooden pipe."

Stephan placed his hand to his ear to make a show of listening. "Mmm-hmm. It does sound nice." The pair sat in silence for a little while, looking out at the stream coming down the mountain.

Rory stared straight ahead. "Reverend Hendricks says if we believe in Jesus Christ, that His Spirit is like streams of living water flowing in us."

Stephan slowly turned toward Rory, though the lad remained focused on the water flow. What caused a boy his age to contemplate such profound thoughts?

"Do you believe that, Mr. Yost?"

Stephan slid his hand back over his hair, his mouth taut. "Ja, Rory. I do." But why did that "living water" inside him feel so stagnant at times? "Is that all the water makes you think of, Rory?"

"I think about my mutter. I did not know her. But she knew me. . . for a few minutes after I was born. My grandparents told me that she loved me and I will see her in heaven. It is the gift of Jesus."

A well of emotion surged through Stephan. He clenched his fists and turned his head away from Rory. He blew out some shallow breaths, hoping the boy would not hear him. Then he stood. "I have a bit of spare time. How about we take a walk down to that cataract, if you think your uncle would not mind, since an adult would be accompanying you."

Rory jumped to his feet and climbed over the edge of the roof onto the boulders. He bounced around on the ground. "Schnell, Mr. Yost, schnell!"

Stephan put his tools aside, and he and Rory tromped down Schooley's Mountain Road toward the waterfall, partway to Hackettstown. The day was yet mild for that final week of October and the trees were a vivid display of red, orange, and yellow. Rory skipped ahead every once in a while, whistling "Yankee Doodle" while he waited on the fence posts that lined the turnpike for Stephan to catch up. At least the whistling could do no harm this time.

Rory hopped off the fence and came bounding back toward Stephan, up the middle of the dirt road, twirling around like a top. Suddenly, the ground vibrated beneath Stephan's steps, and the clopping of horse's hooves and wagon wheels thundered from behind him. Stephan spun around. A stagecoach and six-horse hitch rumbled full speed down the mountain. He turned back with a shout. "Rory!"

Rory tripped and fell on the road and started to get up, but when he saw the stage nearing, he froze. Stephan bolted toward him and swept him out of the road, the two of them rolling toward the fence.

The stage whirred by in a blur of red and black. Stephan's heart thumped wildly within his chest, and gravel dug into the skin on the back of his hands. He looked down at Rory, cradled in his grip, his eyes closed, his face deathly white. *Oh, God, nee!*

✂❧❧✂

Stephan patted Rory's ashen face. "Wake up, son. Wake up!" The boy's eyes fluttered open and Stephan sighed with great relief.

Rory looked about. "Why are we on the ground?" He sat up abruptly. As realization dawned, his glassy eyes widened. "We were almost run over."

"You are safe now." Stephan looked at Rory with concern, scanning his small body. "Are you all right?"

Rory pushed to his feet and stood. "Ja, I think so." He shrugged and wiped the dirt from his sleeve.

Stephan rose, and as he did, he noticed that the stagecoach had come to a stop and the team of horses stood, restless. A man dressed in striped trousers and a tall beaver hat tromped up the hill and called out, "Everyone all right here?"

"We are fine." Stephan nodded, brushing the dirt from his bruised hands.

The man narrowed his eyes at Rory and then glowered at Stephan. "Keep your son out of the road! What kind of father are you?"

Stephan clenched his teeth, glaring at the arrogant man. He stepped forward, shielding Rory from the stranger.

The man swatted his gloved hand into the air dismissively and turned around, heading back to the coach. Stephan and Rory stared at him as he stalked away, his dark coattails flapping as he went. The stagecoach pulled away, stirring up dust in its wake. Stephan released a swoosh of air through his teeth. He glanced down at Rory, shaking his head, and the side of his mouth curved.

Rory grinned at Stephan. "That man thought I was your son."

Stephan slid his palm over his chin. "Ja."

✂❧❧✂

Annaliese sat on a rock overlooking the cataract. Water cascaded over and between boulders and mossy rocks from the steep embankment leading up the side of the mountain. The tranquil setting was what she needed as a retreat from her busy days, but this day she shared it with her assignment from Mr. Marsh to write an advertisement for *The Fashionable Tour*. She sat on a dry rock, basking in the sun of the early autumn afternoon, the sound of the rippling water soothing her. She laid her writing notebook and graphite pencil down beside her. The pencil rolled down the rock and plopped into the stream below. She released a deep sigh as it floated away, disappearing behind some rocks. Her gaze landed on a scattering of brightly colored leaves floating upon the waters pooled within a small gorge. As the water flowed into the pool, two leaves spun around in a magical dance, and she imagined that one of them was she and the other Stephan.

Plop. An acorn dropped from a branch above and splashed into the water between the two leaves, sending them in opposite directions. Is that how it really was with her and Stephan? Annaliese's attention traveled over the tiers of waterfalls trailing from the mountain, and she thought how pretty it would be to see this place in winter, when the waterfall froze in place. With a new home on Schooley's Mountain by Christmastime, she would be able to come and see the curious sight— the flow of water frozen in time. Was that how her life had become? She was hidden away, year after year, in the shelter of this serene dwelling, her life neither retreating nor moving forward. Yet, she was indeed growing older, as was Papa. Was it selfish for her to think that perhaps someday she might have a family of her own? She'd resisted the idea for so long that time had seemed to stand still. But like Rip Van Winkle, would she awaken someday to find that life had passed her by?

Annaliese stood and stretched her arms toward the tree tops, the colorful canopy of splendor overhead. God's glorious creation, His banner of love. *Lord, please help me to be open to Your will, and not seek my own way.*

She placed her small notebook inside her redingote pocket and began her descent down the rocky slope which was laden with leaves, fallen trees, ferns, and other woodland plants.

"Hello!" a voice called from the ridge above.

Annaliese turned back, shielding her eyes from the sun, her abrupt movement causing her to nearly lose her footing.

The man shuffled his way down to help her. With his feet planted at an angle on the slope, he extended his hand to her.

She took hold of his grasp, found firm footing, and let out a little breath. "Thank you, sir. 'Tis slippery."

The man tipped his tall Parisian hat and smiled. "Harlan Beatey, at your service."

Annaliese glanced about and spied Galen where she had tied him to a tree at the bottom of the hill. 'Twas awkward to be alone with an unknown man in the woods, or anywhere for that matter, although it occurred to her how safe she had felt with Stephan when she had first met him. "Annaliese Braun."

"It is a pleasure to make your acquaintance, Miss Braun," the man said. "It is miss?"

"Yes," she said uncomfortably, her eyes scanning him from his fuzzy reddish sideburns to his peculiar, new-fashioned striped trousers.

The man glanced down at a compass in his hand and grimaced. He pulled a paper from his pocket and unfolded it, holding it in his other hand. "I can't understand this thing. The needle spins contrary to my reckoning of this map."

"You are lost then? Perhaps I can be of assistance," Annaliese said.

The man's eyebrows made a subtle dip as his gaze roamed her form. "Perhaps you can."

Chapter 7

"Galen." Stephan glided his palm over the withers of the gelding and looked at Rory. "This is the Brauns' horse."

"What is he doing here?" Rory stroked the horse's neck and answered his own question. "Maybe Dr. Braun is taking a hike at the cataract. He sure has a strange-looking saddle."

"That is a sidesaddle for a lady," Stephan said. "I think it is more likely that Miss Braun is the one visiting the cataract."

Rory jaunted ahead and turned back to him. "Let's go find her!"

Stephan strode forward, calling, "Be careful on that hill." He glanced upward, chuckling. How had he managed to care so deeply for two people within a few days' time?

"Look, there she is! Miss Braun!" Rory shouted.

Stephan and Rory stood on the side of the mountain, almost to the ridge, and beheld Annaliese being scooped into a man's arms, her arm wrapping around his neck. As they came closer, Stephan stared into her eyes. "Annaliese. Forgive us, we did not mean to intrude." He put his hand on Rory's shoulder. "Come, Rory, let us go back."

"Wait!" Annaliese cried.

Stephan turned back. "Is everything all right here?"

"I assure you—" the man began.

"I was addressing the lady." Stephan glared at him.

Rory tugged on Stephan's sleeve. "That is the man from the stage-coach," he whispered. Sure enough, it was the same arrogant fellow in his striped pantaloons.

As Rory took a step closer, Annaliese cried, "Be careful, there is a snake!"

Stephan tugged Rory back by the collar.

"There it goes!" Rory pointed with a stick as the snake slithered away.

Er schuilt een adder in het gras." Stephan locked eyes with the stranger, the Dutch proverb ringing true. His gaze darted around the mulched hill looking for the serpent, but, God forgive him, the one that concerned him the most was the one clutching Annaliese.

"You may put me down now, Mr. Beatey." Annaliese pointed to the large rock near Stephan and Rory. "On that rock, please."

The corner of Stephan's mouth curved in satisfaction. Annaliese preferred his protection over this dandy who was vastly overdressed for an outing in the woods of New Jersey. Stephan took her hand and helped her steady herself beside him.

Annaliese glanced up at him. "Mr. Beatey was trying to save me from the snake."

"How do you know that *he* is not the snake?" Stephan said in a low growl.

"Thank you for your assistance, Mr. Beatey. I would like you to meet my friends, Stephan Yost and Rory Schroeder."

The man tipped his fancy hat. "I believe we have met already."

Annaliese looked from Mr. Beatey to Stephan, raising her eyebrows.

"There it is!" Beatey shouted. He started snapping at the ground with his shiny black walking stick.

The snake slithered toward them. Rory picked it up with a stick and held it up in midair. "It is only a queen snake." He laughed as he looked up at Stephan and then flung it into the woods.

"Not a rattlesnake, eh?" Beatey said. "Well, I am not familiar with these parts."

"Mr. Beatey is lost," Annaliese announced. "His compass misguided him."

"*Een slecht werksman beschuldigt altijd zijn getuig,*" Stephan muttered under his breath.

"What does that mean, Mr. Yost?" Rory asked.

A bad craftsman blames his tools. But he wouldn't tell Rory that. He needed to temper the green-eyed monster that was rearing its ugly head. "A Dutch proverb, 'tis all."

Stephan addressed the strange gentleman. "Tell me, Mr. Beatey, what is your intended destination?"

Beatey held out his map. "I was scouting out this iron mine. The one that is circled."

Stephan surveyed the map. "And you found your way here to the cataract? The mine is on the other side of this ridge, about a half mile down."

"May I see your compass, Mr. Beatey?" Annaliese asked.

Beatey placed the round brass instrument in her palm. She took a few steps around the area.

"Is it broken?" Beatey asked.

"It works perfectly well," Annaliese said. "Come see."

The group came near and hovered over the compass.

"Blasted! It is broken," Beatey growled.

Annaliese looked up at him. "Sir, there is a child present."

"And a lady," Stephan said.

Beatey frowned. "Do pardon. Now, what is the issue with that worthless instrument?"

Annaliese turned the compass around in her hand. "Do you see no matter which direction that I turn, it continues to seek a westerly bearing? The magnetism from the iron in these rocks is attracting the needle."

"Do you mean to say that I found iron?" Beatey gloated.

Annaliese smiled at the man. "No sir. The iron has found you."

"There is iron all throughout this region, Mr. Beatey," Stephan said. "But the iron you are looking for is that way." He pointed over the mound of boulders.

"That is where my interest lies. I am hoping to acquire that mine to add to my holdings at the Van Syckle Mining Company."

"You have no surveyor?" Stephan asked.

"I fired him today, the incapable dolt. The map looked simple enough. . . ." Beatey tapped on the ground with his cane. "What say you, Mr. Yost? Would you care to show me the way? I shall pay you for your services."

"It really is not necessary. You can find the way easy enough. It is at the bottom of this ridge," Stephan said. "If you leave your compass in your pocket and simply follow the map, you will have no trouble at all. There is a trail down there, back out to the main road near the stage stop. I suspect that is how you came in."

"Do you mean to tell me that I already passed it by?" Beatey asked.

Stephan shrugged. "More than likely."

"I have never seen one of the mines before," Rory said.

"There now, Mr. Yost. Wouldn't you like to show your son that iron mine?" Beatey asked.

Annaliese looked from Rory to Stephan. She placed her hand over her mouth to cover a giggle. "He does have the looks of you," she said. "It must be his blond hair and that little cleft in his chin."

"So, Mr. Yost, Stephan, is it? You said it is not far from here. It could not possibly take much of your time. Unless, of course, Miss Braun would like to take a stroll with me."

"I really should get back to my work at the springhouse," Stephan said.

Annaliese's mouth opened, and she looked at Stephan, pleading with her eyes.

Stephan took a deep breath. "Very well."

The troupe made its way down the shallow descent of the mountain. Beatey endeavored to charm Annaliese with his attentions to her, taking advantage of every opportunity to hold his hand out to her, help her over a log, or take her by the elbow. Did she enjoy his attentiveness to her? Did she find a man in striped pantaloons and a fine cutaway frock coat appealing?

"I don't think she likes him," Rory whispered to Stephan.

"What makes you say that?" Stephan whispered back.

"She kept rolling her eyes when he looked away." Rory snickered.

"Ja?" Stephan asked, elbowing the boy.

"Ja." Rory elbowed Stephan back and laughed.

"What is so funny up there?" Annaliese called.

Rory turned around. "Nothing. Mr. Yost is just teaching me how to speak Dutch."

"I thought folks were mostly German in this area," Beatey said.

"Most of the early settlers and their descendants are," Annaliese said. "But Stephan is not from around here, though he now works up at the Heath House resort."

"A laborer?" Beatey asked, sniveling out the words as though it were a disease.

"He is a talented carpenter," Annaliese said.

"I see," Beatey said. "And you, Miss Braun?"

"My father is the resort's physician."

"Do you reside here year round?" the iron baron asked her.

"Not yet," she said, glancing at Stephan with a smile.

The terrain became rocky and Beatey took Annaliese's arm and wrapped it around his elbow. "I am staying at The Belmont. I understand this summer was their first season. They expect the resort will far exceed the spa at Saratoga with all the amenities they have installed—the bowling alleys, tennis courts, the fine cuisine."

"I do prefer the more rustic atmosphere of Heath House," Annaliese said. "It, too, has a great many amenities and has rivaled Saratoga Springs for years. Isn't that right, Stephan?"

"I have not been to a finer resort," Stephan said.

Beatey chortled under his breath, "You?"

I think the New Jersey Devil is in our midst, Stephan thought to himself.

"Folks love coming to the mountain," Annaliese said. "We have the purest chalybeate springs in the country, according to tests that have been done by esteemed scientists."

"Perhaps if my mining interest works out, I may move to Schooley's Mountain. I understand there is some fine property up by Budd's Pond."

Stephan groaned inwardly.

Beatey projected his voice—purposefully, Stephan thought. "Miss Braun, a fine lady like you must enjoy some of the finer things of society. The Belmont is holding their end-of-the-season ball tomorrow night, and I would be most grateful if you would accompany me."

Stephan's ears perked up, and coming to the bottom of the hill, he swiftly turned to wait for the pair. . .and to observe Annaliese's answer.

"Why, Mr. Beatey, that sounds delightful."

❦

"Yet unfortunately, I must decline." Annaliese's heart pattered within her chest. Whether it was due to the exertion of coming down the ridge or from the sudden influx of admiration by this unwelcome stranger, she did not know. Oh, she tried to be courteous, but nothing about the pompous iron baron appealed to her in the slightest.

"That is a pity. May I ask why?" Mr. Beatey scratched his wiry ginger sideburns.

"I am otherwise engaged," Annaliese said, casting her eyes to the ground. "You see, Heath House will be holding its own celebration of the season's end. It is an annual tradition."

"Surely you could miss it this once," Mr. Beatey said.

"I am responsible for planning and preparing for the party. So I must be present," Annaliese said. "Thank you, however, for your invitation."

Mr. Beatey looked at Stephan. "Are you going to be enjoying that party with Miss Braun?"

Stephan stood on the incline, leaning his weight on one boot. He looked steadily at her with his perfect green eyes and hiked his chin subtly. "If she would like me to."

A flurry of butterflies danced in Annaliese's belly. Was that a challenge? Did Stephan want her to clarify her preference of suitors right here and now? She pressed her palm against her woolen redingote and pulled in a deep breath. "All of the Heath House employees will be there. I hope you will attend." Annaliese could feel the warmth rising in her cheeks, despite the chilled air that was quickly descending upon them.

Stephan nodded and issued a satisfying grin toward Mr. Beatey.

Annaliese had the distinct feeling that Stephan had just staked his own claim. She cupped the side of her face with her gloved hand and glanced down. When she looked up again, she caught Stephan looking at her with the hint of a smile in his eyes.

"Perhaps another time, then, Miss Braun." Mr. Beatey looked at Stephan and shrugged. "Or perhaps not."

"Come," Stephan said, motioning for the group to follow. "The mine should be right over there." He looked up. "The cold is setting in and the sky is looking rather bleak. I hope we are not expecting an early snow."

Rory looked up. "Snow!" Then he looked down and held out his foot. "It's a good thing I have my new boots."

Annaliese looked at the lad with the slightly oversized boots, his corduroy breeches, and tiny waistcoat. "Yes, it is, Rory. But you aren't wearing a jacket today." *He really needs a mother's touch.*

"All right, let's get on with it. I'd like to take a look at the mine while there's daylight yet." Mr. Beatey marched forward, digging his cane into the hard ground.

Rory ran ahead, jumping over a log. "Is that it? That cave?"

"It sure is," Stephan called to Rory. "Go easy. And don't go inside until we get there."

In a moment they were all assembled around the dark opening of the mine. The large hole, as tall and wide as the men's height, had no supporting frames. It appeared as a simple hole carved out of the rocky slope. Annaliese walked over the broken rock surrounding the area and peered in. A bat flew out and she gasped.

Rory climbed up on the hill over the top of the mine, his arms stretched high into the air. "Look at me, I'm King of the Mountain!"

"Do be careful, Rory," Annaliese said.

Mr. Beatey proceeded to inspect the area. He took out his compass. "The needle is going berserk again. I guess we are in the right spot."

Rory pointed and called to them, "Hey, look! Your horse!"

Annaliese spun around and saw Galen, his reins dangling on the ground. "Oh no! He must have been frightened and come loose. How did he find his way up here?"

Stephan came to her side. "He must have followed your voice. Let's see if we can surround him." He looked at Mr. Beatey. "Would you help us circle her horse so he doesn't run off again?"

Mr. Beatey grumbled beneath his breath and tossed down a mining tool that he had found. As it hit the ground, it pinged when it landed against a rock. Galen startled, and his head perked up, but he did not run.

The three adults crept forward, encircling Galen. Mr. Beatey made an overzealous attempt and Galen trotted several yards away.

Stephan eyed Mr. Beatey and mouthed, "Slo–ow."

They continued their pursuit, arms held out, closing in on Galen. Annaliese rubbed her finger and thumb together, making some clicking sounds with her tongue as she tried to get Galen to focus on her. She slid her hand into the pocket of her long coat and thankfully discovered a small piece of carrot. She held it out in the palm of her hand and inched closer to him. Finally, she was near enough to grab his reins, but Galen jerked his head and the leather straps slipped through her fingers.

Then Stephan appeared on the bay's other side and gained a firm hold on his halter. He instantly began stroking the horse's neck to calm him.

Annaliese gathered Galen's dangling reins and gave him the promised carrot. "Oh, my naughty boy." She looked at Stephan and smiled relief.

"Are you talking about him, or me?" He cast her a sly grin.

She whispered, "Both."

Annaliese and Stephan walked back toward the mine. Mr. Beatey was far ahead of them, having wasted no time in getting back to his mission.

The iron baron called out as they came near, "The boy is gone!"

Annaliese caught her breath. "Perhaps he is hiding somewhere."

"Do you have the horse?" Stephan asked, his face tense with panic.

"Yes, go!" Annaliese held Galen with a secure grip, and Stephan sprinted ahead. She tied Galen to a low branch and followed him to the mouth of the cave.

Mr. Beatey turned around. "The boy is inside the mine. I can hear him calling for help. The cave floor slopes down and he must have fallen into a crevice."

Annaliese's hand flew to her mouth and she felt as though she would be sick. *Oh, Lord, please save him!*

Stephan came out from the dark entrance and wiped at his face, leaving a smear of moisture and dirt behind.

Annaliese rushed up to him. "Oh, Stephan, it is dangerous in there!"

"It does not matter. I must save my son!" His words froze in the air between them.

"*Your* son?" Her mouth went dry as she attempted to process this revelation.

Stephan pushed his hair back from his tense brow and nodded.

Annaliese couldn't speak. She, too, felt as if she had been sucked into that dark hole.

Chapter 8

Stephan swallowed hard. The pained look on Annaliese's face pierced through him. "I will explain later."

"There is no need, Stephan." Annaliese shook her head, her eyes filled with concern. "What happened to Rory?"

Stephan clenched his jaw and took a deep breath. "Rory is caught in a deep cavity of rock. The opening was covered with boards, but he fell through, and the boards are wedged on top of him. He says he is uninjured."

"Please, tell me what I can do to help." Her eyes darted up, and she looked at him with alarm. "It is beginning to snow."

Stephan glanced about. Indeed, large flakes began their descent like a bad omen. Beatey had slipped past them into the mine and now came out again, rubbing his arms. "It is like an icehouse in there," he said.

"Ja, I saw icicles hanging as the mine goes deeper," Stephan said.

"I could find no tools in there." At least the man had the sense in all of this to be industrious.

"Maybe we'll find something out here," Stephan said. What a time for him to be without his tools. He could go back and get them at the springhouse, but time was running out. The snow was falling and it would be dark before long. The three of them began a frantic search, kicking through the leaves on the ground, looking behind rocks and logs, the moss and peat.

"Over here," Beatey shouted.

Stephan rushed to where an old crate jutted out from a dense tangle of vines, strangling the thick trunks of nearby trees. He tore the slats from the top of the box with his bare hands. Out of the corner of his eye he saw Annaliese wince.

"Mining tools!" she gasped when he succeeded in opening the box.

Beatey reached inside and pulled out the broken end of an auger.

"I don't know what good this will do."

"Bring it anyway," Stephan said, retrieving a crowbar.

"Look! A shovel." Annaliese pointed to the ground where the rusted spade stuck out from beneath a mass of dead leaves.

Stephan uncovered the shovel and then groaned, discovering the handle broken off midway. "At least it is still useable." He pivoted around and dashed toward the mine, the others following.

Annaliese looked around at the light flakes of snow floating down from the sky. "I'm going to give Rory my coat."

Stephan caught her by the sleeve as she stepped ahead of him. "Nee!"

She spun around.

"It is far too dangerous. Do not go in there, Annaliese." He couldn't bear it if anything happened to her as well.

Annaliese nodded.

"Pray," Stephan said.

"I am."

At the entrance of the mine Stephan turned to Beatey. "Ready, Mr. Beatey?"

"Yes. And call me Harlan. Now let's go get the child."

Stephan nodded, but his heart stung. His child. *His* child.

"Please be careful," Annaliese said, looking at Stephan with a wealth of emotion in her crystal blue eyes. She offered him a faint smile, bolstering his hope. Could she really care for him, even though he was such a wretched soul?

Once the men had shuffled down the slanted floor of the mine, Stephan knelt over the opening that Rory had fallen through and called inside. "Rory, can you hear me?"

The lad's mumbled words echoed upward. *"Ja! Erhalten sie mich bitte heraus!"*

"What did he say?" Harlan asked.

Stephan knew not what Rory said, but he knew how to answer. "Do not be afraid. I am coming for you. God will help us."

"Are you sure about that?" Harlan asked, handing Stephan the auger.

"I am," Stephan said, ripping up the worn boards. "Give me the crowbar." With a strong grip on the end of the crowbar, he pried at a wide plank lodged between the dirt and rock walls. With a grunt, he fell backward as the plank released.

Beatey reached and pulled the board up. "It's a good thing that did not fall down and land on the boy."

"Ja," Stephan said. *Lord, please protect Rory. Give me strength and wisdom.* He glanced up at Harlan in the dim light. "We need to widen the opening so he can get back up. Those rocks tumbled in when he fell through."

Harlan squatted down, clearing the boards away. "Does he have enough air down there?"

"I hope, but I do not know how long it will last." Stephan drove the shovel into the pit. He grunted as it lodged in a crevice. "It's stuck. Let me have the crowbar again."

"Good God," Harlan said.

Stephan prodded against the shovel with the long iron tool. "That's who I am counting on." The shovel loosened, but the force slammed both shovel and crowbar against the hard rock lining the cavernous space. Stephan pulled with all of his might, but the tools would not budge and clung to the rock, too far from his reach to get better leverage.

Stephan stood and rubbed his sore hands, which were burning from the friction.

Harlan looked at him with surprise. "Are you giving up?"

Stephan stared at him and then grabbed the auger head and strode over to the wall of the cave. He placed the metal piece against the rock and it clung to it, like a magnet.

Harlan tried to pull it loose, without success. "It is magnetized."

"I am afraid so," Stephan said, wiping the perspiration from his brow. "That is what makes iron mining around here very difficult. I've heard some say that the force is that of a hundred pounds when trying to separate their tools." Stephan leaned back over the hole. "Hang on, Rory. . .Rory?"

"Hello!" Rory shouted back.

"I will return soon, Rory," Stephan hollered down. A burst of air sprang from his lungs at hearing the boy's raspy voice. Had Rory been crying? Was the air growing thin? Were there toxic vapors down there that would harm him?

Stephan dug his heels into the gravel as he ran to the entrance of the mine, Harlan following. The bright white almost blinded him as he took in the dusting of snow covering the landscape. He looked around for Annaliese, but she was gone—as was her horse.

⁂

Stephan's chest tightened as he anxiously scanned the forest. Then he caught sight of Annaliese through the trees in her long purple coat, riding away on Galen.

"It looks like she found some rope," Harlan said, picking up a coil of rope from atop a boulder. "And there is a note." He handed the paper to Stephan.

Stephan read the note aloud. "Gone for help. Found some rope in Galen's satchel."

Harlan looked up at the white-gray sky, briskly rubbing his hands together. "I wonder how much daylight we have left."

Stephan blew warm air into his cupped hands. "We should build a fire. Can you do that?"

"Yes. I have a tinderbox for my pipe in my coat," Harlan said.

"Build it near the mouth of the mine," Stephan said, "and then bring me some light."

"How do you expect me to do that?" Beatey asked.

Stephan took off his neck cloth and gave it to Harlan. "Tie this around the top of a thick branch and rub some sap on it so it will burn slowly."

Harlan looked at the neck cloth in his hand. "What will you be doing?"

"If I can use your cane, I'll continue digging to widen the pit. Then we can lower the rope down and pull Rory up."

"He's your lad?"

"Ja, but I only learned of it recently." Stephan took a deep breath. "I cannot lose him now."

Harlan tossed him the cane. "You already had one close call with him today. I apologize for that. I pushed the driver of my stage because I was anxious to find the mine in the daylight."

"I appreciate your help now," Stephan said, and hurried inside the mine.

Before long, Stephan had cleared the hole, with the help of the iron baron's wooden cane. It proved to be the perfect tool for the task. The hard silver cap on the bottom of the walking stick was not attracted to the magnetized iron embedded in the rock.

The dark space brightened as Harlan appeared carrying the primitive torch. He jammed it into a crevice. Stephan took the rope and knotted the end into a loop.

"Are we ready to do this?" Harlan asked.

"That we are." Stephan tied the other end of the rope around his waist and lay down on the ground in front of the hole. "I'm trusting you to hold on to me to keep me from falling in."

Harlan held Stephan by the legs. "No worries, my friend. Now get that boy of yours."

Stephan called into the dark pit, "Rory, I'm going to bring you up!"

"I'm ready!"

Stephan lowered the rope, and he felt Rory tug on it when it reached him. "Put this rope over your head and beneath your arms, and I will pull you up. But you help me by climbing, the way you do at the spring house."

Stephan secured the rope around his wrists and, hand over fist, hauled Rory out to safety.

Rory threw his arms around Stephan, and Stephan held him tightly, never wanting to let the boy go. "You were very brave, son. Very brave."

"You said God would help us, and I heard some water trickling down there, so I knew I would be all right."

Harlan put his coat around Rory. "That is the best sermon I have heard in a long time."

Stephan chuckled as they stood. "Mr. Beatey has been a great help." He extended his hand toward Harlan. "Thank you."

"It is the least I could do since I almost ran this boy down today." Harlan ruffled Rory's hair. "You are awfully cold, Rory. Let's go out by the fire to get warm."

They made their way out of the mine and warmed themselves by the small fire.

"Ah, the snow has stopped," Stephan said.

Rory looked up at him. "I did not know it was snowing at all."

At the sound of voices, they looked up to see Annaliese, Dr. Braun, Mr. Marsh, and Mr. Schroeder coming up the hill toward them, carrying lanterns and blankets.

Annaliese's gaze met Stephan's from across the firelight. "I met up with them at the springhouse looking for Rory."

Rory ran toward his uncle. "Onkel Rolof!"

"Mein *junge!*" Mr. Schroeder embraced Rory.

Annaliese wrapped a blanket around Rory's shoulders, "Oh, Rory, I am so glad you are all right." She then gave Harlan a blanket, thanking him for his help.

When she met Stephan and handed him a quilt, it took all the restraint he had to keep from taking her in his arms. Instead, he reached beneath the quilt and clutched her hand, whispering, "Thank you." The slight pressure of her fingers against the back of his hand was a soothing balm for his labor.

"Glad to see you are all right," Mr. Marsh interrupted, handing Stephan a bottle of mineral water and his gloves. "I found these with your tools at the springhouse, thought you might need them."

"Thank you." Stephan placed the gloves on his cold hands, though he hesitated at letting go of Annaliese.

"Are you well, nephew? I told you never to come here," Mr. Schroeder said, looking directly at Stephan.

"You told me not to come alone. I was with mein vater," Rory said, to the astonishment of all.

Mr. Schroeder faced the boy, holding onto his shoulders. "You mean your heavenly Father."

"God was with me, but I mean Mr. Yost, Onkel. He is my father. I heard him say so."

Stephan stiffened as everyone faced him. Rory couldn't have heard him from inside the mine.

Rory's uncle glared at Stephan. "Is this true?"

Stephan walked over to Rory, squatted down in front of him, and looked into his large brown eyes. "Rory, I *am* your father. But I only discovered the fact a few days ago. Had I known—" Stephan swallowed the lump in his throat.

"At the cemetery?" Rory bit his lip.

"Ja, how did you know that?" Stephan asked.

Rory gave him a worried look. "I go to my mother's grave sometimes on my way to school. I saw you there and heard you talking to Reverend Hendricks. . . . I did not mean to spy." His eyes became moist pools.

"You heard me say that I was your father?"

"Ja. I was hiding behind the stone church."

Stephan swallowed hard. "I need to tell your uncle something that you did not hear me say." Stephan stood and faced the man who had helped raise his son. "I came to Schooley's Mountain with my cousin in 1809. I fell in love with a beautiful girl named Luisa and we were secretly wed. She feared telling her parents because we were so young, and rightly so. It was an impetuous decision, so I left the resort but regret that I did not know that she was to have a child. Our child." He glanced at Rory, pained at the years he had missed in his son's life.

"Stephan, is that why you came back to Schooley's Mountain?" Dr. Braun asked.

"I came back to find Luisa. To apologize for leaving her to live with the secret of our marriage. I was so wrong." Stephan shook his head and tears streamed from his eyes as he bared his soul in the presence of all.

"If only we'd known. Luisa went to her grave with that secret." Mr. Schroeder shook his head. "She must have loved you very much."

"I have sought the Lord's forgiveness and I now ask the same of you, Mr. Schroeder." Stephan gave Rory a light touch on his shoulder. "And you, son."

"You are whiter!" Rory exclaimed.

"Whiter?"

"Look, it is snowing again, and you have flakes on your shoulders. God has forgiven you and you are whiter than snow!"

Stephan could not help but chuckle at Rory's proclamation, and the others joined in—Annaliese laughing and crying at the same time. No one could deny the truth of what Rory had said, not even himself.

Mr. Schroeder looked at Rory seriously. "Do you want Mr. Yost to be your father, Rory?"

Rory stepped toward Stephan. "Ja! Er ist mein vater. How do you say that in Dutch?"

Stephan pulled Rory into his arms. "I will tell you once we get out of this snow. You go on to the horses with your uncle Rolof and the others, while I put out the fire."

"I can take care of that if you wish," Harlan said.

"Thank you, but I have another matter to tend to as well." Stephan looked at Annaliese, and Harlan grinned. She whispered something to Dr. Braun and he looked back at Stephan, hesitating before he nodded to her.

The others departed, heading toward the trail where their horses and Mr. Schroeder's wagon waited. He would have to make haste. Annaliese came to him, and he pulled her into his embrace.

"Stephan," she said softly. Her beautiful eyes glistened as she stood by the firelight with the snow gently drifting around them.

He placed a finger to his lips. "Annaliese, I have a confession for you. You must allow me to tell you here and now."

She looked at him with concern. "There is nothing that you can say that will change my good opinion of you, Stephan."

"I am unworthy, but I must confess that I have loved you since our first kiss," he said, his voice raspy.

She pressed her mittened hand against the collar of her coat, and a blush crept over her face, though her eyes remained fixed on his.

Stephan touched her cheek. "I have learned that life hastens by—this early snow may melt by the morrow. I do not want to waste another moment of my life."

"Nor do I," Annaliese whispered.

Stephan wrapped the quilt around her shoulders. "I. . .I love you, Annaliese. I need you, and Rory needs a mother. I want to spend this, and every, season with you."

"Oh, Stephan. There is a time to love, and I love you now. . .and have from the time we met."

"I haven't much to offer but my heart, and a home for you by Christmas. Would you be my Christmas bride?"

Epilogue

Annaliese twirled around in the parlor of her new home on Schooley's Mountain Road. "I can hardly believe it is true. A home for Christmas!"

"I did promise you, my love," Stephan said, taking hold of her hand.

"That you did, and I never doubted you for a moment." Annaliese slid her hand along the shelf of the magnificent mantel that Stephan had carved, and faced him. "You did a remarkable job. I am so proud of your fine workmanship and for hiring a crew to complete the house in time. Everyone has been so nice to help us move in, and that includes your uncle Rolof," she said, looking down at Rory.

"I helped, too," Rory said, skipping toward the staircase. "I sanded the railing."

"Ja, and you did a fine job at that." Stephan nodded.

"We worked on it together, father and son," Rory said.

Annaliese walked toward the tabletop Christmas tree sitting in front of the large bay window. She admired the garlands, berries, glass balls, and candles with which they had decorated the tree. She toyed with the tiny pair of Dutch shoes that Stephan had carved and hung by a piece of twine. " 'Tis our first Christmas tree together."

"Ja, a tradition that both the Germans and the Dutch share," Stephan said.

" 'I feel the influence of the season beaming into my soul from the happy looks of those around me,' " Annaliese recited. "That is a line from *Old Christmas* that our friend Washington Irving wrote in his *Sketch Book* and sent to us."

Stephan gazed over her high-waisted evergreen gown with gold netting. "Have I told you this afternoon how enchanting you look—and how enchanting you are?"

She tugged on one of her long, white kid gloves. "Thank you. I am pleased to be escorted to the Christmas party at the Marshes' by my handsome men, dressed in your fine suits and Wellington boots." She walked toward Rory and straightened his cravat and kissed him on the nose.

"Before we attend the party, we have something to tell you, Rory," she said.

"Once we are married you will live here in this house with your new family—Annaliese, Dr. Braun, and I," Stephan said. "But you may visit Uncle Rolof anytime you wish."

Rory beamed. "That is the best Christmas gift ever!"

Annaliese grinned. "Now, please put your coat and scarf on and tell Dr. Braun that it is time for us to leave."

"We will meet you at the carriage, son." Stephan took Annaliese's red cape, trimmed in white fur, wrapped it around her shoulders, and donned his own overcoat. "Come." Stephan opened the door and led her to the front porch. "Reverend Hendricks has agreed to marry us here in your new home on Christmas Eve day, if you will have me. That way you will be my bride by Christmas."

"You mean *our* new home," Annaliese said, smiling. "The timing is perfect. We can be presented to the congregation the following Sunday, on New Year's Eve."

"What is so important about that?" Stephan asked.

"That means I will not have to enter a new year as a spinster!" she said, hugging him.

Stephan chuckled. "*I hou van je*—I love you."

"And I love you—*Ich liebe dich*." Annaliese glanced overhead to the small gable above the porch steps and beheld a ball of mistletoe hanging from a red ribbon. She tilted her chin at Stephan. "Where did that come from?"

"Here on Schooley's Mountain, of course. Do you remember that first day we met, when Rory caught us kissing?"

"Yes, he pointed over our heads and there was mistletoe hanging from that branch."

Stephan nodded.

"Truly? You went out there in this weather to get mistletoe?"

"It is not just any mistletoe." Stephan grinned. "It is our mistletoe.

And you do know what that means?"

She glanced up with her finger on her chin.

"The docktors are harnessed and ready to take us to the party," Stephan said. "You wouldn't want me to whistle, would you?"

"Oh no. I shall have to keep you from doing that. Unless *I* whistle first." Annaliese pursed her lips. Stephan lowered his mouth to hers, claiming her lips like a man who intended to become her husband.

When they pulled away and slowly exhaled, the clouds from their warm breaths mingled in the cold air. "We share the same air, and our hearts become one," Stephan said.

Annaliese gazed up at him. "Ever since you told me that you loved me on that ridge six weeks ago, I have felt as though I am living in a dreamland."

Rory popped out from behind a holly bush. "Papa, is she your liebchen?"

When they both answered "Ja," Rory leapt up the steps and threw his arms around his new mama and papa.

New Englander **Carla Gade** writes from her home amidst the rustic landscapes of Maine. With ten books in print she enjoys bringing her tales to life with historically authentic settings and characters. An avid reader, amateur genealogist, photographer, and house plan hobbyist, Carla's great love (next to her family) is historical research. Though you might find her tromping around an abandoned homestead, an old fort, or interviewing a docent at an historical museum, it's easier to connect with her online at carlagade.com.

I Saw Three Ships

by Pamela Griffin

Dedication

To my critique partners who helped on this project, a warm, heartfelt thank you, especially to Mom who is always there for me, and to my friends Adrie Ashford (O'Mooky) who gave so much of her time and herself to help me with this, and Jill Stengl who did likewise at a moment's notice. *Nollaig chridheil!* (Merry Christmas!)

Who can understand his errors?
cleanse thou me from secret faults.
PSALM 19:12

Chapter 1

Scotland, Mid-Nineteenth Century

With her gaze upon the ever-changing water, Rachel MacIvor sat on the heather-clad hill, aware of a peculiar insight that the pattern of her world would soon change. Yet she did not want her world to change. Once, years ago, perhaps. But not any longer.

She looked out over the simple fishing village, a gateway to the Highlands, near a wide stretch of river that bordered her home. Rose and gold filled the sky, casting a shimmering mantle of vibrant color upon the silvery-black water. The dark silhouette of her grandmother's croft could be seen from this vantage point, and as the colors in the sky slowly faded to twilight, Rachel pondered her weekly visit.

Seanmhair had been pensive this afternoon. Clearly something troubled her mind, as often as she'd glanced at Rachel while together they cleaned and prepared the fish. Normally one to inquire and not a bit apprehensive to speak her mind, Rachel refrained from asking the cause of her grandmother's odd behavior. Without understanding why, she realized that, should she ask, her grandmother's response might upset the everyday order of life as Rachel had come to prefer it. Often Seanmhair's aged blue eyes had turned toward the window that faced the Clyde, and Rachel would follow her gaze to see the graceful bow of a sailing vessel or a flock of birds sweeping over the water. Usually she enjoyed her visit to Seanmhair's, but today she'd felt no compunction about leaving before sunset. Now, however, the gloaming filled the heavens, and she knew a moment's guilt. That she'd sat on this hill and stared at the river for so long might cause concern if she were to return home late.

As she began to rise, a ship's silhouette came into view against the pink and violet sky. Before tonight she'd always looked away. But this evening she watched as the vessel sailed closer, and she recognized it as belonging to the small, family-owned Sinclair Shipwrights.

Inadvertently, her eyes swept to the right to the turrets of the square stone dwelling that perched atop a distant outcropping of rock.

Malcolm.

Bittersweet memories filled the wayward corners of her heart. Rachel had heard he'd returned home two weeks past to attend his father's funeral, but she had yet to see him. Not that she desired to. Far from it. Her dreams were too grandiose, she'd been told, and likely that was true. But her aspirations were never small, and she still couldn't accept the loss. It seemed an eternity since the bitter week Malcolm left for university, something they'd both known he must do, but an action she'd always felt would be preceded by a farewell on his part. But there had been no farewell, no word of explanation as to why he should so abruptly take off without coming to see her. How could he have been so cruel? After all they'd been to one another, how could he just vanish like a nighttime wraith in the emergence of dawn?

Upset, Rachel stood and brushed off the back of her skirts. Gathering her wool plaid tightly about her shoulders before facing the stout wind, she turned her back to the river and the ship it contained. With her teeth clenched in resolution, she climbed the path toward her parents' cottage. She had dallied long enough, dwelling in fantasies. For the most part she'd put such absurd inventions of her mind far behind her, but each time she viewed a ship, she wondered—at one time in her life she had hoped. . .

She shook her head fiercely at the wayward thoughts that broke through the gate she'd long ago erected against them. She'd been a fool to think the son of a wealthy shipbuilder would aspire so low as to seek a permanent relationship with herself, a simple lass, and once nothing more than a shepherdess. That was how she'd met him, all those years ago.

Closing her mind to the memory, firmly shutting the gate upon it once more, she continued her course up the hill strewn with autumn's remnants of heather and milky-golden thistle. Her attention latched onto the silhouette of a man standing in the distant shadows of some pines. Likely it was her father or her brother, Dougal, coming to meet her. As she drew close, her breath stalled in shock and her mind took root in a quagmire of disbelief.

He walked toward her, his stride graceful. She could see by the breadth of his shoulders, the slenderness of his build, and the height of his stature that this dark-haired man was not her brother or father. The cut of his frock coat appeared costly. The angles of his face were as defined and perfect as she remembered them. Faint lines bracketed his nose, but they only served to make him more striking. His lips were slightly parted, as though he would speak, and for one unwelcome moment she remembered the feel of them against hers. She lifted her gaze to his eyes—as stormy green and mesmerizing as the river in turbulent weather—and steeled her heart against him.

"Rachel." The rich timbre of her name from his lips produced an unwanted shiver within her being.

"Malcolm." She said the greeting offhand, as if it had been only minutes since she'd last seen him and not years, though her quickened pulse belied her veneer of indifference. She grabbed both sides of her skirt and moved past in an effort to show that his existence mattered not one whit to her.

He fell into step beside her.

Neither of them spoke.

Rachel's recent thoughts of this man, of all that they'd been and could have been to one another, increased her ire. Her annoyance got the better of her and she whirled to face him. "Why have ye come?"

"I had t' see ye, t' speak with ye."

"Did ye now? And whatever for? I canna think why. To say good-bye, perhaps?"

He winced but did not respond.

His lack of an explanation served only to fuel her irritation. She thrust her palm against his shoulder, pushing him a step back. "You're an unfeeling rogue, Malcolm Sinclair, and that's all ye be, make no mistake about it." Another push with her other hand. "I'd hoped ye would drown in the river the day it took ye!"

After the third time she pushed him, he grabbed her upper arms to stop her. He leaned in close, their foreheads almost touching. "Still made up o' fire and spirit, I see. Yet could I expect any less from me wee Rachel?"

His low rolling words, the intense look in his eyes were almost her undoing—until he added the last.

She jerked her arms free of his hold and retreated a step before her traitorous senses could propel her to embrace him. "I am no' your wee Rachel. Nor shall I ever be. So I'll thank ye t' go back where ye came from and leave me alone!" Turning on her heel, she pivoted away from him.

❧

Malcolm watched Rachel go. The rigidness of her bearing warned him he should not persist, but he must speak with her before she learned the truth from another source. On hindsight, perhaps he should have let her parents divulge the news, but he was now bound by his words.

The moment he'd caught sight of her slight form and the way she walked with such assurance, the striking manner in which the rosy sky glanced off her saucy brown curls—as free and wild as the woman who'd laid claim to his heart years ago—he wondered how he could have left her. At the time he'd been easily convinced it was necessary, and fear of her rejection had been the driving force behind his decision. Now that he'd returned home to Farthay House, he knew it would require every bit of persuasion on his part to get her to listen to him, while the gist of the message would take a miracle for her to accept.

Blowing out a breath, he hurried after her. "Rachel, wait. Please listen t' me."

She whirled around. "Listen to you? Once, I would have desired nothing more than to do that very thing. But three years have made me ears a wee bit deaf to your words, Mr. Sinclair, and I can no longer hear you!"

His lips thinned at her sarcastic retort. "Stop it. You're acting like a wee bairn."

"Och, 'tis a child I am now? Humph. If it's only insults ye be hurlin' me way, I'll have none o' that from the likes o' you."

He forced himself to remain calm, reminding himself that she had every reason to be angry. He was deserving of her attitude toward him and more. "My cause for talking with ye stems from a far different nature than the past. I have a matter that needs discussing; one that involves you."

"Do ye now?" She crossed her arms over her chest and surveyed him with aloof incredulity. "I canna think what ye'd have to say that would involve or interest me in the slightest."

"Enough, Rachel."

Her expression changed to one of somber detachment. "Why did ye leave without a word, Malcolm, without so much as a good-bye?"

He tensed. Confessions were not compatible with her frame of mind, nor was he ready to speak them. He had hoped never to have to admit his faults to her, sure that the truth would only stir hatred, which she now seemed to possess in abundance toward him. Yet disclosure was imminent, though now was clearly not the time. Not if he hoped to gain her assistance, unwilling though it may be.

Her brow perched at a lofty angle. "Will ye no' answer me? Do I no' deserve even the favor of a reply?"

"Now is no' the time t' speak o' the past."

A disbelieving laugh escaped her throat. "My most profound apologies; you are quite correct. Perhaps we should allow another three years t' elapse before we do so." She gritted her teeth, let out a low growl, and started to stomp away again, but Malcolm grabbed her arm to stop her hurried flight.

"I'll thank ye t' let go o' me arm," she clipped.

"No' 'til ye cease with your tomfoolery and listen to what I have t' say."

She tried to shrug out of his hold, but he tightened it. After another vain attempt, her mouth firmed, and she assessed him, her chin held high. "Bein' as I appear t' have little choice in the matter, then say your piece and be quick about it, so I can be on me way."

He'd forgotten what a little spitfire she could be, but this roundabout was getting them nowhere. He released her arm, striving for peace. "Rachel, I am sorry."

"And so ye should be."

He inhaled deeply and let out the breath through his teeth. "Aye, ye are right t' place any scurrilous name on me that ye see fit, but for now ye must listen to what I have t' say." Before he could speak, a girl's cry sailed to them from the craggy slope.

"Rachel!"

They both turned to watch her ten-year-old sister, Abigail, scramble down rocks to the path on which they stood. "Is it true?" Panting, she threw Rachel an uncertain glance. "Are ye really leavin' us and goin' tae live at Farthay House? With himself?" Abigail threw an apprehensive glance in his direction.

Rachel whipped her shocked gaze to Malcolm's and he felt the situation crumble beneath his feet.

"Explain yerself, Mr. Sinclair."

Her words came as frosty as the air that would soon sweep over the land with winter's approach. At that moment, Malcolm would have far preferred to face three long months of old man winter's frigidity than three more minutes of Rachel's icy wrath.

Chapter 2

Rachel crossed her arms over her chest and waited. Abigail also looked his way, and Malcolm pointedly glanced at the small lass and then at Rachel.

"Abbie, run along home now. I'll be there shortly." Rachel relented, not for the sake of the cad before her, but because she didn't want little ears to burn with what she might hurl Malcolm's way should his explanation prove unsatisfactory, as she expected it would. The set of his broad shoulders, the telling clench of his smooth jaw, and the disquiet in his eyes verified she would loathe what was coming.

Abigail looked back and forth between them. "You'll no' be goin' with him, will ye, Rachel?"

Her features relaxed as she glanced at her sister. "Nae, wee lamb-kin. I'll be returnin' home soon."

Reassured, Abigail skipped off.

Rachel firmed her features into stone before facing Malcolm again. "Well?"

"Ye'll have heard about me father's passing, I take it?"

A modicum of remorse riddled her conscience, though she knew he had never shared close ties with his stern father; nor had she liked the man for his treatment of Malcolm and others he considered beneath him, namely those who worked for him at the shipyard. Still, decorum demanded she respond in a polite manner.

"My condolences t' ye and yer *màthair*," she mumbled.

"Thank you."

Decorum was never her strong suit. "So out with it then. Why have ye come t' find me? And what did Abbie mean by askin' if I was to go with you?"

He shook his head slightly, though she saw his mouth twitch. "Ah, Rachel. Your compassion overwhelms me."

His light words and expression carved her waning ire to another sharp point. "Are ye laughin' at me, Mr. Sinclair?"

"Nae, Rachel, never that." He sobered. "Lest ye lambaste me further, I shall speak. I am the new laird o' Farthay House, as ye no doubt realize. Your father has given consent for ye t' come live there. Your presence is sorely needed."

"My presence is needed," she intoned dumbly, struck by his words.

"My mither has been ailing since my father's death. Upon my arrival to Farthay House I found her in a sad state o' despair, and I feel a companion would prove beneficial for her. I spoke with your father and he has agreed."

Rachel blinked, standing as still and forsaken as a castle ruin. As the meaning of his words became clearer, she clenched her hands at her sides. Not only had his years in Glasgow evidently honed him into a pompous *eejit*, they had sapped him of all boyhood kindliness.

"D'ye mean t' tell me, Malcolm Sinclair, that ye've sought me out tae be a servant t' ye?" She could scarcely believe what her ears were telling her. After all they'd been to each other, after the closeness they'd shared. . . "After all these years, ye have the audacity t' stand there in yer fine suit o' clothes and order me tae Farthay House like some, some— mindless ninny who awaits her master's beck and call?"

Tears stung her eyes, and she blinked them back. She would not let him see her cry. "Aye, perhaps me *athair* works at yer shipbuilding company, Mr. Sinclair, and as such is beholden t' ye. But no one—least of all you—manages me!" Despite her best efforts a tear escaped her lashes, and she swiped it away.

"Rachel. . ."

He held out his hand to her, but his tender exclamation of her name sliced at what was left of her pride. She jerked away from him.

"Dinna touch me! I'll no' go tae Farthay House t' be yer slave, and if I never see ye in these hills again, it'll be too soon for me likin'!"

She spun on her heel and marched off in high dudgeon, thankful when he did not follow. Out of his presence, she allowed the bitter tears to run down her cheeks. Despite her best efforts to repress such idiocy, all these years a slight part of her had awaited his return, had hoped, had dreamed—and for what? To be treated as a common peasant by his high-and-loftiness? She could have tolerated and accepted his sudden disappearance those three years ago if he'd been knocked unconscious and shanghaied on a ship to China. That she could have forgiven. Instead, he'd withheld any reason whatsoever for his disappearance. And then he'd had the unmitigated gall to order her to Farthay House, like some incompetent, newly hired servant who had shirked her duties.

An obnoxious, unfeeling ne'er-do-well! That was Malcolm Sinclair.

The view on the walk to her parents' croft was awe-inspiring; the distant mountains, craggy and snow topped, bore thick forests near their bases, and the quiet glen and low hills rolled like waves of a grassy sea. The peace usually found here was absent this evening, however. She could have been walking on blazing hot sand in a barren desert, such as she'd read about in storybooks, and not have known the difference.

Once Rachel opened the door to the cottage, her mother turned from the peat fire where she stirred something in a kettle for the evening meal. Rachel's brother, Dougal, sat on a chair and lowered the paper he'd been reading. Though none of them were educated by tutors or in a public institution such as some of the finer cities had, her mother had insisted all the MacIvor children be taught to read. A skill few in the village possessed. Rachel never told her parents, but Malcolm was the first to teach her the written language; he'd sometimes shared with her words from his storybooks as they sat on the hills for the few hours they'd stolen together each day.

Rachel grimaced at the path her traitorous mind took and forced it to the moment at hand. The aroma of finnan haddock and bashed neeps, the smoked fish and mashed turnips of which she was so fond, tantalized her senses. But the look of anticipation in her father's blue eyes conflicted with the expression of dread clouding Abigail's small features, making Rachel want to retrace her steps out the door.

"Well, lass, did ye meet with Mr. Sinclair?"

"I did."

"Good, good." With a smile, her father rubbed his large hands together. "And did he be tellin' ye of the arrangement and yer new position?"

"He told me."

"Excellent!" He turned to look at her mother. "As this will be our daughter's last evenin' at our table, I'm thinkin' I should bring out the pipes and have a wee bit o' music after the meal."

"That would be welcome," her mother said. "And I have made all her favorites."

"I willna be going." Rachel's quiet words shattered the celebratory mood.

"What's this?" Her father's red brows drew downward. "Of course ye shall go. The opportunity tae live at Farthay House will be befittin' t' ye, as it will for all of us."

"Tae be a servant t' the great Master Sinclair?" Rachel spit out the words. "Bah! I want naught t' do with the man or with his màthair. I would be a scullery maid in an Englishman's castle before I work for the likes o' him."

"Hold yer tongue, daughter!" Her father raised his voice. "Ye speak aboot the family tae whom we're indebted. If no' for the salary the Sinclairs pay, ye would no' be wearin' such a fine dress and would have no time to while away in the hills as ye so often do. If no' for Abbie takin' over the task, likely ye would still be a shepherdess there!"

"I'm thinkin' it be pride and stubbornness that guides oor daughter's tongue, Mr. MacIvor." Her mother spoke with stern calm. "There is nothing petty or shameful in serving others, Rachel. Our good Laird orders us tae do so in His Holy Word. Yet yer fierce pride should cause ye great shame, *inghean*, for 'tis a sin indeed."

Rachel was saddened that her mother thought her a prideful daughter, though the ring of truth pealed in her words.

"Go off with ye tae yer room and think on what yer mither said, Rachel. And while ye're there pack what ye'll be takin' with ye tae Farthay House, for go ye shall. We're beholden to Mr. Sinclair, and that's the way of it. Now that he's taken his father's place in the business, I'll no' have ye be doin' anything to cause us shame or Mr. Sinclair displeasure."

"Aye, Athair."

As she walked toward the small back room she shared with Abigail, Rachel bowed her head with a tinge of remorse for causing her parents grief, though angry frustration ruled her next actions. She carted her battered valise from its corner, moved aside the curtain that shielded their sleeping quarters, and swung the valise onto the bottom cot with a fierce thump.

Had it been anyone but Malcolm who sought her services as his mother's companion, she would have gone, and gladly so. Yet she could not explain such things to her mother or father. Rachel and Malcolm's friendship had been secretive, likewise had their courtship, if one could call it that. A few stolen kisses—which she'd gladly returned—atop the heather-strewn hills far from the village and any seeing eyes.

Since the day eleven-year-old Malcolm had run across Rachel herding sheep, and her no more than nine years of age, they had become fast friends. Yet because of his strict father, who maintained no one of their social status should mix with the common, poorer folk, their friendship remained secret. Malcolm would meet Rachel almost every day on the grassy hills, away from the severe dictates of Farthay House, and they would play and laugh. Sometimes they talked about their lives and dreams. Sometimes they read or sang Gaelic tunes together, learned from her grandparents. Always they enjoyed one another's companionship, until the day it grew into much more than that. As the years progressed and Rachel's father became employed at Sinclair Shipwrights, the need for secrecy became vital.

Half a year before Malcolm left for Glasgow, the summer Rachel turned sixteen, circumstances changed between them. No longer a shepherdess, since Abbie had grown into that task, Rachel nevertheless met Malcolm in the faraway hills. Often they strolled or rode on Malcolm's horse along a nearby lochan, staring out over its waters as they shared dreams, or visited the ancient ruins of a castle from the fourteenth century and the days of Robert the Bruce. On that day fire painted the evening sky as they watched the sun dip beyond the hills. They spoke of plans for the future, and Rachel put one hand to the crumbling wall of the stone castle, staring wistfully out over the lochan as she spoke. She had wanted her future to include Malcolm, though she'd not admitted such. Recalling that day, she could almost feel him draw near again.

"Rachel." Her name on his lips had been a breath, a query, a statement—laced with hope but set in determination.

With a queer sort of breathless anticipation, she'd turned his way. His fingers went to her chin, tilting it up. He'd stared into her eyes as if he'd never seen her before. A moment in eternity afterward, he'd leaned down and kissed her with such tenderness she thought the angels had bent low to the earth and swept her soul to heaven.

"Rachel?"

Dougal's voice at the door snapped her out of her musings. Embarrassed, she lowered her fingertips from her lips and jumped up from her mattress on which at some point she'd sunk.

"Aye?" Her voice came out sharper than she'd intended.

Dougal raised his eyebrows in amusement but limped forward, relying on the crutch he'd used ever since the accident three years ago when a racing wagon had struck him down as he walked along the road one rainy evening. "Ye looked as if ye were takin' a wee *spaidsear* with the fairies. Pleasant thoughts, I be takin' it?"

Rachel let her breath out in a rush. Taking a walk with the fairies indeed! "Was there a matter ye wish t' be discussin', Dougal, or did ye merely come to torment me?" Though he was only ten months her junior, often he acted much younger.

"Torment ye? Me own sister?" The mischief sparking his blue eyes simmered down a notch. "They love ye, lass. Ye know that, do ye not?"

"Aye." The fire seeped from her but she couldn't resist remarking, "And I ken that Athair be fretful about his job and keepin' his new master's favor."

"Then ye ha' not heard?"

"Heard what?"

"Malcolm Sinclair promoted our athair t' the position o' manager. With a raise in salary t' boot."

"Manager?" Rachel's shock eased into disgusted resignation. No wonder her parents were nervous about Rachel causing possible offense. Malcolm had played his hand well. Father would now consider himself indebted to the new master of Farthay House for life. Rachel buried her ire, helpless to speak of how she really felt.

"Ye still have a yen for him, do ye not?"

"For who?"

"Who indeed!" Dougal scoffed but his words were gentle. "The new laird, himself, that's who."

Shock made Rachel stare before sputtering, "Why should ye say such a thing? Now who be *spaidsearachd* with the fairies? A load o' mischief ye'll be hatchin' if ye spread such lies about—"

"Nae." He shook his head. "Calm yerself, Rachel. It willna work. I sometimes would follow when ye met in the hills. I ken what went on betwixt the two of ye."

Speechless, Rachel sought for a reply but found none. She should have known her inquisitive brother would discover her secret; that he had carried it for so long and hadn't told anyone gave her surprise. Or had he? She sank back onto the bed.

As if reading her mind, he spoke. "Ye have naught t' fear. I willna tell a soul, nor have I done so."

Leery as to the reason why, Rachel idly snapped the buckle of the case up and down, studying it. "See that ye keep yer word, Dougal. Such admission could only cause harm. 'Twas a foolish infatuation and no more than that. I have no feelings to spare for the high-and-mighty Malcolm Sinclair."

"Mmphm." Dougal sounded less than convinced. "Ye'll be going tae Farthay House then?"

Rachel released a resigned sigh and directed a look toward her brother. "What with Màthair and Athair practically bootin' me out the door, how can I not?"

He smiled in gentle amusement. "I'll take ye in the wagon. It's little else I have to be doin' these days."

Despite her exasperation with him, Rachel's heart went out to her brother. Since the accident, he could no longer work at the docks, and spent his time whittling or helping around the cottage in whatever labor allowed him to sit or stand while holding a crutch. Yet he wanted no pity, and Rachel respected that, even as she abhorred his sad lot in life.

"Fine, then," she agreed. "I'll be ready t' leave after me mornin' chores are done."

He turned to go, then halted and glanced over his shoulder. "And, Rachel, it might do ye a world o' good if ye whittle that huge chip on your shoulder, as well. It could drag ye down should ye come across a bog, make no mistake about it."

Rachel just managed not to hurl her pillow at his back.

Chapter 3

Weary from perusing the shipyard ledger, Malcolm closed the huge leather portfolio. Except for the need for improving working conditions, which Malcolm mentally made note of when he'd toured Sinclair Shipwrights last week, he could see little else requiring immediate attention. His father had been meticulous regarding the business of shipbuilding, but when it came to the care of his employees Malcolm detected a laxness. Areas were unsafe, the men were forced to work long hours for little pay, and Malcolm sensed their discontent, though none dared speak to his face. Likely they decided he was his father's son and feared repercussions should they air their grievances. His father always maintained that the "underlings" he hired were paid on time and deserved no further consideration—an opinion Malcolm did not happen to share.

The sound of wagon wheels running over pebbled rocks of the drive brought his attention to the casement window. Abandoning his desk, he went toward the glass and pulled back the brocade curtain.

Rachel exited the wagon her brother drove, and he handed her down a satchel. Dougal then withdrew something from his pocket and placed it in her hand, at which point she reached up to hug him around the neck and kissed his cheek.

Relief and regret swept through Malcolm. Once, she'd kissed him in such a way during what seemed another lifetime. After last night, he had assumed that the desired opportunity to renew their acquaintance had passed him by. Yet her presence at Farthay House must mean all was not lost.

His stride swift, he left the study and approached the foyer, where Mrs. MacDonell had just shown Rachel inside. He stood a moment and observed her. She stared, wide-eyed, at the high ceiling, the ornate walnut furniture, and the luxuriant tapestry rugs. It was her first time inside Farthay House, and Malcolm carefully watched expressions of pure awe and girlish delight cross her face—until she saw him. Her rosy lips closed, her elfin chin lifted, and her slim shoulders firmed.

"That will be all, Mrs. MacDonell," Malcolm addressed the housekeeper.

The elderly woman nodded once in her dignified manner. "Very good, sir. I'll just be readyin' the young miss's room then."

Once she left, Malcolm tugged on the ends of his suit coat to seek some measure of equanimity before approaching Rachel, who still bore the look of a Highland warrior princess ready to slay him where he stood.

"I am pleased t' see that ye've changed your mind about coming."

"I assure ye, Mr. Sinclair, 'twas by no decision made on my part." Her tone was as unruffled as the dawn's river waters but just as icy as yesterday. "No' that anyone bothered t' ask for *my* decision, mind ye, but there it is."

Her words pricked Malcolm's conscience. He should have handled the matter differently and given her the option to come rather than the order to appear. Now that he'd assumed the role as master of Farthay House, his attitude at times tended to reflect his position; yet he should have known better when addressing one such as Rachel and curbed his tongue. He had dealt with the matter unwisely, since his chief desire was to regain her friendship and all else lost between them.

Weeks of teeth-gritting silence and barbed retorts didn't appeal, and he decided to amend matters quickly. "I should no' have approached ye in such a manner as I did, Rachel, and for that ye have me most sincere apology. If ye choose t' leave, I'll no' be stoppin' ye."

She looked at him oddly, then gave a stiff nod. "I thank ye for that."

She turned to go, but before she could take more than a few steps toward the door, he spoke. "Still, upon remembering how much ye love a challenge, I would like to offer a proposition."

She turned and eyed him warily. "Aye?"

"Stay and be a companion to me mither for two months, 'til Christmastide. If ye find ye are pleased with the arrangement and life here at Farthay House, ye may consider your position a permanent one." She winced and he wondered what he'd said to cause such a reaction.

He softened his tone. "If, however, ye wish nothin' more to do with us, namely meself, you'll be free t' return to yer parents' home. And I'll never be darkenin' yer doorstep again."

She pondered his words. "And me athair—will me final decision have any bearing on his employment as yer new manager?"

Struck by her words, Malcolm studied the somber tilt of her mouth. She truly believed that of him? That he would be so cruel as to seek some form of petty vengeance? In retrospect, he deserved her misgivings. Nevertheless, her lack of trust in his character stung, much like his finger had when as a boy he'd accidentally sliced it on the blade of his grandfather's forbidden claymore. Rachel had shown by her words that areas of her life were now forbidden to him just as the sword had once been.

"I'll honor whatever decision ye make." He kept his tone formal. "Ye have me word on that."

She thought a moment, her gaze going everywhere else before looking at him. "Perhaps 'tis your màthair who should be makin' such a decision. We may no' be well-suited t' one another; she may prefer a more quiet and staid companion."

"Och, no, Rachel. She'll love ye. Of that I'm sure."

The words slipped out of their own accord. Her eyes opened wider in surprise.

Flustered by his blunder, he quickly sought to rectify the matter. "At present she lies abed."

"Is she ill?"

"Nae; lately she has little desire t' quit her bed of a morning."

He felt as uneasy as Rachel appeared. After almost admitting he still felt strongly about her—a fact that impressed itself upon him when he'd seen her the previous evening—now didn't seem like an appropriate time to offer a tour of the house.

Hearing Mrs. MacDonell's tread on the stairs, he felt a moment's relief. "I'll leave ye to yer own devices; I must return to my bookwork. Feel free to do as you wish 'til tea is served at four. We shall discuss your duties then."

A curt nod was the only parting acknowledgment she offered, but at least she gave him that much in return.

※

Rachel followed the housekeeper to a sparsely furnished room more than half the size of her parents' cottage. She looked at the massive four-poster bed across from the huge fireplace, the wardrobe to the side, the looking glass near the wall, and turned to Mrs. MacDonell. "There must be some mistake."

"Mistake?"

"This canna be where I'm t' stay."

The housekeeper's dark eyes shone in disapproval, and her thin mouth grew even more pinched at the corners. "'Tis no' tae yer likin?"

"Aye—I mean, nae. 'Tis a lovely room."

"His lairdship himself stressed ye were tae have this room. 'Tis the nicest in all o' Farthay House, next t' the family rooms, make nae mistake aboot it."

Rachel did not doubt the woman's words and pondered their meaning.

"Will ye be wantin' anything afore I go?"

"Nae." Rachel came out of her musings. "Thank ye." She felt at a loss. "Aye." At the housekeeper's raised brow, she hurried to explain, "Can ye tell me, exactly what it is I'm to do here?"

"Do?"

Rachel gave a small shrug. "Am I to wait in this room until Mrs. Sinclair summons me?"

"Is that what his lairdship be tellin' ye?"

Malcolm's new title sounded strange to her ears. "He didna say much o' anything at all."

"Och." Mrs. MacDonell eyed her thoughtfully. "Well, if ye dinna mind staying in this room the whole o' the afternoon, that ye may. Though if I were in yer place, I might take a walk on the grounds or in the garden. Last evenin' was a bad night for her ladyship, and I dinna expect she'll be makin' an appearance before dinner."

"Dinner!" Rachel could scarce believe a body could sleep so long. For the past nineteen years, ever since she was a wee bairn, she'd arisen with the first pink fingers of dawn. "Does she have many a bad night?"

"Aye. Since his lairdship passed on tae glory, it has only worsened, poor dear. Ye'll find that oot soon enough, I suppose." She moved closer as though about to unveil a secret. "She's from America ye ken, though her blood runs as Scot as the Clyde. Ye'll find she has some rather odd ways aboot her, though I'd give the life of me firstborn on her behalf, make no mistake aboot it. A finer woman, I've never known."

Mrs. MacDonell bustled out of the room, leaving Rachel to ponder her words.

Malcolm had spoken little of his family. During those carefree days when they'd escaped together to the hills beyond the village, they lived in their own fantasy world where reality was forgotten. But on those occasions when he'd mentioned his mother, his praises for her had been high, and for the first time, Rachel grew fretful that the woman might not approve of her.

She studied her image in the looking glass, trying to perceive what her new mistress would see. The dress her father called "fine" was so—in its day. Now grass stains from whiling away hours on the hills tainted the gray weave and braiding, and no amount of scrubbing had diminished them. Her *arisaidh* was worn thin in places, due no doubt to climbing rocky hills and snagging the long woolen plaid, and her face was too freckled for her liking. At least the faint brown dots—her penalty for enjoying sunshine and never wearing a bonnet—sprinkled only her nose and the apples of her cheeks. Strands of hair had worked loose from her braid, and she wrinkled her nose at her image. She looked like an unruly schoolgirl and little like a lady's companion. Despising the manner in which her hair was bound all around her head, she took out the pins and let her braid swing free, allowing the curling fronds to brush against her waist. If she had her way, she'd loose the entire mass from its thick plait.

With a sigh, she smoothed her skirts, took one last look around the room, wondering what to do, and decided to go exploring. She wished she had dallied a tad longer at her parents' croft but had run out of excuses to delay her departure.

No one had given her directions, but she managed to find the garden. The sight of the cultivated flowers, among the red roses, made her breathe in the perfumed air deeply. A shaft of sunlight beamed through a broken section of wall, and she moved toward the puddle of gold that covered the stone path. Yet the light provided little warmth, and a chill she couldn't explain seeped into her bones. How long she'd been there before she sensed a presence, she didn't know, and she turned swiftly.

The shadow of a man stood in the entrance, and she sucked in a breath.

Malcolm?

The intruder to her privacy moved into the light, and she saw that it wasn't Malcolm, but a man with copper red hair and ruddy skin. His frame was muscular and stocky; he didn't appear the sort to tolerate sitting behind a desk, as was now Malcolm's lot.

"Well, and who might ye be?" His voice was deeper than Malcolm's, grittier sounding, but as he drew close, she saw that he and Malcolm shared the same gray-green eyes. Instantly she knew who addressed her.

"Ye must be Zachary, Malcolm's, er, Mr. Sinclair's brother."

"Aye. Ye did no' answer me question, lass. Who might ye be?"

"I am Rachel MacIvor, and I am to be your màthair's new companion."

"Oh, 'tis that a fact now?" He seemed surprised to hear the news, and Rachel wondered why Malcolm had not thought to share it. "I've been absent from Farthay House for some time or I might have known."

"Zachary. I heard ye were back."

Rachel turned at the sound of Malcolm's voice, noting he didn't seem happy to see his brother. His stance was rigid, his face a mask of displeasure.

"Aye, that I am." Zachary moved toward Malcolm, clapping him on the shoulder. Malcolm didn't return the gesture. "Like a tarnished coin, I am. Canna get rid o' me."

"We had expected ye last week. At Father's funeral."

The mention made Zachary seem uncomfortable. He shifted his gaze away from Malcolm, then back again; his smile disappeared. "I couldna help the delay. I would have been here sooner if I were able."

Malcolm gave no response. Instead he looked toward Rachel. "I came t' tell ye that tea is served and t' escort ye t' the parlor." The look in his eyes bade no denial, and Rachel wasn't sure she wanted to refuse. Zachary dressed in fine clothes, but his manner made her uneasy, reminding her of a few dock workers who'd eyed her as she'd walked home from her grandmother's croft.

Perhaps it was all in her mind, but for the present, she put aside her ongoing battle with Malcolm and took his proffered arm.

⁂

Tea was a strained affair. Malcolm had hoped to have Rachel all to himself, not only to acquaint her with the running of Farthay House, but also in an attempt to rebuild their friendship. To his frustration, Zachary chose to join them and dominated the conversation. And Rachel.

She laughed at his brother's ridiculous jokes and listened with rapt attention to his unruly accounts of life at university. Following that, he regaled her with unlikely stories that took place after he'd dropped out of school last year, shocking the entire family, and engaged in traveling throughout Europe as a seafarer on a ship not Sinclair built. That, to their father, had been the greatest of Zachary's travesties, of which there were many.

When the last of the stout black tea was drained and the bannocks consisted of only a few crumbs on a platter, Malcolm hoped to draw Rachel aside privately for a few moments. But she was bushwhacked by Zachary, who'd learned she didn't yet know the layout of the house. Zachary offered his arm to take her on a tour, a tour that Malcolm had hoped to lead. With perturbed frustration, Malcolm watched his brother steal Rachel away.

Empty hours trailed past until dinnertime, though they were blessedly busy ones for Malcolm, steeped in bookwork. His mother remained absent, and when he inquired, he learned she'd developed another of her headaches. Small wonder, as much as she remained cloistered in her room.

A repeat of tea, dinner was a disappointment. Malcolm clenched his jaw, biting into his food with more fervor than necessary while listening to Zachary manipulate the conversation. At tea Rachel chose to ignore Malcolm, but now he noticed her dart curious glances his way. Once his brother wound down with his extensive version of his near single-handed capture of a humpback whale, Malcolm cleared his throat and spoke before he lost the opportunity.

"I trust that you're enjoying your stay at Farthay House, Miss MacIvor?" He noted that both Rachel and his brother eyed him strangely at his sudden change of topic. The words did sound trite upon hearing them spoken. He drained his glass. "Mither should be down tomorrow; I ken she looks forward t' your meeting."

"Thank ye, Mr. Sinclair. The feeling is mutual."

Her uncharacteristic primness made Malcolm think he'd again wounded her feelings, perhaps by his formal address of her name, which he'd never used before. Yet he wasn't about to speak to her on familiar terms, not with his brother sitting there soaking up every word. Ever since they were lads, Zachary wanted what was Malcolm's though he'd shunned his companionship. And though Rachel wasn't his, he had no doubt his erstwhile brother would try to seize Rachel's heart, too, if he learned Malcolm and Rachel once shared more than friendship—and that he again desired to share more than friendship.

Under his steady gaze that excluded all else in the room, Rachel's skin grew rosy and both she and Malcolm averted their eyes at the same time. He hoped his brother hadn't noticed and looked his way. Zachary busily cut into his mutton and forked the last bite into his mouth. Malcolm expelled a sigh of relief. His peace of mind was short-lived, however, when Zachary abruptly set down his utensils and asked Rachel for a walk in the moonlight.

She seemed flustered and darted a glance toward Malcolm, then to her plate, before looking at Zachary again. "I thank ye for the kind offer, but I am rather weary. 'Tis a long day I've had and I wish tae rise early so as t' meet your màthair." She stood.

"Of course, how thoughtless of me no' t' realize."

Zachary rose as if he would accompany her. Malcolm also rose, tossing his napkin to the table. She looked back and forth between the two men, surprise lifting her brows. Both brothers stared at one another as if they were rival contestants in a game of skill.

"Well then," she hesitated, "I'll be takin' me leave. Good night tae ye both."

"May I assist ye, Miss MacIvor?"

"She can find her own way upstairs, Zachary."

"I merely offered, in the event that she doesna yet ken the layout of the house."

"The staircase is directly outside the dining room," Malcolm argued. "Her room is at the end o' the wing. 'Tis no' difficult to be finding."

"But unless Mrs. MacDonell has lit the lamps, the corridor will be dark."

"That's no' likely."

"Gentlemen," Rachel interrupted before Zachary could fling an opposing comeback, "I thank ye both." She smiled at Zachary. "Mr. Sinclair, your brother is correct in that I can find me own way t' the room I've been given, but I appreciate your concern as to me welfare."

Zachary glowed under her praise, and Malcolm grunted. She turned to look at him. "Mr. Sinclair. . ." She paused, searching for words. Evidently finding none, she shook her head. "I have nothin' more t' say to the likes o' you. All that needs sayin'—on me part anyway—has been said." She gave a slight, dismissive shrug and left the room.

Malcolm watched her go, ignoring Zachary's smile at the manner in which she'd so thoroughly sliced Malcolm to ribbons. The lass needed no broadsword in her hand; had she fought for her clan against England during the Jacobite uprisings over a century ago, the enemy might have turned tail and run back to their lands at the lash of her words alone.

Chapter 4

Rachel undressed for bed then ducked out of the chill air of the drafty room and beneath the counterpane of the four-poster, somewhat bemused by the battle for her favor over dinner. With Malcolm, she felt angry amazement that he assumed he still had the privilege to win her preference; with Zachary, she felt uncertain of his motives, though she did enjoy his conversation and company. At tea and over dinner, she had been more at ease in his presence with Malcolm nearby. But when Zachary offered a tour of the house, she had almost declined. Still, she'd read no ill intent in his eyes and assumed she'd misjudged him in the garden. Sensing Malcolm's displeasure at the idea of her going with his brother, a rebellious imp prompted her to accept Zachary, and gladly.

If Rachel supposed things would settle down with the dawning of a new day, she was sadly mistaken. At breakfast Mrs. Sinclair made no appearance. Zachary and Malcolm continued the struggle for her attention, and after tea Zachary invited her for a stroll on the grounds while Malcolm offered an invitation to go riding. Malcolm's self-assured expression irked her. He knew his offer was difficult to refuse. Ever since the day he'd taught her to sit a horse, Rachel had loved riding with him along the sweeping terrain of barren moors and low hills that belonged to Glen Mell.

Disgusted with the men's childish behavior, Rachel declined each invitation and left the two brothers to share their own questionable company, opting for a book to read from the family library instead. It was there Malcolm found her minutes later.

She looked up from the first page of *Annals of the Parish*, which promised to be a pleasant book set in a small Ayrshire town, and eyed Malcolm with irritation. She lifted her brows. "Ye wish to speak with me, Mr. Sinclair?"

"I. . ." He hesitated. "Came t' get a book." He shifted his attention toward the bookshelves. Rachel returned to her reading, yet couldn't help but feel he was taking an inordinate length of time selecting one of the leather-bound volumes.

"How is your family?" he asked. "In good health I trust?"

She looked at him again. "Bein' as how ye just spoke with them two days past, I should think ye be knowin' the answer to that question. My parents are hale and fit, but I imagine me sister must be missing my presence somethin' fierce."

He flinched. "And your brother?"

"Dougal?" She shrugged. "He's well enough I suppose. He keeps in good spirits, though 'tis difficult for him since he can no longer do what he loves best. He helps around the croft and whittles his sticks, but I ken he be missin' the life he once had."

"He lost his job after the accident?"

"What man be keepin' a cripple for his crew? And what man be takin' one?"

Malcolm was quiet a moment. "Is he good?"

"Good?" She looked at him, uncertain of his meaning.

"At his whittling."

She thought of the gift of the wooden roe deer Dougal had given her yesterday upon their arrival to Farthay House. "Aye." Her tone was soft. "He is that."

"What sort of figurines does he carve?"

With one hand, she slapped the book closed. "May I ask why ye're so interested in me brother's artistic diversions, Mr. Sinclair?"

He inhaled a deep breath and released it swiftly. "My name is Malcolm, Rachel. You used it for seven years before I went t' Glasgow, since ye were a lass of nine and I was eleven."

"Aye, but the passage o' years changes things, as I'm sure I dinna need t' be tellin' ye. And it does no' seem proper for me tae be callin' ye by yer Christian name. Bein' as me athair works for ye—"

"It never stopped ye before."

"—and I'm in yer employ as well."

"When we're alone, as now, I canna see a problem in using informal address."

"And that is yer problem in a nutshell. Ye canna see."

His mouth thinned at the barb that went deeper than a mere discussion of names, and she knew he understood. Satisfied, she rose from the chair and tossed the book to the cushion. "I prefer tae leave things as they be," she said for good measure.

"How long do ye intend t' punish me, Rachel?"

"Why did ye no' say good-bye?" she shot back.

He shook his head. "I didna want t' hurt ye."

She blinked in incredulity and fisted her hands on her hips. "And what did ye think yer fool act would accomplish, *Mr. Sinclair*?" She stressed the name. "Me great and undying joy? Ye dinna ken what punishment is. I lived it for weeks after ye left for Glasgow without a word, and me no' knowin' for what purpose ye suddenly found myself unworthy to speak with on the matter. But dinna concern yerself on me behalf. 'Twas soon over ye, I was, and thankful t' learn what an unfeelin' boor ye really be, before it was too late. I dinna feel a thing for you any longer, make no mistake about it."

They stood staring at one another in a standoff, each unwilling to give an inch.

"Ahem." A woman cleared her throat from the doorway.

Both turned to look. Malcolm immediately moved in her direction. "Mither." He kissed her cheek. "How are ye feeling?"

"I heard voices in the library," she said in an American accent with a tinge of Scot's burr to it, "and had hoped to find my new companion. And here she is. Ye must be Rachel."

"Aye." Embarrassed to realize Malcolm's mother overheard their tiff, Rachel felt her face warm as she moved forward. " 'Tis a pleasure tae meet ye, Mrs. Sinclair."

"What a bonnie lass ye are with all that thick hair and those lovely blue eyes; Malcolm, you were correct in your assessment. And with your gracious appraisal of her character, I'm certain we'll get along splendidly."

Surprise made Rachel dart a glance toward Malcolm, whose own face was suddenly as ruddy as hers must be.

"Aye, well, I'll leave ye two t' get acquainted then," he quickly muttered before leaving the room.

"Och, I seem t' have embarrassed me son. Though I havena clue why." She gave a soft wink, and in that instant Rachel knew they would become fast friends.

Mrs. Sinclair was a woman whose comeliness couldn't be doused even by her wearing of sober black widow's dress. With hair a fiery mix of red and gold to match the spark of mischief Rachel witnessed, and a porcelain sheen to her skin, Malcolm's mother took a person's breath away. Yet an air of fragility settled about her, and upon looking more closely Rachel could discern the shadows that ringed her green eyes.

She may have disliked the woman's husband for his cruelty, but not to speak would be a breach of etiquette. "I'm sorry for yer loss."

"Thank ye, dear child. He was a hard man, but I loved him." She shook off her melancholy. "We met on a ship, ye ken, one of his own, while my family was vacationing in Europe. But come...." She steered Rachel back toward the chair, then took the one close to it. "Tell me about yourself and your family. How did ye meet my son?"

Rachel hesitated. Of course Mrs. Sinclair was ignorant in that regard, since neither she nor Malcolm told their families about their acquaintance. Neither did she wish to reveal the information now. Instead, she spoke of the small croft where she'd been born, and somehow the conversation drifted to the telling of her Highland ancestors who once lived farther north in the mountains, fierce warriors all of them. Mrs. Sinclair seemed not to notice that Rachel refrained from answering her last question, and when the housekeeper came to the door, diverting their attention, Rachel felt relieved that she'd successfully evaded the issue.

"Beggin' yer pardon, Mistress, but there's a man here tae see his lairdship on a matter of urgent business, and I canna find him."

"Very well, Mrs. MacDonell. Show him in."

The housekeeper darted a look toward Rachel. "Ye may wish tae see him privately, if ye wish tae see him at all. He's no' in a good temper; has a mouth on him, that one."

"Oh?" Mrs. Sinclair's brows drew closer together.

"Aye. Threatened t' bring doon the hoose, he did, if I didna fetch ye."

"I see."

Rachel stood. "I should be tendin' to me own matters. That is—if it be all right that I leave you." She hesitated. Just what was expected of a lady's companion? Perhaps she should wait to be dismissed.

Mrs. Sinclair gave a slight nod, her mind clearly on the matter at hand.

As Rachel left the library, she noticed a man standing near the outside door. He surveyed her with a look of superior detachment, though his grubby and ill-fitting clothes confirmed that he was as common as she.

"Are ye the blackguard's sister? If ye've coom tae send me on me way, I'll no' be budgin' from this stoop. Mr. Sinclair thought tae escape what he owed me, but I ken he's back hoom and I'll have what's mine!"

"Mr. Sinclair?" Rachel arched her brows in shock.

"Aye—the welsher owes me a fair amount for his gambling debts, and I've coom tae collect. He thinks his IOUs will keep him in good stead, but he'll no' pull the wool over Angus MacPhearson's eyes. I want what be coomin' tae me."

"Mr. MacPhearson!" The housekeeper's chill voice rang with disapproval. She glanced at Rachel, then back at him. "Her ladyship'll be seein' ye noo."

A smug look on his face, as if he'd won a victory, the irate man followed Mrs. MacDonell into the library. He must not know Malcolm well to assume he had a sister, thinking Rachel was she. However, as Angus MacPhearson's claims settled in her mind, she wondered if perhaps she didn't know Malcolm as well as she'd thought, either.

She had known years ago that he'd taken to drink, as many men of the village did, though she'd never seen him in his cups; but to learn that he gambled stunned her. What other secrets had Malcolm hidden that she didn't know?

❧❧❧

Malcolm gave Solomon free rein as the stallion galloped across the moors. His thoughts, as persistent as the stout wind, flew inside his mind. All of them swirled around Rachel.

He had known it would be difficult to win her favor. Yet his expectations had not included rivaling for her attention with his ne'er-do-well brother. With Zachary there to interfere in Malcolm's plans, the future didn't look as promising as it once might have. Malcolm had hoped eventually to regain Rachel's trust, to woo her, and one day, should the good Lord be willing, to marry his bonnie shepherdess. That was always how he'd pictured her. As his.

Malcolm approached a familiar area and thought of the day they'd first met here ten years ago. Then as now, Rachel's indomitable spirit had drawn him to her. He had been upset, angry, and fearful of his father, whom he never could please. After being victim to a tirade scorning his slovenly appearance and attitude, Malcolm escaped the echoing, bleak chambers of Farthay House to find solace in nature's friendly grandeur that painted the sunny hills of Glen Mell.

Wan and sickly as a lad of eleven, he had panted as he ran and stumbled through the heather, engaging in a mindless race to escape something to which he was forever bound. Thistles scratched his legs below his knee-length breeches and tears clouded his eyes. And then he'd seen her.

When measured by society's dictates regarding comeliness, Rachel was no beauty like his mother. But she possessed an inner fire that made her glow and seem more alive than any person he'd known, even at her scant nine years of age. With a few black-faced sheep around her and a staff in one hand, she surveyed Malcolm as though he'd just crawled out of a bog. Her first words to him had been confrontational.

"Where did ye get sich silly-lookin' clothes?"

Malcolm had looked at his ruffled shirt, ribbon tie, and woolen breeches as if he'd forgotten what he wore, but hadn't seen anything silly about them.

"Ye look like one o' them rich, mutton-headed boys who canna wipe their own noses. Is that what ye be?"

Her taunts had made him angry, and he'd swiped the tears from his eyes with his sleeve. "I am Malcolm Sinclair, and me father is laird o' Farthay House," he'd said proudly, sure that this announcement would incite awed respect in her, as it had in the villagers who had dealings with his father. "One day, I shall be laird there, too."

"Och, noo doubt aboot it. Be off wi' ye then, tae yer grand home. I must tend me sheep." She'd promptly turned her back to him.

Shocked, he'd stared. Hadn't she heard him correctly? Didn't she understand who he was?

She turned all the way around to look at him again. "Are ye still here?"

"Aye." The answer came automatically.

"Then I'll be the one going."

Her saucy attitude made him temporarily forget his own troubles. "Why must either of us go?"

"Me màthair says I maun have naught tae do wi' them tha' live at Farthay House."

"Why not?"

"The laird there is a scurvy and wicked king who eats lassies and laddies for breakfast." She growled the reply, holding her fingers out like claws as if to grab him when she walked closer. Suddenly she leaped forward; instinct made him jump back.

"Aye." Her expression was smug. "Ye are a mutton-head. 'Tis a wonder the king has no' eaten ye!"

"Am not." Her words had stung. "An' me athair is master there, but he's no king."

She'd glanced at the sheep in indecision, then at him. "I ken I could beat ye in a footrace, hands doon."

The very idea of a girl beating him in anything was enough to simmer his blood, and made the ancestral tenets of his boyish pride soar. He'd pulled off his jacket, his jaw clenching. "Tae what hill?"

She'd given a disbelieving laugh, but pointed toward a heather-clad hill some fifty yards away, then let her staff fall to the ground. After a final glance at him, she set off at a dash, her skirts flying and her braids bouncing on her shoulders.

"Hey! Ye canna do that!"

Malcolm sped after her, but even without her few seconds' lead, she would have beaten him by yards. She didn't gloat over the fact, which surprised him. Curious about her, and drawn to her even then, he sneaked out of the manor the following day, and again found her on the hill with the sheep. This time her manner had been more cordial. Within weeks, all aloofness disappeared and they became fast friends.

As the seasons passed, Malcolm lost his gawky boyishness by spending a few hours of almost every day on the hills with Rachel in the fresh air. His health rallied, while his muscles strengthened, and his body became fit and toned. Soon he was the victor in all their footraces and games of strength. As the years added age to their youth, so did it reduce their childhood tendencies, and they began looking upon one another as more than playmates. Malcolm was sixteen when he realized he wanted Rachel for his bride. And that had not changed.

Composed of courageous spirit and passionate fire, Rachel exasperated yet encouraged. She annoyed yet tantalized. Still, what others perceived as flaws, he saw as traits to be admired, even if she did drive him to the point of insanity at times. If not for her bullying persistence and her tendency to speak her mind, no matter the outcome, the milksop of a lad he'd been would have likely grown into a milksop of a man. Yet the one time her support mattered most, he had not trusted her ability to forget his failure. If she were to learn the truth of that night, she would always remember, and a dividing wall would spring up between them. That was what he'd told himself then, and his father's persuasions to mask the horrifying incident had seemed a godsend to Malcolm's tortured mind and anxious heart.

Yet what were these past years, if not living behind a wall of division separate from his Rachel? Would the torment have been so difficult to bear if he'd done the decent thing from the start and taken an old shepherd's advice instead of running away?

Malcolm brought Solomon to a walk as his thoughts wandered to Joseph, a mysterious hermit no one seemed to know much about. His gentle character and tendency to keep to himself caused the townsfolk no alarm, however, and as children, Malcolm and Rachel doubtless had been Joseph's closest companions, though the occasions they saw him were rare. Malcolm knew what Joseph would advise.

He would say that Malcolm must tell her, must ease this burden of guilt from his soul so he could again bear the sight of his face in the looking glass. At the same time, Malcolm didn't want to lose any chance of strengthening the weak limbs of his and Rachel's faltering relationship. Yet for love to bloom between them again, it must be nurtured with the healing waters of honesty. Only then could hope sprout and their love grow anew. Only then. . .

And yet, even knowing all this, Malcolm resisted.

Chapter 5

The days shortened and passed into a week. Winter's abrupt arrival caused evening's shadows to lengthen earlier in the day, and the frosts to increase.

Rachel settled into life at Farthay House as if she'd been born to it, and Mrs. Sinclair's company made Rachel's lot bearable. Malcolm's mother didn't treat Rachel as a servant, but as a friend, stating that if she'd wanted a servant she would have relied on Mrs. MacDonell to see to her needs. Long talks of her childhood and early marriage revealed the woman as considerate, sympathetic, and impetuous, and Rachel was thoroughly impressed with Mrs. Sinclair. Too bad her sons didn't share all the same qualities, though impetuosity did appear to be part of their character makeup.

Rachel's annoyance with Malcolm had waned but not entirely disappeared. She'd once been told that her temper was not unlike striking flint and steel against a tinderbox—sparking into an abrupt blaze to be replaced by a steady, smaller flame that could blow out as abruptly as it had been lit. Zachary, too, tested her patience, and she soon saw that the endless requests for her to accompany him on walks spurred from his desire to torment his brother. Rachel refrained from correcting Zachary's assumptions that Malcolm had any interest in her—other than as a servant, that is.

The Saturday after the week she'd arrived at Farthay House, she was surprised when Malcolm stepped into the parlor, where she was taking letters for Mrs. Sinclair. He looked at her, then at his mother.

"Have ye told her?"

"I thought I would let you do that." Mrs. Sinclair eyed Malcolm with a steady smile.

"Tell me what?" Rachel looked back and forth between them.

"We have discussed it and decided that your Sundays should be spent with your family," Malcolm explained. "I'll be takin' ye to church tomorrow, and ye can go home with your family once services are over. Before sunset, I'll return for you."

Flabbergasted, Rachel could find no words. She missed her family but never reckoned she would be granted leave to see them. When she only gaped at Malcolm, he gave an abrupt nod, seeming uneasy. "Well then. So that's settled." Without another word, he left the room.

The next day, Rachel kept quiet as he drove her to the village church.

"I am no' an ogre, ye ken," he said at last, breaking the silence. "I never intended for ye t' be strangers to yer own family."

Rachel had no idea how to respond. "Then I'll be thankin' ye for that," she managed. The heat of her anger against him had sputtered to a low flame, and his thoughtfulness made it difficult to fan it to life again. Not that she was sure she wanted to. She still didn't understand what prevented Malcolm from satisfying her questions about his leaving, but these past days in his company kindled far sweeter memories. When he'd been absent, it was a fairly easy matter to push all such recollections aside; but seeing him every day forced those memories to resurface.

Ironically, the entire time she was at her parents' home, all she could think about was Malcolm. When she almost buttered her smoked salmon instead of her bannock, she didn't miss the amusement dancing in Dougal's eyes, nor the lift of his brows that told her he knew exactly about whom she'd been thinking. She pointedly ignored him and answered the many questions aimed her way from the rest of the family about her life and the people at Farthay House. Thus, when Malcolm came to collect her that evening, she found herself eager to see him.

She said her good-byes to her family and accepted Malcolm's hand into the wagon. Soon the horse clopped along the rocky path to Farthay House while the dim moon made a crescent in the purple twilight.

"Is that King David?" she asked suddenly, speaking of the animal they'd ridden as children.

Malcolm swung his head her way. "Nae. Solomon is his offspring."

"And what of King David? Is he still alive?"

"Aye." Despite the shadows, she detected confused surprise on his face. "Tell me, why this sudden interest in horses, Rachel?"

"I would no' like t' think something happened t' King David. We had such good times, riding him along the moors." Rachel held her breath, waiting. By her admission she was letting Malcolm know she'd decided to bury the hatchet—and not in his head.

A smile lifted the corners of his mouth. "Then it is t' be a truce, Rachel?"

"Aye. If ye want t' be calling it that. A truce, Malcolm."

His smile lit up the dusky evening light. "More finer words I havena heard! I have missed ye, Rachel. Missed the moments we shared."

She almost ruined the present moment then by insisting on hearing why he refused to confide in her if he'd missed her so much. But she curbed her tongue before the question could spill from her mouth. Her mother would have been proud.

Malcolm let the reins go slack. The wagon took longer to reach Farthay House than their trip that morning, an obvious ploy on Malcolm's part to spend more time with her, but Rachel didn't mind.

Settling back against the hard seat, she listened as he recounted humorous moments of his university days. She couldn't help but note how his recollections differed from his brother's. Zachary's tales centered on himself, while Malcolm gave credit to others, sharing their admirable traits as well. After the telling of one prank against a professor, not instigated by him, or so he said, he let out a rich, deep throaty laugh, and Rachel's heart gave a tingling jump upon hearing it again. She hadn't realized until that moment just how much she'd missed his laugh. To her chagrin, her eyes grew moist at the thought of the years they'd lost and could have shared. Swiftly she turned her head to look at the water reflecting the colors of the sky.

"Rachel?" His tone was concerned.

Blast him, he always could read me well. "'Tis nothing. A speck o' dust blew in me eye, I expect."

He grew quiet and she knew he'd discerned the true reason for her melancholy. Not until they approached Farthay House and the stable did he look at her again. He opened his mouth as if he would speak but remained silent.

"Aye?" she prodded.

His manner seemed intensely grave. "I wanted t' tell ye. . ." He hesitated. "That I enjoyed talking with ye tonight."

"As have I." Rachel sensed a peculiar awareness that this wasn't what he'd intended to say.

"And I should like very much to go riding with ye tomorrow. If ye be willing."

Rachel's heart jumped, though outwardly she remained calm. "And yer màthair, what of her?"

"As I'm sure you've noticed, she prefers to lie down in her room of an afternoon. Ye'll no' be missed."

To be with Malcolm again, to relive her idyllic dream of three years ago, was all she'd ever wanted. Yet she wasn't so foolish as to suppose she could return to the days of their youth. Such carefree times were behind them now. Still, if only to relive those days for one hour, for one cherished moment. . .

She couldn't resist the opportunity. At the same time, she promised her heart she wouldn't allow it the pleasure of trusting him again.

⁂

The next morning couldn't pass quickly enough for Malcolm. He flew through the notices needing payment and upon seeing a familiar name, frowned at the retelling of his mother's meeting with Angus MacPhearson. That was a season in his life he wished to forget but a time he would always be forced to remember.

A movement at the door that stood ajar made him look up. He grimaced as his brother strode into the room and stopped in front of the desk. "A word with ye?"

Zachary's infringing gaze lowered to the strewn papers and then hit upon the open ledger. Malcolm swiftly gathered the missives into a pile, stuffed them between the pages, and closed the book. "Aye?" He set the quill in its holder and stopped the jar of ink.

"Mither wishes tae go to the village, and for me t' take her."

Malcolm's brows shot up at the surprising news. "And Rachel?" He could have bitten his tongue in half at his slip of her Christian name and the instant note of awareness in his brother's eyes.

"Mither wishes tae go alone to visit auld widow Lachlan."

Malcolm recognized the name of a fishwife in the village whose arthritic bones barely enabled her to continue her living. "Ye need me permission?" Malcolm didn't understand the reason for Zachary's visit.

An expression of disgust clouded Zachary's face. "I dinna need yer permission for any sich thing. I only thought tae mention it as we'll be takin' the horses."

"Leave Solomon."

Zachary looked surprised. "And take King David?"

"He's a sturdy horse."

"He should have been put out t' pasture long ago."

"I'll no' argue the point with ye, Zachary. But for today, I need ye t' leave Solomon behind."

"Plannin' a ride?" Shrewdly he narrowed his gaze. "She is a bonnie lass."

"Leave her be, Zachary." Malcolm dropped all pretenses. "She's no' for you."

"Because she's under yer employ? Or because ye have a desire tae take her for yerself?"

Malcolm didn't respond, and Zachary gave a victorious laugh. "Aye, I thought so! Well, she doesna seem t' return yer regard, dear brother, and unless I see a ring circling her finger, I consider her fair game."

"She's no' 'game.'" Malcolm detested Zachary's coarse appraisal of the fairer sex. "And she's more woman than ye could ever handle."

Zachary seemed surprised at Malcolm's response. "Ye offer the challenge so boldly? Perhaps I should be takin' it an' no' look a gift horse in the mooth."

" 'Twas a warnin', no' a challenge, *dear brother*."

"To me they are one and the same. Or do ye fear the risk that I might win our bet?"

"I dinna speak of a gamble. I am no longer a gambling man."

"Och. But I am."

Malcolm rose from his chair, his knuckled fists resting on each side of the ledger as he leaned his weight onto the desk. "Ye'll no' hurt Rachel, or ye'll have me t' contend with. Do I make meself clear?"

"I didna say I would hurt the lass. Only that I would make her mine. By Christmas week, is that no' the bargain ye made with her? And ye no longer a betting man. 'Tis a shame."

Realizing Zachary knew about the private proposition he'd struck with Rachel, Malcolm opened his eyes wide.

"Servants have a way of talkin' when they think no one is aboot," Zachary explained, his manner nonchalant. "Take Solomon if ye must, but in the end I will have Rachel. And judgin' from what ye maun tell her, I canna say the same for you."

"What I maun tell her?" Malcolm was confused.

"As to the wee matter of why ye left here so abruptly three years ago. And it does no' take a genius t' figure out 'twas her that ye be leavin' behind." With a self-satisfied smirk, Zachary headed back to the door, leaving Malcolm in shock to stare after him, his blood running cold.

Chapter 6

Malcolm had been quiet ever since they'd left Farthay House. At first, Rachel was uncertain about riding with him when he'd explained they had only the one horse, and he was in the process of purchasing more. Yet the desire to share his company again, much like their childhood days, lured her to sit on the gray stallion in front of him. She had not reckoned being so close to Malcolm would again stir within her feelings she'd thought put to eternal rest. With relief she dismounted once they reached their destination, though she couldn't help but question why he would choose this place.

The castle ruins stood as forlorn as they had three years ago, facing the shimmering lochan that enclosed the gray stones of the abandoned fortress on three sides. The small lake appeared calm today, but Rachel wondered if untold mysteries seethed beneath its depths like the unspoken emotions that churned within her heart.

Her hand on the castle wall, she kept her expression placid and turned from looking out over the water to give him a sidelong glance. "Why did ye bring me here, Malcolm?"

"Do ye remember when last we were here?" He countered her question with another. "And what we discussed that day?"

His query probed the sensitive lining of her heart. How could she forget? And how could he be so unfeeling as to force the memory to resurface? " 'Twas years ago. I have forgotten much of that time." Her gaze went back out over the lake. She heard him draw close beside her.

"Have ye, Rachel?" His large hand went to her shoulder and he turned her around to face him. "I dinna believe you."

The pull toward him now was as great as it had been then. Her breath caught. His smoky green eyes held the same promises they had on that last day they'd come to this place, when they shared dreams of the future and Malcolm led her to believe he wanted her to play a significant part in his. What a fool she'd been.

"I canna help what ye do or dinna believe," she said, not allowing herself to yield. " 'Tis yer choice to believe as ye will. As it has always been yer choice t' do as ye like on numerous occasions. Ye are the master of Farthay House, after all, and need answer t' no one." She couldn't resist the small dig; she still smarted that he chose not to share with her his reasons for leaving.

He sighed, briefly shutting his eyes. "After last night, I thought we were beyond this. Can we no' leave the past behind us, Rachel?"

Rachel released a soft breath. His deliberate evasiveness irked her, but she, too, was weary of continuing down this bitter course she'd first chosen to travel with him. The flame of her anger had burned low and sputtered out. "Aye. Perhaps 'tis best."

She turned away, seeking stable ground for both her feet and her heart. Walking over the wild grasses, she pulled her plaid close about her as the chill wind bit through the weave, then she came to a sudden stop.

"Are ye cold?" Malcolm asked when she briskly rubbed her arm with one hand. The woolen dress did little to keep out the chill. Before she could answer, Rachel felt his cloak swathe her shoulders. The warmth of his body and his masculine scent permeated the fine woolen texture of the cloth, assailing her senses with shivering delight.

What are ye doin', Malcolm? What is yer purpose for all this? Why have ye crashed back into me life like a wave of the sea? Again the questions peaked inside her mind, begging release.

"Perhaps we should walk," she suggested. Trying to relive a moment from their childhood had been a mistake. Having him stand so near to her addled her brain. Christmas suddenly seemed far away, though it was a matter of weeks. She had agreed to remain at Farthay House until then, but she planned to stay no longer. And it would be wise for her foolish heart to bear in mind the folly of anything else.

His steady look gave her reason to believe he'd read her mind. He knew how much he was affecting her, and that frustrated her all the more. Not waiting for his reply, she began walking, eager to escape.

"Any faster, lass, and we'll be in a footrace," he called after her.

At the moment, that didn't sound like an objectionable idea.

"Rachel?"

"Aye, then a race it shall be, Malcolm Sinclair," she muttered under her breath. "Only this time ye willna turn out the victor." She spoke of much more than footraces.

Pulling the edges of his cloak together with one hand, she took off at a sprint.

"Rachel?" Worried confusion riddled his tone, and she heard the grasses swish with his rapid footsteps behind her.

She ran faster, though she was no match for him and she knew it. Within seconds, he grabbed her arm to stop her and swung her around. "What foolishness is this?" His eyes opened in shock when he saw the moisture covering her cheeks. Swiftly, he pulled her into his arms and held her close, resting his chin atop her head. "Rachel."

Confused about her toppling emotions, even more confused as to why she had acted so childishly as to run from him, she allowed herself the brief respite of pressing her cheek against the warm linen covering his chest. His hand smoothed down her back. The wind whipped against them as they stood silent, sharing exultation in the feel of being held in one another's arms again, while lamenting the past that had kept them apart.

"I would have told ye, then, but I couldna do so," he said quietly.

"Because of yer athair?"

"Aye. In part, 'twas due t' something he said."

She pulled slightly away. "Did ye tell him about us and he didna approve?"

"Nae. Though I would have told him soon." His smile was slight as he tenderly pushed back the hair blowing into her face. "But even then me athair's feelings on the matter could no' have kept me from ye, lass."

"Then what did, Malcolm? What caused ye t' run from me? Why should ye want t' run, when days before we'd shared such lovely dreams of a life together?" With all awkward pretenses behind them, the long-held questions burst forth in waves.

His expression sobered. "I didna run from ye, Rachel. Never think that."

"Then what?"

"One day, I'll tell ye, but today is no' that day."

"Why, Malcolm?"

He shook his head. Cradling her face between his large hands, he bent to kiss her brow, as one might do to placate a child. The touch of his lips on her skin did something unexpected to Rachel. Her heart gave a little jump, and she tilted her face upward as he moved away a fraction. His mouth parted in shock as he correctly read the unspoken message in her eyes. Tense seconds that rivaled an eternity elapsed as they stared at one another. Then, bending down once more, he covered her lips with his.

Warmth spiraled through Rachel, and she realized a part of her had been waiting for this since his return into her life. His lips moved over hers tenderly, slowly, as if rediscovering something very precious. When he pulled away, it was all she could do not to grasp his head and draw him back to her.

"I want t' begin afresh, Rachel," he said softly. "To start today as if the past didna exist and we had only just met."

She drew her brows together. "I ken that willna work."

"Nae?" His expression grew troubled.

"I would never kiss a stranger."

Malcolm laughed, the rich sound of his voice carried by the wind, and Rachel smiled at hearing it again. She would have to content herself that he'd promised to explain in the future his reasons for leaving, and let it go at that. He could be as stubborn as she, and it was useless trying to make him speak before he was ready. All arguments aside, she desired his companionship, and being with him today, like this, patched the hole that had been left in her heart three years ago.

❧

Over the next week, Malcolm and Rachel spent pleasant hours together, as often as their duties would allow. Twice Malcolm almost told her the truth, but each time she had looked at him with a sweet, questioning smile when he'd begun to broach the subject. To see the trust again glimmer in her eyes, eyes that revealed the depth of her heart for him—an expression he never again thought to see—curbed his confession. He could not speak of treachery and deceit and duplicity when she looked at him in such a tender manner. He could not risk what he'd worked so hard to restore, only to have her heart turn bitter toward him again. At the same time, he knew the more time that passed, the more difficult it would become to tell her.

The sound of a step on the tiles shifted his attention to the study door. His mother walked inside.

"You're workin' late into the night," she said, her tone both curious and concerned.

Malcolm shrugged and tossed his quill pen to the desk. "I'm workin' on plans for improvements at the shipyard." He hesitated. "Of course such developments will require funds to set them in motion, but unless we want a strike on our hands, I see no other choice."

"I have nothing but the greatest faith in ye, Malcolm. And I know that your father approved of your business acumen."

Had his father known of Malcolm's plans to put the workers' needs above the demand for supply, Malcolm doubted he would have approved, but he smiled in gratitude and rose from his chair to approach his mother. "What are ye doin' up so late, Mither? Can ye no' sleep?"

"Och." She waved a hand dismissively. "Too many pastries before bedtime have made me quite restless. I am wide awake and have now come t' pester you."

He chuckled and took her arm, leading her to the fireplace and one of the chairs there.

Roses again bloomed in her cheeks where before they'd been sallow, and he knew that was partly due to the walks Rachel insisted his mother take with her. The subtle bullying to persuade his mother to go outdoors had worked well, and Malcolm was thankful he'd thought to acquire Rachel as her companion.

"I like her," his mother said, as though reading his mind. "And unless me eyes deceive me, you do, too."

Malcolm had no need to ask about whom she spoke. Nor was he surprised by his mother's straightforward manner; in many respects Rachel and she were a lot alike. "Then I imagine it would be no surprise if I were to admit t' more than merely liking the lass, would it?"

"Not in the slightest." She leaned forward. "Do ye plan on taking it further is what I'm wantin' to know."

He laughed. "Mither, your subtlety is astounding."

"Humph. I never pretended t' be anything other than what I am. That is one reason yer father proposed to me."

"Aye, and an intelligent man he was. I canna imagine anyone dearer I'd rather have for me mither." He grinned boyishly.

"Posh! Enough of yer mollycoddling. I ken when you're trying to change the subject, and dinna think ye will succeed!"

He sobered. "In truth, I have thought much about the prospect, aye. Yet there is a matter which first must be addressed."

"You're talking in circles. To what matter do ye refer?"

He looked at her steadily. "The matter of three years ago."

The confusion etching her face gave way to understanding. "Malcolm Sinclair! Do ye mean to tell me she has no knowledge of what truly happened? That in all this time ye never told her?"

"I tried many times but it never seemed the proper time."

His mother let out an unladylike snort. "And will there ever be a 'proper time'?"

"What if Father had confessed such a thing to you? Would ye have been so willin' to forgive him?"

She thought a moment. "I would have been angered by his stupidity and actions, aye, but after my blood cooled I would have forgiven him." Concern returned to her eyes and she reached out to cover his hand with hers. "Son, ye canna keep such a thing from her. 'Twould be far worse if she were to hear from a stranger. The incident happened years ago, 'tis true, but someone might have seen or heard something that will one day slip out in conversation. Can ye risk having her learn the truth in such a manner?"

That was the fear Malcolm had carried with him every day since that night. "Nae." He closed his eyes. "I ken I maun tell her. I will. Tomorrow."

" 'Tis best. And now I shall attempt to sleep again." She rose from her chair and Malcolm walked with her to the door. As he neared it, he heard footsteps hurrying around the corner.

He would have followed to see who'd been eavesdropping, but before he could, his mother reached up to give a parting kiss to his cheek.

"It will work out, Malcolm. I'll pray that it does. And it would no' harm ye to do the same."

Malcolm gave a vague nod. His relationship with his Creator had suffered over the years, and it wasn't until university and speaking with a professor about the Savior that his life began to change. None of the Sinclair males had been praying men, and it was difficult for Malcolm to learn, though he knew his mother was right.

Only the power of God could repair this muddle that Malcolm had wrought with his foolish decision of bygone days. Had he listened to the advice of the shepherd Joseph, who surely would be considered a wise man had he lived in the time of Herod, Malcolm would not be struggling to fashion in his mind the words he must now tell Rachel.

Thinking of her fiery spirit, he winced. Tomorrow would prove whether his confession would aid in the restoration of their relationship or bring about its swift demise.

Chapter 7

The day dawned fresh with promise. Even the chill rain failed to dampen Rachel's spirits. She stood beside the parlor casement window and looked out over the sweep of waving grass that came to an abrupt halt beside the river.

Last night Malcolm had seemed distant, as though something plagued his mind, making Rachel wonder. After breakfast hours ago he mentioned his wish to discuss something of great import with her, and to meet him in the garden once his mother took her nap. Rachel assumed the reason he chose not to speak of the matter then was because Zachary had entered the room. But Malcolm's eyes had glimmered softly as he held her gaze before turning to go, so she felt the news couldn't be all bad, despite his grave countenance at the time.

Smiling, Rachel thought of these past weeks in Malcolm's company. Often she spied the boyishness still so much a part of Malcolm, while admiring the man he'd become. His arrogance at their initial reunion had departed, to be replaced by a gentle strength of character that attracted her. He no longer took to the drink, unlike his brother who imbibed a snifter of whiskey each evening. But Rachel hadn't seen a glass of liquor in Malcolm's hand since she'd arrived at Farthay House.

As time permitted, they rode together or took walks, reminiscing about their childhood while getting acquainted with the man and woman each of them had become. Twice in that time he had kissed her, sending her heart careening into the sunset-laden clouds. But afterward he always drew away, distant, an expression of unease lining his brow. The manner in which he slipped his fingers midway into the pockets of his frock coat while staring out over the water with clenched jaw testified he was keeping something from her. He only answered her queries of what troubled him with a wan smile, and then changed the subject. She had never demanded he speak, but now felt that must be the matter of import he wished to discuss. At first, she toyed with the idea that his revelation might be of a personal matter, as in a proposal. Yet she didn't dwell on that possibility long, lest disappointment steal the wind from her sails should engagement not be the topic of conversation.

Eager to arrive ahead of him, Rachel made her way to the door leading to the garden where they were to meet. Hearing a tread, she turned expectantly, and masked her disappointment when she saw it was only Zachary. He came to a stop in front of her, a little too close for her liking. Still, she tried to be polite.

"Good afternoon, Mr. Sinclair."

His brow arched. "So formal. I should like ye t' call me by me Christian name, as I've heard ye use with me brother—Rachel."

His forward manner made her uneasy and she moved to sidestep him. His hand slapped the wall beside her head, blocking her escape. She looked up in shock.

"Now then, dinna be impolite," he purred in a slimy voice. "I only wish to spend with ye a wee bit o' the time ye spend with himself. Surely ye canna deny me the privilege. Ye might find ye even prefer me company."

"Mr. Sinclair," she said, stressing the words, "if I've given ye the wrong impression, then 'tis sorry I am, make no mistake about it. But ye are sorely mistaken if ye think I am the sort of girl who divides her time between brothers in the unsavory manner your tone suggests."

He let out an unpleasant, amused laugh. Rachel was distressed to see her earlier assessment of his character was correct. Yet she would not be bullied; moreover, from what she'd learned of Zachary these past weeks, the man was all bluff. She doubted, despite his bold words, that he would carry his actions further. At least, she hoped that was the case.

In one swift movement, she ducked under his arm while pushing him away with her other hand. He grabbed that hand.

"I'll thank ye to let me go," she ordered.

"Why will ye no' go for a walk with me, Rachel?"

"I'm no' a fish or a duck." She referred to the pouring rain, trying for levity, though she failed to see humor in the situation. "Regardless,

I wouldna care to walk with you in any case."

His lips compressed. "Because of me brother?"

"Aye, if ye must put a label on it, then there it is." She figured it best to let him know where she stood now before he took his infatuation with her any further.

He scowled. "And did he happen tae mention why he left so suddenly three years past? Did he tell ye how far he was in his cups the night yer brother was injured?"

His shocking words made her both keen to hear more and appalled to learn even the slightest bit of information in such a manner. To stand and listen felt like a betrayal of Malcolm, but she found she could not move, as if rooted to the spot.

He took her silence as affirmation to continue. "I speak the truth, lass, a truth he didna bother t' share with ye. I overheard me father and brother discussing the matter that night. Malcolm was gambling and drunk. Lost a fair amount o' money, he did, tae Mr. MacPhearson. He was upset an' driving the wagon fast, payin' no attention tae the road— nor the fact that he drove off of it and knocked yer brother doon. And then he drove away, leaving him lying there, bleeding and unconscious in the freezing rain."

Horror ripped through her heart. "They never found the driver! Your athair suspected one of his workers ran down Dougal. He even said so."

" 'Twas all a lie, Rachel. Our father didna want the scandal that was sure t' come if Malcolm's folly was discovered; Father was having problems with his workers and didna want more. Malcolm would have gone tae jail, ye ken."

Her brain raced with what he told her though her mind felt sluggish, not wanting to absorb the revulsion of it all. Sensing someone draw near, she looked past Zachary.

Malcolm halted several feet away, his expression one of dread. But in that glance, she read the truth of Zachary's words. She walked around Zachary. Malcolm watched her approach, his expression wary.

"Tell me 'tis no' true, Malcolm." Her tone begged him to deny Zachary's claims, begged him to say that Zachary was only making this up because of jealousy. "Tell me ye didna leave me brother there to die. The accident I could forgive, even the drinking and the gambling, but tell me ye didna run away like a coward an' leave me only brother t' lie wounded alongside the road. Tell me, an' I'll believe ye."

Sadness filled his eyes, making her want to scream. His jaw clenched, his face remained gravely calm. "I canna do so, lass, for 'twould be an even greater lie. And I'll no' be party to a lie any longer. All that Zachary said is the truth of what happened that night."

Rachel blinked, wide-eyed and aghast. Instinctively her hand swung up and made sharp contact with his jaw. He winced, but showed no surprise.

"He almost died that night," she seethed. "If no' for Joseph findin' Dougal, he would have died! How could ye, Malcolm? Could ye no' at least have had the decency t' fetch aid? Ye almost killed me brother! An' then what? Ye ran off t' school and yer privileged life to escape yer crime, while Dougal lost the job he loved and will always be a cripple because of yer stupidity and selfishness and cowardice." She shook her head, the truth of her bitter words making impact with her mind. Tears clouded her eyes as she stepped back from him. "I dinna know you. The Malcolm I loved never would have done such a despicable act. I—"

Angry dismay choking off her voice, Rachel hurried away, lest she break down in front of him. One thing was certain; promise or no, she would not stay at Farthay House another minute.

◈

"Malcolm, think before ye act. Was this no' your trouble before?"

His mother's concerned words stilled his actions a moment, but he merely shook his head and went on with the last of his packing. "I maun spend time at the shipyard, t' better understand the problems there. I plan to acquaint myself with the workers, work alongside them—get me hands dirty for a change. One tour and reading the accounts in the ledger isna of great help when determining what improvements maun be made."

"Are ye certain that's the only reason you're leaving?"

His heart constricted with pain at the reminder of Rachel's absence. "It isna far, Mither." He turned toward her, resting his hands on her shoulders. "Zachary is here to keep ye company. I'll no' be gone long." The bitterness toward his brother had waned, though Malcolm only blamed himself. Had he had the courage to speak of his folly sooner, things might have gone differently.

"You'll be back in time for Christmas?"

"I wouldna dream of spending the Yule away from me family."

"You'll take care of yourself?"

"Of course." He dropped a kiss onto her brow, then closed his satchel and picked it up.

"She'll come around, I'm sure of it."

Malcolm attempted a smile. "Of that, I'm no' so certain."

"You're not the same rowdy young man ye were then. You have matured—she's seen that. Give her time."

"Ah, Mither. I wish I had your faith."

"It begins by dropping to one's knees." Her eyes were loving but steady.

"Aye." With a vague smile, he left Farthay House on foot. Since there was nowhere to stable Solomon near the shipyard, he had decided to walk the few miles.

Along the road, he approached a shepherd herding three sheep. Malcolm squinted in the late afternoon sun behind the man.

"Joseph?" he asked as he came abreast of the shepherd who didn't look as if he'd aged in the eight years since Malcolm had last seen him. His ash gray hair hung almost to shoulder level, and his beard matched his hair but was speckled with bits of remaining red. His face bore no more lines than before, and his strange eyes were as they'd always been—sparkling with merriment, while at the same time managing to be serene with gravity.

"Malcolm, 'tis a pleasure tae see ye. I had heard ye were back hoom. Is all well with ye?" His words rolled like the gentle lull of ocean waves, bringing to mind an angel's song. A strange comparison to the rugged man before him, but Malcolm couldn't help applying his boyhood thoughts to the shepherd.

"All is well."

"And how is Rachel?" Joseph countered. "No' such a wee lassie anymore, I'm thinkin'. Are matters well between ye?"

Malcolm eyed him sharply. Had Joseph looked into his heart and found the truth written there? "If I were a drinking man, I would buy ye a whiskey and speak t' ye of me woes," he admitted, "but I frequent the pubs no longer."

Joseph nodded. "A good thing, too. Me home is over that rise. I havena had a visitor in a long while, but ye are welcome."

Surprised curiosity led Malcolm to accept. As far as he knew, no one had ever been to Joseph's home. Minutes later, Malcolm found himself sitting on the lone chair the humble one-room croft boasted. The sleeping cot was fastened to the wall and partitioned off with a clean tattered curtain. A simple but beautiful carved wooden cross hung on the wall above the table, and Joseph followed Malcolm's admiring gaze.

"Dougal made that for me a few months after his accident."

The reminder brought the stabbing pain back with a vengeance.

"Now, tell me lad." Joseph's voice was soft. "How can I help ye?"

Chapter 8

Since the day Rachel walked home in the pouring rain, threw open the door, and wordlessly hurried to her sleeping quarters—ignoring the shocked stares of her mother and siblings—her family was careful not to probe too deeply her reasons for leaving Farthay House. Thus it was with surprise that Rachel regarded Dougal as he hobbled to the table and demanded to know what was wrong and why she'd left.

She laid her quill over the list of items needed from the market for the densely fruit-laden black bun, sticky-toffee pudding, and other treats she would help Màthair prepare for the Yuletide. "Why should ye think something be the matter, Dougal?" she hedged.

"Because ye've been walkin' about like a wraith since ye left Farthay House. A wraith with a look o' reckoning in her eye."

At least Abbie was in the hills with the sheep and their mother was outside so they couldn't hear. "I would rather no' speak of that place nor of the scoundrel who runs it."

Dougal's jaw firmed. "Did he harm ye in any way, lass?"

At the fierce protection that blazed in his eyes, she put a gentling hand on his sleeve. "Nae. No' of what ye speak. This goes back three years. Something he did that opened me eyes to what a deceiving coward the master o' Farthay House truly is."

Dougal relaxed and nodded. "Then ye ken the truth o' what happened."

"What truth?"

"That Malcolm Sinclair was the unknown driver responsible for me accident."

Rachel stared in stunned disbelief. "Ye knew this?"

"Aye. I saw his face before he drove off that night."

"And ye told no one?" Rachel asked incredulously. "No' even me?"

"It wasna me place t' tell. What would have been the point? Once I remembered, he had already left for Glasgow. Since his return these few weeks past, I learned he is a changed man, no longer taken tae the drink, and he has plans tae benefit the workers, including our athair."

"Brought on by guilt, no doubt," she countered with a huff.

Dougal shrugged. "Whatever the cause, I do no' question. He came t' see me, t' speak with me two weeks ago. He apologized for injuring me and offered me a job."

"A job?" Rachel blinked. Dougal was full of surprises today.

"Aye. He said he could always use a good carpenter, one who can carve no' only well, but also creatively. He looked at me handiwork and liked what he saw. I start work at Sinclair Shipwrights after the New Year, when he hopes some o' the renovations have been made." His smile was bright. "I'm t' have me own wee office where I may sit and whittle tae me heart's content."

Rachel could scarcely take it all in. "But 'twas Malcolm who crippled ye and left ye t' die. How can ye forget that?"

Dougal pondered a moment. "I have no' admitted as much tae our parents, but 'twas a time when I took me own share o' the whiskey. Seanmhair was right tae call it the devil's brew. Too much, and a man forgets his own name. Such was the case with Mr. Sinclair that night. He and his athair had a row, and he went t' the pub tae get guttered. His mind went into a black fog. By the time he remembered the accident, Joseph had found me, and Malcolm's father convinced him all must be kept quiet. Shortly afterward, he sent him away tae Glasgow."

"If what ye say is true, why did he no' tell me?" Rachel countered.

"Did ye give him the chance?" Dougal's eyes glowed, but were steady. "Yer tongue can be as swift as a whip and flail a man at ten paces, make no mistake about it."

She arched her brow. "Was that supposed to be funny?"

His smile was nothing but mischievous. "Simply observin' a fact."

She rose from her chair and grabbed her cloak, flinging it around her shoulders. "I maun go to market before it closes and make me purchases, or there will be no black bun for yer Christmas." She considered. "No' that ye deserve any—make no mistake about that!" She finished tying the ribbons in a bow at her collar with a jerk.

His laugh still carried to her ears as she briskly closed the outside door behind her.

A light, wet snow was falling, but that didn't deter Rachel. She needed time alone to think about all Dougal had said. Once she arrived at the market, she knew she sounded scatterbrained as she read off the list of ingredients they would need. Mr. Watt boxed the items into a small crate. Rachel barely observed his curious farewell as she departed with her purchases.

Outside, she shook her head as she went over the facts again in her mind.

"Rachel, is that ye, lassie?"

Startled out of her reverie she turned to look behind her and instantly broke into a smile. "Joseph! How good it is t' see ye." She hadn't seen him since her brother's accident, and marveled that he hadn't changed from the time she'd first seen him when she and Malcolm had fallen into an argument while playing in the hills. Joseph had approached, putting an end to their spat with his calm words and habit of talking in parables. Since that day in their childhood, Rachel and Malcolm had seen him rarely, but each time the impact the gentle shepherd left on them was astounding.

"And how be ye, lass? Is all well with yer soul?" He reached for her crate.

Taken aback by the manner in which he'd phrased the question, Rachel allowed him to carry her purchases. She craved counsel, and Joseph had always proven to be a worthy listener. Knowing this, she told him everything from the day Malcolm reappeared in her life until now.

They walked for some time before Joseph spoke. "The road t' complete forgiveness is often hard t' travel, lass. 'Tis filled with bogs that can suck a man doon, and briars that can scratch him. Yet for those who persist, the rewards be great."

Rachel threw him a sidelong glance, considering the wisdom of his words.

"Likewise if one refuses tae leave the fog o' the past, he can no' appreciate the clarity of the present life with which God has blessed him. A child thinks as a child, but maturity brings wisdom. There is a time when one must let go o' fantasies and embrace the truth."

"And ye think I live in the past?" Rachel asked.

"From what ye tell me, I ken ye do, but 'tis more than that." He halted on the road and she did likewise. "With Malcolm, ye both escaped tae an imaginary world as children. Ye came t' see him no' as the boy and the man he truly was, but as the person ye wanted t' see. Neither of ye spoke much about matters concerning ye; instead ye both lived in a world of escape."

"How do ye ken this?" She hadn't spoken such things to him.

"Malcolm told me."

"He spoke with you about me?" A quiver of tender amazement touched her heart.

"Aye; he was distraught, he was. But more distraught that he'd let ye doon and could no' be the man ye wanted, the man ye thought him to be afore he left for Glasgow."

"Perhaps he wasna then, but he has become such a man," Rachel mused.

"Still, he has failings."

"Aye, but he's trying t' amend his athair's wrongs and do what is right with his company. And he no longer takes to the whiskey."

"So ye're saying there be worth in the man?"

Stunned to realize she'd been defending Malcolm, Rachel blinked and averted her gaze to the snow that began to coat the grasses. Dougal's earlier words, and now Joseph's quiet ones, forced a dark curtain to sweep from her mind. "Aye," she agreed softly. Despite his shameful actions concerning Dougal, despite his abrupt departure without saying good-bye—though now she understood his reasoning—her heart had never stopped loving him.

She grabbed the crate from Joseph's arms. "Forgive me, but I maun go; I have a matter that needs tending."

"Tae Farthay House?" Joseph asked before she could do more than turn around.

She again faced him. "Aye."

"He isna there, lass."

"No' there," she repeated, dread weighting her heart with a heavy millstone.

"Nae, nae, dinna look so forlorn," Joseph soothed. "He hasna left Glen Mell."

The stone fell away and a ray of light flickered. "Where has he gone?"

"I canna tell ye, lass. But when next ye see him, and ye will, of that I'm certain, let him be the first tae speak."

With a blithe parting smile, Joseph turned and walked away.

❦

Christmas arrived and hope birthed within Rachel that she would see Malcolm soon. While Abbie and Dougal hung boughs of holly around the croft, Rachel and her mother baked the black bun, the sweet puddings, and meat pastries of *bridies*. Seanmhair sat on a stool making her famous *cloutie* dumpling, and Athair was outside preparing the birch that would serve as the long-burning Yule log, stripping it of its leaves and bark.

Rachel sidled up to her grandmother. "Ye knew Malcolm would come for me that last day I came t' see ye; that is why ye acted so oddly, isna that so?"

"Aye, lassie, I had heard of his plans in the village." She took Rachel's hand between her blue-veined ones. "I often spied ye goin' tae the hills when ye be children. Yer heart was then his, and still is, I ken."

"Aye." No longer surprised to find her secret was no secret after all, Rachel bent to kiss her grandmother's thin cheek.

Once the meal was ready, everyone ate to their heart's content, Dougal taking thirds. Rachel hoped that Margaret, a bonnie lass from the village, was expert at cooking, for she knew Dougal favored Margaret and she him, judging by the looks Rachel had seen the two share. A wedding was sure to be announced soon, since Dougal would again have income; and though Rachel was pleased he'd found a measure of happiness, she wished for her own portion.

Until recently, it had been unlawful for people to keep the Yule, due to an edict from the sixteenth century, but Rachel's mother had always insisted they observe Christmas since it was the day the Laird Jesus came to earth as a wee bairn. Prince Albert and Queen Victoria recently brought to Scotland new traditions, though Rachel's family kept a few of their own.

Athair brought out the pipes. Soon the lingering, soul-stirring notes reverberated through the croft. To Rachel's surprise, Dougal brought out their grandfather's fiddle that *Seanair* had bequeathed to him, but Dougal had not played since before the accident. When he first brought the bow across the strings the sound was discordant, but soon he played skillfully as he'd been taught by their seanair. Rachel noted the happy tears in her grandmother's eyes.

As the men played, the rest of the family sang songs of tradition. They played "*Taladh Chriosta*," "God Rest Ye Merry Gentlemen," and ended with a spirited chorus of "I Saw Three Ships." Abbie pulled a grudging Rachel up from the chair and linked elbows with her sister, forcing her to dance a jig.

> *"Then let us all rejoice amain,*
> *On Christmas day, on Christmas day;*
> *Then let us all rejoice amain,*
> *On Christmas day in the morning.*
>
> *"And all the souls on earth shall sing,*
> *On Christmas day, on Christmas day*
> *And all the souls on earth shall sing,*
> *On Christmas day in the morning."*

Dougal played the last verses faster and faster, and soon the two girls fell into a heap on the floor, dizzy and laughing.

"If ye could have it, what would ye wish to be on those ships all three?" Abbie asked Rachel from where she sat on the floor.

Rachel looked into her little sister's merry blue eyes. She thought of the past weeks, and especially the last two without Malcolm by her side. "Peace, love, and forgiveness."

"Aye," her mother said softly from the corner. " 'Tis a worthy answer. Mr. MacIvor, I do believe our daughter is growing up."

Chapter 9

New Year's Day brought with it another sprinkling of snow as the women engaged in *redding*, a thorough housecleaning, while Abbie took out the ashes from the coal fire in preparation for the Hogmanay celebration. Dougal regaled Abbie with tales of when he used to engage in the tradition of *firstfooting*, a custom wishing family and friends prosperity for the coming year. Always the first to beat his peers and race to the Sinclairs' door before midnight, Dougal arrived bearing simple gifts, while hoping the cook would give him a feast and a coin in return. He was never disappointed.

"But isna the first foot over the threshold supposed tae be bonnie, male, and dark?" Abbie wanted to know.

"No' bonnie, lambkin. Braw. And aye. So, I be two out o' three," Dougal amended, and Abbie giggled, looking at his red hair.

"Why does no one come through our door?" she wanted to know.

"Because we dinna live in the village," their mother was quick to explain.

"Why is that?"

"Because yer sheep prefer the hills," Dougal teased, lightly tweaking her nose.

She giggled and went back to helping stir the mixture for the pudding, satisfied with the reply. Rachel knew it was more than that. As was a common saying—"he's as bare as a birk on Yule e'en." The firstfooters, most of whom were young men like Dougal, desired a rich man's feast in return, not a poor man's supper, which was usually all the MacIvors could afford. Though this year, with her father's promotion and more bounty than they'd had on the table in years past, circumstances promised change.

They shared a leisurely meal late that night, as was their custom to see in the New Year. As the village bells began pealing, heralding midnight, Abbie hurried to the window to see.

"No one is out there," she said sadly.

Rachel knelt to hug her sister. "Never ye mind. We can still celebrate, aye?"

Abbie gave a dejected nod and smile.

The sound of a step outside the door brought their attention to it, and Rachel watched wide-eyed as it opened.

A tall figure in a fine kilt and cloak stepped over the threshold, the view of a face obstructed by the many parcels he carried. The hair was definitely dark, he was most certainly male, and. . .

Rachel inhaled a swift breath as Malcolm's smoky green eyes met hers once he set the parcels on the table.

"Oh!" Abbie squealed in delight. "He's braw *and* dark—we're sure tae have good luck this year!"

"Shush, Abbie," their mother gently scolded.

Malcolm broke eye contact with Rachel, and, as was the custom, wordlessly set about adding coal to the fire from the mounds in the sack he'd brought with him. He stirred the embers to life, then rose to face her parents.

To Rachel's astonishment, he issued an apology, admitting his part in Dougal's accident and his cowardice in following his father's imprudent advice. Her parents blinked in astonishment. Dougal was the first to rise and hobble with his crutch over to Malcolm. He stuck out his hand. Malcolm gave it a hearty shake, then pulled him into a swift embrace.

This broke the solemnity of the moment and everyone talked at once, welcoming Malcolm with warm hugs or hearty backslapping as if he were a family member. Rachel glanced at the table, stunned to see *all* the desired gifts present, though many firstfooters brought few. But Malcolm had brought everything—coal, salt, shortcake, a sprig of greenery, a bag of coins, and other traditional symbols to bless them with warmth, light, and prosperity for the coming year.

"Rachel, a word with ye in private?" Malcolm looked to where she still knelt on the floor by the window. Her mother smiled in approval, and Seanmhair motioned with her head toward the door.

"Go on with ye," she urged. "We will prepare Mr. Sinclair a meal."

Rachel needed no persuasion. She slipped into her cloak and

followed Malcolm outside, into the chill night.

"Rachel," he began, "I canna tell ye how sorry I am for all that happened betwixt us. Both in causing Dougal's accident and in keeping it from ye—"

She pressed her fingers to his lips to halt his words. " 'Tis in the past, Malcolm. What needed t' be said has been said. I hold no grudge toward ye any longer."

His eyes brightened with surprised hope. He circled her wrist with his hand, kissing the fingertips before he lowered them from his mouth so he could speak. He didn't, however, let go of her hand. "Rachel, lass, ye are me heart and always have been."

Her own heart jumped at his words. "Malcolm, I ken I've loved ye all me life, but 'twas no 'til Joseph spoke that I understood it."

He grew alert. "You spoke to Joseph? When?"

"The day before Christmas. Why?" She was confused at the sudden change in topic.

"He's gone, Rachel."

"Gone?" She blinked.

"Aye. His croft doesna appear as if anyone ever lived in it. I went to thank him for his counsel—he helped me regain footing with the Laird and also convinced me to see ye again. All that remained was the cross Dougal carved, sitting in a ray of sunlight, it was. Joseph's croft is bare, as if the man, himself, never existed."

Rachel's eyes widened as she tried to take it all in. "He did exist, did he no', Malcolm?"

"We both spoke to him several times. He must have."

"Aye."

From inside, her father's pipes began the haunting tune "Auld Lang Syne."

"Rachel, me love. . ." Malcolm reached into his waistcoat and pulled out a stunning sapphire pendant. It shimmered in the light that the moon cast upon the snow. "This was my seanmhair's, given to my t' give t' the woman I would one day take for my bride." Opening her hand, he laid the heirloom in her palm with care, then closed her fingers around it and held them.

Her mouth parted in shock at what she knew was coming, what

she'd always wanted, but up until minutes ago, never dared dream could actually be.

"Would ye consider becomin' my wife, Rachel?"

Here was the question she'd anticipated for years, and she couldn't find her voice. She swallowed hard and searched for it. "Aye, Malcolm, I most definitely will."

His smile stretched wide. "Come here, my wee bonnie lass." He pulled her close and Rachel yielded, wrapping her arms beneath his cloak and around his waist. She laid her ear against his swiftly beating heart, reveling in his warmth and protection.

From inside, her family's voices sailed to them:

"Should auld acquaintance be forgot,
And never brought to mind?
Should auld acquaintaince be forgot,
And auld lang syne?"

"For days gone by, Rachel," Malcolm whispered, tilting her chin up with his fingers and thumb.

"And for days yet t' come, Malcolm," she answered, her heart in her eyes.

Her three ships had come in: Peace, love, and forgiveness sailed into their lives that night, and Rachel knew all would be well with their souls. Sheltered from the cold in the warmth of Malcolm's arms, she felt her dreams were realized at long last.

Malcolm's lips touched Rachel's tenderly, then more firmly as their kiss deepened into one of shared love and promise.

"For auld lang syne, my jo,
For auld lang syne:
We'll tak' a cup o' kindness yet,
For auld lang syne."

(*jo*: "dear"; *auld lang syne*: "old long since" or "days long ago"— original lyrics by Robert Burns from Scots Musical Museum—1796, public domain)

Sticky-Toffee Scottish Pudding

Pudding:
8 ounces self-rising flour
1 teaspoon baking powder
10 ounces boiling water
6 ounces dates, chopped

1 teaspoon baking soda
1 teaspoon vanilla
2 ounces butter, softened
6 ounces sugar
1 egg

Preheat oven to 350°. Sift flour and baking powder in bowl; set aside. To saucepan of boiling water, add dates, baking soda, and vanilla; set aside. Cream butter and sugar in separate bowl; beat in egg and sifted flour mixture. Blend in date mixture. Pour into buttered 9 x 9-inch square baking pan. Bake until firm, about 40 minutes. As pudding cooks, prepare sauce.

Sauce:
4 ½ ounces butter

7 ½ ounces brown sugar
5 ounces whipping cream

Place ingredients into saucepan and melt slowly. Boil for one minute. Once pudding is removed from oven, poke a few holes in it with fork, and pour a bit of sauce over top. Place under broiler until it bubbles, but be careful not to let it burn. Serve pudding warm with remaining sauce.

Nollaig chridheil! (Merry Christmas!)

Pamela Griffin lives in Texas with her family. Her main goal in writing is to help and encourage those who know the Lord and plant a seed of hope in those who don't, through entertaining stories. She has over fifty titles published to date, in both novels and novellas, and loves to hear from her readers. You can contact her at words_of_honey@ juno.com.

Colleen of Erin

by Tamela Hancock Murray

Jesus said unto him, If thou wilt be perfect,
go and sell that thou hast, and give to the poor,
and thou shalt have treasure in heaven:
and come and follow me.

MATTHEW 19:21

Chapter 1

Dublin, 1820

Finn Donohue stood behind the counter of his store, filling out an order for more horse blankets. Cold weather had brought about a demand that had almost depleted his supply. Finn never wanted to turn away a customer for lack of merchandise. His aim was for Donohue's Mercantile to be known for stocking the largest variety of quality goods in Dublin. His formula so far had proven successful.

The front door bell tinkled, signaling that one of the last customers of the day had arrived. Finn shivered as a burst of cold air blew in before the door shut. He spun around on his heel. Just as quickly, warmth filled him as he watched Colleen Sullivan approach the counter in a graceful stride. His heart skipped a beat. Colleen was the prettiest girl in all of Dublin, what with her hair as black as coal and her eyes as green as the emerald grass of his beloved Erin.

Finn noticed that she had made sure the heavy wooden door closed behind her. No doubt she valued the heat from the store's pot-bellied stove. Seeing such caution pleased him on a cold December day. Though a small gesture, it proved that the wealthy Sullivans knew the value of a farthing.

As soon as her glance caught his, he greeted her. "Top o' the evening to you, Miss Sullivan." Finn tipped an imaginary hat in her direction and let his lips form his most engaging smile.

"Top o' the evening to you indeed, Mr. Donohue." Her eyes danced above cheeks that were as rosy as spring cherries no matter what the season. Her speech, while still conveying a soft Irish brogue, possessed a refined polish cultivated during her Swiss finishing school years. "I'm glad to find you are still open. I was afraid I might have been too late."

"Aye, you are out a bit late today. But even if you had knocked on the door at the stroke of closing time, I would have kept the store open for you." Like Colleen, Finn owed his precise speech to travel abroad.

Unlike Colleen, he didn't come from a wealthy family. His *máthair* had sacrificed to provide the means and knowledge to lift him up to the merchant class, and he wasn't about to forget her dedication to him.

Colleen smiled. "Thank you for your kindness, Mr. Donohue, but I would never impose upon you to keep the store open for me, especially since my own carelessness caused my delay. I was setting out my supplies for tomorrow's mending, only to discover I had run out of white thread."

"Well, we can't have that now, can we? Let me fetch a nice big spool for you."

She smiled and brought the sun with her.

As Finn moved toward the rack that housed the spools of thread, he heard her add, "Oh, and after that, I'd like my usual order of candy."

He turned and grinned at her. "For the orphans, eh?"

"Of course. And I'm hoping the doll for Kathleen's birthday will be arriving soon from London."

"Any day now, Miss Sullivan."

Colleen stared at the toy display, but Finn discerned that her concentration wasn't on his current offerings. Instead, her countenance radiated wistfulness. "Oh, I do so hope Kathleen likes the doll I chose for her."

"Why, I'm sure she will. What little girl wouldn't love a doll with auburn hair and a green velvet dress? But if the one you chose doesn't meet your expectations, you may certainly choose another one. I ordered several in anticipation of Christmas."

"Then many little girls in Dublin will be happy on Christmas morn. But I'm sure I'll be very pleased."

He set the spool of white thread on the counter for her approval.

She inspected the thread and then nodded.

"Little Kathleen should be grateful for anything she might get, if you ask me," he commented. "Without you and your generosity, those orphans would have lean birthdays. No birthday presents at all, I would conjecture. You are kind to remember each one."

"The Lord has blessed me beyond what I deserve. It is my duty and obligation to share with those less fortunate. A duty and obligation I fulfill with great joy." She broke out into a genuine smile.

" 'God loveth a cheerful giver,' " Finn quoted from scripture. "Considering how much you give again and again to His glory, I'd say that you can rest assured He loves you."

"And He loves you, too."

"But I am not nearly as compassionate as you. You're softhearted, Miss Sullivan. No wonder you're well thought of by us mere mortals in Dublin. And not just by the orphans."

A slight blush colored her cheeks.

Finn decided to change the subject to minimize her embarrassment. "Oh, I have something I'd like to show you. You mentioned that you'd like to give a set of pearl earrings to your máthair. I took the liberty of ordering a pair. See if you like them." After withdrawing a key from his pocket, he unlocked a drawer under the counter where he kept special treasures. A little purse containing a dainty pair of pearl earrings awaited. He opened the purse and presented the earrings to Colleen. "I hope they please you, Miss Sullivan."

She gasped when she viewed the small but nearly perfect pearls. "I am delighted, and my máthair will be, as well. She always likes to say that a buckle is a great addition to an old shoe."

Finn and Colleen shared a laugh. The emotion made him feel good, and he wondered what it would be like to share mirth with Colleen all the time. Seeing her admire the pearls, he allowed himself the briefest fantasy of giving her an emerald pendant one day. Such a stone would match the color of her eyes.

Colleen pulled the string on the purse to secure the pearls. "Thank you, Mr. Donohue. Please add these to my bill. I'll settle with you at the first of the month, as always."

"I know you will. If only my other customers were as faithful as you. There's no excuse for not paying a bill, I always say."

"But sometimes there is a good reason," Colleen pointed out. "Hard times and unexpected circumstances can occur to the best of us."

"I suppose a few bad debts are inevitable, but I have little patience with those who can do better. Forgetting a debt doesn't mean it's paid." He made a mental note to add Colleen's amount to his ledger and noticed her eyes had taken on a distressed light. "I'm sorry. I have no business bothering a pretty lass with the problems of business. I'd much rather pass the time of day speaking of pleasant matters." He regarded Colleen's purchase. "I hope you don't mind me for complimenting you on your taste. In fact, I'm giving my own máthair a string of pearls to mark the occasion. You inspired me, if I may say so."

Her face softened. "You may say so. Oh, speaking of Máthair, that reminds me. She's baking today, and so I need four cinnamon sticks if you have them."

"Indeed I do. Of the finest quality." He hadn't meant for the pride to show in his voice, but it had. He wondered how many other nearby merchants could boast as much. He reached into a spice box and withdrew the number requested. Their sweetly pungent aroma pleased him.

Colleen inhaled delicately as she watched him pack the spices. "Ah, that cinnamon smells delightful."

"I was just thinking the same."

She lifted her dainty forefinger. "Oh, and one other thing. Has the silk I ordered arrived yet?"

He pursed his lips. "Not yet, I'm sorry to say. Next week, I hope."

A flicker of disappointment visited her pretty features before she composed herself. "That is quite all right. Nothing you can do to change that. I won't engage the seamstress until I have the fabric in my own hands."

"That is a wise practice." Still, he hated that he couldn't make the order arrive a moment sooner than it would. "What I can change is how quickly the silk gets to you once it arrives at the store. When it does, I'll deliver it to your house myself. In person."

"You will? Oh, don't let me trouble you so."

" 'Twould be no trouble at all, Miss Sullivan. Your farm is only a few miles out of my way. I enjoy the excuse for a drive in the fresh air. I find it invigorating."

"I hope that's not just blarney you're speaking to me, Mr. Donohue. But delivering the silk yourself would be mighty kind of you."

He smiled, pleased that he could help. "And how else may I be of assistance to you on this fine day?"

"I believe that will be all. My order is never a large one. 'If you buy what you don't need, you might have to sell what you do.' "

"A wise proverb," Finn agreed. " 'A heavy purse makes a light heart.'"

His own reference to money reminded him that plenty of work needed to be done and he hadn't heard any movement from his worker as of late. He swept his gaze over the store, looking for his employee. Finn wasn't known to be lenient, expecting from his assistants more than an honest day's work for an honest day's wages.

His gaze captured Darby, who was once again staring out the window instead of going about his chores. The idea that the boy wasted time on the job vexed Finn to no end. "Darby!"

The young man lurched out of his daydream. "Yes, sir!"

"You're getting a late start. Lose an hour in the morning and you'll be looking for it all day. I need you to make sure we are fully stocked on fabric. You know Mrs. O'Malley bought several yards to make clothes aplenty for her brood yesterday. I wouldn't want to miss a sale because we can't lay our hands on the appropriate broadcloth."

Darby nodded.

"And then be quick about the sweeping. Indoors and out."

"Yes, sir. I will." Darby nodded in several quick motions and hurried toward a table overburdened with fabric.

"Mr. Donohue, he looks like he's scared to death of you!" Colleen chastised him, although in a voice too low in volume for Darby to hear.

Finn felt a tinge of embarrassment, but not enough for him to give any ground. "You know me, Miss Sullivan. I have little patience for ne'er-do-wells. Darby would rather spend the day chasing leprechauns than working."

Colleen looked at Darby and shook her head. "He's but a boy."

"Then he should learn sooner rather than later that poverty waits at the gates of idleness." Finn looked in his employee's direction and tried not to sneer. "That lazy boy will be finding himself out of work if he doesn't mend his ways."

"Have you no compassion?" Colleen's eyes darkened.

"I have compassion for those who work, I do." Finn clenched his fist around the pencil he was using to record Colleen's purchases. Slothful men reminded him too much of his *fáthair*, who'd abandoned his máthair when Finn was an infant to pursue idle dreams. That was almost three decades ago. Finn had never seen his own fáthair.

"You'll never hear me speak ill of the laborer," Colleen conceded, reluctance coloring her tone.

"I am a firm believer in working hard, as you know. Through work, I am determined to give my máthair the life she deserves. The life my fáthair denied her." Though he had always loved Colleen, moments such as this reminded him why he had never asked to court her. Resisting the urge to wag the pencil at the young woman, he settled for tapping it upon the counter. "You, Miss Sullivan, could learn a lesson or two from me. To wit, why you keep that no-good overseer on your farm, I'll never know."

She stiffened and lifted her chin ever so slightly. "Ross O'Hara may not toil with the diligence you think he should, but he needs the job and I'll keep him on at my place as long as he's willing to stay."

Finn observed Darby picking up the broom and gave himself a mental pat on the back for getting through to the boy. "See how Darby is working now? One need not be harsh to encourage employees to work. And he knows he'll be getting his pick of gifts from the store to give his family this Christmas, courtesy of me. But I'm not as gullible as you are, Miss Sullivan. Ross O'Hara is taking advantage of your soft heart, he is."

Colleen huffed. "Might I ask you to tend to your own affairs?" She grabbed her order from the counter and tilted her head at him once. "Good day, Mr. Donohue."

Alarmed by her upset tone of voice, Finn snapped his attention back to Colleen. "Miss Sullivan, allow me to help you get those goods to your carriage."

She lifted her nose. "Good day, Mr. Donohue."

With those words, she left. He thought of pursuing her, but another patron passed Colleen on her way through the door.

Finn turned brief attention to Joey. The well-dressed man, wearing a fine walking suit, was one of his best customers. If he could multiply Joey tenfold, Finn would be the richest man in Dublin. Deliberately putting aside his frustration in allowing Colleen to see him in a poor light, Finn cleared his irked expression and replaced it with one of an eager merchant.

"Good evening, Joey. You're just in time. I was almost ready to call it a day." Though he addressed his customer, Finn's gaze remained on the door through which Miss Sullivan had exited. Watching her pass by the front window, Finn wished he could have nailed his lips shut. Why did he have to let down his guard and irritate her?

He exhaled. Colleen Sullivan would never understand why Ross O'Hara vexed him so.

She didn't know that Finn loved her.

As Joey browsed, Finn mused to himself. How could he expect Colleen Sullivan, a woman born of privilege, to understand how he had come up from nothing? Not only had his máthair toiled, but Barney O'Conner had taken an interest in him. When Mr. O'Conner offered young Finn a job as a shipping clerk for his importing business, Finn didn't hesitate to take the opportunity. For seven years, Finn labored and learned the business, going abroad, thanks to his máthair's largesse—money she earned by scrubbing floors in Dublin's fine homes.

Later, when the mercantile came up for sale, Mr. O'Conner helped Finn purchase the business. For the past nine years, Finn had built his customer base to where he turned a fine profit and had long since paid back Mr. O'Conner, with interest. The rewards had been long and slow in coming.

Only in recent times had Finn felt he made a living good enough that he could consider taking a wife. Colleen Sullivan was his first choice. An image of her loveliness floated into his consciousness, making him smile.

"Do you have the cinnamon sticks I ordered, Mr. Donohue?" Joey asked, interrupting his thoughts.

Finn took his gaze from the window. Colleen had passed long ago, anyway. "What's that?"

"The cinnamon," Joey repeated without the least bit of vexation. "I ordered cinnamon sticks last week."

"Oh. Those. Yes, I have a few. I just sold four to Miss Sullivan. I hope her request won't disfurnish you."

"I'm sure it won't. I only need three."

Finn counted what remained in his supply. "I have more than three. And superb cinnamon it is, too."

"I have no doubt about that." Joey paused. "And the other spices?"

Finn searched his brain and recalled that the previous week, Joey had requested pepper and licorice. "Not yet, I'm afraid. My spice merchant has proven unreliable as of late. The situation has gotten so dire that I'm thinking of taking my business elsewhere."

"Oh, don't make such a decision on my account. I can wait."

"You are generous as always, Joey."

He shrugged. "And why shouldn't I be? I've been blessed."

Finn nodded, remembering how Colleen had uttered almost the identical phrase moments before.

"I see behind you the bolt of linen I ordered. A mighty fine shade of purple it is, too. I can always depend on you for quality wares."

Such a compliment delighted Finn. "Pleasing the customer has always been my aim."

"If you could provide me with a few other items, I would be pleased. First, two pairs of silk stockings. And some bay rum scent. Then I'd like to see the fragrance on display—the one in the opaque bottle." Joey nodded toward costly floral perfume and, after inspection, agreed to take it without expressing concern about its price.

Finn remembered another item his customer might like, since he was in the habit of buying expensive gifts for a woman. Finn wondered if Joey purchased such lovelies for his wife, sweetheart, or máthair. He had hinted that he'd be pleased to be privy to such information, but Joey was never forthcoming about the woman in his life. Still, Finn could make some reasonable deductions. "I received some fine silk fans this morning. I put aside a lace one I thought you might especially like for your—wife?"

"Yes, I would like to take a look at the fans."

As usual, Joey made the purchase without offering any clues. Instead of asking for credit, he paid his bill in full. For such promptness, Finn was grateful. He hated to extend credit but knew such a practice was a necessity if he hoped to stay in business.

He bade Joey good day as curiosity struck, and not for the first time. Who exactly was Joey? Why didn't he ever tell Finn his last name? Did he live in Dublin or out in the country? Perhaps seeing the man's conveyance would offer him a clue. "I know that bolt of cloth is heavy. Might I help you take your goods to your carriage, Joey?"

"No, thank you. Your offer is quite generous, but I assure you, I can take care of myself."

Finn lifted his finger, hoping to stop him. "But—"

"I shall see you early next week, in hopes that those spices have arrived." With that, he made a quick exit.

"That's the second instance in less than an hour," Finn muttered. In spite of himself, he ran after his customer. For the first time, he wished he hadn't attached a bell to the door of his establishment. He hated that the clanging sound would alert Joey he was being followed.

Finn stuck his head out and looked left, then right. Since winter was deep, night threatened. He saw not a single being in the twilight. He wanted to take a chance and, after choosing a direction, run after the elusive customer. Yet he couldn't. No use in having everyone in Dublin think him daft.

Chapter 2

Holding her shopping basket, with her free hand, Colleen pulled her redingote trimmed in ermine more closely to herself to ward off the cold. She rushed to her awaiting carriage at the side of the store. She couldn't get out of Finn Donohue's sight soon enough. The man exasperated her. All she had wanted was to go into his store and procure a few goods to last her through the week and perhaps engage in pleasantries with the proprietor. Why did he insist on upsetting her with his meddling? She wondered if she deserved to be vexed for not allowing her driver to accompany her on her errand, wanting to see Finn without being under her driver's watchful eye.

Yet gladness joined vexation. She thought back to how her steps felt lighter, her heart merrier, in Finn's presence. How handsome he was! As if it weren't enough that he possessed a fine abundance of wavy black hair, a pleasing complexion, and eyes as blue as the sea—no, that wasn't all. He had told her she inspired him! She sighed. He had kissed the Blarney stone, that one had.

Then she recalled how he had criticized her compassion, calling her gullible. Gullible!

Too exasperated by the remembrance to be gracious, she ignored the driver's offer to assist her in boarding the carriage. Stomping up the step, she let out a sigh and thrust her goods toward the side of the carriage, not caring in what position her reed basket landed on the black leather seat.

Colleen plopped down with more force than needed, sending her garments flying. The driver gave her a curious look and opened his mouth slightly as though he planned to ask what had put her in such a mood. She shot him a glance dark enough to discourage questions, before he shrugged and shut the door.

As she smoothed her skirt with gloved hands, she thought about Mr. Donohue. Everyone, including her máthair, thought Colleen to be the perfect match for the merchant. The cherished daughter of a deceased gentleman farmer and his wife, Colleen was denied nothing by her doting máthair.

That fact evidenced itself in her style of dress, sewn according to the latest pattern from Paris. Her decorative bonnet was fresh and elegant, and her redingote reflected a military style beloved by the French at the time. The garment boasted many buttons and cords and, in Colleen's case, ermine trim at the hem, collar, and cuffs. Underneath such a fine coat, her pelisse was equally fashionable, sewn of richly dyed cotton and featuring a high waist.

Mrs. Sullivan had suggested more than once that a merchant would appreciate—yea, even benefit from—such a fashionable wife. Known to be a fine dresser, Colleen possessed the attire and superb confidence to wear clothing well. Such a reputation would attract more business for Finn should they wed. Surely, Mrs. Sullivan suggested, the ladies in town wanted to look as elegant as Colleen, and they would be certain to buy expensive cloth and fine lace from the store in an effort to emulate her mode of dress. Aware of the luxuries Sullivan money afforded, Colleen could see such logic. Yet she wanted to marry for love, romantic that she was.

So why did she love such an uncompassionate ox?

The question remained unanswered as the carriage passed the milliner's shop she patronized regularly, a druggist she hardly ever saw thanks to robust health, and two pubs she had never entered. All the storefronts, including Finn's, had been whitewashed in anticipation of the celebration of Christ's birth. She spotted a couple of acquaintances and sent them a friendly wave. Her family farm was located just outside the city, so soon they had passed the outskirts of town and were clip-clopping up the lane to the farmhouse. Visions of Finn rolled through her head. If only she felt free to give him her most ardent affections. Could he love her, too? But it was no use.

Lord in heaven, why did Thee give me feelings for a man with so little mercy for others? Or am I being disobedient to want to be near him? I am ready for Thine answer, whatever it may be. In Jesus' precious name, amen.

Moments later, after Colleen disembarked and made a special effort to show the driver courtesy to amend for her previous rudeness, she entered the farmhouse she had always called home. The dwelling, whitewashed, as were the stores, looked fresh and ready for Christmas. She smiled, heartened to see such a vivid reminder of the Babe's purity.

Though Colleen never considered the house imposing, it was larger than most in the area, with several ample rooms. The structure had been solidly built by Colleen's ancestors.

Anticipating Colleen's arrival, Mrs. Sullivan greeted her at the door. "Did you get that thread you were after?"

"Yes, I did, and the other things on your list, too." Colleen kissed her máthair on the cheek as was her custom whenever she returned from a journey, no matter how long or short. Remembering the pearls, she slipped them in her pocket so her máthair wouldn't spy them.

Mrs. Sullivan took the basket and gave the goods a quick inspection. "Good. I see he even had the cinnamon. Now we can bake our Christmas cakes for the church dinner and make some wassail on Christmas Eve, too."

"Aye." Colleen braced herself for the next question she knew to be inevitable.

"And how was Mr. Donohue?" Lively emerald eyes, identical to Colleen's, took on a light of mischief.

"He was well." Colleen didn't look at her máthair but concentrated overly on removing her bonnet and redingote with the help of a maid.

"Waited on you himself, did he?"

Colleen nodded. "As always."

A look of satisfaction crossed Mrs. Sullivan's features. "You know, if you play your cards right, I believe he could be yours."

"Máthair, you know how I feel about that. Why, he was after that boy in his store—Darby, I think his name is—to sweep the floor as it was. He'd work me to death."

"Afraid of a little labor, are you?"

"Nay. But Finn's a hard man. Complaining about those who aren't able to pay their bills on time." Colleen didn't hold back a grimace.

"You must remember that you've never had to worry about money, but Mr. Donohue has not been so fortunate. A merchant must collect on his debts, or he won't be in business long. Try to see things from his point of view."

"I suppose you're right," Colleen admitted. "It's just that I'd like to see him demonstrate a wee bit more compassion for his fellow man."

"He might come around one day. You never know," Mrs. Sullivan said. "So did you see anyone else of our acquaintance?"

"Mrs. Kelly was shopping with her daughters, and Mr. Fitzgerald sends his regards. And I passed Joey on my way out of Mr. Donohue's store."

"Joey. Did he have anything to say beyond a greeting?"

"Nay. He is a mysterious one," Colleen conceded. "Funny, no one ever mentions seeing him except at the store. Not at church, not about town, just at the store."

"Oh, I'm sure people have seen him here and about. We just don't know about it, that's all." Mrs. Sullivan smiled. "Maybe he wants to be secretive, rich as he is. I understand he keeps the Donohues in fine style with his purchases. Surely Mr. Donahue is grateful."

"No doubt. He told me again today how he wants his dear old máthair to have a better life than he had—a life she earned many times over. She worked so hard to make the money to send him abroad so he could learn his trade and make contacts with importers."

The older woman's eyes darkened, and she flitted her hand as if dismissing a fly. "That fáthair of his was no good."

"Máthair!"

" 'Tis true. But enough of that. I know it isn't right to gossip. Besides, it's almost time for dinner. And Cook has made my favorite—mutton stew."

⊱❈⊰

The following day, Colleen knocked on the door of one of the city's orphanages, Mallory House. Ian Mallory, an orphan who grew to be wealthy, had bequeathed his ancestral home upon his death to the benefit of the city's parentless children. Colleen enjoyed her visits to Mallory House. The number of children never grew past twenty, so she could learn each child's name and disposition.

"There ye are, Miss Sullivan. 'Tis good to see ye once again," the gray-haired mistress, Miss O'Leary, greeted Colleen. "The children are waitin'. Yer visits are the highlight of their week, they are." She stepped aside for Colleen to enter.

"And they are a highlight of mine," Colleen assured.

"Miss Sullivan is here!" she heard little Dylan say.

His announcement brought forth a tidal wave of children. They shouted greetings, their voices echoing in the foyer.

"Now, mind yer manners!" Miss O'Leary cautioned.

Colleen laughed. "I don't object to a little noise all in fun. But I must say, if you are all good during story time, there will be a piece of candy for each one of you. Special from Donohue's Mercantile."

Whoops and hollers echoed.

"I'm not sure ye'll be able to calm them now that ye've made such a promise," Miss O'Leary warned, a teasing light dancing in her blue eyes.

Still laughing, Colleen withdrew a book from her satchel, saying a silent prayer of praise for the children and their joy. As the hours waned, her thoughts turned to Finn. What would he think of spending an afternoon with the orphans? Surely he could find compassion for such tenderhearted little souls, their plight no fault of their own.

Or could he?

⁂

"Back again, I see." Finn smiled at Colleen the following day when she returned to the store. "You must be anxious about that fabric."

In spite of herself, she felt her heart lighten. This time she had allowed her driver to accompany her into the store, so she knew he would be listening even while pretending to be otherwise occupied. She made sure her voice sounded nonchalant. "Yes, after my last visit to the orphanage, I realized more than ever how much in need they are of fresh clothing. I hope to fashion a simple shirt for each of the children. They will enjoy something new."

"They are sure to welcome such efforts."

Colleen looked yearningly at the toy display. "No doubt they'd each like a toy, too." She looked Finn straight in the eyes. "You know, Mr. Finnigan is donating a crate of oranges so each child might have a fresh piece of fruit on such a special day."

Finn let out a low whistle. "Oranges, eh? The grocery business must be fine for Finnigan to go to such extravagance."

She chose an apt proverb as a response. " 'Keep your shop and your shop will keep you.'"

"Aye, the proverb cannot be bettered," Finn conceded. "Finnigan is doing a good thing. A nice orange will help keep the orphans healthy."

Once again, Colleen made a point of eyeing a stock of toys lined along shelves on the far wall. A selection of dolls with painted china heads, wearing colorful dresses and matching bonnets, sat side by side, their eyes of black lacquer seeming to beg for a little girl's love. Wooden pull toys, shaped like ducks, dogs, and cats, were painted in vibrant colors. Colleen visualized the children playing with any number of games Finn had on display, and running with the balls. She cast her gaze toward him and caught his conflicted expression.

Finn crossed his arms and leaned against the counter. "I know what you're going to say next, Miss Sullivan. You're wanting me to donate some toys, aren't you?"

"Well, now that you say so, it would be lovely for each child to receive not one but two gifts each." Colleen glanced at the top of the counter and back. "I'm supposing that would be a nice thing for you to do."

"But I was hoping to sell those toys." His voice sounded plaintive.

"Of course you were. But surely you have time to order more to replenish your stock before Christmas, eh?"

He shifted his weight from one leg to the other. "How many would you be needing?"

"Oh, not many," she replied, stalling for time as she went down her mental list. "Eighteen?"

"Eighteen!" He swallowed and adjusted his collar.

"That's not such a large lot. If the orphanage were full, I'd be asking for twenty."

"Twenty! In that case, eighteen doesn't sound so great a number." He let out a labored sigh and glanced at the dolls, wagons, pull toys, balls, and wooden hoops. "Oh, all right. I believe I can find it in my heart to let the children have a few toys."

She exhaled an unrestrained gasp. "Oh, Finn—I mean, Mr. Donohue—that's very kind of you. Very kind indeed."

"Well, as you say, when the Lord has blessed a man, he can give back a few farthings."

Suddenly she felt led to pursue the thought that had occurred to her earlier. "Won't you help me take the toys to the children? It will mean much to them—and to you, to see who'll be benefiting from your generosity."

"Really? You want me to accompany you?"

Regret seized her. Perhaps she had been too bold. "Well, I—"

"Why, certainly. I can do that. Now that you mention it, I wouldn't mind seeing the little ones myself."

"Tomorrow, then?" Her tone of voice sounded too eager to her ears.

"I can do that. Now go on and choose the toys you want."

"That would be delightful." Regarding the selection of wares, Colleen revisited her own childhood. Choosing a toy for each child, be it a new doll or hoop for a girl or a wooden pull toy or ball for a boy, pleased her. After a few moments, she had completed her joyful task. "Thank you, Mr. Donohue."

A moment later, Colleen didn't bother to suppress her smile of victory as she left the store. Maybe there was hope for Finn Donohue after all.

Chapter 3

As soon as he told Colleen he'd take toys to the orphans, Finn regretted the promise. He liked children, at least the idea of children, but the thought of entertaining them made him feel like the goose sent with a message to the fox's den.

He didn't know much about children of any age or description. He realized—not for the first time—how odd he and Colleen both were as only children in a country full of large families. Brothers and sisters could have helped him. As it was, he felt lost. Had his fáthair stayed, Finn no doubt would have enjoyed the companionship of many siblings. Another reason to resent him.

He remembered the apostle Paul's admonition in Colossians 3:8: *"But now ye also put off all these; anger, wrath, malice, blasphemy, filthy communication out of your mouth."*

The last ones on the list troubled him little. Anger at his fáthair, well, that was another matter.

"To put off repentance is dangerous," he muttered under his breath.

"Sir?" Darby asked. "Did ye say somethin'?"

Startled, Finn looked over at the boy and noticed that, for once, he held a broom in his hand. "Just muttering to myself. Go on about your business."

"Yes, sir."

Resolving to be more careful with his musings, Finn decided to put together a few orders for delivery. The task, though not thoroughly engaging, took his mind off his fears.

Concentrate on Colleen.

Colleen! His admiration and fondness—even love—grew with each encounter. He took in a breath at the thought of her beauty, her kindness, her soft voice, her confidence. . . . Colleen possessed every attribute he wanted in a woman, and more. But could he fit in her world? He had to show her he could.

But how? Finn didn't want to make a fool of himself. The only way he thought he might avoid that was to let Colleen do all the talking the next day. Maybe then he could survive the afternoon at the orphanage.

⚜

Colleen heard hoofbeats slow from a trot to a stop and wheels rolling, then braking, against the dirt path leading to the farmhouse.

Finn!

She set aside her embroidery and rose from her chair to peer out the window.

"Sounds like your beau is here," Mrs. Sullivan called from the kitchen.

"Máthair! He's not my beau!"

Mrs. Sullivan approached her, wearing a wide grin. "Maybe one day he'll be asking to court you."

Colleen let out an exasperated groan that she hoped would conceal her feelings for her visitor. All the time she'd been engaged in household tasks, images of Finn stayed close at heart. "Máthair, please. I'm not looking for a suitor."

"If not, then you'd better be thinking of it." The older woman inspected her daughter. "You are lovely now, with an abundant head of hair and smooth cheeks. And with such a slim figure, you wear your clothes well. If I may say so, you remind me of myself at your age. But remember, you won't be young and beautiful forever. One day you'll look like me, with gray in your hair and wrinkles around your eyes."

"Oh, but you are still beautiful," Colleen protested.

"To a daughter, maybe. But as to marriage, well, don't delay forever. I'm wanting grandchildren. If your fáthair were still alive, God rest his soul, he'd be saying the same." She tapped Colleen on the shoulder in a cautionary but kind gesture.

"I know, I know. But I don't want to marry any man who doesn't understand my compassion for others."

"Give him time. If I know you, Colleen Sullivan, you'll have him seeing the light faster than a rabbit running from a wolf."

"I may try," Colleen admitted, "but the waiting man thinks the time long."

A knock on the door hushed the women. Mrs. Sullivan, still spry, rushed to answer. "Mr. Donohue!" she greeted as though she hadn't seen him in a decade. "So good to have you here."

Charmed, Colleen exchanged greetings with Finn. Her delight waned as she shifted her concentration from her máthair to the man before her. She hadn't expected him to be dressed in a crisp morning suit. True, she had chosen to don a flattering pink frock trimmed in white fur, but Finn looked smarter than she'd ever seen him. She wondered if the orphans would think him a visiting dignitary instead of a merchant. Still, he looked too handsome to deserve any admonishment.

"Come on in and have a cup of tea," Mrs. Sullivan offered.

"Aye, if only I could spare the time. But the orphans await." He smiled at her máthair in a way she had seen him look at his best patrons.

The stars in Mrs. Sullivan's green eyes showed Colleen that the older woman was captivated. "You'll have to be sure to stop in for a good long visit and some tea with us next time. Cook made some fresh bread, too, and we have plenty of clover honey. Maybe you can partake with us when you bring Colleen back later today."

"For you, Mrs. Sullivan, I will make the time."

"I'll wager you wouldn't close the store for me, though," she teased.

He rubbed his clean-shaven chin and looked up at the sky as though he were in deep contemplation. "I don't know. I might have to think on that proposition awhile."

Colleen's máthair laughed, giving rise to an unwelcome flash of jealousy. *What am I thinking? 'Tis my own máthair, and Finn must soften his heart before I could even think of him as a husband for me. Oh, what is wrong with me? What gives me the idea he'd even consider me? Pride has reared its ugly head. Lord, please stop such uncomely emotions in my heart!*

"Mr. Donohue, we'd best be going, or the mistress of Mallory House will wonder what became of us," Colleen managed to say.

"To be sure," Finn agreed. "We wouldn't want to disappoint her— or the little ones."

The ride to the orphanage wasn't long. For the first time,

Colleen wished miles rose between them and Mallory House. She found that she enjoyed sitting beside the storekeeper. His fine countenance turned more than one woman's head as their carriage passed. Perhaps part of their curiosity resulted from wonderment as to why she rode with Finn. Yet Colleen had the distinct feeling that the women were admiring his comeliness—and might have been feeling a wee bit of envy. Though she and Finn didn't touch, she sat closely enough to enjoy his nearby warmth and the manly scent of his spicy shaving lotion, whereas they could only peer from a distance.

As she expected, Finn didn't say much along the way. Colleen, not wanting to bore him with mindless chatter, restrained herself to remarks on the weather and a few mutual acquaintances from church they spotted. Otherwise, she enjoyed the companionable silence. She had a feeling that he did, as well, although she also sensed a nervous spark. She wondered why.

Before long, their carriage approached Mallory House. The home looked like a large, uncomplicated box. Like other houses in the area, it had been whitewashed for Christmas. Shutters of dark wood made a splendid contrast with the light hue.

"There they are!" called one of the orphans, Sean, running across the lawn as their carriage approached.

Two other boys, Joseph and Patrick, ran toward them, calling out greetings as Colleen and Finn disembarked. From the corner of her eye, Colleen observed Finn, monitoring his response. The boys looked clean, but their clothing had been mended several times. At least Miss O'Leary kept them all in shoes during the winter.

"Miss Sullivan, did you bring us Christmas toys? I heard that's what you were plannin' to do." Patrick tugged on the sleeve of her redingote.

"Hey, that's not polite," Joseph admonished with a poke to the little boy's ribs. "Miss O'Leary would take to ye with the wooden spoon if she heard you say that."

Patrick flinched. "Sorry." His eyes grew wide, and he drew closer to Colleen. In a whisper he asked, "Well, did ye?"

Colleen laughed. "I cannot tell."

"She did! She did!" Patrick bounced up and down, red curls flying.

Finn's hearty laughter filled the air. "Word gets around here fast, I see."

"Yes, sir. No fella can keep a secret around here, at least not for long. Too many ears around," Sean informed him.

"Say, mister, who are you?" Patrick asked. "Are you one of them big London soli—solipticures?"

"Do you mean 'solicitors'?" Colleen guessed.

Patrick nodded. "Aye, that's it. Are you one of those? The last time one of them came by, Mary and Agnes left."

"Nay, he's the storekeeper, you dunce," Joseph said. "Don't ye know anything?"

"He's not old enough to go to the store. You know that." Sean shoved Joseph gently enough for a reprimand, but not enough to strike him off balance.

"You didn't come to adopt one of us, did you?" Patrick persisted.

"No, I'm afraid not." Colleen felt compassion tug at her heart. If she could adopt the entire lot of orphans, she would. But she could make their lives in the institution easier, so she did as she felt the Lord leading her.

Colleen noticed that Sean held a ball she had given him for his last birthday. "Were you getting ready to play a game, boys?"

She saw Finn eyeing the ball. "Boys, I haven't played a game of football since I was but a lad. What say you to a game after I help Miss Sullivan unload—I mean, after Miss Sullivan and I visit with Miss O'Leary?"

"Aye!" Patrick exclaimed.

"Aw, he just don't want to do his chores," Joseph said.

"Chores await, eh?" Finn answered. "Well then, let's put off our game. Work always comes first."

"It can wait," Sean said.

"Unwillingness always finds an excuse," Finn countered. "I wouldn't want to get you in trouble with the mistress. We can play another time."

"Oh no, Mr. Donohue." Colleen pulled him aside and spoke in

a voice that couldn't be overheard. "It's quite all right. Miss O'Leary would be happy to let them play for a time. You go along. There isn't that much for me to do. I'll tend to our errand."

Finn looked back at the carriage. "I can't allow a lady to fend for herself. What say I deliver the goods to Miss O'Leary? Then the boys and I can play while you read to the girls—after I help them with one of their chores, that is. Miss O'Leary may think it's fine to delay work for company, but never let it be said that I encouraged sloth. Laziness is a heavy burden."

"Oh, I'm sure they would be delighted for you to help before they play." Colleen observed his suit. "You're not quite dressed for work, I must say."

He regarded his attire. "Never mind. I'll choose a chore that's not so messy."

"Well then, that's a splendid idea. I'll send out the other boys to take part in the game."

"Other boys?"

"Of course. You didn't think this was all of them, did you?" Colleen jested.

"Oh. I—I suppose not."

She thought she spied a frightened look on his face. Why was he afraid?

If the boys noted Finn's unease, they didn't let their expressions show it.

Joseph didn't miss a beat. "They should be finished with school soon. We're out because our lessons are done!" He beamed.

Finn laughed. "The schoolhouse bell sounds bitter in youth and sweet in old age."

"School will never seem sweet to me," Sean said.

"Me, either," Joseph concurred.

Colleen chuckled. "I'm glad to see you boys agree on something." With that, she left Finn with his new friends.

Later, after Colleen had visited with the girls, reading to them and assisting with their candlewick projects, Colleen bade them farewell and ventured to the front lawn. Seeing Finn having such a good time running back and forth, she held back, hating to interrupt.

He looked like such a little boy himself, playing as though years had melted. After Finn scored, he looked up and seemed surprised to see Colleen standing near. He sent her a victorious look then rushed to her.

"Are you finished with the girls already?" His cheeks were ruddy with winter air and exertion, and his breath looked like steam when he exhaled.

"I'm afraid so. You can come back and visit another time. I know the boys would love to see you again," Colleen said.

Patrick joined them. "Do we have to stop?"

"Well, let's see now." Finn consulted his pocket watch. "I'm afraid we must. I didn't realize the time had flown so quickly. I hope the girls don't feel neglected that I didn't stop in to say hello to them, as well."

"Aw, who needs a stinkin' ol' girl?" Patrick asked.

The adults laughed, and after Finn bade farewell to the boys, he escorted Colleen to the carriage.

"Your gifts pleased Miss O'Leary," Colleen said. "And they pleased me, too. I hope now that you've visited the orphanage you aren't sorry you made the donation."

Finn smiled. "I'll never regret anything I can do for the orphanage. Those boys touched my heart. I hope you don't think me less of a man for saying so."

"Oh no!" She placed her hand on his sleeve but didn't let it linger too long. "I think you more of a man for admitting you can have—can I say—compassion for others."

Had she just uttered such a thing about Finn Donohue?

He grinned. "Didn't think I was capable, eh?"

She felt her face blush hot. Could he read her thoughts? Then again, Finn's outpouring of kindness had extended to the boys only upon her suggestion, and so far, just for an afternoon. Surely a life of hardheartedness would be more difficult to change than what could be accomplished in so short a time.

Meanwhile, her own heart throbbed with pain. She wanted Finn to learn compassion not to please her but to make his life better. She prayed that being with the boys was only the beginning of Finn's yearning to look beyond himself and his hurts and extend kindness to others.

Having mused enough, Colleen responded, "Oh, I think you always have been capable of compassion. Then again, who couldn't feel sorry for those poor children, parentless as they are with no place in the world to go but Mallory House? I thank the Lord every day that Miss O'Leary is kind to them."

"Yes, and they are there through no fault of their own," Finn pointed out. "Surely they deserve a little joy on Christmas morn."

"Yes, they do." She realized they had reached her house. "Here we are. I hope you will accept Máthair's invitation to dine with us."

"I'm not so sure she offered me a meal," Finn pointed out.

"Maybe she didn't. But I am."

<hr />

Mrs. Sullivan greeted them at the door, surrounded by the aroma of the muttonchops and parsnips that would be the evening's meal.

"Finn accepted my invitation to dine with us," Colleen told her.

"Good." Her jolly smile confirmed that she was pleased.

Though Finn was pleasant to Mrs. Sullivan during dinner, Colleen noticed that his gaze stayed on her most of the time. She didn't feel uncomfortable. Instead, she found she wanted this man—a man she thought she had known all these many years—to remain near her.

Mrs. Sullivan excused herself to package a plate of leftovers for Finn's máthair. Colleen's heart beat faster when she realized they were alone in the parlor.

He shifted his weight from side to side and spoke in a shy tone she didn't recognize from the usually confident storekeeper. "I—I had a fine time today, Miss Sullivan."

"As did I. The boys certainly took to you. That pleases me very much." She paused, working up the nerve to ask him something she'd been contemplating. Courage gathered, she looked him in the eye. "I have a request. Please call me Colleen."

His face brightened. "I may?"

Suddenly feeling shy and hoping she wasn't making a mistake, Colleen glanced at her shoes and then returned her gaze to his face. She nodded.

"Colleen." He sighed. "How sweet your name sounds on my lips."

"Yes, it does. Say it again."

"Colleen." He smiled. "Say my name. My Christian name."

"Finn." Just uttering his name aloud brought joy to her heart. A heart she still had to protect, lest she lose it forever.

Chapter 4

After bidding Colleen farewell, Finn whistled as he all but skipped across the Sullivans' lawn. Fresh with joy from being granted such a privilege—the privilege of calling Colleen by her Christian name—he was in an exhilarating mood. He leaped into his carriage and urged the horses homeward. Could Colleen ever love him enough for him to ask her hand in marriage one day? The looks she sent his way hinted that she could, yet something about the way she carried herself told him that the time to declare his love to her wasn't right. Not yet. One day, maybe. Hopefully that day would be soon.

Daydreaming of the present and future with Colleen, Finn wondered why the horses came to an abrupt stop without his say-so.

Then he saw it—a fluffy white form in the path.

The sheep bleated.

"A sheep! What's that sheep doing out and about?" He jumped from his conveyance and headed toward the stray animal. "How did you get out, boy?" A bleat from another sheep caught Finn's attention. It, too, had escaped and wandered down the path. Finn noticed two more not far off. "What is the meaning of this?" he asked no one in particular.

He picked up the sheep and surveyed the part of the fence that shielded the Sullivan farm from the path. Soon he discovered his answer. A gap in the wooden fence had proven too much for the sheep to resist. Several had escaped from the pen, and Finn had no doubt the entire flock would be headed for freedom before all was said and done. Colleen's overseer, Ross, would need to summon the dogs to gather them back up and repair the fence in haste. In the meantime, Finn returned to the pen the one sheep he had rescued himself before he hurried back to the house to let them know what had happened.

Colleen greeted him. "What are you doing back so soon? Is something wrong?"

"I'm afraid so. Your sheep are escaping from the pen as we speak."

Colleen gasped. "Oh no! Did Ross leave the gate open again?"

"He leaves the gate open? Why, such carelessness is inexcusable for a farmhand, much less an overseer."

An embarrassed look covered her face. "I know. But I'm afraid he does take spells of carelessness from time to time."

Anger reared its head in Finn's heart. How could Ross be so uncaring about the property he had been charged to protect? Thinking there was no time to debate the issue, Finn decided to get right to the point. "The gate isn't the problem. I found a gap in the fence."

A flicker of disgust—something Finn had never seen cross Colleen's face—appeared before she composed herself. "I mentioned that to him when I saw it earlier today. I thought he would have mended it right away, as I asked. He knows the sheep will get out if there's a break in the fencing."

Finn tightened his hands into fists, though he kept them at his sides. "That man ought to be throttled."

"Let us not condemn him."

Finn appealed to fact and reason, as much to keep himself calm as to convince Colleen. "I know his reputation. He loves the bottle more than his work."

"He means well."

"So you say. You'll never plow a field by turning it over in your mind," Finn pointed out. "Surely after this, you'll consider firing him."

"My farm help is none of your concern, Finn Donohue." Her strong voice brooked no debate. "Let me concentrate on the task at hand."

He wanted to argue that he was concerned about the woman he loved, but her expression remained steely. Chastened, Finn's guilt spurred him to help Colleen summon the dogs to gather the stray sheep.

"The first thing we need to do is find Ross." Finn tried to keep disgust out of his voice. "Where is that worthless farm manager when he's needed?"

"I'm not sure where he might be at present." The edge had returned to Colleen's voice.

Finn withheld further comment. "Since we're not sure, why don't I take to fixing the break for you? No point in gathering up all the sheep if we just put them right back in the pen with a torn fence." Finn's motive wasn't pure. A tough chore would give him the chance to spend some of his ire in a productive way and keep himself in Colleen's good graces, too.

"Making that repair would be kind, but are you sure you have time?" She looked at him, concern and admiration in her eyes. "And what about your suit?"

He didn't flinch. "A suit is only raiment. And for you, Colleen, I have all the time in the world."

She blushed and looked down at her skirt as though it had become interesting. He wasn't sure if her response was good or bad.

He cleared his throat. "Have you got a hammer and a few spare pegs in the shed I can use?"

"As far as I know, yes. Look on the top shelf in the back."

He nodded and set about his errand.

Inside the shed, he found more than tools. Not expecting to see anything living except perhaps a dog or cat, he jumped back to see a lump on the floor underneath a brown horse blanket.

The lump snored.

Moving closer, Finn knelt beside the form and moved the blanket away from the source of the snoring. The face revealed belonged to Ross O'Hara. The man clutched an empty tankard, keeping it near his lips even as he slumbered.

Finn shook him by the shoulder. "Ross O'Hara!"

The balding man, who looked older than his fifty years, stirred and groaned.

"Wake up, Ross! What are you doing asleep back here, and with a cup at that? Have you been drinking?"

Eyes fluttering open, he came alive. "Finn Donohue? What are ye doin''ere?"

Finn stood to his feet and looked down at the idle man. "I had dinner with the Sullivans. But never mind that. Why are you sleeping instead of doing your work?"

"The workday's long over, that's why. And what business is it of yers?"

"It's my business when you don't mend the fence."

"The fence?" A twinge of remembrance crossed his craggy features, but he recovered by taking the offensive. "This ain't yer farm. It's the Sullivans'. I do as they say, not as you wish."

"If only. Miss Sullivan just told me she asked you to repair the fence. Why didn't you?"

"I'll get to it tomorrow." Ross settled back in as though he planned to return to slumber.

Finn knelt down far enough to slap Ross on the shoulder. "You'll get to it, all right. But tomorrow is too late. The sheep are already out."

"Huh? What sheep?"

How could he ask such a ridiculous question? Finn stood erect. He folded his arms in a conscious effort to hold back his temper. "The sheep you were supposed to be tending. Those sheep."

Surprise lit Ross's dulled eyes, and he sat upright. "They got out? I didn't mean for that to happen."

"Sure you didn't. Now get up and help us get them back into the pen. If you can."

Ross tried to stand but wobbled.

"I'd tell you to fix the fence, but you're in no condition. You should have done your job before you took to the bottle. Better yet, you should have done your job and left the bottle alone."

"I—I'm sorry. I'll look around and see if I can find some of the sheep. How many's missin'?"

"We're not sure yet. Where are the other hands? Can't they help us in the search?"

"No, I let 'em all off."

"All of them? What were you thinking?"

"I didn't mean to. They asked one by one for this reason and that, and before I knew it, I'd told them all they could have the day off, and the night, too. They've all gone into town for some fun, I imagine."

"You'll have to look for the sheep alone, then. Maybe this will be a lesson to you," Finn couldn't resist adding.

"I'll do me best."

Finn wanted to retort that he wasn't sure that Ross's best was good enough, but Finn had already vexed Colleen as it was. With rancor, he gathered the hammer and pegs and made his way to the fence. Though repairs weren't his profession and he wasn't donned in work clothes, he completed the chore quickly. As he predicted, the exertion released some of his anger toward the drunken farm manager. Even better, he felt good when he rose to his feet and eyed his handiwork, knowing he had done a good deed for Colleen.

As he admired his achievement, Colleen and the dogs approached. A few sheep followed in turn.

Finn counted five sheep. "Is that all of them?"

"I'm still missing four," Colleen said.

"That's four too many. Let's keep looking."

Ross approached from the woods. "Three. Ye're missin' three."

Finn noticed that no sheep accompanied the farmhand. "It's already back with the flock?"

Ross shook his head and stared at the ground. "Wolves got him."

"Wolves! Oh no!" Colleen groaned. "What a horrible death. The suffering that sheep must have felt. The poor animal."

"That's a misfortune, sure enough, but there's no use in standing around moaning and crying," Finn said. "Let's hurry and see if we can find the others."

An hour later, Ross, who had sobered thanks to embarrassment and forced exercise, gave up the search. Finn concurred.

"I'm sorry, Mr. Donohue," he said, breaking the silence on the long walk back to the farm.

"Don't go telling me you're sorry. Tell that to Miss Sullivan. And if I were you, I'd be ready to pack my bags. I know you'd be out on the street if you were working at my store. You wouldn't have lasted a day."

Ross sneered. "I believe it. Ye're not known for mercy, Mr. Donohue."

"I dispense mercy to those who deserve it." Finn remembered the orphans and ignored Ross's disdain.

Back at the house, Colleen awaited their return. She greeted them at the back door, an anxious look on her face. "Were you able to find the sheep?"

The men shook their heads.

"Oh, those poor animals."

"Those poor animals have lost you some income," Finn pointed out. "All because of this lazy farmhand. If he had done his job, none of the sheep would have gone astray."

Colleen looked at Ross. "You are dismissed for the evening. I'll see you tomorrow morning." Instead of sounding a reprimand, her voice was weary.

Ross slumped and nodded, then turned to go back to his quarters.

"Dismissed only for the evening?" Watching Ross depart annoyed Finn all the more. He tightened his lips so hard he could feel the blood rush. "Don't be afraid. Fire him if you like, Colleen. I warned him on the way back from the search that he could expect to lose his position over his negligence."

Colleen stiffened. "I have no doubt you'd fire him if you were me, but you are not. I thought I told you that I have my reasons for keeping him in my employ."

"I'd like to know what those reasons are."

She crossed her arms, the motion matching her lips twisted in vexation. "All right, since you were kind enough to fix my fence and look for my sheep, I suppose I owe you that much. Ross is a distant cousin. We keep him here because his penchant for drink keeps him unemployable by strangers."

"I can testify to that. I found him asleep, clutching an empty cup, and his breath reeked of ale."

She slumped. "Usually the farmhands under his supervision realize his weakness and try to do what they can to make up for Ross's inconsistencies. I don't know what happened this time. He seems to be getting more and more careless. So you see why no one else but family would hire him."

"So you say. But why should you even put up with such laziness? Family or not, he should be of some use if he's being paid." Finn felt rage boil up to his neck. "You can't allow yourself to take in every stray. You cannot save the world."

"I know. The Lord has already saved the world."

Her answer, delivered with the serenity of an angel, irked him all the more. "I know that, Colleen. But being a good Christian doesn't mean you should allow everyone to take advantage of you." Seeing her chin drop, Finn decided he'd better leave before he said something he might regret. "I'm sorry. Perhaps I should not be so free with my opinion. I only want what's best for you."

"And I believe, in your way, you do. But for now, I must bid you a good evening."

Colleen's words sounded frosty, and her expression looked nothing as it had earlier when she'd granted him leave to call her by her Christian name. Finn's heart, so warm before, felt petrified. He wanted to protest, but Colleen shut the door. Gently. Yet firmly.

Chapter 5

The next day, Finn could hardly concentrate on work. Every time the bell at the store rang, he looked up, hoping Colleen might have decided to stop by. Noon came and went, and no Colleen.

His thoughts ran wild. Maybe she was avoiding him on purpose. Maybe she could never love him. Maybe she was even thinking of asking him to return to calling her "Miss Sullivan." Maybe he had been too harsh on Ross.

So many regrets and speculations. If only he could turn back the clock!

He thought of Darby. As instructed, the boy was taking account of the pickles. Finn swallowed. "You can go on to lunch, Darby. And take two pickles for yourself and your sister. I know how much you both like them."

Darby nearly dropped his pencil. "Really? You'd let me take two pickles? And grant me leave to go to lunch early, too?" As soon as the words left his mouth, Darby looked at the ceiling and back and tightened his lips as though uttering the words would void the privilege.

Finn's heart warmed in spite of himself. The favor to his faithful—albeit slow-paced—shop boy must have meant more to Darby than a new pony to a child. "Aye. But mind you, I can't extend such a gift every day."

"Oh, that I know, sir. Thank ye. And ye can be sure I'll be back on time from lunch."

Finn chuckled as Darby handed him the account, then scurried to lunch, clutching two fine pickles he wrapped himself with the care one would usually reserve for diamonds.

Darby kept his promise of a prompt return after lunch. Finn's lightheartedness upon doing a good turn made the afternoon go by more swiftly, despite his disappointment that Colleen didn't appear. Only his regular customers obliged him with a stop by the store. Not that he wasn't grateful; he was. But only Colleen could mend the rip in his heart.

He noticed Joey entering. "Top o' the evening to you," Finn called with forced cheerfulness. "Be right with you, Joey."

He tipped his stylish hat. "Take your time."

Finn completed Mrs. Callahan's order, after which Joey brought several expensive items to the counter.

"You're buying quite a few things today, Joey. Expecting a big Christmas, I see." Joey's bill would keep Finn living in style for a month.

"I have many gifts to give. I must not let anyone go without during the season of our Savior's birth."

"Those on your list will be happy indeed." Finn inspected Joey's selections. He placed a forefinger on a diamond-shaped silver trinket box. "I can't help but wonder if this is for Mary McGuire. She's been eyeing this box and the heart-shaped one for a while now, but I know she can't afford either on her own. You wouldn't be having eyes for her now, would you?"

"No indeed. I don't even know who she is, if you want to know the plain truth."

Joey's evasive answer left Finn more puzzled than ever. How could such a wealthy and attractive man as Joey not appear to know anyone in town, nor be known by anyone? Usually a rich man had more friends than he could count. He remembered the old Irish proverb: "Sweet is the voice of the man who has wealth." Surely Joey's voice was sweet to people other than Finn.

He tried again. "I'm sure some pretty lassie around here has caught your eye."

Joey chuckled. "I'm afraid not. No, 'tis a bachelor's life for me."

"Not if the women around here have anything to say about that, I'd venture."

The men enjoyed a hearty laugh before Joey brought up another topic. "I heard Miss Sullivan had a bit of trouble with some stray sheep last night. Is that so?"

"'Tis so." Surprised, Finn leaned toward Joey. "Where did you hear such a thing?"

"Fences have ears."

"If only they had mouths as well, then they could have reminded Ross to fix the gap." Finn let out a breath. "I didn't know you were acquainted with Miss Sullivan." He observed once again Joey's magnificently tailored attire and otherwise impeccable appearance, along with his poise. The idea that he knew Colleen caused jealousy to visit.

"I have never spoken to her. I only know of her and her máthair. And Ross."

Finn took in a breath with such exertion that a whistle escaped his lips. "You know Ross?"

"I know about Ross. He is one who needs mercy and grace more than the average man."

Finn snorted. "If he did a lick of work, I would have sympathy for him, and showing mercy would be easy."

"Agreed." Joey's tone carried such weight that, feeling chastised, Finn shifted from one foot to the other. "I know Miss Sullivan needs more help. Managing the farm has gotten to be too much for Ross."

"Ross and the bottle, that is," Finn muttered.

"Never mind that. I know someone who can help."

"You do?"

"Yes. You are familiar with the Wild Boar and Grey Goat Inn?" Finn nodded.

"Go there now and ask for Patrick. He's an excellent overseer, and I happen to know that he's in need of work. He was just let go from his old job."

Finn wasn't sure exactly which Patrick Joey meant, but there was no arguing with the man. No sooner had he issued his edict than he turned on his heel and disappeared.

Feeling compelled to obey, Finn grabbed his coat, asked Darby to keep a close eye on the store, and rushed four blocks to the inn. When he entered, several men he recognized waved their greetings. Normally Finn would have stopped to talk, but he knew his mission was too important for him to allow himself the luxury of exchanging pleasantries. He had to find Patrick.

He looked and could identify almost every man present. He had known most since childhood. Others he recognized from church.

Almost every man patronized his store at one time or another. Yet—unusual for such a gathering in Dublin—none of them went by the name of the beloved saint who'd brought Christianity to Ireland.

"What can I get fer ye?" asked the burly, unshaven innkeeper.

"Nothing to drink, thank you, Bryan, but you may be able to help me. I seek a man by the name of Patrick."

Bryan shifted his glance from one side of the room to the other. "Patrick? I know a lot of Patricks."

"I'm looking for the Patrick who's an overseer."

"Oh, that Patrick. Why do you want to meet with him? Would he be owin' ye money?"

"No." Finn was glad he wasn't on a mission to collect a debt since Bryan protected his patrons. "I understand he's looking for work. He was just let go at his old job, if my source tells me right."

"So ye're lookin' to hire him at the store?" Bryan narrowed his eyes. "I don't know if that would work out so good. He's used to the outdoors, not bein' inside all day."

"Shouldn't you let him speak for himself?" Finn snapped, then thought better of it. "Anyhow, it doesn't matter. I'm not looking for help at the store. A friend of mine who owns a farm needs a new man, and Patrick was recommended to me by one of my best customers."

"Oh." Bryan cocked his head and looked at Finn squarely. "That changes things. I'll see if he wants to talk to ye." For the first time since he'd offered Finn a drink, Bryan grinned.

Finn waited until the innkeeper emerged from the back with a strapping young man with a full head of straight red hair and muscles evident beneath his shirt. Even before introductions were made, Finn recognized Patrick Dempsey as an employee of the successful Douglas farm.

"I understand you are looking for farmwork?" Finn ventured.

"Sure I am. The sooner the better, I say. The wife is gettin' low on food for us, and our brood's not wantin' to live on love," Patrick answered in a brogue as thick as clotted cream.

"Weren't you working on the Douglas farm?" Finn sought to confirm.

"Aye, but not anymore. The old man let me go. Seems he had a nephew he liked better. I'd like to see him do my job half as well." Spitting the words, Patrick squinted his eyes and peered at a group of men gambling on a game of cards.

"I hope you can live up to such a bold statement." Though Finn's words offered a challenge, he could discern from the man's muscles that he knew how to work a hoe.

"Aye, I can, and I do. I can fell a tree faster than a beaver and coax more milk and offspring out of the livestock than most of the other farmhands in the parish."

"That's good to hear."

"So who's lookin'? Certainly not you."

"No. But Miss Colleen Sullivan's overseer could use a hand."

"You mean Ross O'Hara?"

"Aye."

"I don't know. I understand he loves the bottle more than he does his work. Or maybe I shouldn't be confidin' such a thing."

" 'Tis no confidence. Everyone knows Ross doesn't do his job. That's why they could use some help out there. Ross is pretty easygoing. He shouldn't give you much trouble. Not if you do an honest day's work. And from the looks of you, I think you do."

"Aye. I've worked with drunkards before. I can do it again. Ye want me to go an' see her about the job tomorrow mornin'?"

Though Joey had insisted that Finn take on this errand, suddenly he realized that he had no right to tend to the affairs of the Sullivan farm, especially without mentioning his intentions to Colleen first. "Uh, you might better let me put in a good word for you."

"I'd be obliged. Can I buy ye a drink in return fer the favor?"

"No, thank you. I must return to my store."

Finn's stomach churned as he left the inn. He had followed Joey's advice without question, feeling compelled. In his heart, he knew Joey would never mislead him, yet now he had regrets. Would Colleen be upset with him for interfering? Debating was useless now; he had made a promise to Patrick, and he had to keep it. He would just have to face the music, that's all.

Later, after he closed the store, Finn didn't delay in going to the Sullivan farm. *Lord, please let her be grateful, not angry.*

⁂

Busy discussing the week's menu with Cook and granting her permission to take home leftovers from lunch to her family, Colleen didn't realize she had a visitor until the maid announced Finn's arrival. Her heart started to beat in a noticeable way. All day she'd been fighting the urge to go to Finn's store and apologize to him for being cold when he chastised her about Ross. Much of what Finn had said about Ross was right. Yet she had to show Finn that he needed to see her side of the story—even if that meant not seeing him in spite of her yearning.

Not expecting guests, Colleen hadn't taken time to look her best. She wished to freshen her appearance, but making Finn wait too long would be rude. Colleen instructed the maid to fetch a cup of tea for Finn and make him comfortable in the parlor. That would buy her enough time to give Cook final menu approval for the next day and to smooth her hair.

Moments later, when she saw him sitting straight in a velvet chair, enjoying the tea, she stopped her pace for an instant. She could imagine greeting him each evening after a day at the shop, asking about his customers and about the popular patterns and fabrics from abroad. She dreamed about pleasing him with his favorite dishes and sharing time by the fire each evening. But such fantasies were just that—only fantasies.

He arose when she entered. "Good evening, Colleen."

"Good evening." She sat in her favorite chair across from him.

"I ask your forgiveness for appearing unannounced. My news is important."

"Of course." She knew if she expected compassion from him, she had to demonstrate it in kind. "You are welcome here anytime."

His countenance brightened. "So you forgive me for the unkind words I had for Ross last evening?"

"Your words were said in a state of vexation." She cast her gaze upon the floor. "They held a grain of truth, I'm sorry to say."

"I want what's best for you, though I'm sorry if I appeared to be harsh."

"You mean well," she said in all truthfulness. "So tell me, what is your news?"

"No need for me to delay in telling you. I—I asked Patrick Dempsey about working here. He'd like to take you up on the offer, if you'll have him."

She didn't know whether to feel grateful or vexed by his interference. "You did what?"

"I spoke to Patrick about working with Ross. I wouldn't have known he was available, either, except that Joey told me." He tapped the bottom of his mug a few times on the arm of the chair.

"Joey? You mean that customer of yours who comes in and buys enough goods to keep a brood of twenty and a staff of servants fed and clothed in fine style?"

"That's the one."

She shook her head. "He certainly is a mysterious one. No one seems to know anything about him."

"Maybe not, but he seems to know everything about everyone else. Patrick is a mighty good overseer. I'd hire him myself if I owned a farm. And just think—you'd be doing a good deed. He has a wife and children, and he needs the job."

Colleen thought for a moment. "I suppose I can afford to pay another man, especially if he'll do a good job."

"I think he will."

She decided to be pleased with Finn rather than vexed. After all, he had taken a risk to do her a favor. "Please tell him to report for work tomorrow morning at six."

"I will." Finn paused. "Your trust means much to me."

"Of course I trust you. You are an honorable man."

"I did a good deed myself today for Darby. A small thing, really. But it made him so happy that I felt happy, too."

She wondered what he meant, but details weren't forthcoming. But did the deed itself matter? Only Finn's compassion did. The idea that he had changed his ways toward his shop boy warmed her heart. "Aye, you are seeing that the rewards of Christian charity flow both ways."

"Indeed they do."

A spontaneous thought occurred to her. "Oh, I do have a question for you."

"Aye?"

Though a sudden feeling of shyness visited, she didn't let it stop her from posing her query. "Would you be so kind as to accept our invitation to Christmas Eve dinner?"

"Christmas Eve dinner?"

She didn't expect him to seem so taken aback and decided to mitigate his unease with jesting. "Aye. On December twenty-fourth, it is. At least I'm pretty sure that's the date."

"Indeed!" He laughed.

"You won't need to tend the store, since Christmas Eve falls on Sunday this year," she coaxed.

"But it's back to work for me on Christmas Day."

Why did he stall? Bowing to etiquette, she offered him an escape. "Your hesitation suggests you have other plans. I understand."

"No!" he rushed to assure her. "I have no plans at all."

"Are you sure?"

"Yes, I'm sure."

"Good." Her expression revealed more relief than she intended. "I hope your máthair will join us as well."

"I would be delighted to accept your invitation, and I feel confident in saying that my máthair will consent."

After the door shut behind him, she could hear him whistle a cheery tune. Happiness had made itself abundant among the Sullivans and Donohues.

Chapter 6

M rs. Sullivan entered the house, back from posting letters in town. She didn't bother to give her usual account of the people she saw there, but came straight to the point. "I passed Finn Donohue turning out of our lane. He must have come by for a visit?"

"Yes, Máthair. You needn't worry. All was right and proper. I did invite him in to sit by the fire and partake of tea. He was the perfect gentleman. The servants will attest to that."

"Aye," Cook said.

"I find no call for such dramatics. You are a lady, and he is a gentleman," Mrs. Sullivan confirmed.

"I know." Trust between Colleen and her máthair had never been in question, so she pitied Finn for his admission of pain suffered at the hands of his fáthair's negligence. She mused about how blessed she was to have such a devoted parent. She could only hope that she could imitate her máthair successfully once she married and, if it pleased the Lord, that He would bless her with children.

Colleen addressed Cook. "Mother and I shall depart to the dining room. Please see that dinner is served."

"Aye, Miss Sullivan."

As soon as she and her máthair were seated at the modest table, Colleen filled her in on the rest of the conversation. "I did invite Finn and his máthair to Christmas Eve dinner. I knew you wouldn't mind."

"Not at all. We are blessed, and I am grateful for any opportunity to share our blessings with others." Mrs. Sullivan gave her a sly look. "But surely our local merchant didn't come by to get himself invited to dinner."

"No. He wanted to tell me about a new farmhand who can help us around here. Patrick Dempsey. He was let go from the Douglas farm and is looking for a new position." She regretted the need to express her next sentiment. "After the incident with the sheep, I think it's time

243

we hired someone else."

"With reluctance, I agree." She sighed. "So you're going to do just as Finn says? You're going to hire this man Patrick?"

"With your permission."

"Aye, I give my permission. We've been in need of a reliable overseer around here for a long time. I just didn't have the courage to tell Ross."

"We don't have to let Ross go. We'll let Patrick help him, that's all."

"Because Finn Donohue told you so."

"Aye." The idea that a man cared enough about her to make such a suggestion didn't offend Colleen, even though she considered herself an independent. Instead, she felt strangely safe. She liked that feeling. She liked it very much.

⁂

Colleen didn't relish her next task, but she needed to let Ross know what was happening before Patrick's arrival the following day. She sent a messenger to the farmhands' quarters and summoned Ross to her study. He wasn't long in appearing. To Colleen's surprise, he had combed his hair and wore a fresh change of clothes.

"I know what ye're goin' to say before ye even say it," he said without accepting the seat she offered. "Ye're goin' to let me go. Well, I s'pose I deserve it. Ye've been kind to me long enough."

Ross, whom Colleen's máthair had told her was once a proud man, appeared beaten. Colleen could look into his face and see that he had once been comely, but drink, to which he took in sorrow after losing his wife and young child to illness, had taken the joy from his being. He looked at his shoes and slumped his shoulders.

"We're not firing you," Colleen said.

"Why not?" He looked up, defiance in his eyes. "I deserve it, just like your man Finn Donohue said."

"Don't you remember the apostle Paul's letter to Titus? 'Not by works of righteousness which we have done, but according to his mercy he saved us.'"

"So?"

"So how could we turn you out when the Lord has been so merciful to us? I only ask that you accept the help that we are offering you."

"Help?" Suspicion colored his voice.

"Aye. We have employed Patrick Dempsey to take over the main duties, but we want you to stay on and show him the ropes."

He narrowed his eyes. "And then what?"

"It will be as it always has been," Colleen assured him. "You may stay as long as you like."

"Are ye sure?"

"I am."

Ross fiddled with the brim of the hat he held in his hand. Staring at it, he nodded. "Thank ye." Though his voice was barely audible, Colleen knew he meant his expression of gratitude as surely as if he had shouted it from the rooftops. "I–I'll try to do better by ye."

"I know. And I'll pray for you," she promised.

"I wish ye would. God prefers prayers to tears."

✦✦✦✦

On Christmas Eve, the Donohue carriage rolled down the rutted lane of the Sullivan farm, toward their whitewashed house that appeared both large and inviting. Mrs. Donohue lurched to one side, almost bumping her head.

"Seems to me any family with as much wealth as the Sullivans could do a better job o' keepin' up their road," she remarked in her lilting Irish brogue. "I don't know if we should have come 'ere for dinner tonight. I don't expect to suffer bodily harm all in the name o' dinner, even if 'tis Christmas Eve."

"You'll recover, sure as I'm sitting here." Finn's voice remained gentle.

She righted the basket she held in her lap. "I just hope my pie survives the trip."

"No amount of bumping will affect its taste," he assured her.

Finn knew why his máthair seemed out of sorts. Reclusive except for trudging to and from work since his fáthair abandoned them, she wasn't accustomed to sharing any meal, even a holiday dinner, with others. Finn had taken a risk in agreeing to the dinner on behalf of his máthair.

As he predicted, she had acted withdrawn and irritable ever since he told her about their plans. He half expected her to feign illness that night. To his surprise, she had instructed her maid to style her thinning gray hair in a flattering manner. For the first time, she wore the new bonnet Finn had ordered from the same milliner Colleen employed. He noted she seemed uncomfortable in her redingote, tugging now and again on the fur-trimmed sleeves that no doubt seemed bulky and unnatural to her. As the maid helped her with the redingote, he had been pleased to see she had even chosen to wear her new blue winter pelisse.

Employing her own maid and wearing stylish attire were two aspects of her new life that Mrs. Donohue had not adjusted to readily; serving came to her more easily than being served. But she had earned what little bit of luxury he could now afford her, and Finn planned for his máthair to become even more accustomed to living well as the store grew more and more prosperous. According to his ledgers, prosperity wouldn't wane soon.

Looking over at his máthair, he wondered if she secretly was glad he had suggested they have dinner with the Sullivans and was only experiencing nervousness and regret now that the time had arrived. Finn sent up a silent prayer that she would relax.

He decided to help by distracting her. He pointed to the house. "Look. There's a candle lit in the window."

"So 'tis." She nodded. "Pretty. Colleen is the youngest in the family; am I right?"

"Right you are, Máthair. It's just her and her máthair. No doubt Miss Colleen is the one who lit the candle, being the youngest family member. They are very traditional folks, you know. I can tell by the wares Miss Colleen buys at the store and the tales she tells me."

Mrs. Donohue harrumphed and looked out the window. "The tradition seems more comely in a house where there is a child."

Finn didn't answer. Instead, he thought about Colleen's innocent ways. Her angelic face gave her the aura of a beautiful child, but she was so much more. He couldn't resist thinking about being married to Colleen. Thoughts of her had only increased since she agreed to hire Patrick without any reticence. The fact of her trust told him that her heart was growing softer toward him. She would make a good wife.

At the same time, his increased compassion toward others was being rewarded even though prizes were not what he sought. Since he had grown kinder toward Darby, the youth had been quick about his chores, and the store looked cleaner and tidier as a result. Finn had also resolved to be more patient with those in arrears with their payments to him, praying that he would strike the right balance of mercy and justice. Surely Colleen would have been proud of his progress had she been able to look over his shoulder, but he had a feeling he didn't need to boast. No doubt his demeanor revealed his new way of thinking.

Colleen. His thoughts never had trouble returning to her. If they wed, one day she would bear him beautiful children. Their first girl would be named Mary. She would light their Christmas Eve candle. The candle acted as a symbol of welcome to the Virgin and Joseph as they traveled looking for shelter, just as they had done on the night of the Savior's birth.

"Ye're quiet. Deep in thought, eh?" Mrs. Donohue interrupted his musings. "Ye are quite fond o' Miss Sullivan, ain't ye?"

No point in not telling the truth. "Aye."

"Ye think she'd consent to be your wife?"

The thought, one he had dwelt on for so long, sounded so permanent falling from his máthair's lips. He gulped. "Would that please you?"

"Aye. She'd be lucky to have ye."

"I think she can make me happy. Very happy."

She chuckled. "Ye know what they say. Marriages are all happy. It's havin' breakfast together that causes all the trouble."

He laughed. "I can imagine having breakfast with her with no trouble at all." He cut his glance to her and noticed a slight smile on his máthair's lips. Her approval meant so much. With her blessing, he knew pursuing Colleen was right.

The carriage stopped.

Mrs. Donohue clutched the basket that contained the dessert she had prepared and stared at it. Finn noticed that her eyes appeared to be blank.

"What's wrong, Máthair?"

"I'm not feelin' so well, Finn. I think I'd like to go home." Her smile had vanished.

He knew that her fears, not illness, spurred this new protest. "You'll be thinking nothing of the kind. You'll dine with the Sullivans and enjoy every minute. 'Tis not as though you'll be among strangers. You know Mrs. Sullivan from church."

"Aye, I suppose she's pleasant enough." She kept her gaze on the pie.

With a gentle motion, Finn took the basket from his máthair and then helped her disembark from the carriage. She stepped slowly toward the house, as though she faced execution rather than a pleasant meal. In moments they had arrived at the door and were greeted by Colleen and Mrs. Sullivan.

No matter how many times he saw Colleen, Finn had to control himself to keep from sighing in admiration. This night she looked especially lovely. Though dressed in the most superb of her finery—a picture of perfection in red and green—she could have been wearing the milkmaid's rags and still presented the image of beauty. Her eyes shone and sparkled just like the stars. Burning candles offered a flattering light to her form, catching the sparkle of her hair and pearl-like teeth. When she greeted him with a hello, the world melted.

"I brought a mincemeat pie," Mrs. Donohue informed Colleen, bringing him back to practical matters. Mrs. Donohue's voice sounded tentative, as though she wondered if her offering would be accepted.

"Splendid! It will be a wonderful accompaniment to our Christmas pudding." Colleen sent them both a gracious smile.

Finn watched his máthair's reaction. As he expected, Colleen's pleased expression caused her posture to relax. Even better, if Colleen noticed that Mrs. Donohue felt uncomfortable, she didn't let on in her countenance or conversation. Mrs. Sullivan was just as welcoming.

Relieved, Finn was determined to keep all the women, especially Colleen, smiling during the entire visit. He tried all night to be witty, and Colleen's repeated laughter and smiles rewarded him, convincing him of his success. When Colleen asked him if he would offer grace before the meal, Finn felt grateful that he had used his foresight to memorize a few words of gratitude. Yet his planned speech didn't materialize. Instead, the blessing he offered came from his heart and, to his ears, sounded lovelier than anything he could have written on his own.

Afterward, Finn stuffed himself on spiced beef and a variety of accompaniments and partook of both the mincemeat pie and Christmas pudding. After dinner, he patted his belly and inwardly congratulated himself on the way, in spite of the setback he'd suffered as a child, his prosperity allowed him to enjoy such fine company and food.

After the meal, Colleen again set the table and placed on it a loaf of bread made with caraway seeds and raisins, a pitcher of milk, and a candle of beeswax that was large enough to offer light for several hours. The back door was left unlocked so that Mary and Joseph, or any wandering traveler, could partake of the dinner.

"The two o' ye have set out a fine meal, ye have," Mrs. Donohue commented. "Mary and Joseph would be proud to eat here if they passed by."

Finn sent his máthair a smile, noting that her evening was progressing as well as the greeting had promised. Despite her initial anxiety, she had taken well to Colleen and Mrs. Sullivan. Soon the older women chatted like old friends. Earlier that evening, Mrs. Sullivan had even suggested that Mrs. Donohue join the church sewing circle. To his delight, Finn's máthair accepted with little hesitation. Surely the Lord had a hand in getting his reluctant máthair to become involved with new friends.

He said a silent prayer, thanking the Lord that his máthair, who had spent her youth as a servant, was accepted by the Sullivans without reservation. Then again, Colleen and her máthair were known for their free expressions of Christian charity.

Finn returned his thoughts to the present. "I hope someone stops by to eat such a fine meal." He admired the table. "Perhaps a traveler on his way out of town."

"Do you really hope someone stops?" Colleen asked. "I didn't think you cared enough about people you think of as ne'er-do-wells to wish they would partake of a free meal."

"Colleen!" Mrs. Sullivan chastised. "What are you thinking, insulting our guest in such a way?"

"I'm sorry, Máthair. And I'm sorry, Finn." Genuine regret colored her face and voice.

"No matter, Colleen. I deserved that remark, and more. I never have had much patience with laziness." He glanced at his máthair. She knew why Finn felt the way he did about irresponsible men.

"Don't let past pains affect the present," Mrs. Donohue said. " 'Tis time to let all that go." She reached over and patted his shoulder.

Finn wasn't so sure. He changed the subject. "Has anyone ever stopped by in past years?"

"No, sadly." Colleen shrugged. "I don't expect anyone to stop by tonight, either. But we put the food out, all the same. And we hope. And pray."

Chapter 7

As the evening waned, Finn wished he could think of a reason to prolong the festivities. The four of them had just about run out of conversation, but he was comfortable by the fire in the parlor, and he didn't want to leave Colleen's presence.

Finn was ready to express regret that the evening needed to come to a close, when they heard a knock on the door.

"Who might that be?" he asked.

"I think I know. Excuse me." Colleen rose from her chair and disappeared. A few moments later, she reappeared with a young girl who looked to be on the cusp of womanhood.

Finn studied the girl. Her eyes were a stunning shade of blue, and her hair an appealing shade of red. He recalled an old proverb: "If you meet a red-haired woman, you'll meet a crowd." No doubt the boys in Dublin fought over her, even though beside Colleen, not even the girl's brilliant hair could put her above the beauty of the one Finn loved. Only after he had made that silent observation did he realize that the girl's clothing, though clean, showed signs of repeated mending and her shoes were well worn.

"This is Mary O'Connell," Colleen explained.

"Oh. Mary." Finn realized what was happening. Mary had been engaged to extinguish the Christmas Eve candle. According to tradition, only a girl bearing her name could extinguish it. No doubt Mary had several other houses to visit that evening. Though her name enjoyed popularity in Ireland, not every house was blessed with a little girl by that name.

The family followed Mary to the window. She extinguished the candle with a delicate breath. After the light ceased, everyone present stood in awed silence. Finn observed the deep night, lit by twinkling stars, its silence broken by the occasional bleating of a sheep and braying of a goat. The animals reminded Finn of the way angels announced the Savior's birth to shepherds watching their flocks. How magnificent and startling their glory must have appeared amid an otherwise silent night.

After a moment, Colleen's sweet voice broke the silence. "Thank you, Mary."

The girl nodded. " 'Tis beautiful, isn't it?"

"Aye," Mrs. Sullivan agreed.

Colleen handed the girl a sack that Finn had watched Colleen prepare earlier. Mary's family would enjoy the several slices of meat, potatoes, and two slices each of pie and cake. Colleen also handed the girl a few coins. Finn thought Colleen paid too well for the small task Mary performed but realized that Colleen's generosity was essential to her nature and part of the occasion.

Mary's eyes lit with gratitude. She curtsied. "Aye, mistress. Thank ye."

"Thank you," Finn added.

Mary's glance caught his gaze, and in the look he discerned desperation. Perhaps the food Colleen provided would be the only Christmas feast Mary's family would know that year. Without warning, his heart moved toward the girl, and he reached for money in his pocket. Surely his máthair and he could do without a few extra coins. He surrendered a few pence, and her open mouth and her eyes lit with thankfulness were a far greater reward than he felt he deserved. Suddenly he wished he could do more.

"Oh, thank you, sir!" Mary curtsied to him.

Soon the girl disappeared into the frigid night. Finn wondered what type of home she might be going to at evening's end. He said a silent prayer for Mary, her family, and the world's disadvantaged. He remembered the Savior reminding His disciples that the poor would always be with the world. Truly Finn could not help everyone, but he could touch the few people the Lord might see fit to place in his path. He prayed for future discernment.

A thump sounded just as he finished his impromptu prayer.

"What was that?" Colleen turned her head in the direction of the noise.

"I don't know," Mrs. Sullivan answered. "It sounds as though it came from the dining room."

"Surely no traveler is visiting us, after all these years of having no one stop by on Christmas Eve," Colleen wondered aloud. She took Finn by the forearm and looked into his eyes. "Oh, I am glad you are here."

Finn felt his courage emerge, thanks to her touch and the dependence on him that her look demonstrated. "I'm sure whoever our visitor is means us no harm. Indeed, he could be a wandering traveler who is aware of our tradition of offering a meal. Or perhaps it's simply the cat knocking over a bowl."

"Perhaps," Colleen agreed. She relaxed. "I suppose it's not even worth investigating."

They resumed conversation until a sound that seemed to be the foot of a chair dragging across the wood floors drew attention. Finn sensed the others in the room stiffen. With a tone that conveyed more confidence than he experienced at that moment, Finn said, "I'll see who—or what—it is. Ladies, please stay here. I would not wish harm to come to you, should our visitor be a thief."

"Be careful, Finn," Colleen begged.

Her words fortified him enough that he could smile. "I will."

Finn felt a touch of fear but managed to tiptoe into the hallway leading to the dining room.

Lord, I petition Thee for protection.

Once he reached the threshold, he peered into the room.

What is this?

Curiosity and fascination left him immobile. A man, dressed in a coat that had more holes than cloth and a shirt missing the two top buttons, had accepted their unspoken invitation and sat at the table. At that moment, he ate bread. The way he tore at the food, ripping it with his teeth, reminded Finn of a hungry dog. After the man had finished the slice of bread, he picked up the pitcher of milk and poured a goblet full, ignoring spillage on the table. He then gulped down the liquid so quickly, Finn wondered if he even tasted the milk.

Napkins were provided, but the man paid them no heed. Instead, between every few bites he wiped his mouth on his sleeve. Finn wondered if he could even find a clean spot amid such dirt. He contemplated offering the ragged man a suit of his own clothes but decided against it when he saw that the other man's frame, though thin, was larger than his own. A beggar would give little thought to precise tailoring, but this man wouldn't be able to squeeze into any of Finn's garments. Perhaps he would offer to let the man come into the store for a new suit of clothing on Monday.

The thought startled him. Would such a thought have occurred to his mind only days ago? He realized that his heart had changed. The change felt good.

Reluctant to disturb the man since he obviously hadn't eaten for some time, Finn watched him devour the remaining milk and bread.

"Is everything all right, Finn?" Colleen called from the next room.

"Aye. Please don't worry. All is taken care of." He expected the man to look up, but he kept eating.

"Is there anything we can do?" Colleen asked.

"Stay where you are." Realizing the beggar must have heard their exchange, Finn knew the time had come for him to speak with the man.

When Finn entered the room and approached the table, the man set down the goblet with a thud. "Afraid of me, eh, Finn?"

The voice sounded familiar, and the man knew his name. But he didn't know any beggars. At least, in the past he'd never looked when he passed them on the street, and he'd blocked his ears from hearing their cries for spare farthings. He decided that his indifference to the plight of others would change.

He screwed up his courage. "I'm not afraid. I—I thought I might offer you a suit of clothes, or a blanket from my store if you need one."

"Ye did, did ye?" Even through the dirt caked on his face, Finn could see that the man was both pleased and surprised. "Well, ye seem to 'ave made some progress in your attitude toward those less fortunate than yourself."

"Less fortunate? Fortune has nothing to do with my success. I work hard for everything I get and put my faith in the good Lord that

He will see fit to reward my puny efforts." Despite his sympathy for the pathetic soul, Finn's anger grew. "I'm not a rich man's son. Any success I have, I owe to my máthair's hard work—demeaning work she had to take on to support us and lift us out of poverty. I'm not about to throw away my money. I have finally reached the point of prosperity where I can provide my máthair a more leisurely life, a life she deserves. I see no reason to waste my hard-earned money on people who are too lazy to work."

"Too lazy to work, eh? Is that what you think about me?"

Suddenly Finn felt nervous. Something seemed strangely familiar about this man, and Finn's confidence in his answers was starting to wane. "I—I don't know about you."

"You don't? Are you sure?" The man stared into his face.

Finn gasped. Those eyes! He had seen the same eyes just yesterday. No. It couldn't be. It couldn't be! "Joey?"

He nodded. " 'Tis I."

"But—but what happened to you?" Finn couldn't help but stare at the man's attire. "Where is your fine hat, your beautiful suit? Why are you dressed in rags not fit for a dog's bed?"

Joey shrugged. "Like the apostle Paul, I can live with much or with little, whatever is the Lord's provision. I have found that people respond to me more favorably when I pose as a rich man than when I appear like this." He looked down at his clothes and chuckled, but Finn heard no rancor.

"But only yesterday, you bought many fine Christmas gifts. And you paid in gold."

"Aye, and those gifts will be loved by the little children who have nothing else."

"Little children?"

"Aye, and their parents, too." Joey looked into Finn's eyes. "So what do you think of me now that I'm not dressed in finery? Now that I have not a pence to me name?"

"Did you lose your fortune so quickly?"

"Aye, I did, and I don't miss it," Joey confessed. "So now that I am poor and can no longer patronize your store, has your opinion of me changed?"

"What can I say? Can't you see I'm too flabbergasted to speak?"

"So the Blarney stone vanished, did it?" He chuckled in a kind way. "I know, lad. This must come as quite a shock. But ye must learn from seeing me here tonight that not every less fortunate person is a ne'er-do-well like your fáthair."

"How—how do you know about my fáthair?"

"Your resentment about him has eaten at ye like a tapeworm. Ye've let his actions affect your outlook on life, and because of that, ye've thrown away much happiness and peace that could have been yours, had ye been more trustin'. The time has come to forgive your fáthair and to enjoy the abundant life that can be yours. Can ye not see that now?"

"There must be something you're not telling me. What is it? What do you know about my fáthair?"

Joey shook his head.

"You mean you don't have some sort of story to tell me that will make things right, some facts I didn't know that will prove me wrong about his character? Some evidence that shows I should forgive him?"

"That would make ye happy, wouldn't it? To think that your fáthair had some good reason for leavin', other than to follow the leprechauns? If he did, that reason 'asn't been revealed to me. Nay, I'm sorry, but ye must be stronger than that. Without any explanation or increased understanding, I'm askin' ye to forgive him and let go of the past. If ye don't, ye'll never find the true happiness God has planned for your life."

Finn hesitated. "What you're asking isn't easy."

"I know. Ye've been carrying around a lot of bitterness for years. Too many years. If ye're not cautious, that bitterness will keep on eatin' at ye 'til ye're an old man, gnarled with anger and alone in the world."

Finn swallowed.

"Ye don't want that for yourself, do ye?"

"Nay." His voice was but a whisper.

"I leave you with Psalm 145:8: '*The Lord is gracious, and full of compassion; slow to anger, and of great mercy.*'"

Finn nodded. "I understand."

"I'm glad to hear it."

"I'll never see you again, will I?"

"Whether or not you see me again is not for me to decide."

Chapter 8

Wpered. "He's been in there a long time."

Colleen didn't want to give her máthair reason to fret, but she was concerned, as well. What if Finn faced trouble? Her heart beat faster with the thought. Like it or not, she couldn't control the fact that her world would be turned upside down if anything happened to Finn.

"Why don't I go take a look?" she suggested in a whisper.

Mrs. Sullivan hesitated. "I don't know."

Mrs. Donohue intervened. "Please?"

Colleen nodded then tiptoed into the doorway of the dining room. When she saw the scene, she froze. Finn conversed with a man in rags, a man whose relaxed posture showed he was no threat to anyone. Yet his face looked familiar. She squinted. Could it be?

Joey!

Though she hadn't spoken aloud, Finn turned to her, obviously sensing her presence. "Colleen."

"Finn, what is the meaning of this?"

Finn looked into her eyes. As soon as he did, she could see that something in him—to his very soul—had changed. "It seems I learned a lesson today."

"A lesson? How? Why is Joey dressed in such tattered clothing? Why did he stop at our house to eat humble food, when surely he must have a fine Christmas meal to go to anywhere he likes in Dublin? I don't understand."

"I don't understand everything, either. Perhaps Joey will enlighten us."

Following the turn of Finn's head, Colleen peered in the direction of the dining room table. Joey had vanished.

A look of puzzlement and alarm colored Finn's expression. "Joey! Where are you?"

Colleen watched as Finn strode through the kitchen and flew out the back door. She could hear him calling Joey's name, his voice carrying over the fields. Colleen didn't move. She sensed that Joey didn't want to be found, and wouldn't be.

Mrs. Sullivan approached from behind and touched Colleen on the shoulder. "Whatever is the matter? Who is Finn looking for?"

"Joey. He was here, and then he just disappeared." Colleen snapped her fingers. "Like that."

"Joey?" Mrs. Donohue parroted. "The same Joey who patronizes the store?"

"Aye," Colleen responded.

Mrs. Sullivan's eyes widened. "Why, I never heard of such a thing. Where are our manners? He's been so good to Finn, we must invite him to partake of some of our food. There's plenty left."

"No, Máthair, he has already partaken." Colleen pointed to what little remained of the bread and milk.

"He ate the meal we set out?"

"He certainly did," Colleen affirmed.

Mouth hanging open, Mrs. Donohue put her hand to her chest. "Are you meaning to say that Joey is actually a beggar?"

"I don't know," Colleen admitted. "All I know is what I saw, and the change I see now in Finn's face."

Finn approached, bringing the outside frost with him.

"Did you find Joey?"

"No. He melted into the night. He has always had that habit. Except this time, I don't think we'll ever see him again."

"'Tisn't so!" Mrs. Donohue protested. "Why, he was one of our best customers, he was."

"Yes, Máthair," Finn agreed. "But my business is thriving, and while I'll miss seeing Joey, I now have many wealthy patrons. But I know he came here to teach me a lesson about life, not to fill my coffers. From now on, I'll make an honest profit from the store, as I always have, but there will be a change. I won't be stingy any longer. I'll be generous with my time and money."

"So that's what he came to teach ye, eh? To throw away your money?"

"I won't throw it away, Máthair. There will be plenty for us, but I will use more of what I have to God's glory, not simply hoard it."

Mrs. Donohue smiled. "That's a right good thing, 'tis."

"And there's something else. I tell each of you here tonight, I'll never again look down upon anyone less fortunate. First, Colleen took me to see the orphans, and even though they didn't have a mind to, they worked on my cold heart. And now, seeing Joey as he was caused me to realize all the more that it is not a person's wealth that matters, but what is in his heart."

"But your fáthair. Can ye forgive 'im?" Mrs. Donohue asked.

Finn's face softened. "I know you forgave him long ago, Máthair. 'Tis high time I did the same. So yes, I forgive him. And from now on, I will pray every day for him, wherever he might be."

Colleen felt as though a long-standing burden had been lifted from her back. When Finn reached for her hand, she allowed him to take it.

"I think 'tis high time you and I share in a cup of tea, don't you, Mrs. Donohue?" Mrs. Sullivan asked.

Mrs. Donohue studied Finn and Colleen, a tickle of light entering her eyes. "Aye."

As the older women departed into the kitchen, Colleen and Finn took a seat in the parlor.

"Finn, I must say, I cannot believe your change of heart. Surely there is more to this than meets the eye. I can't help but wonder if Joey might indeed be an angel."

"An angel?" He stroked his chin. "I hadn't thought of that. He does have a habit of disappearing without a trace. But I tell you what. It doesn't matter who or what Joey is. What matters is that God used him to teach me a lesson I needed to learn."

"I knew your heart was never so hard as you let on, Finn," Colleen said. "You were hurt, and pain can be an awful thing to overcome on your own."

"True. I suppose I needed help. You, for one. Taking me to the orphanage like that. Those boys touched my heart that day. And they're the first ones I have a mind to help more, Colleen."

"Oh, that would be wonderful. The more you speak, the more

convinced I am that Joey is an angel."

"It matters not. The only angelic being I care about is sitting beside me."

Colleen felt a blush rise to her cheeks, and she retreated to the shield of formality. "You exaggerate, Mr. Donohue."

"Let me find out. I'd like to court you in earnest, if you'll have me."

Colleen felt her mouth grow dry and her heart beat swiftly. "Court me?"

"Aye. I wasn't worthy before, and I'm really not worthy now. But all the same, I hope you'll give a humble shopkeeper like me a chance."

"Oh, I'll give you more than a chance."

He took her hands in his. "How your words fill my heart with glee, my beautiful Colleen of Erin. I love you now more than ever. I have always loved you, from the very first time we met."

"And I have always felt the same about you." Her voice came out in a whisper. Suddenly she felt awed by the radiance left by his true repentance. "How I love you, Finn Donohue!"

He took her in his arms and brought his lips closer to hers. Closer, closer, until they made sweet contact. The kiss, so warm and gratifying, was all she dreamed it could have been. The touch expressed and revealed their love for each other better than words ever could.

Epilogue

Finally, the wedding day had arrived, and after a lovely church ceremony, Colleen and Finn were man and wife. Frolicking abounded at the reception, as the popular couple had invited many friends and family to celebrate their special day with them. Patrick, the farmhand Colleen hired, and his family were among the guests. Under his stewardship, the Sullivan farm had become more prosperous than ever.

"Are you ready to give up your bouquet?" Finn asked, looking like royalty in his fine wedding garb. "The girls are waiting."

Colleen regarded the pink and yellow wildflowers in her bouquet, marveling at the way they complimented the filmy pink and yellow gown she had chosen to wear for the ceremony. More wildflowers were woven throughout her dark hair, standing out brightly amid her shiny locks. She had never felt lovelier, and judging from Finn's expression, she had never appeared to be more beautiful in his eyes.

"I don't blame anyone for wanting such a magnificent souvenir of this day." She let out a happy sigh. "I'm ready." She looked at the throng of young women.

"Toss it to me! Toss it to me!" Colleen heard from several as she prepared to toss her bouquet of spring flowers and shamrocks.

Laughing, she shut her eyes and tossed. The smallest girl, a cousin no more than five years of age, caught the bouquet.

"'Tis a good thing the superstition of the bouquet is just that—a superstition," Finn joked. "Otherwise, we'd have a lot of spinsters in the family while they waited for her to grow up and marry."

Colleen laughed. Mirth came easily to her that day, and every day since she and Finn had agreed to court, and later to marry. They chose St. Patrick's Day to wed, which proved to be lovely in the spring. Ireland was dressed in her finest greenery. Colleen and Finn liked to think that such a glorious afternoon had been made by the Lord, just for them, to bless their special day.

Pipes and fiddles played in the background, sending out tunes the guests had known since childhood. They feasted on a wedding cake decorated with shamrocks, symbolizing the Father, Son, and Holy Spirit. Even without such traditional symbolism, all who knew the young couple were aware that God was central to their marriage.

Finn took her by the hand. His face radiated exuberance. "I love you, Colleen Donohue."

"Colleen Donohue." Laughter escaped her lips once again. "How many times I said that name to myself, but now it sounds so new and strange—but lovely—coming from your lips."

"Shall I say it until you become accustomed to it?" Finn teased. "Colleen Donohue. Colleen Donohue. Colleen Donohue. Is that enough?"

"It will never be enough."

As Finn drew her close for a kiss, she could only imagine the happiness she would feel being Mrs. Finn Donohue for the rest of her days.

Irish Soda Bread

4 to 4½ cups flour
1 teaspoon salt
3 teaspoon baking powder
1 teaspoon baking soda
¼ cup sugar

2 cups currants or raisins
¼ cup butter
1 egg
1¾ cups buttermilk

In large bowl, stir together 4 cups flour and the rest of the dry ingredients. Cut in butter with a pastry blender or two knives until crumbly. In separate bowl, beat egg slightly and mix with buttermilk. Stir into dry ingredients until blended. Place dough on floured board and knead 3 minutes or until smooth.

Divide dough in half and shape each half into a smooth, round loaf. Place each loaf in greased 8-inch cake or pie pan. Press down until dough fills pans. With sharp, floured knife, cut crosses about ½ inch deep in tops of loaves.

Bake in a 375-degree oven for 35 to 40 minutes or until nicely browned. Makes 2 loaves.

Tamela Hancock Murray is the author of over thirty novels and non-fiction works. She feels honored and humbled that her books have placed her on bestseller lists and that one of her Barbour titles, Destinations, won an RWA Inspirational Readers Choice Award. Tamela has been a literary agent since 2001 and is with The Steve Laube Agency.

Tamela lives in Virginia with her husband of over thirty years. They are the parents of two lovely daughters. Tamela enjoys church, reading, and spending time with her immediate and extended family and friends. Tamela is passionate about edifying and encouraging other Christians through her work. She always enjoys hearing from readers. Please visit her on Facebook and Twitter.

A Right, Proper Christmas

by Jill Stengl

Dedication

To Jill Eileen with love and thanks from Jill Marie

"The people that walked in darkness have seen a great light. . . . For unto us a child is born."
ISAIAH 9:2, 6

Chapter 1

Midlands of England, 1860s

Icy wind cut through Dan's threadbare jacket and drove straight to his bones. Hunching his shoulders and tucking his hands into his armpits, he forged ahead. His feet felt like stinging lumps within his boots. Each breath formed a frosty cloud that settled on his turned-up collar and sculpted icicles on his cap's brim.

He must find shelter for the night. *God, have You noticed Your servant freezing to death?* God had always provided for his needs in the past. . . .

If it's time for me to die, I'm ready. But something inside him stubbornly clung to life, to the belief that God would provide one more miracle. Why would God call a man to preach, then allow him to die of exposure? That would make no sense.

A sign loomed ahead at the side of the road with Little Brigham—One Mile painted on a rough board in white letters. There he might find shelter of some sort, though he had no money and no prospect of earning any. Teeth chattering, he moved on.

Only one year ago, he had looked forward with longing to a Christmas back home in England. But during his absence, his mother had left the old house. And when he did finally locate her living with a butcher on the south side of Birmingham, she had greeted him with an invitation to leave her be and go make a life for himself.

Home? Ha! For him, no such thing existed.

Why, God? Why do I have no love but Yours in my life since Granny died?

Even now, the memory of his mother's hard voice and bitter face made him grimace. Why had he imagined that she would have changed for the better? Why had he thought she might offer him a glimpse of maternal affection just because he returned alive from the Crimean peninsula?

Because he was a fool and dreamer.

God, if any goodness remains on this wicked old earth, please show me, and that soon. I'm nigh on ready to dive into the pit.

He hiked to the top of a rise and looked down upon the village set in a gentle vale. The rectangular tower of a church stood black against the twinkling lights of cottages, rising high enough to block out the lowest stars. Wind whistled past Dan's ears and pushed him forward.

"The church?" he asked aloud. A recent encounter with a sneering bishop back in the city caused him to hesitate. That clergyman had not even tried to conceal his amusement at the suggestion of Dan's ever becoming a minister of the Gospel.

But if the church would not aid the lost and lonely, who would?

He scrunched up his face and shook his head. Stubbornness would be the death of him. "All right then." At the very least, the church building should offer protection from this wind.

As he walked up the church path, a faint cry drifted amid the gravestones. Dan stopped short. A shudder, not caused by cold, rippled through his frame, and the hair on his nape stood on end. Slowly, he let his gaze shift right and turned his head to follow. No ghostly form appeared. He swallowed hard.

Again the thin wail gripped his attention and tightened his throat. This time he pinpointed it to a particular headstone. He took one more step toward the church door, then turned back. Curiosity compelled him to approach that marble slab. Something living must have made that noise.

Teeth clenched, he stepped off the walkway and crunched across frozen sod. A dark form huddled at the base of the gravestone. He touched it with his boot and felt it give. Again he heard the cry. Dan squatted, reached out his hand, and touched cold fur. Gently he moved the creature into full starlight. A cat, its eyes half closed, its teeth bared in a death grimace. The small body was already stiffening.

But as he set it down, something moved and wailed. He felt at the base of the stone again and found a tiny body. A kitten. Two—no, three kittens crouched behind their mother's lifeless form. He picked one up. Its eyes glinted in the starlight, and its mouth opened in a surprisingly loud *meow*.

Without another thought, he tucked two of the kittens into his jacket pockets and the third inside his waistcoat. Rising with a crackle of joints, he continued along the walkway and entered the porch. The door creaked as it opened, then closed behind Dan with a ringing *crash*. The nave of the church was cold and still. "Hello?" he called. His voice rang hollow in a vast empty space. The clerestory must be very high. Dan reached out in the darkness, moving slowly forward until his hands touched smooth stone. More exploration revealed intricate carvings and the outlines of a human face. He jerked his hand away and shivered. A tomb. He was not yet lonely enough to relish the thought of cozying up to the stone effigy of some departed lord or lady.

Quickly he turned away. As his eyes adjusted, the gray outline of windows appeared high above, and he located rows of pews. Taking care not to squash the kittens, he lay down on a wooden bench and stretched out. If he died during the night, perhaps the townspeople would let his body rest with the remains of their ancestors in the yard. That way at least he would have company on Judgment Day.

An unmarked grave. God would know where his body lay, but no one else. No wife, no family would mourn him. Loneliness gnawed like a canker at his heart.

Only Granny had ever loved him. Almost, he could feel her gnarled hand on his head and hear her fervent, trembling prayers while he knelt beside her stool in the chimney corner. A love light for him had always shone in Granny's faded eyes, and her faith had been his solid rock.

The kitten inside his waistcoat had curled into a ball against his belly. He felt the tiny vibration of a *purr*. The kitten in his left pocket twisted and turned against his hand and sucked weakly on his fingertip. The kitten in his right pocket didn't move. He cupped its body in his palm and rubbed the soft fur with his fingers.

Heaving a deep sigh, he stared up into darkness. Three motherless babies. He should have left them to freeze. He had nothing to give them but warmth and sympathy.

※

The thatching on Winchell Cottage glimmered in the starlight, rimed with ice. Light glowed in one window. Dame Winchell and her half-wit son would surely enjoy hearing Christmas carols, Charlotte assured herself, although they were unlikely to offer wassail in return.

The boisterous group of carolers assembled in ragged rows. By this time, the youngest among them had lost interest in singing and entertained themselves by punching, poking, and otherwise tormenting each other.

Charlotte's patience ebbed.

"Let us begin with 'Joy to the World,' " she announced in her firmest tone, separating the two Popkin boys, who had engaged in a hair-pulling battle. Why wouldn't the other young adults help her control these children? Charlotte sent Clive Brigham a pleading look, but he was too busy grinning at Hattie Holloway to notice.

Although Charlotte started the song in a comfortable key, two of the singers picked their own range and hurried ahead of the rest. Choosing to ignore them, she closed her eyes and sang her loudest.

The cottage door cracked open. "Ger out," snarled a woman's low voice. "Let a body rest, whyn't ya?"

Several of the older carolers laughed. Little Sally Whitesmith began to cry.

Charlotte drew the child close in a comforting embrace. "We crave pardon for disturbing you, Dame Winchell. We thought only to spread some Christmas ch—"

The door clanked shut. Crestfallen, Charlotte herded her flock away, shushing questions.

"Ain't we done yet, Charlotte?" Sammy Johnston whined. "The wind is awful cold."

"The last house on our list is the rectory," she said. "The rector mixed up his best wassail for us tonight, and I baked scones, and we'll play blindman's buff."

"Can't we play games first? I'm tired of singing."

The other children echoed Sammy's plea and added, "It's so cold!"

"But don't you see? We must earn our fun by singing the best carols we've sung this night," she said brightly.

Clive and Hattie laughed at some private joke of their own. Charlotte could not even console herself with the possibility that Clive was attempting to make her jealous. Only pride kept her from bursting into frustrated tears. She might as well be invisible for all the notice he took of her.

The day had begun so beautifully. That morning Mother had allowed Charlotte and her three younger sisters to deck the rectory halls with greenery, bows, and candles. Furthermore, she had allowed the girls to bake scones and biscuits, though Christmas Day was yet a week off. Father provided songbooks for the caroling, and he mixed a great pot of steaming wassail. Eighteen youths, girls, and children had assembled for the caroling—including Clive Brigham.

Charlotte had been in love with Clive for almost as long as she could remember. Now, while he was home from Oxford for the holidays, would be an ideal time for him to notice her and realize that she was the woman of his dreams.

That afternoon, when he'd first arrived at the church, the carolers' meeting place, Clive had told Charlotte she looked like a Christmas angel. Her joy had spiraled to giddy heights, even though he did pat her cheek and call her "little sister." It was surely just a term of endearment. They were no blood relation, after all.

But Hattie Holloway had joined the group, looking stylish and lovely in a new bonnet, and ever since then, Clive couldn't seem to take his eyes off her.

George Wendell, one of the bigger boys, grabbed Charlotte by the elbow. "Les and me are going on, Char. We got places to go. It was delightful. Thank you for asking us." He gave Charlotte a broad wink, clucked twice as if she were a horse, and then the two youths jogged up the street before she could draw breath enough to protest.

The icy wind seemed to wrap around her heart. Would Clive desert her, too? He was the last baritone in the group. *Please, God, don't let him leave!*

As Charlotte arranged her remaining singers before the rectory steps, she could scarcely breathe around the lump in her chest. The sight of Hattie's arm linked through Clive's elbow nearly provoked her to tears. *How could he?* How could he be so sweet and kind to Charlotte yet flirt openly with Hattie?

"Let us begin with 'Hark! The Herald Angels Sing,' " she said stiffly. Little Sammy surprised her by starting out with a pure, clear

"Hark!" and the remaining carolers joined in.

Mother opened the rectory door and called Father to come listen. They stood framed in the light and warmth pouring from the house. A tear trickled down Charlotte's cheek while she sang, "Glory to the newborn King!"

❧❦❧

Dan felt as if he had no sooner dozed off than a hand gripped his shoulder and shook, hard. "What d'ye mean by sleeping 'ere, man? This be the Lord's 'ouse, not an inn."

"No room at an inn for the likes of me," Dan mumbled, sitting up and blinking in the light of a lantern. "I reckon the good Lord must know how that feels."

The man's broad, black-bearded face split into a grin. "That He do, lad; that He do. Like the foxes, ye've no place to lay yer 'ead. Be that the tale?"

Dan nodded. The kittens were warm and motionless against his fingers.

"Ye've no call to freeze in the church whilst there be fire and food at the rectory. I 'appen to know the rector will be glad an' all to take ye in. The reverend Mr. Colburn is a kindly man, as like unto the Good Shepherd as earthly man can be. Come wit' me, lad. Ol' Joe'll see ye're fed and bedded down for the night. I've no wish to be diggin' ye a permanent bed in the yard come morning."

Joe wrapped his arm around Dan's shoulders and turned him toward the door. "Just a step once we get outside. O'er the stile and through the 'edgerows. You'll think ye've entered the pearly gates once Miz Colburn takes ye in, lad. A fine woman be that one. And four pretty daughters to charm your eyes whilst ye regains your strength. Been in the army, lad? I thought as much. Ye've the look—worn of heart and bone, and your face that leathered by the sun."

A mist rose among the tombstones and dulled Dan's vision. He saw light ahead, brilliant light that made him blink. Music rang in the darkness—angelic voices proclaiming Christ's birth. Dan stopped in his tracks. "Angels!" he whispered.

"Wha's that you say?" Joe inquired. "Angels? Well, true enough as may be." A deep chuckle rumbled through his chest. "Move along now, lad, and introduce yourself. No call to be shy; you'll be right welcome."

Dan clambered over the stile and staggered toward the light. Shapes appeared through the mist. People bundled against the cold, mostly rosy-faced children, singing bravely in puffs of steam. Carolers! How long had it been since he last heard Christmas carolers? He turned to thank Joe, but the stranger had disappeared without a word of farewell. Or if he had spoken, Dan was too tired and confused to remember.

❦

"Now to the Lord sing praises all you within this place,
And with true love and brotherhood each other now embrace;
This holy tide of Christmas all others doth efface.
O tidings of comfort and joy, comfort and joy; O tidings of comfort
and joy."

Her sister Eleanor plucked at Charlotte's elbow and pointed. "I see someone coming. Should I call Father back?"

Charlotte saw the dark figure emerging from the mist of the churchyard. Apprehension tightened her body. "Yes." Eleanor pushed her way inside, making hurried excuses. Mother was welcoming the carolers into the rectory, thanking and greeting the children as they filed past. Charlotte kept a close eye on the approaching man—his halting gait indicated drunkenness—while she herded her carolers toward the door. Clive had already ushered Hattie inside.

"Mother, please send Father out here." Charlotte tried to keep her voice calm as she followed close behind the last child.

Mother didn't understand her urgency. "He's in the kitchen, child." She trotted after the children, waving her arms and cheerfully calling orders about where to hang up coats and scarves. Chunks of icy mud melted on the entry tiles.

Charlotte nearly pushed Sammy through the door, intending to close it before the stranger could force his way inside. She turned, grasping the door's handle, ready to pull it shut. A man stood on the doorstep, one hand in a frayed fingerless glove clutching a cap to his chest. Charlotte glimpsed his eyes—and could not close the door.

"Is the rector in?" His voice was gruff and raspy.

What to do? She could not ask the man into the parlor where the party was being held. Neither could she leave him out in the cold. "Please step inside. The rector will see you shortly." She held the door open.

"Thank you kindly, miss." He stepped past, and she smelled his unwashed body, but no alcohol. He stopped beside the coat stand already piled with hats, coats, mufflers, and dripping mittens. She saw his wondering gaze flit about the entryway over polished walnut paneling, wreaths and bows on the staircase's banisters, and mirrored candle sconces. "I'd as leave not muss the floor with my dirty boots."

Charlotte allowed herself to smile. "The children have already tracked mud from one end of the house to the other. Would you—would you care for a cup of wassail, sir?"

Gratitude flickered across his smudged features. He had large dark eyes underlined by heavy dark circles as if he not slept in days or weeks. The deep lines cut into his black-whiskered cheeks framed a grim mouth. Yet for all that, it was not an unappealing face.

"You're very kind, miss. I have—kittens." He blinked as if confused.

Charlotte thought she must have misunderstood. "Come again?"

He pulled his hand from his pocket and held out a furry bundle. "Found them in the churchyard. The mother is dead. I. . ." He swayed on his feet, and a dazed expression came over his face.

Charlotte reached out to take the squeaking kitten just as the man's eyes rolled up in his head and he swayed like a falling tree. She rushed forward to catch him, but he was a dead weight in her arms, and she crumpled to the floor. He sprawled across her lap, his head lolling against her shoulder. The kitten scaled her arm like a tree and tried to hide in her hair, its claws raking her neck and ear.

"Father!" she called in a panic. Another kitten poked out its head from beneath the man's waistcoat, stared up at Charlotte, and hissed.

Unhurried footsteps approached the hall. Father paused in the drawing room doorway. Candlelight glinted off his spectacles. "Oh, my dear!" He hastened forward. "Is he alive?"

Chapter 2

The poor chap looks half starved," a man's quiet voice said. "Let me try the sal volatile."

With a gasp and a start, Dan opened his eyes. The smelling salts' fumes burned his sinuses. He coughed, and pain knifed through his chest.

"He is ill, Father. Whatever will Mother say? But I couldn't leave him outside on a night like this; I simply couldn't!"

So she wasn't a dream after all. He focused on her face.

"I think he is not so much ill as weak from exposure and near starvation—as were his kittens. You did the right thing, Charlotte, my dear." The speaker was a balding man with spectacles perched near the end of his long nose. He wore a clergyman's collar. "What is your name, my friend?"

"Dan Jackson." His voice was a croak.

Dan looked at the girl again. Charlotte. Pink and white skin, soft brown hair in bunches of ringlets near her cheeks, and sparkling eyes tilted up at the corners, giving her a lively air. Angry red scratches marred her white neck.

Remembering, Dan felt the front of his waistcoat.

"Your kittens are safe, Mr. Jackson," Charlotte said. And she smiled. Dan looked away, feeling dizzy all over again.

"I am Mr. Colburn, rector here in Little Brigham." While speaking, the rector rose from his knees and settled into a side chair. "And this is my eldest daughter, Charlotte."

Dan glanced around. He lay on a settee in a small study, bundled beneath a thick woolen blanket. A small fire glowed on the hearth, and an oil lamp glowed on the desk. Charlotte sat near his feet; the rector sat near his head. "I swooned?"

"You most certainly did. Where do you come from, Mr. Jackson?"

"From Birmingham, most recent." His head felt thick. "Never

done that afore—swoon, I mean."

"The Crimea before that?"

"Yes, sir."

"I thought as much. You seem stretched thin of spirit and soul. Were you wounded?"

"Only a few scratches, since healed."

His gaze returned to Charlotte's neck, and she smiled again, this time with amusement. "Scratches can be painful," she said.

"When did you last eat?" the rector inquired softly.

Dan shifted his gaze to the fire. "I don't recall. Two days, maybe. Times are bad in the city. I headed south on a canal barge, but ran out of money. Offered to work my way. No luck. So I walked."

"Until tonight," Charlotte said in a near whisper.

"Until tonight. I found a dead cat in the churchyard and picked up its kittens. A fool act. I had naught to offer."

"Except kindness and warmth," Charlotte said. "It was a Christmas thing to do."

"Charlotte dear, will you fetch our guest some food and drink?" the rector suggested.

"Yes, Father." She rose, paused to look down at Dan, then walked from the room, her full skirts rustling.

Dan forced his gaze back to the rector's face. "A party of people—I saw them come inside. Singers."

The rector smiled. "Yes, my daughters prepared a party for the carolers."

"I should go. You have guests. She should be with them." Dan made a move to rise, but the rector gently stopped him.

"Your presence gives us only pleasure, Mr. Jackson. If my daughter did not wish to bring you food, she would have said as much. She is a forthright young woman, yet she has a kind heart," Mr. Colburn remarked. "Are you married, Mr. Jackson?"

Dan felt his face grow warm. The rector had seen him looking at Charlotte. "No, sir. Few decent women in the Crimea, and the good Lord kept me from the other kind. You needn't fear; your daughter is beyond my touch, and I wouldn't presume to think elsewise." He coughed, then continued, "I hope sometime to marry and have family, but first a man's got to find work. You wouldn't know of an opening hereabouts, would you now?"

The rector pursed his lips and wrinkled his forehead. "Times are hard everywhere, Mr. Jackson. But I shall keep my ears open. Do you have experience?"

"I was an 'ostler before I went to war, and I worked for the cavalry in the Crimea. Horses are my only skill, though I haven't got so much as a swayback nag to my name." He tried to smile. "Just cats."

"Horses." The rector rubbed his chin and pondered. "A useful skill. We shall see."

Charlotte hurried back into the room. "I set soup on to boil for you, Mr. Jackson, but I thought a scone or two might hold you until the soup is ready." She offered a plate of raisin scones with thick cream. "And Father's wassail."

He took the steaming cup and the plate from her hands. "Thank you kindly, miss." He met her gaze.

She sat down abruptly. "I fed the kittens in the kitchen and put them in a basket near the stove. They're sleeping."

"Good." He felt self-conscious about eating while she watched, but hunger overcame his qualms. The scones filled the edges of his aching void, and the spicy wassail warmed him from the inside out.

"How did you find us?" Charlotte asked.

He gulped the last drop and wiped his hand across his mouth. Too late he remembered his napkin. "I saw the church and thought I might sleep inside for the night." He shook his head to drive off a creeping lethargy. "But your sexton found me sleeping on the pew and told me to come here. He showed me the way through the churchyard and over the stile."

The rector and his daughter exchanged glances.

"I heard singing and thought it was angels." Dan heard his voice begin to slur. "God sent me to the light. Found an angel."

❧

Charlotte watched Dan's head sag to one side. His deep breathing filled the silence. "I fear he won't want his soup tonight," she said.

Her father smiled. "I believe you're right. I hope he doesn't wake cramped after sleeping on that settee. It's barely long enough for him, though he isn't a tall man. I wonder who directed him here. Odd—we have no sexton at present."

"Do you think he'll be warm enough?" Charlotte rose with her father but lingered, studying that shadowed face. "The poor man."

"I shall stoke the fire before I retire for the night." Father patted her shoulder. "You should attend your remaining guests, my dear."

She gasped. "Oh, the carolers! I completely forgot them." Picking up her skirts, she hurried away. What might Clive and Hattie have done in her absence? How could she have allowed a common stranger to distract her from things of genuine importance? Things such as winning back the interest of her future husband.

Charlotte, her three sisters, and their mother sat around the parlor, staring blankly at the party clutter their guests had left behind. "Clive kissed Hattie under the kissing ball," Priscilla announced.

Charlotte's heart gave a painful wrench.

"Only on the cheek, silly," Priscilla's twin, Drusilla, corrected with a knowing air.

"It was still a kiss, and Charlotte's jealous."

"Young ladies, we do not speak of such things," Mother said firmly. "Help your sisters carry out the dishes."

"Why can't Molly do that in the morning?" Drusilla grumbled.

"Molly does enough work around this house to earn twice what we can afford to pay her. I have four daughters with strong, healthy bodies, and there is no good reason on this earth why they cannot do honest labor." Mother set the example by carrying out a tray loaded with empty cups and tumblers.

Charlotte began stacking plates. "I used to grumble about Mother making us learn how to run a household by doing all the work ourselves, so I know just how you feel, Dru. But now that I am older—"

"Do, please, spare us the now-that-I-am-older-and-wiser speech, Charlotte," Eleanor said. "If you marry Clive Brigham, you'll never need to lift a finger. No blacking stoves, no polishing fire irons for you. You'll have an army of servants at your beck and call."

"But Clive didn't kiss Char, he kissed Hattie," Priscilla said, "even though she does have freckles."

"I have a surprise for you in the kitchen," Charlotte said. "Something cute and furry."

The twins instantly fell for the diversion and pelted her with excited questions.

After the clutter had been cleared away and the kittens were bedded down for the night, Charlotte climbed the stairs, watching her hand slide up the polished walnut banister. Heaviness seemed to weigh down her spirit. Where had the joy gone? No matter how hard she tried to recapture the spirit of Christmas, nothing brought back the joy she remembered so vividly from her childhood holidays.

Inside her tiny bedchamber, she set her lamp on her dressing table, sat down, and regarded her reflection. Earlier in the day she had gazed into her mirrored eyes with confidence and anticipation, knowing that she looked attractive. Real-lace flounces and tiny tucks on the bodice of her burgundy gown enhanced her curves, and a wide sash hugged her waist. Fashion and cold weather dictated the necessity of multiple flannel petticoats which added inches to her waistline, but then, Hattie's waist was no slimmer.

She pulled pins from her hair and shook her head. Glossy locks tumbled down her back.

Clive, why do you ignore me? He was so handsome and aristocratic with his flashing smile, his gray-blue eyes, and his smooth, yellow hair. He could not be in love with Hattie—could he? What was Hattie's secret? Charlotte considered asking her mother how a woman contrived to fascinate a man, but Mother would only read her a lecture about modesty and propriety, and adjure her to trust in the Lord.

Christmas this year simply must be perfect. Tonight the children had been uncooperative, and then the stranger's arrival had distracted Charlotte from her purpose. But she would have other opportunities to impress Clive before he returned to college. She loved that boy with a passion that nearly consumed her—surely he must respond sooner or later! Somehow she must show him a glimpse of the cozy, comfortable home they two could share if only he would marry her. . . .

Kneeling on the bed, she pulled its curtains closed. Her sheets felt clammy as she gingerly slid her toes, her feet, and her legs down beneath her covers. Would the stranger sleeping downstairs be warm enough?

Cold feet drove away sleep. She tucked up her legs and curled into a ball.

A dog barked somewhere in the distance. *Mother should let us get a dog to guard against intruders.*

Like Dan Jackson.

And kittens.

She chuckled softly, picturing that little furry head bobbing from beneath the man's waistcoat. The waistcoat also concealed a tender heart. Yet, such a coarse manner of speaking he had. Poorly educated.

What if he wakes in the night and walks out with Mother's silver candlesticks?

Such a nice, deep voice. A kind voice.

Could be a murderer.

Such beautiful dark eyes. . .

⁂

Clang. Clatter.

Dan sat up, blinking.

A figure rose from the fireside. "I beg your pardon, Mr. Jackson. I intended to sneak in here and stoke your fire before our maid arrives this morning, but I am as stealthy as cannon fire, apparently." The reverend Mr. Colburn smiled in apology.

"This is your study. I'll be on my way."

"Nonsense, lad. You should remain where you are. Your voice sounds congested. Are you feverish?"

Dan pondered his condition for a moment. "I feel weak." His voice caught; he coughed a sharp, barking cough and winced at the pain of it.

"Ah, Mrs. Colburn will make a poultice that should draw out that cough. She'll be here in a trice, if I'm not greatly mistaken."

Shoes clicked in the hallway, and a woman's harried yet pleasant face peeked around the door. "May I enter?"

"You may enter, my dear," Mr. Colburn said. "Did you hear his cough?"

"I did, Mr. Colburn, and I know just the treatment." She bustled forward and placed her hand on Dan's forehead. "I am Mrs. Colburn, of course. You are most welcome in our home, and I trust you will stay as long as your needs require."

Dan recognized sincerity in the woman's soft brown eyes. Charlotte had not inherited her beauty from her mother, yet Dan saw family resemblance. "Thank you, ma'am." He could manage no more without coughing.

"We must move our guest to a bedchamber where he will not be disturbed," she declared. "I'll have Charlotte move in with Eleanor."

Guest! Dan wanted to protest, but his voice would not cooperate. Shivering, he lay back on the settee and huddled beneath the blanket. The notion of staying on as a guest in this warm and welcoming household struck him as nearly ideal.

⚜

Mr. Jackson asked to take a bath before he set foot upstairs. Mother feared he would take a chill and die, but he insisted, so she enlisted Charlotte, Molly the housemaid, and the twins to haul water from the cistern into the scullery. Eleanor escaped the chore by pleading a headache.

"This bucket is too heavy for me," Priscilla grumbled. She switched its weight from one hand to the other. Water splashed over her feet.

"Mr. Jackson will appreciate your help," Charlotte assured her.

"Why should I care? Eleanor says he's just a beggar."

Charlotte stopped to glare at her little sister. "That is unkind. He is our guest, and we shall treat him like visiting royalty. As Father often says, 'We may be hosting an angel, unaware.' Do your work to please Jesus."

Despite their parents' careful training and frequent admonitions, Priscilla followed Eleanor's lead and seemed to delight in making everyone else's life difficult. Drusilla, the quieter twin, emulated Charlotte.

Priscilla snorted. "Little wonder Clive prefers Hattie to you. She doesn't preach sermons at him three times a day." She grimaced and stuck out her tongue.

Heat rushed to Charlotte's face. She set down her buckets, grabbed the girl's arm, and drew a deep breath for a scathing retort. Her hand itched with desire to slap the smug look off Priscilla's face.

Slow footsteps approached from the hall. Mr. Jackson appeared in the doorway, his expression hesitant.

The two sisters stared at him in shamed silence. Drusilla emerged from the scullery with an empty pail and asked, "What's wrong?" Molly appeared in the doorway behind her, looking equally curious.

Charlotte released Priscilla and felt her face burn hotter than ever. "Not a thing. Please sit here while we finish, Mr. Jackson. It will be only a few minutes more." She copied her mother's most gracious manner.

He sat carefully on one of the kitchen stools.

"Do you want to see the kitties?" Drusilla asked, looking directly up into his face. "One of them is kind of weak and doesn't move much, but the other two are lively. We call them Fluffy, Fuzzy, and Purr because we don't know if they're boys or girls."

He smiled and nodded slightly. Drusilla ran to the stove and pulled the basket from behind it. Making a pouch of her apron, she bundled the kittens into it and returned to him.

Mr. Jackson lifted one kitten, checked under its tail, and set it on his knee. He inspected each protesting kitten in turn, then stroked all three furry backs with one sweep of his hand. "Three brothers," he said hoarsely and turned his head to cough.

The harsh sound of that cough made Charlotte frown.

"They eat lamb if we grind it up good and add broth. Charlotte told us to try goats' milk, and they suck it up pretty well. They want to suck everything, though," Drusilla told him.

Priscilla appeared at his other side and took one of the kittens. "This one is my favorite. Father found the dead mother cat and buried it behind our stable. He said she was black with white paws, like this kitten."

Drusilla held up another kitten. "This one is dressed like a bishop. He's the quiet one. I want to call him Harvey now that I know he's a boy."

A smile softened Mr. Jackson's face. He lifted the third kitten. "Mine looks like a butler with a high white collar. Humphrey."

Priscilla grinned. "Mine is Hubert."

"On'y the hot water is yet needed, miss," Molly said, as she again returned from the scullery carrying an empty bucket. "D'you want that I should fetch it?"

Charlotte felt blood rush into her face; she had neglected her work to watch the little scene. "I'll get it, Molly. You go ahead with your regular chores. Thank you."

Molly gave her a genuine smile. "You ain't never no trouble, miss."

Charlotte used two towels to protect her hands and lifted a steaming kettle from the stovetop. Mr. Jackson returned his kitten to Drusilla and started to rise, his expression troubled.

"Don't worry; I can do this. I'm stronger than I look," Charlotte assured him. "You just rest there." After emptying two kettles into the tub, she tested the temperature. Good and hot.

"Your bath is ready, Mr. Jackson!" she called. "The soap and towels are close at hand, and Father left a razor for your use." She met his gaze as she stepped into the kitchen, drying her hands on her apron.

"Thank you, miss. Me being so dirty—I couldn't—" He coughed again. "Your room, I—" Another bout of coughing bent him over.

Priscilla and Drusilla stared at him, frightened, the kittens clutched in their arms.

At last he looked up, shivering, eyes watering, and Charlotte felt tears burn her own eyes. "You poor man, I think you should just go straight to bed. Sheets and blankets will wash."

He shook his head, closed his eyes, and pinched the bridge of his nose. "I'll rest better once I'm clean. Like Mr. Wesley said, 'Cleanliness is next to godliness.'"

While Mr. Jackson bathed downstairs, Mrs. Colburn and her two oldest daughters quickly turned Charlotte's bedchamber into a sickroom. They aired clean sheets before the peat fire glowing on the hearth in order to remove any lingering dampness, turned and plumped the feather bolster, then made the bed. Eleanor had already brought up a pitcher of well water and a clean tumbler to set on the bedside table. When the entire chamber smelled fresh and every last speck of dust or dirt had been eradicated, Mrs. Colburn pronounced it good and headed downstairs.

Charlotte glanced around her room, looking for anything else she might want or need during her stay in Eleanor's room. Would the guest be comfortable here? Would he enjoy sleeping in her bedchamber with its ruffles and lace and the strong scent of lavender?

A silly thought. Why should he care? Dan Jackson might be married and have several children, for all she knew. He looked to be a hard sort of man, the type that would scorn frills and furbelows. Then she pictured him with that kitten cradled in his big hands, and a smile touched her lips once more.

Judging by the clamor and activity below, Mr. Jackson was now on his way upstairs. Charlotte smoothed the pillows and the counterpane, then hurried to the head of the staircase. Mr. Jackson had one arm over Father's shoulder, and he wore one of Father's nightshirts and an old bed gown. Daylight from the staircase window caught in his damp, tousled hair and reflected off Father's bald head as they climbed one slow step at a time.

Mr. Jackson glanced up as they passed her on the landing, but no recognition glimmered in his eyes. He appeared drawn and exhausted. The shadows beneath his eyes looked stark on his clean-shaven face, no longer blended with soot and grime.

"Charlotte!" Mother's exclamation spun Charlotte around. "Child, have you no delicacy? Get to your room and stay there."

Charlotte wanted to protest—she was nineteen years old, no longer a child—but she hastened off to Eleanor's bedchamber.

Chapter 3

Dan awakened, feeling motion on the bed. His eyes opened, but he saw no one. Another little *thump*. He turned his head to one side and looked into a kitten's startled face. It froze.

He smiled and tried to speak. "Hello." To a kitten, that raspy voice probably sounded like a monster's snarl. His arms were tangled in the bed sheets. He found a way to get one hand free and reached for the kitten. It was too young to run far; it squalled as he lifted it.

He settled the little creature on his chest and began to rub its head and neck with his thumb. Almost immediately it began to purr.

From beyond the bed curtains he heard a whisper: "What are you doing in here? If Mother finds out, you'll not sit down for a week!"

"No, no—he likes it!"

"He likes what? Priscilla, did you wake Mr. Jackson?"

Dan saw the curtains rustle. The child must have been watching him through a gap.

"I didn't wake him, Char. Humphrey did."

"Humphrey? You brought one of the kittens in here? Oh, Pris, what will Mother say?"

"But he likes it, don't you, Mr. Jackson?"

"I do," Dan croaked. He weakly pulled the curtain aside, hoping for a glimpse of Charlotte.

Priscilla smirked at him, her eyes alight. "I thought you would want to see Humphrey. He eats almost as much as Hubert does. Harvey is the smallest. They're all three quite intelligent. Father brought in a tray full of sandy dirt, and they know just how to use it."

Dan smiled. His eyes hurt, but he felt significantly better. "How long have I been sleeping?" He had lost track of time since the rector helped him into this bed. For all he knew, Christmas had come and gone, and the New Year, as well. He had slept away the hours, waking only for meals and necessities.

To his satisfaction, Charlotte pulled the curtain farther back along its rail. "You came to us two days ago. This is Sunday. Mother says you were out of your head for a time yesterday, talking to invisible people. But other times you were lucid."

"I don't remember." A feeling of warm pleasure crept through him. He wished for more light, the better to see her shining hair and smooth cheeks.

The kitten curled up beneath Dan's chin, still purring. Its tiny paws kneaded his neck, its claws like tiny pinpricks. He saw Charlotte's lips curve into a sweet smile as she watched.

"Do you want me to bring Harvey and Hubert, too?" Priscilla asked.

"Maybe later." Dan was already getting sleepy. "Do I have a fever?"

Charlotte laid her hand along his cheek. He closed his eyes. "You feel warm, but you're no longer burning up. Father nearly called in the physician, but Mother told him to let you sleep. She said your own strength would best fight this fever."

"I'm hungry."

"Good! I'll try to bring you some food. You stay here, Priscilla. I'll tell Mother you're awake, Mr. Jackson." Charlotte rubbed her hands down her apron, smiled again, and hurried from the room.

"Would you open the bed curtains?" he asked Priscilla.

The girl leaped into action. Soon, winter daylight spilled across the bed. Dan looked around the room, really seeing it for the first time—a small, gabled chamber with whitewashed walls and a warped wooden floor. Heavy, old-fashioned walnut furniture should have given the room a sober aspect, but white ruffles and embroidered flowers softened the effect. Pink, purple, blue, yellow—bright blooms of every hue were sprinkled across the counterpane, the bed curtains, and the pillow tops. Someone had even painted flowers on the wall like a little garden.

The door opened, and Mrs. Colburn entered. "I beg your pardon for the intrusion, Mr. Jackson. Priscilla is a lively child, and Charlotte cannot seem to restrain her. Priscilla, remove that animal from this room!"

Dan covered the kitten with his hand. "Please leave him. He—he keeps me warm."

As if the tiny body offered significant heat.

Mrs. Colburn lifted one brow. "I hope you are not feeling worse." She laid her slightly clammy hand on his forehead.

"No, ma'am. I could get up, I think." He wanted to cough, but restrained it, fearing he would disturb the kitten.

"Really?" She stared into his eyes. "You do look and sound much better. But I'll have you know, you were a very sick young man, Mr. Jackson. The Lord brought you to us for good reason."

"Yes, ma'am, and I'm grateful to Him and you both."

"I think you should wait until tomorrow before you attempt coming downstairs, but you might sit beside the fire here. Oh, the fire has nearly gone out! Molly!" She called through the door. "Where is that girl?" She left the room and called down the staircase. "Charlotte, tell Molly to bring peat! What? She's gone home? Then you bring it up, or send Eleanor! Mr. Jackson's fire is dying, and it's cold in this room!"

Dan closed his eyes while she bustled about.

"Are you very hungry?"

He looked up. "Yes, ma'am. Dreadful hungry."

"Then I'll fetch your tea."

She vanished into the hallway. Dan dozed until he heard footsteps on the stairs. Charlotte appeared, toting a lumpy sack. She glanced his way and smiled. "I hope Priscilla and I didn't bother you too very much."

"You bothered me not in the slightest." He could speak proper English when he made an effort. The kitten slept on, ignoring the rumbling voice coming from its sleeping spot.

Charlotte knelt beside the hearth and carefully arranged peat bricks on the grating. "Mother is unhappy about the kitten in your sickroom. She gave Priscilla a talking-to."

"I like having him here."

She smiled at him over her shoulder. "The twins insist that the kittens have no fleas."

"Glad I am to hear it. What will your family do tonight?"

"Probably sit in the kitchen and read. We try not to work on the Sabbath. Father believes our day of rest should be pleasant and restful, not onerous. Most evenings we do handwork while Father reads aloud.

I am making knitted mufflers and lace cuffs for Christmas gifts." She poked at the peat and blew on the embers.

"My grandmother tatted lace."

"Did you live with your grandmother?"

"She lived with us until she died five years ago. My mother worked, so Granny mostly raised me. She was a fine Christian woman."

Charlotte settled back to sit on her heels. "My grandparents are all dead now, but I dearly loved my grandmum Colburn. She taught me to make crocheted lace. What did your father do?"

"I never knew my father." He steered the subject back to handwork. "Did you make all these pillows and things?" He waved his hand to indicate the room's decorations.

She looked slightly embarrassed. "I did."

"I thought as much. And you painted the walls?"

She nodded. "It's silly, I know, but I do love flowers."

"I like it. Makes the room feel like springtime. Like you." He captured her gaze and held on until he thought his heart might give out.

At last she looked away, color flooding her cheeks. "I must go, Mr. Jackson. I'll send one of the twins up to take the kitten soon. I hope you recover quickly." She scrambled up and left the room.

Later that evening, the twins sneaked all three kittens upstairs. Dan sat up in bed and watched the tiny brothers tumble, squeak, stalk, and pounce upon each other. Their pink paws and pink noses contrasted with their fuzzy black coats and white markings.

"All three the same colors, yet each so different from his brothers," he commented after Drusilla rescued her Harvey from a mock attack by Humphrey. "Just as you twins are alike yet different."

The two girls had climbed up on the foot of the bed to play with the kittens. Dan thought their mother would undoubtedly object, but the girls ignored his subtle hints. He scooped up his favorite kitten and held it near his face. Solemn gray blue eyes gazed into his, and the kitten patted his nose.

"Humphrey says he's sleepy and needs his supper. Best take all three down to the kitchen afore your mother finds you here," he said. "I thought Sunday evening was a time for quiet reading."

Drusilla frowned at him. "Mother fell asleep, and Father is out visiting a sick parishioner. We're having fun, and Harvey isn't sleepy."

"Neither is Hubert." Priscilla lifted the kitten, and her apron came with it. "Hubert, let go." The kitten mewled and held tighter. One by one she released its claws from her apron. Tiny snags marked the fabric.

"Girls, Mr. Jackson is the tired one." Charlotte suddenly stepped into the room. Had she been watching from the hallway? Without one glance at Dan, she started fussing with the fire. "You need to be thoughtful of his wishes and take the kittens downstairs now."

Priscilla looked quickly at Dan, and she must have seen exhaustion in his face, for her shoulders slumped. "Oh, very well. We'll bring them back tomorrow, Mr. Jackson. Humphrey misses you when he's in the kitchen." She picked up two kittens and slid off the bed. Drusilla clutched her Harvey and followed.

"And I'll miss him. Thanks for the company." He listened to the clatter of their shoes on the stairs before he said, "And thanks to you for the rescue, miss."

Charlotte faced him, rubbing her hands down her apron. "Do you need water or food or anything else tonight?" She sounded breathless.

He paused to study her, then slowly shook his head. "I meant no harm; they climbed on the bed without my leave and stayed—"

"Mr. Jackson, I know my sisters. You need make no explanation. Thank you for your patience with them, and I'll do my best to prevent a repeat invasion."

Relieved, he rested back against the pillows and spoke in his best English. "They're no real bother, but I'm right sure your parents would disapprove—as they should. Your family is what God must have intended a family to be. I'm thankful to have made your acquaintance. I'd nigh given up on life and love afore I met you."

❧

Charlotte quietly closed the sickroom door and leaned her forehead against its panels. Her heart raced, and her chest felt tight. Never, ever should she have sent the twins away as if maneuvering to be alone with Mr. Jackson! As soon as the girls left the room, she had become intensely aware of him, a strange man sitting on her bed in Father's nightshirt, with her knitted green bed scarf draped incongruously over his shoulders. Although he had said and done nothing untoward, the room had suddenly become small and stifling.

This stranger brought out astonishing feelings—reactions no man had ever induced in her before, not even Clive. She felt feminine and alive, yet also somewhat frightened. Not so much of him as of herself.

Slowly she moved along the hall and entered Eleanor's room. The fire had burned low, so she poked it back into life and added fuel. Then, seating herself at the dressing table, she pulled out her hairpins and stared at the floor.

How many men would react so mildly to a pair of intrusive little girls? When Charlotte first glimpsed her sisters through the open chamber door—the two of them and three kittens clambering about on the sick stranger's bed—her heart had nearly stopped. Of all the foolish, ignorant tricks!

Yet she had paused to observe and found herself amazed by his patience. More than once he had hinted that the children should get off the bed and take the kittens downstairs, but never had he raised his voice or spoken unkindly. No suggestion of disrespect entered his voice, words, or gaze.

What an unusual man! If only he were more than an unemployed ex-soldier of no social standing. If only—if only Clive had such velvety dark eyes full of mystery and magic.

Chapter 4

The following afternoon, Dan washed at his basin then pulled
on an oversized pair of trousers and a faded wool tunic that
someone had left folded on a chair in one corner of the room. The
tunic hung on his frame, its sleeves were too short, and the fabric
abraded his skin. He wrapped the bed scarf around his shoulders,
glanced at his reflection in Charlotte's dressing-table mirror, and
laughed aloud. Like an incredibly ugly woman he looked in that
scarf, with his black growth of whiskers and wildly insubordinate
hair.

His limbs were shaky; otherwise he felt good. He could breathe
deeply without breaking into a fit of coughing.

Slowly he descended the staircase, mistrustful of his rubbery knees.
The house seemed empty, yet he heard voices from somewhere.

He headed toward the back of the house and entered the kitchen.
Laundry dried on racks before the fireplace, and the room had a humid,
misty atmosphere. He smelled soap and bluing. Following the clatter
of a mangle and the hiss of steam, he peered through the doorway of
the scullery where he had bathed days earlier.

The small room seemed filled with laboring females. Not one
of them noticed Dan. All were clad in cotton shifts and faded old
skirts, their sleeves rolled up against the oppressive heat. Charlotte lifted dripping garments from a steaming copper and stacked
them near the mangle, which Mrs. Colburn operated, cranking the
garments through, one at time, to wring out excess water. Sweat
beaded on Charlotte's flushed face, and damp hair stuck to her
cheeks and neck.

Feeling like an intruder, Dan backed away unseen and sought out
the rector's study. He knocked on the closed door.

"Enter."

Mr. Colburn looked up from his desk and rose to his feet as Dan stepped into the room. "Ah, what joy to see you on your feet, Mr. Jackson!"

"Call me Dan, if you please, sir."

"Does my wife know you are up and about?" The rector's eyes held a conspiratorial glint. He pulled two chairs close to the fire. As soon as Dan sank into one armchair, the rector sat across from him.

"No sir, although she said last night that I might get up today. I found your womenfolk doing laundry. Thought I might best help by standing clear."

Mr. Colburn laughed aloud. "Perspicacious of you, son."

Dan grinned and scratched his forearm where the tunic's sleeve rubbed his skin. "I'm that if you say so, sir."

The rector's smile changed into a considering look. "It means you are perceptive. Things that others might not observe, you see clearly. How much schooling did you receive, Dan Jackson?"

"I did four years at the National School but never took my exams. My Greek and Latin are weak. I know geography and sciences from reading, and I can use proper grammar if I set my mind to it. My officer on the peninsula, Major Sykes, brought half his library with him and gave me leave to use it."

"Indeed." The minister spoke slowly, as if thinking deep thoughts. "Are you well acquainted with the Holy Scriptures?"

"I first learned to read from my grandmother's Bible, sir. I can quote whole psalms and list every book of the Canon in order. I still know my catechism." He coughed. "More than anything, I wish I could study more about God."

"Do you now?" Mr. Colburn looked gratified. "For your own edification only, or for some greater purpose?"

Dan rubbed the back of his neck. "My heart is burdened for my people back home in Birmingham. Most have no way of hearing the gospel. Sure, there are churches in town, but none close enough. People haven't got time nor strength to travel far to hear a preacher. I told them what I know, for sure, and some I've led to Christ's salvation, but I need more training in the deeper things. The people need more than the weak 'milk of the Word' I can give them."

The rector studied him with shining, yet sober, eyes. "Daniel

Jackson, I believe you've heard the Macedonian call—although in your case 'tis the Birminghamian call. You're an evangelist by the Lord's almighty power and gifting."

"I hear His call but have no way to answer it. No college would take me, so I've no chance of wearing a collar like yours. My speech is rough, and I've no proper manners." Yet Dan felt a flutter of excitement. If God called, would He not also grant the means to answer?

"You are exactly the right messenger for the people you're called to serve," the rector said firmly. "God is never mistaken about these things. If 'tis only training you lack, I'll gladly share my meager store of knowledge. Your fervor inspires me, son. Why should I not be Paul to your Apollos?"

Dan lifted his brows, uncertain of the analogy. "Why not indeed, sir?"

Mr. Colburn chuckled. "Soon you'll fully understand my meaning. Dan, I offer you full access to my library for as long as you need it. Take books back up to your room if you like, or remain here and discuss them with me. And one thing is certain: We must find you proper clothing before you appear in public. An ascetic monk craving self-abasement would doubtless prize that tunic, but no guest in this home should be subjected to such humiliation."

Dan scratched at his collarbone and silently agreed.

"You may have my spare razor, and I'll find you a more comfortable shirt while you peruse the bookshelves." The rector rose. "If you enjoy reading aloud, you'll find an appreciative audience this evening."

⁂

Mrs. Colburn and her daughters gathered around the hearth in the sitting room, pursuing their fancywork by the glow of an oil lamp on the side table. Charlotte's fingers flew as she crocheted the last inch of an intricate cuff intended as Molly the housemaid's Boxing Day gift, but only half her mind focused on her work.

The muffler she had knitted for Clive kept dangling into her thoughts. Clive already owned several mufflers. As eldest son and heir of the local squire, he lacked for no possible creature comforts.

Mr. Jackson would make much better use of a thick woolen muffler. Charlotte might possibly even eke out a pair of mittens from the leftover yarn. If Mr. Jackson departed the rectory before Christmas Day, she could bestow them upon him as parting gifts. Charity gifts, of course.

But then what gift could she offer Clive to make him see her ideal-wife qualities? She could bake treacle-ginger biscuits, her own special recipe. Or pecan pastry with black currant filling. Clive was fond of sweets—perhaps a bit fonder than was good for him. However, to his way of thinking, baking was servants' work. He would probably mock her efforts and accuse of her aspiring to hire out as someone's cook.

According to Father, Mr. Jackson's childhood had been nearly devoid of treats like biscuits and tarts. Charlotte recalled his obvious enjoyment of her scones that first evening. . . .

"Why are you smiling, Char?" Priscilla asked. "You look smug."

Charlotte's smile vanished. "I simply enjoy my work, that's all." She glanced up and leaped to her feet. Thread and needles dropped from her lap.

Dan Jackson stood in the sitting room doorway, clad in baggy trousers and an old shirt and waistcoat of her father's. He held a book and wore a hopeful expression.

"This is a sewing circle," Eleanor said in unwelcoming tones.

Dan brushed hair out of his eyes. "No men allowed? I'll be off then. Sorry to intrude."

Mother found her voice. "Mr. Jackson, certainly you may join us. But should you be out of bed?"

"I'd go stark mad if I stayed there any longer," he said, coughing a little. "Thank you for washing my clothes. I saw them hung up in the kitchen."

"You are most welcome, Mr. Jackson."

Charlotte seconded her mother's statement with a quick nod and a smile. "On Monday nights the house always feels damp, except by the fire. And our hands are wrinkled and chapped from the water." She held up her own reddened hands, realizing that she would have hidden them from Clive. To Mr. Jackson she somehow wanted to prove her usefulness around a household.

"You carry a book." She indicated the volume in his hand. "Might you read aloud to us?" Or would such a request embarrass him?

But he nodded. "Sure. That's why I brought it: *A Christmas Carol*."

"Charlotte is mad about that book," Eleanor said. "It's like the Bible to her."

"Eleanor, do not be blasphemous. Drusilla, bring Mr. Jackson a chair," Mother ordered.

"I'll do it, Mother, since I'm already up." Charlotte stepped over Eleanor's feet and brought one of the side chairs into their circle, close to the fire screen.

"Thank you." He moved forward so quickly that their shoulders brushed. He smelled nice, he had shaved, and his hair was combed. It was still too long, and it stuck up in places, but he had made an attempt.

"On Christmas Day we're having a party of friends and family. If you're feeling well enough by then, I trust you will join us, Mr. Jackson," Mother said. "Our dinners are never formal affairs. We simply enjoy the good company and fellowship."

"Thank you kindly, ma'am."

"We intend to host a proper Christmas party this year," Charlotte added. "With all the traditional foods and games, like Mr. Dickens writes about."

"I like Dickens," he said quietly. "Especially this book." He held up the thin volume. "I used to read his books aloud to my grandmother. Before that, she read them aloud to me."

"Then you understand the importance of preserving our holiday traditions," Charlotte said with a pleased smile.

"Charlotte is fanatical about this; but then Charlotte is fanatical about nearly everything," Eleanor said, sighing. "I am Eleanor; I'm fourteen. I know you're Mr. Jackson."

"Call me Dan." He scanned the twins. "No kittens tonight?"

"They attack our threads and yarns and snag things," Drusilla explained.

"Mayhap we could visit them once you're finished working. Should I read now? I should think we all know the start of it." He opened the book carefully, turned the first few pages, then slid his big hand gently down the page. Before reading the first line he glanced up once more and caught Charlotte's gaze. Again she smiled. She couldn't help it— he was just so nice.

He coughed softly then began. " 'Marley was dead: to begin with. There is no doubt whatever about that.'"

Chapter 5

Christmas dinner at the Colburn house was unlike anything Dan had ever before experienced. Squire Brigham was in attendance along with his wife, a son, and a daughter near Eleanor's age. An elderly spinster and her widowed sister also joined the party, and then there was Dan.

Scarcely a square inch of tablecloth could be seen between the myriad serving trays piled with food. An immense roasted turkey graced the center of the dining table. A rabbit stuffed with oysters held down one end of the table, balanced by a large baked fish at the other. Oranges and grapes spilled from a silver bowl. Tarts, biscuits, sauces, pastries, jellies, and buns filled every available space.

Dan mostly sat quietly and observed. Seated at the rector's left hand, across the table from the squire, and beside old Mrs. Benton who was slightly deaf, he occupied himself by tasting moderate portions of each dish. He overheard snatches of conversation from the far end of the table; Charlotte kept up a lively banter with Master Clive Brigham, seated across from her. Dan could see the young man's grinning face and hear his occasional quip.

Clive was tall, handsome, wealthy, educated, articulate, and seemed to be sincerely fond of Charlotte Colburn. She deserved a man like him. She deserved the best of everything.

That pain in Dan's chest must be lingering effects of his illness. Instead of Christmas peace and good cheer, he felt a heaviness of spirit. All these rich trappings—the greenery, the red velvet ribbons, the candlelight, and the colorful fruit—none of them brought back the quiet joy he had experienced earlier that day at the Christmas church service.

The rector had read the Christmas story from the Gospels of Luke and Matthew, and the worshippers had sung a few carols. Sharing a songbook with Drusilla, Dan had glanced over the child's head and met Charlotte's smiling gaze more than once. Joy welled up in his spirit, as well as thanksgiving, for God's provision, for His Son, and especially for the company of one lovely young woman.

How beautiful she was in a gown of deep green! A crocheted-lace collar accented her delicate features and soft-looking skin. "Eyes like doves"—where had he heard that poetic description? It suited Charlotte. All day long he had struggled to keep his gaze averted; all too often he had failed.

Now Dan fervently wished for the day to end. He should leave the rectory in the morning; he had trespassed on this family's hospitality long enough.

At last Charlotte produced the flaming plum pudding and set it down before her father with evident pride. "And here we have the final tradition to complete a right and proper Christmas dinner," she said.

The blue flames slowly flickered out, and everyone clapped.

"What a lovely pudding, my dear," said Mrs. Brigham. "I've never seen a finer."

"Charlotte and her 'proper' Christmas traditions," Eleanor said, rolling her eyes. "That's all she talks about."

"You sneer at me, yet you enjoy the Christmas joy and cheer as much as any," Charlotte snapped back. "Traditions are important; they strengthen our country, and they make Christmas the loveliest holiday of all."

Dan studied Charlotte's flushed cheeks and heard the tension in her voice. "While traditions surely have their place in a home," he said clearly, "Christmas is the celebration of Christ's birth, and with it His death and resurrection. God's love and sacrifice are what sets this holiday apart."

All eyes turned to Dan. He read varying responses, from scorn to approval.

"There you go, Char. Finally, someone puts you in your place," Clive Brigham said with a chuckle.

"Thank you for this timely reminder, Mr. Jackson," the rector said, smiling. "I'll take a small slice of pudding, my dear, and no sauce."

Charlotte pulled her stunned gaze away from Dan and began to serve her pudding.

Dan accepted a slab of pudding on a china plate but felt too miserable to eat more than a bite or two. He pulled the rest apart with his fork and tried to respond politely to the rector's comments.

"Would you light the candles on the tree?" A voice spoke almost into his ear. He turned to meet Mrs. Colburn's eager gaze and nodded. She led him to the hallway, handed him a lighted taper, and put her finger to her smiling lips.

Dan slipped into the parlor. A fir tree stood on a side table, its branches draped with strings of beads and laden with little gifts. He climbed on a chair to light the top candles, working quickly and cautiously.

What would the Colburns say if he were to admit that this was his first Christmas tree ever? Although this particular tradition was relatively new to England, brought from Germany by Prince Albert, the fashion for Christmas trees had swept throughout Queen Victoria's realm and beyond.

Just after he lighted the last candle, the parlor door burst open and the twins rushed inside. Dan smiled at their exuberance. Together they inspected the gifts hanging from the tree branches while the adults followed at a more sedate pace.

He retreated to a quiet corner to watch the family and friends receive their gifts. Seeing Charlotte's shining eyes as she held up a delicate pair of earbobs and thanked the Brigham family, he felt a twinge of anger at his penniless state.

He could offer her nothing. Nothing at all.

The rector stood in front of the parlor door, blocking Dan's only possible exit. He met Dan's gaze and smiled in his benign way, then approached. "Thank you for taking part. Your presence with us is a great blessing."

"My presence?" Dan said. "I contribute nothing important."

"On the contrary, you contribute much. Your timely reminder that Christmas is the celebration of Christ's birth—"

"I embarrassed her."

"Perhaps, yet the hurt was unintentionally given."

Dan shrugged slightly. "I enjoy beauty, good food, and tradition as much as the next man, but without Christ it all means nothing."

Mr. Colburn thumped Dan's shoulder. "Amen and amen!" He chuckled, then sobered into thoughtfulness. "Charlotte often mistakes the traditions for the truth. She strives to produce Christmas joy by doing everything perfectly, like a holiday version of Martha. True joy can be found only in worshiping at Jesus' feet, like Mary. In a few succinct words, you corrected her error. To my pleased surprise, she accepted the reproof from you without a murmur."

"Only because I am a stranger and a guest," Dan said.

"Hmm. I think not." The rector's smile held a mysterious glint. He moved on to visit with the squire, leaving Dan to wonder.

After the guests departed and the little fir tree stood dark and empty, Dan and the rector both helped clean up the kitchen. The family members sang as they worked, choosing lively carols at first and closing with "Silent Night."

Dan no longer wished to escape upstairs. He wanted the day to last forever. He wiped dishes and handed them to the girls to put away. Once Charlotte gripped his thumb along with a platter. Did she even notice? He couldn't be sure.

But when at last the work was done, he could think of no excuse to linger. He said his good nights to his host and hostess, and winked and waved at the twins. Eleanor ignored him, but Charlotte met his gaze. She quickly looked away, and his spirits plummeted.

At the base of the stairs, with his hand grasping the newel post, he stopped and stared at the bottom riser. Charlotte should have her own room back. He was no longer ill. Tomorrow he must take leave of this wonderful family and strike out to find work. Somehow he would find a way to pay them back for their hospitality and generosity. As if love could ever be repaid.

"Mr. Jackson, please wait!"

He turned, gripping the post until his knuckles whitened. Candlelight from a wall sconce caught in Charlotte's gleaming curls and glowed upon her skin as she gazed up at him, both hands behind her back. Suddenly shy, she lowered her gaze. "I wanted to thank you—for what you said today over the pudding. You were right, and as soon as you spoke I knew it. These past weeks I've been trying to manufacture Christmas cheer instead of simply enjoying Christ."

She looked up into his eyes, and a great lump filled Dan's chest. He gave a jerky nod. "Not to say that the greenery and the tree and all weren't beautiful; they were." His voice sounded like iron scraping over gravel. "And the food was delicious. I've never eaten better in my life. God blessed us, every one, as Tiny Tim would say."

She smiled. "I'll never again read that story without thinking of you. The voice you used for Marley's ghost gave me gooseflesh!"

He held her gaze and tried to return the smile.

"I want you to have this." She brought her hands from behind her back and held out a dark lump. When he merely looked down at it, she took hold of his hands and pushed the soft something into his grasp. The touch of her slim fingers shocked him so that he nearly dropped the gift.

"For you." She looked abashed, yet determined.

His hands were shaking so hard that he could scarcely control them. A knitted muffler unrolled from his grasp and dangled nearly to the floor. He caught a pair of mittens just in time.

"They are dark blue, though you cannot tell by candlelight. I thought you—you might like to have them." Suddenly she sounded uncertain, even worried.

"I can think of naught I'd like better," he said firmly. He met her gaze. "I have no gift for you."

Her sudden smile dazzled him. "I'm so thankful you like it! I've wanted to give it to you all day but never found the right time. This is the best part of Christmas." She appeared ready to touch his hands again, but caught herself. "May Jesus fill your heart with great joy, Dan Jackson."

"And you, Miss Charlotte." He had never spoken her name aloud before. It sounded like a caress.

She stepped back, rubbing and twining her hands together, then turned and hurried toward the kitchen. He heard a quiet "Good night" before she vanished.

❦

After the house was dark and everyone else had retired to bed for the night, Charlotte sat on the kitchen floor beside an oil lamp turned low and cuddled the kittens. Once roused, they were eager to play and socialize. Her favorite was Humphrey, not only because Dan favored him and had named him, but also because the kitten liked to look into her eyes and pat her nose and cheeks with his soft paws. He seemed aware of her as a person and a friend, not merely as a pair of hands that stroked and played.

Again and again her mind recalled two scenes of the day.

The first scene had played out in Father's study. When she closed her eyes she could picture Clive's amused grin. "Char, you can't mean it. You're like a sister to me; you always have been. I know our mothers talked about us marrying someday, but it was all a game. You're a pretty girl, for certain, but I could never see you—that way. *You* know."

Charlotte buried her nose in the fluff of Humphrey's back and grimaced. The idiot! If she had already known, why would she have questioned his feelings for her?

The second scene: her encounter with Dan Jackson in the front hall. That memory brought a different kind of heat into her face and body. His mysterious dark eyes, the attractive lines of his face when he smiled, his rough hands trembling in her grasp, his deep voice speaking her name. Oh yes, he found her attractive. A selfish part of her heart exulted in Dan's admiration, the same part that resented Clive's immunity to her charms.

However, Dan Jackson was not only of a social class several steps below Charlotte's, he was also destitute—without a penny to his name. Why had she flirted with him? Why, when she touched his hands, had she felt that shock of attraction? She was no siren, deliberately enticing a man she could never consider taking as a beau. The danger, the hazard of luring a man, then spurning him—such things had never thrilled her before.

And they did not thrill her now. Shame burned a path up her throat and emerged in a sob. A loving relationship with a man she could respect and adore—that was her heart's desire. Wasn't it?

A tear burned a path down her cheek. She wiped it away with Humphrey's soft head. He purred.

Chapter 6

On Boxing Day morning, Dan rose early, washed, and shaved. Staring out the window, he imagined Charlotte as his wife, seated behind him at the dressing table, brushing out her shining hair. A wave of longing for a home and family of his own flowed over him until he nearly drowned in it.

Ice rimed the windowpanes. Cold filtered through the cracks around the frame. Below lay the winter-dead garden, its gate, and the path leading to the church. Beyond the church ran the north-south highway. His hands clenched in dread. Soon he would walk that lonely road once more, never to see this house, this family—Charlotte—again.

Slowly he turned away from the window and left the room that had been his haven for eight days. His tread upon the stairs was equally slow. Clutching the newel post at the base, he pictured Charlotte and felt again the grasp of her hands on his.

"You're not planning to leave us, I hope."

Dan lifted his gaze to see the rector standing in his study doorway. "I am, sir."

"On Boxing Day? You'll not find work today, my lad. Wait a few days and see what the Lord brings."

Looking into the rector's kindly eyes, Dan recognized genuine affection. "You truly wish me to stay? But why?"

"There would be a great outcry if you were to disappear this morning. I believe a few hearts might quietly break. I believe mine might be among them. I had greatly counted on training and teaching you. So seldom do I find a student willing to subject himself voluntarily to my lectures."

Dan smiled at the jest. "But I cannot live on your charity when I am well and strong."

"I dare say you've not yet regained your full strength. Which brings to mind—I mentioned your work experience to the squire yesterday. He needs a good man in his stables. The beginning position and salary would be small, but there is great potential for future advancement." He beckoned. "Come into my study, have a muffin, and discuss business. I insist."

❧❧❧

As soon as Charlotte stepped into the upper hallway that morning her gaze fell upon the open door to her bedroom. She rushed to look inside and saw no evidence that Dan Jackson had ever inhabited it.

She clattered down the stairs and rushed to the kitchen. Startled kittens scampered behind the stove. Molly dropped a wooden spoon on the flagstone floor and clutched at her chest. "Miss Charlotte, how you frightened me!"

"Has he gone?"

"Has who gone? The rector?"

"Mr. Jackson."

"Not that I seen, miss. He and the rector was holed up talking in the study when I got 'ere and built the fires. Did you have a nice Christmas, Miss Charlotte?" She picked up the spoon, almost returned it to the porridge pot, then thought better of it, and selected a clean one.

Recalling her lost manners, Charlotte smiled. "We had a lovely holiday, Molly. How is your family? Happy Boxing Day to you."

Three little heads appeared from beneath the stove and the china dresser. Seeing no cat-starved monsters, the kittens dashed back out to play. Harvey leaped after Molly's apron strings and fell on his face.

Molly tried to ignore him. "Thank you, miss. My family is thriving right well. My sister, what ailed over summer, has picked up some color and fat on her."

"I'm so pleased to hear it, Molly." Thinking of the lace cuffs waiting in Molly's gift box, Charlotte smiled again. Her mother would give Molly her Boxing Day gifts later in the morning. "So Mr. Jackson and the rector are in the study?"

"They was last I seen."

"Thank you."

Humphrey rubbed about Charlotte's ankles, hidden beneath her

307

petticoats. She scooped him up and held his soft purring body to her cheek, then draped him over her shoulder. He flopped there like a tiny scarf with his legs and tail dangling. She placed one hand on his back, but he seemed secure enough.

On a whim, she headed toward the study and knocked at the closed door.

"Enter," her father said.

He and Mr. Jackson were seated at the desk, bending over open books. Mr. Jackson appeared to be taking notes. He looked up, and his quill tipped sideways, blotting ink across the page. Both men rose to their feet.

"Good morning, my dear," her father said, beaming with satisfaction. "As you see, Mr. Jackson and I have begun our theological studies. We have come to an agreement. Although I have offered to teach him simply for the pleasure it will provide me, he insists upon paying for the instruction and finding separate lodgings."

"But where will you stay?" Charlotte asked, gazing into Mr. Jackson's eyes. "And where will you work?"

He opened his mouth, but Father spoke first. "The Lord will supply. For the present, he will sleep over the kitchen in the empty servants' quarters."

Charlotte nodded, trying to think of an intelligent comment. She smiled and bobbed a curtsey. Humphrey chose that moment to jump down from her shoulder. She grasped at him, but he used her bouffant skirts as a safety net, slid down, and hopped to the carpet. With a chirping *mew* and fur standing on end, he scuttled under the sofa.

"What prompted that display, I wonder?" Charlotte said, smoothing the snags caused by tiny claws in her gray wool gown.

"A sudden burst of kitty high spirits, I reckon." Mr. Jackson went down on his hands and knees to peer beneath the sofa. "Humphrey— here, kitty, kitty."

Charlotte knelt beside him, pushing aside her ballooning skirts. "I don't see him. Where did he go?"

Mr. Jackson tipped his face toward her. "Exploring." His tone held a hint of thrills and adventure.

She met his gaze and grinned.

Charlotte found it difficult now to imagine her life without Dan Jackson in it.

⚜

The following week passed quickly for Dan. Whenever he considered applying for a position at Brigham Grange, the thought of working for young Clive galled—so he waited. His life of study fell into a pattern that seldom linked with Charlotte's social plans, yet he usually glimpsed her several times during the day, and she seemed to enjoy conversing with him. It would be pure foolishness to imagine that she found him attractive. He was well aware that Clive Brigham held Charlotte's heart; although, he was equally aware that Master Clive regarded her affection with slightly amused, slightly irritated indifference.

One afternoon, his head so full of information that it began to ache, Dan finally closed the theology books and replaced them on their proper shelves. The timeline of Old Testament patriarchs, judges, kings, and prophets enthralled him, though he saw more practical use in the study of God's attributes. So much to learn!

Rubbing his temple with one hand, he closed the study door behind himself. It must be nearly time to dress for dinner. Not that he had fine clothes to change into—his version of dressing was a quick wash and comb. His first purchase, when he did find work, would be a decent suit of clothes and new boots.

"Mr. Jackson."

He looked up to see Charlotte descending the stairs. She looked exceptionally lovely. His face must have revealed his thoughts, for she smiled shyly. "I am attending a charades party at Brigham Grange tonight. Would you like to join us? It is not a formal occasion—Clive didn't even send invitations."

"I think not."

"I wish you would." She reached the bottom step and stood there, her eyes level with his. "The party will be more fun if you come."

He caught himself looking at her mouth as she spoke. Quickly he averted his gaze to the wall. "I haven't proper clothes for a party."

"I don't care what you wear."

Did she have any idea how she affected him? Whenever she

309

spoke with him, he forgot his low social status and his doubtful future. Whenever she spoke with him, he felt like a man whose world held no limits—in fact, like a man who could *conquer* worlds!

"I—I can't. If you'll please excuse me. . ." He bowed slightly and headed toward the kitchen.

Once in his garret chamber, he went to his knees beside the bed and held his head with both hands. "Lord God, help me!"

≪∽⧉∽≫

Disappointment rippled through Charlotte, and her anticipation of the party faded. Clive would treat her like a younger sister. Some of the village boys would flirt with her and flatter her, but they would mean nothing by it.

She should just stay home. Perhaps Dan would read to her beside the fire again. They could play with the kittens and talk, and he would catch her gaze and hold it until her heart filled her chest.

But no matter how much she enjoyed Dan's companionship, there was no avoiding the fact that their paths would soon diverge. He would do the Lord's work in a big city, preaching and evangelizing among the poor. She would marry Clive or some other dull, well-to-do, middle-class fellow, settle down in a drafty barn of a house, raise a brood of children, and grow bored and fat and melancholy.

Gloom settled over her spirit like a mist on the moors.

Chapter 7

Dan puffed out a breath and watched it dissipate against the dark backdrop of the church tower. His boots crunched in a light fall of snow. The eve of a new year had arrived, and he felt no closer to a solution to his problems. The temptation to accept Mr. Colburn's offer of scriptural training as a gift tormented him night and day, almost as often as the temptation to remain near. . .

Charlotte. She seemed to like him well enough; they conversed easily, and she listened with interest while he spoke of his missionary calling. At times he recognized a singular light in her eyes when she met his gaze—but he could easily be mistaken. He was no expert on women and their ways.

Again he sighed deeply and coughed. The cold air bit at his face and fingers but no longer ached in his lungs. He felt strong, well fed, healthy—ready to work, if any work could be found.

Lord God, I don't know what to do or where to go. I can't accept charity schooling and be a burden on the rector; a man must carry his own weight. But the opportunity to learn and study Your Word—how can I pass it by? Guide my steps, Lord. I am at a loss.

The sound of scraping caught his attention. Circling the church building, he saw a large and well-bundled figure shoveling snow from the church walkway. "Joe?" Not loud enough. Moving closer, he called again. "Joe!"

Joe paused and looked over his shoulder. "Aye, man? How can I be helping? If you're needin' the rector, he'll be in his study at the—" He paused and frowned. "Do I know ye?"

"I'm the man you found sleeping on the pew and took to the rectory."

Joe's wrinkled brow cleared. "And so y' are. Recovered your sleep, I see. Fine people, them Colburns. The good Lord sets store by them such people. Always looking out for others, they be. Summat troubling ye, lad?"

Dan brushed snow from a marble headstone and decided to unload his burdens. "I need work. The rector has offered to train me in the scriptures—has already started educating me so I can return home and preach—but while I'm training I need work and lodging. I can't live any longer off the minister's bounty. He's been generous—they've treated me like family—but if I stay longer I'll feel like a tick on a dog, sucking it dry."

Joe rested his enormous hands on the shovel's handle and frowned in concentration. "Ye might ask at the Red Stag, or maybe at The Bell in Culverton, up the road a piece. Or Mr. Brigham might take on a gamekeeper or groom."

Dan straightened his shoulders. "I'll try the first two, but I can't see myself working for—for the squire. I can't help believing that God must have something else in mind."

"You keep believing, lad." A smile gleamed through Joe's bushy beard. "You keep right on believing."

"Thank you for the help." Dan started off, then stopped at the end of the walkway and turned back. "Thank you also for helping me that night—" He blinked. How could a man Joe's size vanish that quickly? He must have ducked inside the church. Dan shook his head in wonder. The walkway was neatly shoveled and swept, ready for the end-of-year worship service that night.

Dan headed into town. Houses and shops jutted into the narrow road through Little Brigham, scarcely leaving room for a carriage to pass. Just this side of the market square, Dan saw the sign of the Red Stag hanging above the door of a gabled, half-timbered building. Beyond the inn, an arched-stone gateway in a block wall undoubtedly conducted travelers to the stables behind the inn.

The public room held a few customers—travelers, judging by their appearance. The stout woman wiping out tankards behind the bar gave Dan a short look. "Fresh out o' shepherd's pie," she said.

"I'm looking for the innkeeper, ma'am," Dan said, doffing his cap.

She rested her forearms on the counter and spoke gruffly though not unkindly. "He's around back at the stable, but I wouldn't bother 'im iffen I was you. He be in a right foul mood, him." She laughed without humor, then squinted her eyes and gave Dan an assessing look. "You'd be that drifter what the rector took in. Come to think on it, you might be in luck if you're looking for work."

"I am."

She sniffed. "I 'eard you was sickly. You don't looks it. Do you know 'orses?"

"I do."

A smile transformed her face into cherubic sweetness. "Tell Mister Cuttlesworth that the missus sent you round. Go on with you now." She swept her towel at him. "Through that door and on back."

Encouraged, Dan searched until he located a short, stout man harnessing a pair of grays to a fine brougham. "Mr. Cuttlesworth?"

"That be my name. Don't bother me; I'm right busy. Gentry passing through, wanting fresh 'osses and that fast."

"Yes, sir." Dan stepped forward to hold one of the skittish horses steady enough for Mr. Cuttlesworth to hitch it to the carriage. "Easy there, lad," he soothed. The horse stopped tossing its head and sniffed Dan's breath, its nostrils fluttering. "Aye, you smell the mint I chewed." Dan grinned.

He ran his fingers over the animals' headstalls and blinders, settled the collars more comfortably over their shoulders, and checked their legs for swelling. He looked up to see Mr. Cuttlesworth observing him through narrowed eyes.

"You knows 'osses then?"

Dan nodded. "Worked as 'ostler at the Lion & Unicorn in Birmingham before the war. Tended cavalry mounts and gun mules in the Crimea. I'm seeking a job. Mrs. Cuttlesworth sent me to find you."

"What's your name?"

Dan told him. "The sexton, Joe, sent me here to ask about work."

"Never 'eard of him. You living in town?"

"I've been lodging with the rector, but I need a room."

"We got better than a room. The 'ostler here gets the cottage at the end of the stable block—or he did 'til he run off last night with the haberdasher's wife. Let's see what you can do, lad."

A short time later, Dan drove the team to the front of the inn. A fine gentleman and his lady emerged from the inn's double doors and mounted their carriage. "Thank you, my good man," the gentleman said and flipped Dan a shilling.

Dan returned to the stable and located the exhausted job horses that had needed replacing. Mr. Cuttlesworth had thrown a blanket over each of the beasts, but they were both still sweating and shaking. Dan led the geldings around the yard until they cooled; then he prepared bran mash, warming it on the cast-iron stove in the tack room. The animals ate gratefully, then dozed and nibbled at hay while he brushed dried sweat and mud from their shaggy winter coats. Only afterward did Dan let them drink and put them away for a well-earned rest.

After cleaning up the tack room, splicing a broken bridle, and rinsing out some soiled blankets, he brushed off his hands and wondered whether or not Mr. Cuttlesworth intended to hire him. He nearly ran into the innkeeper as he stepped into the passageway. Mr. Cuttlesworth lifted his lamp.

"You been 'ere three hours, and the place looks like new. You're hired, Jackson."

Dan walked back to the rectory late that night, carrying a package under one arm and softly whistling "God Rest Ye Merry, Gentlemen."

Charlotte met him at the door. "There you are! We were growing worried."

"I sent a message boy." He pulled off his cap as he stepped inside.

"That was hours ago. But, Dan, I'm so pleased you found work! You'll still live here, of course." She took his cap and hung it on a hook, then unwrapped the muffler from his neck.

"Nay, I've a cottage of my own. Four rooms and a loft. I'll soon set it to rights." He could smell himself—sweat, dust, and horses. "I'm in need of a wash."

"Come to the scullery and wash up for a late supper. Soon we shall all walk over to church for the New Year sing and prayers."

He obediently followed her through the house, trying not to watch her too blatantly. In a plum-colored gown of shiny-striped fabric, she looked too pretty for words. She set her lamp on the scullery table, tied on an apron, poured water into a basin for him, then laid out clean toweling. "The water was scalding just minutes ago.

It should be comfortably warm now. I'll prepare a plate while you wash."

"Thank you." He wondered where the other family members might be hiding. This being alone with Charlotte felt too right, almost as if they were husband and wife in their own cottage.

She lighted a candle from the lamp, set it in a holder, and left him alone in the scullery. Her candlelight faded into darkness. Dan stripped off his soiled jacket and shirt, plunged his hands into the warm water, and began to scrub his upper body and head.

While he was toweling off, Humphrey wandered into the scullery and mewed in greeting. For such a tiny beast, the cat had a lot of awareness and personality. Dan bent over to pick him up. Humphrey purred and kneaded his shoulder.

"Mr. Jackson, my father found garments for you." Charlotte's voice indicated her approach. "They're from the missionary barrel and far from new, but we thought you might like another change of clothing. Especially now that you have a—"

"Miss Charlotte," Dan called, "unless you wish to see a man without a shirt, you'd best come no farther!" He had little patience with modern women and their ridiculous sensibilities, yet neither did he wish to shock or embarrass the girl. "I purchased new garments today."

A pause. "Oh," she squeaked. "Very well." He heard her skirts rustle as she retreated.

She wasn't in the kitchen when he passed through it on his way to the tiny staircase leading to the servants' quarters. He shook his head and smiled ruefully. How would a lady like Charlotte survive in the crowded slums of Birmingham, where people often dispensed with their outer garments on hot summer days? Could she adapt and accept people for who they were instead of judging them by their attire? Or would she wither away like a rose plucked from its garden? He would never know, of course.

In his bedchamber, he unwrapped his parcel. When had he last owned new clothes? He changed into clean cotton drawers and a starched white shirt. Never owned a white shirt before. The suit seemed well made, though its fabric was rather coarse. The jacket's fit was tight across the shoulders, but otherwise the garments were adequate. He knotted his tie beneath his chin and tucked it into the waistcoat.

"Your supper is ready, Mr. Jackson!" Charlotte called from below.

Was it his imagination, or did her voice betray a quiver of anticipation? He ran the comb through his shaggy hair one last time, straightened his shoulders, and descended the creaky stairs into the kitchen.

She stood before the china dresser with her hands clasped at her waist. The kittens frolicked around her skirts. Her gaze inspected Dan from head to new boots. "You look very fine," she said at last.

"Fancy feathers," he commented. "Hope I tied the neckcloth right."

She approached him slowly, her eyes on his necktie, and reached to straighten it. He swallowed hard. "Didn't you have one on your army uniform?" she asked.

"Not like this."

"You must have looked handsome in uniform." She gave the tie a final pat, and he thought he might fall over backward.

While he ate cold pork pie, rye bread, and boiled cabbage, she settled across the table from him. "My father tells me you are learning quickly."

Dan was careful to keep his mouth closed while he chewed.

She continued. "Now that you have work, how can you continue your studies?"

He swallowed. "I'll find time. A man makes time for things that are important to him."

"So you'll still come to the rectory? For studies, I mean?" She lowered her gaze to her clasped hands. "I hope you'll dine with us occasionally, too."

A stinging pain in his leg distracted his attention. "Oww!" Humphrey climbed his trouser leg like a tree and hopped into his lap. "You little beast!" Dan couldn't help grinning as the kitten poked its face over the tabletop and batted at the cabbage with one white paw.

"Humphrey!" Charlotte cried. "These kittens are becoming spoiled beyond imagining. The twins allow them too much license."

"I've scarcely seen the twins lately."

"They spend much time at their cousins' house, and you've been lost in your world of books." Charlotte rose and circled the table. "Do you want me to take him away?"

What he wanted was to wrap his arm around her and draw her close. "No, I don't mind him."

The front door closed, and voices filtered through to the kitchen. Charlotte hurriedly moved away. "Mother and the girls are back. Father is already at the church."

It suddenly dawned on Dan that he and Charlotte had been alone in the rectory all this time, chaperoned only by three kittens. He suddenly felt short of breath.

⁂

Charlotte stood between her mother and Priscilla, trying to listen to her father's sermon. Despite her best efforts, her mind kept wandering. Since she first became fully aware of Clive, years ago, she had never noticed any other boy or man. All her plans had focused on him, all her efforts went into attracting his notice, all her dreams of the future took place inside his hereditary home, Brigham Grange.

Until Dan Jackson swept into her life. Each encounter with him was more exciting than the last. According to her father, Dan had an exceptional mind, a remarkable understanding of theological mysteries, and a close relationship with the Lord Himself. He was a man who would love his wife and lead his family in godly ways—a man much like her father, for all their external differences.

Adding to his appeal was the fact that Charlotte felt more attractive and more of a woman in his presence than with any other man of her acquaintance. This might be the result of his obvious admiration, but Charlotte thought not. Between them lay a strong and mysterious bond.

Could it be that God intended Charlotte to exchange her grand dreams for a short, hard, sacrificial life in a drafty shack in the big city? No! She gave her head a sharp shake. God knew better than to ask such a thing.

Mother looked over at her in surprise. Charlotte tried to smile reassuringly. But then she caught Dan's quick glance over Priscilla's head, and her heart leaped. Why did he have to be so attractive? Life with him would bring nothing but hardship and pain.

The New Year peal of bells rang out from the church tower.

Chapter 8

Dan forked manure and soiled bedding into the dung cart, then wheeled it to the refuse heap in the inn's courtyard. Steam rose from both the cart and his body as soon as he stepped outside.

While he worked, his mind dwelt on intriguing topics. The infinity and omnipotence of God, the inerrancy of scripture, the question of free will versus predestination—he loved it all. The joy he found in discussing and debating such topics with the reverend Mr. Colburn had taken him by surprise. Who would have thought that a latent theologian could dwell in the form of a humble hostler? Who would have thought that opportunity to study such holy topics would ever come the way of Dan Jackson?

He smiled while dumping the cart. Gratitude toward God put lightness in his steps and strength in his body even as he performed the most mundane of chores.

"Mr. Jackson?"

Drusilla and Priscilla Colburn trotted across the brick courtyard. Bundled in warm clothing until they each appeared twice normal size, they beamed at the sight of him, big eyes glowing in their pointed little faces.

"Good morning, ladies. What brings you here? Where's your mother?" He brushed his grimy hands down his trouser legs. Despite the cold, he worked in his shirtsleeves.

"Mother let us come to town with Charlotte and Eleanor, who are shopping for fripperies. Tonight is the big Twelfth Night party, you know."

"That it is."

"Just now we saw Millicent Brigham carrying an enormous wreath. The hall at the Red Stag will be glorious!" Drusilla sighed and clasped her mittened hands beneath her chin.

"You're coming, aren't you?" asked Priscilla. "We want to dance with you."

Dan smiled at her blunt pronouncement. "You honor me, ladies; but nay, short of a miracle, I'll not be attending the party."

"But why not?" Priscilla said. "You live right here at the inn."

"I'll be doing my job, that's why not. All the people traveling to town for the party will need someone to care for their horses. That someone would be me." Dan kept his tone light and tipped his cap. "Now, if you'll be excusing me, I must attend to my labors."

The girls followed him back into the stable. " 'Tis most unfair," Drusilla insisted. "You should have your chance at fun like everyone else. Couldn't you get the horses settled, then come to the party for even a short time?"

"Mr. Cuttlesworth hired me to do this job. I'll not be leaving the stable until every last guest has departed for home. That's the way of it, little friends. I'm a workingman, not a gentleman." He smiled at the girls to remove any sting from his words, then picked up his pitchfork and shifted another load of muck into the cart.

Priscilla frowned, and Drusilla looked ready to cry. Both girls walked along the row of stalls, inspecting the backsides of the resident horses. "You need Humphrey to come live with you," Priscilla said, "as soon as he's grown. I just saw a mouse."

"There are mice enough here to keep a dozen cats employed," Dan said, grateful for the change in subject.

"Charlotte will be sad that you're not coming tonight." Drusilla refused to be distracted. "She likes you as much as we do."

"I don't know that she does anymore," Priscilla said. "She gets all red and irritated when we talk about him much, and she drops things."

Feeling red and irritated himself, Dan tried not to hear the girls' chatter.

"Yesterday she cried all over Humphrey. His fur was wet and gloppy."

"But she might not be crying about Dan. She's been dismal all week and talks only to Father in his study," Priscilla said. "Can you picture Char living here?" She waved her hand to indicate the stable and its environs. "She might like Dan extremely, but she'd never marry an 'ostler. She wants to be lady of the manor."

Keeping his face averted, Dan grimaced. Trust Priscilla to

summarize the entire matter in a few concise words. He paused to draw his sleeve across his forehead and his suddenly burning eyes.

⁂

Charlotte regarded her reflection in the blotchy, wavy mirror. Glossy curls framed her sober face. Noticing the pronounced droop to her lips, she attempted a smile and immediately felt tears spring to her eyes. Annoyed, she turned away from the mirror and smoothed her long gloves.

Other young ladies clustered behind her in the small space, smoothing their hair and arranging their necklines to show as much of their shoulders as they dared. Charlotte felt lost in a sea of rustling, colliding skirts. Excited chatter assaulted her ears.

What had become of her joy in the season? Laces and ribbons and silks no longer satisfied her desires. The prospect of dancing with Clive left her heart unmoved by either dread or happiness. The Twelfth Night party, anticipated for months, now loomed before her as a trial to be endured.

Despite a cold wind, the Colburn family had walked to the inn from the rectory. Pattens protected the girls' dancing slippers, and frozen mud could not soil their skirts. Father saw no reason to hire a carriage when they could easily walk the distance.

So the girls had found no excuse to visit the inn's stables. Dan was undoubtedly too busy for conversation anyway. Charlotte would only be in his way.

She returned to the ballroom and observed her surroundings with a sense of detachment. A new certainty awakened in her heart, spreading warmth throughout her body. Closing her eyes, she pressed her hands to her hot cheeks and recognized the truth.

A lifetime of poverty and hardship with Dan would be preferable to splendor and comfort without him.

⁂

Dan barked orders to a stable boy hired to assist him for the evening. A pair of dapple grays hitched near the pump whinnied, and the squire's handsome Cleveland bays answered with ringing neighs that echoed through the courtyard. Dan heard a snatch of orchestra music before another carriage rattled into the yard.

Many drivers left their horses hitched in the courtyard or street, gave them nosebags, and covered them with blankets for the duration of the party. Dan had actually stabled only the few beasts belonging to those responsible for setting up the party. He glanced up at the inn and shivered.

"Why ain't you a-dancin' at yon party, lad?"

The deep, gruff voice startled Dan out of his reverie. "Eh?"

"A young buck oughtn't to be cooling 'is 'eels in the stableyard whilst pretty ladies be without partners inside." Joe, the sexton, tipped his shaggy head toward the inn. "Why not step inside for an hour and tramp the boards? I kin 'andle things out here for ye."

Dan shook his head. "Thank you, but Mr. Cuttlesworth wouldn't take to that. He hired me to do the job." He tilted his head and gave the hulking giant a closer look. "Why do I never see you about town?"

Joe's teeth flashed in a beam of lamplight. "Turn about, how's come I seldom see *you*, lad? I reckon you and me walks different paths. But ye needn't try to shift the subject. I know for a fact that Mr. Cuttlesworth wouldn't object to ye leaving the 'osses to my keeping for an hour. Ask 'im yourself, if ye can't be taking my word on it."

An overwhelming desire to make the attempt caught Dan by surprise. His entire body shook, and not with cold. He glanced down at himself. By the time he washed and changed—

"Clothes be 'anged. It's you the lady wants to see."

Dan's rational mind rejected the plan, yet his heart wanted to heed Joe's advice. "But Mr. Cutt—"

" 'Ere be the man 'isself. Ask 'im."

Joe faded into the shadows as Mr. Cuttlesworth approached. "Dan, you're a wonder, a fair wonder. I never seen the like!" He glanced around the courtyard at the quiet, contented horses, the few drivers conversing or dozing on their boxes, the starlit sky above. "The Bethlehem stable could ha' been no more peaceful!"

"If I might ask, sir, would you take kindly to my stepping inside for a time? I'd greatly care to dance one or two dances, and Joe the sexton offers to watch things here for me—"

Mr. Cuttlesworth waved his hand airily. "If ever I met a lad deserving of his chance at happiness, it's you. Only mind you're back afore the rush."

Dan closed his gaping mouth, blinked twice, and nodded. "Certainly, sir."

Mr. Cuttlesworth trotted on back to the inn. Joe reappeared at Dan's elbow. "Best wash up quick-like and find your young lady. She'll be pining for ye."

As if in a dream, Dan hurried to his cottage, washed, shaved, and changed into his good clothes. Dark hair hung almost into his eyes and waved on the back of his neck. Fine clothes didn't change his nature, but no matter. If Charlotte couldn't accept him for his true self, her regard would be worthless.

Doubt assailed him as soon as he stepped into the hall. Greenery, ribbons, candles, and strings of beads adorned the walls, and large kissing balls hung above every arch. He saw one laughing young woman ducking in and out of an archway while her persistent suitor endeavored to catch her beneath the ball.

Dan searched the crowd for a familiar face. There was Charlotte on the dance floor, performing some kind of country dance opposite Clive Brigham. He was talking to her with animation, but she seemed strangely apathetic, lacking her usual sparkle. Nevertheless, her beauty built a lump in Dan's chest until he could scarcely breathe.

What had he been thinking? Why would a woman like that want to dance with him? He prowled the edges of the throng, overhearing snatches of conversation, dodging a running child.

"Dan!" The twins emerged from a group of children in one corner.

Priscilla nearly tackled him in an exuberant hug. "You came! I knew you would come. Has Charlotte seen you?"

"No."

"She's been in the Slough of Despond all evening, just because you weren't here."

He lowered his brows in disbelief. "Did she say that?"

Drusilla joined them, hands folded decorously at her waist. "She never said so, but Mother chided her for sulking. Mother said something else that might have been interesting, but she said it too low for us to hear."

"And then Charlotte got very quiet. She has danced every dance, but she doesn't talk much," Priscilla added, tugging at his arm. "You must ask her for the next dance or she may never be happy again."

The exaggeration lightened Dan's spirits for only a moment. "I don't know many dances."

"Can you waltz? Most of the dances are waltzes."

"I can waltz—well enough." Not so well, but he should be able to avoid treading on Charlotte's feet.

"Then get ready and go ask her! They finished the set."

As Clive escorted Charlotte from the dance floor, Dan squared his shoulders, coughed, and stepped forward. "Miss Charlotte."

She glanced his way, her eyes widened, and she stopped short. "Dan!"

Another young man moved in to address her. "Miss Charlotte, may I—"

She brushed past him without heed and reached to take Dan's hand. "However did you get away? Father said you must be terribly busy tonight and I shouldn't expect to see you."

"Joe offered to spell me for a time. I—I—Will you dance with me?"

Her face turned pink. "I shall be honored to dance with you, Mr. Jackson."

The orchestra struck the first few notes of a waltz, and Charlotte led Dan to the floor. His boots suddenly felt two sizes too large, and sweat broke out on his forehead. Charlotte placed her hand on his shoulder. He gently laid his callused hand on her little waist, clutched her other hand, and swallowed hard. Would he even be able to move his feet?

Charlotte followed her partner's competent lead, amazed at how light he was on his feet. He never stepped near her slippers. They floated over the floor, and her skirt bobbed and swayed to the rhythm.

"Will it suffice?"

She blinked. "Will what suffice?"

"My face. You've stared at it these five minutes without speaking a word. I hoped you might have come to a conclusion." He smiled. "I find yours most pleasing to behold."

"You must know how handsome you are," she said faintly. "I imagine many women have told you so."

His eyes widened. "But for my grandmother, you are the first."

"Surely not!" She slid her hand higher on his shoulder, then back into its proper position. "How old are you?"

"Twenty-four."

The orchestra concluded the waltz with an instrumental flourish, and the dancers slowly emptied the floor. "Dance with me again?" Charlotte asked, then blushed at her own boldness.

"I'll dance with no other," he said quietly, standing close. Somewhere within the folds of her skirt, he still held her hand. Charlotte moved her fingers, and he linked his through them.

People brushed past on both sides, but she paid them no heed. Dan held her full attention. What was he thinking as he gazed so deeply into her eyes? Dared she hope he might ask her father for her hand? But what real use would she be to him in his ministry, a spoiled country girl?

I could do it, Dan. She gently squeezed his hand and leaned closer. *I could make any shack into a home, and I would love my life if you were always in it. Dear God, please let him love me!*

The strength of her longing caught her by surprise. For Dan she would do anything, give anything, only to have him near.

Now his gaze questioned her as if to inquire: *But would your affection last through fire and ice and deprivation? Could you, a delicate flower, thrive in my chosen field?*

"I am strong, Dan. I survived many childhood illnesses, and I can work hard." She spoke her thoughts aloud.

He answered in kind. "It would be harder than you think."

"I enjoy a challenge."

His expression softened. "I know. You're a stubborn little creature."

Strong hands caught them both by the arms and shoved them two steps to one side. Startled and angry, Charlotte tried to jerk out of Clive's grasp, but he laughed and pointed up. "Now you're in the right spot. Kiss her, Jackson! She wants you to."

Dan looked up at the mistletoe kissing ball, then lowered his gaze and sought Charlotte's. She smiled and gave him a tiny nod. To the cheers of a surrounding crowd, Dan kissed her gently. At the touch of his lips on hers, Charlotte lost all doubt.

"Pick a berry, Dan," Eleanor said, laughing and bright for once. "One berry for every kiss."

He reached up to pluck a mistletoe berry from the ball, but two fell into his hand. "I best pay for that with another kiss," he said. This time Charlotte rose on her toes and kissed him back.

Whistles and cheers rewarded them.

Charlotte pulled Dan's head down and spoke into his ear. "Now this is truly a right, proper Christmas—the most joyful ever—because God planned it for us."

Chapter 9

Dan stepped back to admire his handiwork. A coat of whitewash brightened the humble cottage until it fairly sparkled in the spring sunshine. Mrs. Colburn's and Charlotte's hard work in the garden, planting shrubs and roses and flowers, also gave it the look of home. A honeymoon cottage, he thought with an irrepressible smile.

No longer drafty, free of mice thanks to Humphrey, brightened by colorful blooms, and furnished with an assortment of pieces donated by Charlotte's relatives and the Cuttlesworths, the cottage filled its position alongside the inn's stables with pride.

Throughout the winter and well into spring, the rector had taught Dan and counseled the young couple. Their courtship had progressed largely under the watchful eye of Mrs. Colburn.

Dan intended to continue his scriptural training for at least another year before he and Charlotte moved to Birmingham. He wanted to purchase a comfortable house in the city for his wife, which meant he must continue to work and save every penny. Already he owned a dogcart and a venerable, but healthy, Cleveland bay gelding. Charlotte loved to drive the modest vehicle on country picnics with Dan and her sisters.

The young couple would probably always be obliged to economize, but Dan had long since realized that his fiancée thrived in challenging circumstances. God had provided him with the ideal missionary's wife.

"So the wedding be this night, eh?"

Recognizing that deep voice, Dan slowly turned. "Joe?"

The burly giant grinned affably. "Reckon 'twere Providence brought ye to town that winter's night?"

"I know He did. And He prompted you to send me to the rectory. But, Joe, when did you get back in town? I've mentioned you to several people, including the rector, but no one seems to know you. I had assumed you were sexton at the church, but Charlotte tells me they have none at present."

"I'm here and there, lad. Hither and yon. Ye'll likely not see me again soon, but I'll ne'er forget you and your lovely bride. The Lord will bless ye with long and fruitful years of ministry together. Sorrows, alas, will come, but ye'll carry few regrets. Generations to come will rise up to call ye blessed, and ye'll dandle your grandbabies on your knee."

Dan nodded slowly and removed his cap. "As the Lord wills."

Joe reached over the gate to clap Dan's shoulder with his beefy hand, then walked on down the village street. Dan stared after him. A tingle ran up his spine. Joe turned a corner and was gone.

Feeling pressure on his ankle, Dan looked down. Humphrey twined between his boots. "What are you doing outside, cat? A carriage will run you over, or a dog will swallow you whole."

Humphrey, still a leggy kitten, trotted back to the house and waited for Dan to open the door. "You're right. I'd best wash and dress for the wedding. I'll wear my best suit—black and white like yours."

Church bells rang in celebration over Little Brigham. Children frolicked and shouted in the streets as the wedding party streamed from the church doors. Charlotte clung to her new husband's arm beneath a shower of flowers.

Eleanor ran up to give her a kiss. "You'll be happy, Char. I know you will."

Priscilla and Drusilla nearly strangled Dan with hugs. He squeezed them both and gave them matching kisses. "I love my little sisters."

The twins transferred their hugs to Charlotte. "You got the best husband ever," Priscilla said with confidence. "Treat him nice."

"And Humphrey, too," Drusilla added. "We'll feed him every day while you're away. But try not to stay away too long!"

Just before the young couple climbed into their waiting carriage, on loan from Mr. Cuttlesworth, Charlotte's parents claimed their share of hugs. "May God bless you richly as you enter His service together," the rector said, wiping tears from his eyes with his thumb.

Charlotte's mother clung to her a moment longer, kissed Dan's cheek, and stepped back to wave.

Dan climbed to his seat, then threw handfuls of coins into the air.

Children squealed and pounced, including the twins. Priscilla's piercing cries of triumph rose above the rest.

With a *cluck* and a slap of reins, Dan started the pair off at a trot. Charlotte turned back to wave as the carriage bumped over the road.

"Who is that man?"

Dan glanced at her. "What man?"

"The big, black-bearded man standing on the church porch. He waved to us. I don't believe I've ever seen him before."

Dan turned around and returned the stranger's wave. With a shrug and a smile, he drove on. "I really couldn't say. A well-wisher, I suppose."

Charlotte faced forward and leaned on his shoulder. "*Now* will you tell me where we are headed? I know Father made the plans, but no matter how I pleaded he gave me not one hint."

He shifted the reins to one hand and wrapped his arm around her. "We're headed to a comfortable inn in a quiet little town nestled amongst the hills, where none will find us. Your parents honeymooned there twenty-four years ago. We'll have an entire week to ourselves. How does this please you, my love?"

She replied with a fervent embrace.

English Scones

2 cups unbleached flour
1 tablespoon baking powder
2 tablespoons sugar
½ teaspoon salt
6 tablespoons butter
½ cup milk
½ cup dried cranberries and

½ teaspoon lemon extract
(You may subsititue ½ cup
raisins and ½ teaspoon
almond extract)
1 egg, lightly beaten
Sugar

Mix first four ingredients. Cut in butter until mixture resembles corn-meal. Add milk until dough clings together and is a bit sticky—add more milk if necessary, 1 tablespoon at a time. Add desired fruit and extract. Turn the dough onto a floured surface and pat until about 1½ inches thick. Either cut into wedges or use a biscuit cutter to cut circles. Handle as little as possible. Place scones on ungreased cookie sheet—don't allow them to touch each other. Brush with egg, then sprinkle tops with sugar. Bake at 425° for about 15 minutes or until light brown. Serve with preserves or jam and Mock Devonshire Cream

Mock Devonshire Cream:
2 tablespoons powdered sugar
1 (8 ounce) package cream

cheese, softened
½ cup sour cream

Stir sugar into cream cheese. Fold in sour cream and blend. Makes 1½ cups.

Jill Stengl is the author of numerous romance novels including Inspirational Reader's Choice Awardand Carol Award-winning *Faithful Traitor*, and full length historical *Until That Distant Day*. She lives with her husband in the beautiful North woods of Wisconsin, where she enjoys spoiling her three cats, teaching high school literature classes, playing keyboard for her church family, and sipping coffee on the deck as she brainstorms for her next novel.

Mercy Mild

by Gina Welborn

Dedication

For my precious girls—Jerah, Rhyinn, and Niley. You are my Polly and Irena, and I hope you see in them little glimpses of yourselves.

*Let us therefore come boldly unto the throne of grace,
that we may obtain mercy, and find grace to help in time of need.*
Hebrews 4:16

Chapter 1

Schooley's Mountain, New Jersey
December 22, 1868

The home of eccentric Essie Hasenclever was *not* an option for the child.

As the stagecoach rocked and rolled up the Washington Turnpike, Deputy Sheriff Ezekiel Norcross winked at the three boys on the opposite bench, earning a smile in return. He then tapped the nose of little Irena next to him. She glanced away from the badge on his lapel long enough to exchange a grin.

On the other side of Irena, Polly Reid drummed her boot on the coach floor. Her troubled gaze focused on the gold streaks in the sky created by the setting sun. The nine-year-old urchin's shoulder-length blond ringlets hung loose under a dark blue glengarry with a red torrie on top and pink ribbons added to the red ones hanging down the back. Instead of being steeply angled atop her head like a Scotsman would wear it, the boat-like "bonnet" rested level on her head and low enough to reach her eyebrows. How it came in her possession, Polly wouldn't say. Nor did she have even a hint of a Scottish burr.

The coach hit a bump in the road, and the children bounced on their seats. The boys laughed, and Irena giggled.

Polly uttered an elongated "ugh."

"How much further, Mr. Norcross?" she asked for the eighth time—and he was counting—since they passed Chester, five miles back.

"All the way up the mountain ridge," he answered, even though in a quarter mile they'd be at their journey's end.

Polly groaned. Her foot-tapping resumed.

Zeke smiled yet didn't tell her he was only teasing.

Unlike the other children whom he'd had to coax responses from, Polly had jabbered freely during the three-hour ride to the orphans' new parents and new life. Until now. The closer they came to their destination the more agitated she'd grown. Her lips pursed tight, hands clenched together and twisting.

Not that he faulted her.

Despite his external calm, his stomach was doing its own inner handwringing. No matter how persistent Essie Hasenclever was—and he fully expected the aged woman to be—in offering to care for Polly, he refused to allow it to happen. His duty as a Morris County deputy, and as a man of God, demanded he protect all under his wings.

Especially widows and orphans.

The court had charged him to escort these orphans to the potluck dinner at the German Valley Inn. Not to claim them for himself. Since the war ended, he'd dreamed of coming home to a passel of children. The boys as towheaded as he. The girls with dark brunette locks like their beautiful mother. Lately, every time he saw Marianne Plum, he'd think the reasons he had for not courting the reserved widow weren't worthwhile reasons at all.

He gave his head a shake.

No sense fantasizing about a life he could never have.

"Stop!" Polly stood and banged on the ceiling. She leaned out the window and yelled to the driver, "Sir, I must attend to the necessary. If you don't stop immediately, I will—"

"Whoa!" came from the driver amid the rattling and squeaks as the carriage slowed.

Before it came to a complete stop, Polly yanked open a door, scrambled down the steps, then darted into the woods.

James deRoses and the Adams twins looked beseechingly at Zeke.

"Do you three need *necessary attending* also?"

They nodded vigorously.

Zeke opened the door on his side of the carriage. "Get on with your business." As they scrambled out, he looked down at little Irena Barimore. "And you, sweetheart?"

She nodded.

Holding her close, he climbed out and walked to the side of the forested road to where Polly had disappeared. If she'd been able to wait a few minutes longer, they'd have been at the Inn just around the curve in the road.

"Polly," he yelled, "I need you to finish up and come help Irena."

"Might be a minute!"

"Better hurry. Bobcats live in these woods, and I can't shoot what I don't see."

"Really?"

"Really."

"Deputy Norcross?" the driver called out. "I am already behind schedule. Folks are waiting to be picked up at the Inn, and the Heath House will pay extra for this delivery if I get it there before seven."

Zeke removed his watch from the pocket of his red plaid vest, the metal warm against his palm. Nearly a quarter to six. They needed to hurry before the valley was consumed by darkness. His black wool suit suited him well during the day, but once the sun set. . . He wasn't any more dressed for freezing temperatures than the children were.

"Go on," he ordered, sliding his watch back in his pocket. "Leave the children's luggage in the Inn's coatroom."

The driver tipped his hat. With a flick of his wrists, the horses resumed their path to the last stage stop before heading up Schooley's Mountain.

Zeke patiently waited for the children to return. Instead of a ten-foot walk off the stage and into the Inn, now they'd have a hundred-yard one. Could be worse, he reasoned, with the temperature in the forties (or lower), instead of the pleasant upper fifties and no wind. He presumed all the children in the Highlands of New Jersey were praying for a white Christmas three days from now. While he'd known Polly Reid all of three hours, he *knew* she would soon start praying for snow, too, if she hadn't begun already.

"Sorry about that," Polly said, grinning broadly as her boots crunched the fallen leaves. "Ma says sharing your need to attend the necessary isn't polite, and I tried not to, but I figured it's better to spew your words than things that are not proper to mention."

Proper or not, she had him there.

She took Irena from Zeke, who pressed his lips together to keep from laughing.

"I'll take Irena," Polly said. "We will be back shortly."

Then they were gone, into the woods.

⟡

The violin quartet played. The people in the hall chatted. And Marianne Plum stopped shifting the order of the food on the serving table to look to the open double-door entrance to the Inn's dining hall. She fanned her neck with both hands.

He was going to be late.

True, the clock had yet to strike six, the time the potluck was to begin, and no one else seemed bothered that the guests of honor had yet to arrive. But she knew Ezekiel. He was either early or late, never on time, and never consistently one or the other.

Marianne placed her palm on the bodice of her blue silk gown. Her heart raced, and she felt out of breath and a bit damp, which was either from the heat from the bodies filling the hall or in expectation of Ezekiel's arrival. Likely the heat. After all, she and Ezekiel had spoken just a week ago when she had been in the General Store buying mineral water, and he had stopped in for a bottle, too. There had been no way he could have known she was there. Yet, they were there. Together. Unplanned.

Warmth swept underneath her skin.

"Stage!" someone yelled.

She turned to her friend, Ruth Schroeder, who was standing next to her and holding an apple pie that smelled more of cinnamon than apples.

"Oh dear," Ruth muttered. "Why am I so nervous?"

"You are to meet the child you and Lemuel are adopting." Marianne took the pie from Ruth and gave her a sympathetic grin. "Your life is about to change. Go wait with Lemuel."

"Should I?"

"Yes."

Ruth's gaze focused longingly where her husband stood at the dining hall's entrance, where Ezekiel and the orphans would soon appear. Yet she didn't move.

Surprised at her friend's uncharacteristic hesitancy, Marianne walked to the end of the serving table. She placed the pie on the table then noticed the trembling of her own hands. *She* wasn't adopting a child. Her life wasn't about to change, so she had no cause to be nervous or expectant or out of breath from anticipation. Yet she was.

And the curiosity of it all sent her fleeing into the kitchen for serving spoons.

As the rocks crunched under his polished-to-a-shine low boots, Zeke glanced over his shoulder. The orphans trailed him like ducklings around the curve of the desolate Washington Turnpike. At the back of the line, Polly looked at him with a crooked smile and a hop to her step. While the hem of her pink calico gown hung uneven midcalf, her white socks were as soiled as Irena's bonnet, and the red cashmere shawl wrapped around her twice clearly was one made for a woman not a child, Polly still bore an aplomb he found captivating.

"Mr. Norcross," she prompted, "how much further?"

Ahead was their destination—the German Valley Inn, a white-framed three-story building with steam rising from chimneys and music from a violin quartet filtering from the open windows. A dozen or so rocking chairs sat unoccupied on the wraparound porch. When he'd been a child, the black shutters that framed the windows reminded him of eyes warning, *God is watching*.

Which was why he had never misbehaved near the German Valley Inn, but once he'd made it up the mountain. . .

Every summer of his childhood, his family had left their home in Camden and come to Schooley's Mountain for the "magical" spring waters. After earning a degree from Rutgers, he'd journeyed out West and ended up scouting. Then came the war, and more traveling. For the past couple of years, he had been living in the county seat of Morristown, and yet Schooley's Mountain, with its businesses and homes nestled between the trees, would always be the place he considered home.

Tipping his bowler hat back an inch, Zeke schooled his grin, turned in a circle, and looked around as if he were a new arrival to the area, even though he'd been born on the second floor of Belmont Hall.

"Uh, children, where was it we were headed?" he asked, pretending to be lost.

A small hand gripped his fingers. He looked down at little Irena Barimore chewing on the end of one of her chestnut braids and smiling up at him with all the trust a four-year-old could give. An impressive feat, considering she appeared ready to fall asleep at any moment.

His chest tightened.

If he were her adoptive father, for Christmas he would give her a doll and paints and a new white bonnet.

He felt another grip on his other hand.

"Yes?" he said, looking from Irena to Polly.

"You don't remember?"

He gave Polly his best panicked look. "You still have the map, right?"

As he expected, Polly eyed him as if he were trying to sell her an elixir to cure all ills. "Sir, you never gave me a map. You have to know where we are going. Don't you live here?"

"I think I live in Morristown."

"You aren't sure?"

"I am getting old," he answered with a shrug. "They say your memory is the first to go." Considering how often he awoke at night from dreams of the war, he rather wished his memory would start to go.

Polly's nose scrunched. "How old are you?"

"Thirty-seven come spring."

Her blue eyes widened. "That *is* old."

Restraining his chuckle, he released her hand then scooped little Irena up in his arms. "Do *you* remember where I am supposed to take you?"

Irena placed the tip of her finger in the cleft of his chin. Her gray-green eyes looked at him adoringly. "I go home with you," she said in that soft-spoken voice of hers that sounded like a loud whisper.

He placed a kiss on her nose. "I would take you home with me, sweetheart, but God has a new family prepared for you. Let's go meet them."

They hadn't traversed another ten yards when Zeke heard a timid question.

"What if they hate us?"

Chapter 2

Zeke wasn't sure which Adams twin had spoken, so he stopped and turned to face the children. Any other time he would have continued jesting, but with the six-year-old twins and seven-year-old James deRoses looking as exhausted as Irena, he knew he needed to allay their fears.

"Remember in the stage what I read to you? The information about your new families?" While he hadn't shared who was going to which parents, he'd at least given names.

James nodded.

The twins looked ready to cry.

Polly stepped between them and gripped their hands. "Sir, what if our new parents aren't good people?"

Zeke knew almost everyone in Morris County. Those he considered good people and those he wouldn't give even a snake to. Under orders of the orphans' court, he'd investigated all the adoption applicants. But a crazy feeling told him that if he couldn't convince Polly of the goodness of their new parents, she'd grab the twins and run.

"I know them. Will you trust my judgment?"

"People lie," one twin said.

"People die," the other added.

James nodded again.

Still clutching Irena, who was now gently snoring, Zeke knelt in front of the children. He touched the top of James's black hair. "Mr. deRoses, who is the Father of the fatherless?"

James whispered, "God."

"That is right." Zeke moved his hand to the top button of the boy's frayed tweed coat, over a heart that he could feel beating against his palm. "Who will never leave or forsake you?"

"God," the twins and Polly answered in unison.

"Correct. God has never left me, so I know He will never leave you."

Polly and the twins smiled.

James didn't. "How do you know?"

"Because I am fatherless, too."

James stepped forward, wrapping his arms around Zeke. Immediately Polly and the twins followed suit.

"I trust you," one of the children whispered. Which one didn't matter.

Zeke closed his eyes, aware of the intense ache in his chest. He no longer grieved for his father or stepfather, or how he'd been unable to earn their approval in their lifetimes. God had healed those wounds. Yet in the last three hours, a crucible of emotions had seized him. He felt ripped asunder. On the tip of his tongue was the promise that he would take these orphans home with him, that he would be their father, that he would never leave or forsake them.

But they also needed a mother, and he had no wife.

Unless he could have Marianne Plum, he would do without a wife. But even if he had her, he would still have to do without the only other thing he desperately wanted this side of eternity—children. Marianne simply didn't want any.

The irony of it all.

With tightness in his voice, Zeke said, "Let's get on inside."

He led them up the Inn's front steps, past delighted-to-see-them townsfolk milling about the foyer, to the lavatory where they cleaned up, then to the spacious dining hall brimming with a violin quartet and more people than he'd ever seen in one place since the last Independence Day celebration. He guessed upward of two hundred, all applauding their arrival. A row of chairs circled the white wood-paneled room—added seating needed for those unable to find a seat at one of the round cloth-draped tables. A cloud of smoke floated in the far corner of the room where several prestigious men in the county, including Judge Fancer, the man whom he needed to speak to about Polly, stood enjoying their cigars near two open windows.

While those around him took turns welcoming the children, Zeke's gaze sought for and found the lovely brunette near the serving table. He knew her well enough to know that she was making sure the silverware in the bowls and on the platters was in a uniform pattern.

Every so often she would adjust one. Her brow furrowed enough to deepen a worry line in her forehead.

Her head tilted, her lips pursed ever so gently as, he knew, she counted the number of serving pieces on the table. As many as were out would be the exact number returned. Marianne would ensure it. No one valued order like Marianne Plum. He loved her for it. He loved her. And that mole near the upper right side of her mouth—

He couldn't breathe.

He wanted. . . . Well, he wanted her to resume wearing that atrocious black crepe mourning veil so he'd feel less tempted to kiss her.

A year after her husband's death, Marianne had discarded her widow's weeds. Tonight, she wore a light blue gown. She could afford new dresses, yet she seemed content with the older ones. Content with her lot in life. That was the only reason Zeke could figure why none of the bachelors in the township had tried courting her after her year of mourning ended. It was partly why he hadn't.

No one else could possibly know what Henry Plum had shared with Zeke about his wife.

Zeke felt his cheek twitch.

Henry Archibald Plum.

Not the only enlistee in Company K of the 7th New Jersey who'd died during the war, but the only one he'd grown close enough to during their three years of soldiering together to consider a brother. As always, on Marianne's bodice, pinned over her heart, was a silver locket holding a strand of Henry's hair.

Marianne abruptly looked up from the table of food, her brown-eyed gaze meeting his unwavering one. A faint smile played across her lips, as if to say, *Good to see you are well.*

His heart leapt in his chest.

Zeke did his best to match her smile with an unaffected yet charming one that said *likewise.*

"I hear your heart breathing," Irena whispered.

"Sweetheart, that's my lungs taking in air."

She tilted her head to look at him. Her nose touched his cheek, nuzzling him. "Your lungs sound happy."

Polly laughed and turned away from the person who'd been

shaking her hand. "That's because he's looking at—"

"Evening, Norcross."

Zeke looked to the shorter yet brawnier man standing on his right, near the dining hall's entrance. Last time Lemuel Schroeder hugged him, Zeke had felt his spine pop in three places. His father, Rory, was just as exuberant with his welcomes.

"Evening," he answered with a nod. "You just arrive?"

When Lemuel grinned, the tips of his cheeks raised his spectacles. "Been standing here this whole time, but you never noticed." His knowing gaze momentarily shifted in the direction of Marianne.

Zeke uttered a quick prayer of thanks that he wasn't one to blush.

Lemuel stepped close to Zeke and whispered, "Ruth fears our child won't like her. Would you say something to ease her nerves?"

Zeke gave a slight nod, more to confirm he heard what Lemuel had said than to agree. Ruth needed words of comfort from her husband, not him. But knowing Ruth Schroeder as he did, the lovely redhead wouldn't stop helping Marianne in the kitchen long enough for anyone to offer encouragement.

Lemuel turned his attention upon the children. "Who do we have here?"

Polly stepped forward, smiling. "Sir, I'm Miss Polly Reid." She exuberantly shook Lemuel's hand then introduced the other children. With a raised brow, she remarked, "Your name sounds familiar."

"I have the honor of becoming the father to one of you. Or two of you."

The Adams twins looked at each other and shared front-tooth-missing grins.

Zeke held back confessing that they were going to Lemuel and his new bride. Some Christmas gifts ought to be surprises.

Lemuel looked back to Zeke. "We were told there were four orphans. Who gets the fifth one?"

Zeke didn't have to glance at Polly to know she had tensed up. "Christmas came early this year, and someone has been very good."

"Deputy Norcross!" Mrs. Cottrell barked above the noise in the dining hall. The woman whose black gown emphasized the abundant gray in her hair pushed through the crowd with one hand, holding onto her husband's arm with the other. "It is about time you arrived!"

By the bitter edge in her words, Zeke knew she hadn't yet forgiven him for not choosing her to be an adoptive mother. Eliminating her hadn't been his choice, or Judge Fancer's. It had been her husband's. Zeke would go to his grave withholding that information from Mrs. Cottrell.

Everyone looked his way, and the hall quickly quieted.

Across the room, Marianne pointed their way, spoke to pale-faced Ruth Schroeder, then gave her friend a nudge forward. Ruth started working her way through the crowd.

"Children," he whispered, feeling the warmth of the room, "stay close to me now."

Mrs. Cottrell and her husband came to a halt in front of him.

"You poor, *poor* children," Mrs. Cottrell said, her scowl deepening the frown lines on her face. "I cannot believe he allowed the stage to desert you a mile back down the turnpike."

"We only had to walk around the curve," Polly clarified.

"Child, that is no way to speak to your—"

"Lavina," her husband warned.

Mrs. Cottrell fell silent. She clenched her hands together in front of her.

"Norcross, nice to see you." George Cottrell shook Zeke's hand.

While the reverend and his wife were in their early forties, only Cottrell looked it. Zeke suspected their son's death at Gettysburg had changed Mrs. Cottrell for the worse.

As soon as Cottrell released Zeke's hand, Polly secured it in hers. Zeke gave her fingers a reassuring squeeze.

To Cottrell, he said, "Sir, the children and I are ready to begin whenever you are."

Reverend Cottrell nodded. He withdrew a paper from the inner pocket of his coat. Zeke presumed it was the telegram he himself had sent moments before meeting the children at the rail station, asking the reverend to begin praying for each child by name.

Polly was not on the list.

Before Zeke could ask Cottrell to add Polly's name to the paper, Ruth stopped next to her husband.

"Say hello," Lemuel whispered.

Her mouth opened, yet she said nothing.

Mrs. Cottrell stepped forward and gripped Polly's shawl. "Dearie, let me take this."

"All right," Polly said, "but I'll keep my hat."

Mrs. Cottrell gasped. "Certainly not! That appalling thing—"

"Looks pretty on you," finished Lemuel.

Before Polly could give Mrs. Cottrell her shawl, Zeke took it from her. He handed the soft cashmere to Ruth then gave her his bowler hat and Irena's bonnet. "Would you put these in the coatroom for us?"

"I should—" Her gaze shifted to Mrs. Cottrell then the children then back to Zeke.

"All is well." He hoped she understood his implied *trust me*.

"Darling, I'll come with you," Lemuel offered.

"No, Lemuel, please stay with the children." In a voice Zeke barely heard, Ruth added, "I know you want to."

Zeke grabbed Lemuel's arm. "Corporal, I order you to escort Mrs. Schroeder to the coatroom and stay there as long as necessary to ensure the children's belongings are safe and secure from enemy hands." *Go ease her nerves.* He waited until understanding dawned in Lemuel's eyes then released his hold.

Lemuel clicked his heels together and saluted. "As you command, sir!"

Once the Schroeders left the dining hall, the ever-watchful Widow Decker claimed the spot next to Zeke that Lemuel had vacated. Zeke's mother's gray-blond hair had an additional streak of white at the temple, something new since he had seen her on Thanksgiving Day. Like Marianne, she wore a light blue gown, which, he knew, she'd debated returning home and changing upon seeing what Marianne was wearing. The two women were more alike than either would admit.

When his mother didn't speak, Zeke focused on Reverend Cottrell who, in that booming seminary voice of his, was explaining the first order of business to the crowd.

"Following the explanation of events for the evening, Justice of the Peace Rorick will pray for the meal. According to Mrs. Plum, the food is ready."

While Cottrell rambled about seating (the lack of it, to be precise), Mother leaned close, her shoulder against the sleeve of Zeke's frock coat. "It is a wretched day when a woman turns fifty-five and the only visitor she receives is her reticent neighbor."

"My apologies," he whispered back. "Sheriff Briant had me delivering warrants last week."

Irena touched the older woman's cheek. "Pretty."

"Thank you, sweetie," Mother softly cooed in a voice he knew was sincere. She adored children as much as he did. Her bejeweled hand cupped Irena's jaw. "You are as enchanting as spring's first flower. What I would give to have a granddaughter like you." Without looking away from Irena, she as-charmingly cooed to Zeke, "Did you not explain to Briant what day it was?"

"He did not need me to tell him it was Friday."

She gave him a look of mild disdain, yet she cradled Irena's hand in hers.

Zeke restrained his smile. "I'm confident your neighbor's actions were intended to be gracious."

"Gracious? She gave me pickled radishes and her blue-ribbon preserves."

"You must have felt like a prizewinner." He felt no remorse over how his comment increased the irritation in her expression. It'd take a miracle to convince his mother of the lack of vileness in Marianne Plum.

"I abhor radishes, and blueberries give me hives." Her eyes narrowed to slits. "Ezekiel, I will have you know that woman wishes ill upon me."

"Would you have me arrest her? Cart her off to Morristown?" A tempting thought.

"I would have you—"

"Shhh," came from Mrs. Cottrell.

Zeke looked away from his mother to the good reverend.

"And please remember," Cottrell was saying, "to collect your dishes after the meal because. . ."

Zeke's attention faded from the man speaking and back to his mother. One of these days he'd bring about reconciliation between Widows Decker and Plum. To say anything would first require he have a heart-to-heart with his mother, something easy to avoid now that their relationship was the best it had been in years. He couldn't lose that. He had hurt her enough during his misbehaving childhood and the almost decade he'd spent out West when he never sent word of where he was or what he was doing.

Reverend Cottrell cleared his throat and moved on to the next order of business.

"Eating will commence following the announcements and the opening prayer." He momentarily glanced at the dining hall entrance. "Since the Schroeders haven't returned, let's go ahead and have the two other adopting couples go to the front of the line. Mr. Schroeder, you get on up there, too."

The crowd parted for the Kains, Sharpensteins, and a reluctant Rory Schroeder, who everyone in the hall knew preferred to let others go before him.

"Once the adoptive parents have their food and are seated, Deputy Norcross will introduce Irena Barimore, James deRoses, and William and Phillip Adams to their new parents. The ladies from the German Valley Missions Society will distribute gifts that have been contributed in support of the adoptive families. Thank you to those who donated. If you wish to send potluck leftovers home with adoptive families, let Mrs. Plum know." Cottrell looked around the room. "Benediction will be offered by the honorable Judge Fancer. Finally, don't forget the Christmas Day dedication of our war memorial! Sergeant Ezekiel Norcross of Company K of the 7th New Jersey Volunteer Infantry will be speaking."

While the crowd broke out into applause, Zeke froze. Internally, he winced at the reminder of the speech he had been drafted into giving. The very same speech he kept waking in night sweats about. He could think of at least a handful of veterans more deserving of the honor.

Justice of the Peace Rorick waited until the applause died down before offering the prayer.

Unlike Polly, James, and the twins, who closed their eyes and bowed their heads, Irena stared straight at Zeke. She placed her hands on his bristled cheeks then nuzzled her nose against his. She smiled, he smiled, and she rested her head on his shoulder and fingered his badge.

Zeke looked across the room to where Marianne stood.

Like him, her head wasn't bowed in prayer.

Unlike him. . .she wasn't smiling.

Chapter 3

"A men" resounded throughout the hall, and people began moving to the serving tables. Yet Zeke kept his attention on Marianne. He tried not to make presumptions on why—*or delight in the fact that*—she was watching him.

He gave her a look hoping to imply *what is it?*

She shook her head and turned her attention to the table of food.

They had a connection. He felt it. She had to have felt it, too, so why did she retreat every time he made the smallest step in pursuit?

Polly tugged on Zeke's hand. "Sir, can we go eat?"

"Not yet."

He wanted to take them to supper as much as he wanted to chase after Marianne to see what plagued her, but he needed to inform Judge Fancer of Polly's arrival.

Looking around the hall to find the judge, Zeke noticed Essie Hasenclever limp over next to Mrs. Cottrell. The at-least-three-score woman spoke to Mrs. Cottrell, yet her greedy gaze was upon the children. If he placed Miss Hasenclever in a fairytale, she would never be on the side of the beautiful, tragic princess. He wouldn't say she was evil. Neither would he say she was of the soundest mind. She was merely wealthy enough to be allowed to go her way.

Zeke turned to his mother. "Would you see that the children's plates are filled?"

"I would think *you* would want—" Her confused gaze shifted in the direction of his. "Certainly!" She scooped Irena out of his arms and into hers, then, smiling, she offered an outstretched hand to the Adams twins. "Shall we?"

The four older children looked to Zeke.

"Stay together," he ordered. "This nice lady will help you put more vegetables on your plate than you will eat in a year."

"But what about you?" Polly asked, still clinging to Zeke's hand.

"I do not eat vegetables. Ever," he said matter-of-factly. "Too vegetable-y."

"Children, ignore him," his mother chided, yet her blue eyes twinkled with amusement.

Zeke motioned them toward the serving tables. "I'll introduce you to your new parents in a few minutes."

"But—" Polly broke off. She then drew in a breath and pointed at Reverend Cottrell. "Mr. Norcross, that man didn't pray for me like he did for Irena, James, and the twins. He mentioned three sets of adopting parents, and you said the twins would stay together." She patted her chest. "I'm number five. No one was expecting me, were they?"

Zeke's throat tightened. How was he to answer her? Even he hadn't known she was coming, and he was under the jurisdiction of the orphans' court. Until he found the distant cousins of hers that supposedly lived over in Pleasant Grove, he had been ordered not to say anything to her.

"I told you, Christmas has come early for someone who's been very good."

Her eyes watered up. "I am not a present, sir. I'm a person."

"I know, sweetheart. You will have a home *and* a family. I promise."

"But I don't have a family to go home with tonight."

"What is this?!" Mrs. Cottrell stepped forward, her face flushed.

Essie Hasenclever followed step and practically yelled, "That orphan said she has no home to go to tonight."

The two women placed their hands on the twins' shoulders. The boys tried to jerk free, but Mrs. Cottrell and Miss Hasenclever held firm. The twins immediately began crying.

In a heartbeat, Polly moved from Zeke's side, frantically slapping at the women's hands. "Let them go! I said *I* have no home. They do!" Polly freed the boys then shoved them behind her back. They huddled together in front of Sarah Howe Norcross Decker, who had a look in her eyes Zeke hadn't seen since he'd been unfairly (albeit logically) blamed for using the billiards sticks at Heath House as javelins on the front lawn.

With Irena clinging to her neck, his mother, Polly, and James formed a protective circle around the twins. According to their records, the boys had been at the Soldiers' Orphanage in Richmond for two years, Irena a year, and Polly five months.

Reverend Cottrell ended his conversation with the men next to him and turned toward Zeke. "Norcross, what is this commotion about?" His question came as the noise in the room decreased.

"We have an extra orphan," Mrs. Cottrell announced for all to hear.

"An extra orphan?"

Recognizing the gravelly voice, Zeke stayed silent and waited for Judge Fancer to push through the crowd. Fancer stopped next to Mrs. Decker and the children.

Removing the cigar from his mouth, Fancer's gaze settled on Zeke. "Well?"

"We have an extra orphan," Mrs. Cottrell repeated before Zeke could speak. "She needs a home. I will take her."

"No, I will," Essie Hasenclever offered. "My house has more room than yours."

Judge Fancer twisted his fingers around his cigar. "Norcross, I knew of four orphans coming to this county. Why am I learning about a fifth only now?"

From his inner coat pocket, Zeke removed the papers he had been given on each child, as well as the ones on the adoptive parents Judge Fancer had chosen for them upon Zeke's recommendations. Among the papers was a letter from the orphanage's director detailing everything he had told Zeke on the train platform while the children and the director's wife had eaten their lunch inside the rail station.

He unfolded the letter and handed it to Judge Fancer. "Your honor, what you need to know is right here."

He waited as the judge read about how an orphan's investigator for the Commonwealth of Virginia discovered that Polly's mother had cousins in Washington, DC. The man traced their travels after the war to the Highlands of New Jersey. He then contacted the Morris County Sheriff's Department about a Victor and Eliza Ralston living in the county. Recent tax records placed them in Pleasant Grove. The orphanage's director had asked Zeke not to inform Polly of the existence of her cousins perchance they could not be found. Sheriff Briant had agreed.

Yet the director had apparently assumed the cousins would be found, because at the last minute he had added Polly to the train. If the cousins weren't found and no suitable couple came forth to adopt the child, she was to be placed in a state orphanage.

Feeling a hand on his back, Zeke turned his head to see Ruth standing beside him, a renewed confidence in her expression. Lemuel gave Zeke a nod. He acknowledged them both with a tip of his chin.

Judge Fancer scratched his bearded cheek. His gaze shifted to the children, still huddled in front of Zeke's mother.

Zeke looked around the dining hall. He couldn't see the Sharpensteins from Springfield who were to adopt Irena, but James's soon-to-be parents, the Kains from Hackettstown, were holding their food-filled plates at the end of the serving table, near where Marianne stood. All three sets of adoptive parents would graciously offer to care for Polly—*that* he knew with confidence. As long as Miss Essie Hasenclever wasn't chosen, Zeke would be content with whoever was given temporary care.

"Deputy," Judge Fancer said, folding the letter, "how long will it take you to resolve this situation?"

"Two days, sir."

Fancer offered the letter back to Zeke. "What we need is someone to provide Miss Reid a home for the duration of your task."

"I will take her," Essie Hasenclever offered again.

And ensure she spends the next two days scrubbing every inch of your home. Zeke replaced the letter along with the others inside his coat pocket. Until the judge asked for his advice, the law—and his duty as an officer of the court—required he remain impartial.

"Your honor," began Mrs. Cottrell, "I would like—" Her husband wrapped his hand around hers, drawing her attention. He shook his head.

"Your honor," Reverend Cottrell said, "presuming the child will be going to a set of parents in the next two days, would it not be wise to place her in the care of an individual?" He paused. "Someone who would not pin hopes on a permanent relationship. Someone who would have the financial wherewithal to support the child until Deputy Norcross finds a permanent home for her."

"I said I'd take the extra orphan," Essie Hasenclever bellowed. "I've made it sixty-three years without becoming attached to a child. Doubt I will start now."

A few murmurs rose in the crowd.

Although Mrs. Cottrell clearly looked ready to argue a case in her own favor, she stayed silent. Likely because of the continued hold her husband had on her hand.

Judge Fancer nodded at Zeke. "Your thoughts?"

Zeke didn't have to look at his mother to know she'd already grown attached to the children. The home of eccentric Essie Hasenclever was not an option either. Only one person could fit the wise and practical parameters Reverend Cottrell had set *and* be a caregiver that Judge Fancer, not to mention Zeke, would approve.

Only one.

And Zeke was in love with her.

The problem was, Marianne fled *from* children quicker than he fled *to* them. Even though she baked sweets and mended clothing for the orphanages in German Valley, Chester, and Pleasant Grove, she always had her housekeeper's husband make the deliveries.

She will never allow Polly in her home.

Polly would be good for her, he argued, silencing his inner doubts.

Despite—or more aptly, because of—all the unexpected, magnificent, and insanely frustrating emotions he bore for Marianne, Zeke kept his attention focused on the judge.

"Your honor, I recommend the widow Mrs. Henry Plum to be temporary caregiver."

Chapter 4

The attention of those in the dining hall shifted from Deputy Norcross to her—a literal (action if not sound) *whoosh* of heads turning. Marianne's heartbeat increased. She clasped her hands in front of her to keep anyone from noticing them shaking. The moment the discussion turned to providing the child a temporary home, she should have grabbed her shawl and made for the buggies.

Her chest felt like a giant was standing on her.

Take a child into her home?

Her home?

To care—no, to provide care for it?

No. It did not matter if it was for two hours or two days; absolutely she would not do it. Anyone who truly knew her would know that was her answer. Children were messy. Children disrupted the order in a home. Children were needy, noisy, and nuisances.

She shook her head. No.

Yet everyone in the dining hall still looked at her in expectation of a response, as if they hadn't noticed her reaction. Or maybe they had and they couldn't believe she'd say no.

Oh, that rather vexed her.

For twelve years she had lived on Schooley's Mountain. Twelve! The worst bit, of all the people in the community who knew her best—the only one who knew of her past—Ezekiel Norcross should have known better than to recommend her as a temporary caregiver.

"Mrs. Plum," Miss Hasenclever grumbled, "we all know your dislike of children. Tell them you will not take the orphan so we can be about our business finding someone proper and loving like myself to care for her. Instead of someone cold and heartless like you."

Marianne placed a cordial smile on her face, despite the frustration building inside. Agree to care for the child being thrust upon her, or decline the request, the easier decision of the two. Judge Fancer, of course, would insist she give reason for her refusal, whereupon she would have to admit she had no good reason, which would make her look selfish.

She could not share the truthful reason without exposing how inadequate she was to be a mother. The truth that kept Ezekiel from seeing her as something more than a friend.

The truth can set you free.

No, Lord, it would change how they all feel about me.

To save her good name, she had to take the child. Had not Ezekiel confirmed it would be but for two days? For a night or two, she could feign mothering skills. After all, she wasn't being asked to offer love to the child. Her heart wasn't capable of that, anyway.

She drew in a steadying breath.

"I will do it," she said loud enough for all to hear.

"You will?" her neighbor, Widow Decker, said, staring wide-eyed. The little girl she held shifted in her arms to look at Marianne, her head tilting, a smile growing.

The three boys and the older girl smiled as if they accepted Marianne, too. Why that made her feel strangely pleased wasn't something she had time to ponder.

"Certainly I will, Mrs. Decker, presuming Judge Fancer accepts Deputy Norcross's recommendation." Marianne didn't look at her neighbor's son out of fear he would see the hurt—no, anger—she felt toward him at the moment. She'd hoped he cared for her.

If he did care for her, he would not have trapped her in this situation.

Judge Fancer turned to face Marianne, blocking her view of Ezekiel. "Mrs. Plum, are you sure you can do this?"

"Why wouldn't she be?" Ruth Schroeder asked, as a faithful friend would.

Many heads nodded in support of Ruth's question.

Essie Hasenclever shook her head yet stayed silent.

Mrs. Decker, for all her criticisms of Marianne, surprisingly stayed silent, too.

"Then by order of the court," Judge Fancer said, "I appoint Mrs. Henry Plum, widow, as temporary guardian to Miss Polly Reid until

Deputy Ezekiel Norcross secures permanent guardianship in accordance with the dictates of the Soldiers' Orphanage of Richmond, Virginia."

A round of applause followed his announcement.

Before Marianne knew it, enjoyment of the evening resumed. She made herself a plate of food. The tables were all filled, as were the chairs about the dining hall. Determined not to speak to Ezekiel, she found a chair in the kitchen and awaited the introductions of the parents to the children. *Oh, dear Lord, what have I done?*

꧁꧂

Later that evening, when the dining hall was nearly empty—save for Marianne, the newly expanded Schroeders, and Polly Reid—Ruth swept the floor while Marianne washed the tables, likely more times than they needed it. Once the hall was clean, they would all leave for home.

She and Polly would leave for home.

Together.

The two of them. Alone.

True, her housekeepers, Jacob and Charlotte Graff, lived at the Plum house, too, so she and the child wouldn't be completely alone, but the thought did little to ease the tension growing in Marianne's stomach. She'd barely eaten a bite. How could she, knowing what fate awaited her? Two days with a child to care for. She should have said no. She really should have.

Ruth nudged Marianne's shoulder with the end of the broom handle. "She is watching you."

Marianne stopped wiping the table. Polly Reid sat at a table next to Lemuel, who held a sleeping twin. His other newly adopted son sat with Lemuel's father, Rory, talking a mile a minute despite the lateness of the hour. Polly's blue eyes were fixed on Marianne. There had been times throughout the evening when Marianne had felt someone watching her. The first time was Ezekiel right after he arrived with the orphans. Later, during the meal and the distribution of gifts for the orphans and adopting parents, she'd turned to see him staring at her. But he looked away both times.

Hopefully, a response in shame over the quandary he had put her in.

She had noticed the orphan girl staring, too; only at those times, Marianne had been the one to look away. They hadn't spoken a word to each other after their initial introduction, when the other children had met their new parents. Holding the little girl's hand while Reverend Cottrell prayed for a blessing on the children had felt. . .peculiar.

Had there ever been a time when she'd held her own mother's hand? Her memory held no reminders. Her heart held no hope that there had been a time.

With her father, the last time she had held his hand had been the day—

Marianne's fingers tightened around the wet cloth, and she blinked to clear the tears from her eyes. She wasn't going to cry. The past was past. No sense reminiscing.

"I imagine the child is wondering who the strange woman is who has been assigned to care for her," she finally answered then corrected, "to provide care for her."

Ruth stopped sweeping and did her own staring at Marianne. Neither of them had been asked to clean the dining hall. Yet Marianne didn't feel right leaving the room dirty. Besides, she enjoyed cleaning and putting things back in proper order, and Ruth enjoyed helping. What brought them together as friends was their desire to *see a need, meet a need.* That, and the fact that both of their husbands had left for war and later died during the same battle.

Ruth placed her hand on Marianne's arm, stilling her from moving to another table to clean. "Marianne, we need to talk."

"About?"

"I saw you shake your head when Ezekiel first suggested you," she whispered, even though her husband's and new son's laughter echoed about the room. "Why did you change your mind?"

"My reasons are complicated."

"Because of Deputy Norcross?"

How was she to answer? So many of her life's choices in the last year had been influenced by Ezekiel Norcross. He was constantly on her mind, from sunrise to sunset, to the point of distraction. She could still remember the tingle from his hand pressing against the small of her back as they'd climbed the church stairs to attend the Schroeders' wedding. Had that been eight months ago? It felt like yesterday.

She felt her cheeks warming.

"Perhaps," she murmured.

Ruth turned Marianne so that their backs were to the table with the men and the children. "Do you have feelings for him?"

"Perhaps," she muttered again, because she had no inclination to lie. Yet the depth of her feelings scared her too much to admit.

"Does he know how you feel?"

"He has given no indication."

"Men are slow-witted when it comes to deducing a woman's romantic feelings," Ruth said matter-of-factly. "Do you think he feels the same for you?"

Marianne stared absently at the damp cloth she held. "Sometimes I believe he does. Mostly I am unsure."

"You could ask him."

"That would not be proper."

"I know." Ruth sighed. "And there is his mother."

This time Marianne sighed. Despite her attempts to make peace with Mrs. Decker, the woman refused to forgive whatever it was Marianne had done to offend her. And she wouldn't tell Marianne what her offense was, which added to the tension between them. If Ezekiel attempted courtship, his mother would demand he choose between them.

Yet, even if his mother were not a conflict, Marianne had watched as he'd doted on the orphans, and how they'd doted on him. One thing she knew for certain about Ezekiel Norcross: he wanted to be a father. He'd make a wonderful one, too. And she had no yearning to be a mother, and. . .well, that put an end to any possibility.

"Wife," Lemuel called out, "our boys would like to see their new home."

Ruth nodded. To Marianne, she said, "We have room in the wagon for you and Polly."

"Jacob left the buggy for me."

Ruth took a step.

Marianne didn't follow.

"Are you coming?" Ruth asked over her shoulder.

"Oh, Ruth, I can't." Fear weighted her legs to the wooden floor. Feeling the blue eyes of the child still staring at her, Marianne wrapped her fingers around her friend's hand. She pulled Ruth to her. "I have made a grave mistake."

"In agreeing to take Polly?"

"I have no idea how to be a mother."

Ruth smiled softly, giving Marianne's hand a little squeeze. "Oh, Marianne, I know exactly what you feel, because I felt that way earlier until Lemuel reassured me. Do what your mother did and all will be well. You turned out just fine."

Marianne nodded because doing so was the expected response. She released Ruth's hand and started to the serving table to collect her empty dishes. She could be a caregiver. She could do all things through Christ. Yet Ruth's advice brought no abatement to the tension and fear taking root inside. Do what her mother did?

No child should have to endure what her mother had done.

Chapter 5

I like cats." The child swung the basket holding two empty pie tins as they walked down the hallway to the Inn's coatroom. "I've always wanted one for a pet. Do you like cats, Mrs. Plum?"

Moonlight streaming through the heavily curtained hallway windows left shadows on the walls. The wind caused the trees to move and sway and shift, like a person moving. Watching. Waiting.

Marianne swallowed at the tightness in her throat. The Inn had guests. Even though it was midnight, they weren't alone in the building. The shadows weren't anything but trees.

Still, her pulse raced. Why hadn't she left with the Schroeders?

Desperate to distract her mind, Marianne focused on the child's strangely comforting cap, with the fuzzy red ball on the top and pink and red ribbons streaming down the back. Someone in the serving line had mentioned the girl being highly possessive of it. Called it Mr. Toodles, like it was a pet. In all her thirty-two years, Marianne had never had a pet, and none of her neighbors ever had pets either. Even Mrs. Decker.

Marianne nervously fiddled with the silky blue fringe on the hem of her bodice. That she was fearful was ridiculous. No one was in the hall with them; her mind was merely playing tricks. Not to mention, she was the adult. She was the one who was supposed to be fearless and brave. Not someone listening for squeaks, bumps, and screams in the night, like she'd done every day of her childhood.

"Mrs. Plum?" the child prompted. "I asked if you liked cats."

"Yes," she blurted, despite having no idea if she truly liked felines or not.

She knew without a doubt that she disliked the darkness. And shadows. And hearing her heart pound between her ears. Her mouth was dry. Why was it so dry? Had they missed the turn to the coatroom? They should be almost to the front door. *Fear not,* she chided herself.

Be calm for the child's sake. The silence only enhanced her non-calmness. She needed to fill it. Talk about something, anything.

What did one talk about with children?

"Do, uhh, do you like dogs?"

"I love dogs!" The child stopped and blocked Marianne's path. "Do you have a dog? Please say you do. Please, please!"

"No dog." Then feeling a curious rush of sympathy, she added, "I'm sorry, I wish I had one for you to play with. I have never had any kind of pet."

"Really?"

"Really."

The child's sudden smile filled her face. She grabbed Marianne's hand, and they resumed walking. "I used to have a rabbit named Arthur and a hog named Randy, but we had to butcher Randy after. . .well, the war and all. Ma made me eat him, and that made me cry, but he tasted good. I wished he hadn't, because he was my friend. Do you have a rabbit or a hog?"

"She has a goat," a voice whispered.

Marianne bit back her scream before it could leave her mouth.

"Mr. Norcross!" The child dropped the basket and ran to Ezekiel leaning against the Inn's front door.

He caught her up in a hug, yet his bowler hat amazingly stayed perched atop his head. "Surprised to see me, Pollywog?"

"Nope." She wrapped her arms and legs around him. "I knew you wouldn't leave without saying good-bye."

He held her as if she weighed nothing. "You are right in that."

Breathing slowly, Marianne covered her heart and waited until the rapid pounding under her fingers abated to a natural rhythm. She had never been more relieved to see Ezekiel. She scooped up the discarded pie basket and, as she walked to them, noticed a red shawl atop a carpetbag on the floor.

"Evening, Deputy," she said, in her best attempt not to sound pleased upon seeing him.

"Mrs. Plum," Ezekiel answered in a tone that said he was *delighted* to see her.

Which vexed her even more. The man conscripted her into

agreeing to be caregiver to an orphan, almost scared the wits from her, and now was gazing upon her as if she were his everything. If she were less of a lady, she would slap him.

After she kissed him. But they had an audience, and no proper Christian woman kissed a man in public. Nor would Marianne allow passion to dictate her actions.

Ezekiel shifted the child until she was on his back. "Hold on, sweetheart." He then grabbed the shawl and frayed carpetbag from the floor. "Ladies, shall we go?"

"Go where?" the child asked, her arms around his neck.

He opened the door. "Home."

"Home?" Marianne repeated as her heart flipped in joy at the thought he actually meant *their* home.

"I had thought of a moonlight ride to New York City, but since you insist upon home, ma'am, then home it is."

She stepped across the threshold. "You mentioned home first."

"Did I?"

Marianne refused to let his faux innocence charm her. "You needn't have come. Jacob left me the buggy."

"About that. . ." Ezekiel followed her outside then closed the door. "I sent him on home with it." He hurried down the steps to Mrs. Decker's covered buggy at the bottom.

On the tip of her tongue was the question, *Why?* Yet there, in the tenderness of his gaze, was the answer, and her heart flipped. Because he knew how her mother used to leave her tied to the porch at night. He knew her fears of the dark.

The child slid off his back and onto the middle of the bench. Taking the red shawl from him, she wrapped it around her shoulders. "You're funny, Mr. Norcross."

"You're funny, too, Miss Reid." Ezekiel placed the carpetbag at her feet. He then rested an arm on the side of the buggy and looked to Marianne again. "Are you coming? The walk home is all up mountain."

Marianne started down the stairs then halted three steps from the bottom. Could the tenderness in his eyes have meant something more?

"Why are you here?"

He looked at her with eyes as blue and frank as his mother's. "Same reason you are—for Polly."

She shook her head. "No, here. Right now. At midnight."

"Ahh, at midnight." He shrugged absently. "The spell."

"The spell?"

When he said no more, Marianne gave him a look. Truly, he was a vexing man. *That*, and charming, joyful, and noble, but his virtues notwithstanding, she was still rather peeved at his actions this evening and his cryptic answer just now. The spell? What was that supposed to mean? His head tilted to the side, and he peered at her as if the answer was obvious and he wondered why she couldn't see it. But she couldn't see it! What was it he knew and she didn't? Even the child was smiling as if she knew.

"What spell?" she demanded.

Ezekiel walked forward. He stepped onto the first stair, to where their eyes were level. "My lady, your coach turned back into a pumpkin. I brought a buggy so you would not have to walk up home in your glass slippers."

"Into a pumpkin?"

"That often happens"—he winked—"at midnight."

Ezekiel Norcross, with his even features and cleft chin, was undoubtedly a handsome man. Even with the day's growth of blond bristles on his face that she ached to touch. Even when he wasn't taking things seriously. Even when he was oblivious to how much she loved him.

How much she *loved* him?

She nervously dropped her gaze to the top brass button on Ezekiel's red plaid waistcoat. Henry had wanted her to find love again. In the letter she'd found packed in his belongings, he had insisted on it. *Be brave, darling,* he had written five times throughout the letter. Maybe she should be a little less proper, a little braver, and take the initiative. If she descended one step, she would be close enough to kiss Ezekiel.

Could she do it?

Needing to know if Ezekiel was feeling as she was, she looked up from his vest. His gaze was on her mouth. Then he looked up and whispered something. Her heart was pounding so loudly that she didn't hear what he had said.

"What happens," she whispered back, "at midnight?"

His foot moved to the step between them. He leaned forward a fraction. "The prince chases after the woman he loves."

Marianne parted her lips. She wanted him. She wanted a kiss. She most desperately wanted to be the beauty he would pursue. And by the look in his eyes, she believed he wanted that, too, even with what he knew about her.

She eased her shoe to the edge of the step.

"He's pretending you're Cinderella," the child called out, breaking the magical spell Ezekiel had woven around them.

Ezekiel drew back.

Marianne blinked. Who was Cinderella? Fearful they would realize her ignorance, she released a nervous giggle then, lifting the front of her skirt, stepped around Ezekiel and hurried into the buggy. She set the pie basket at her feet.

As cheerfully as she could, she patted the child's leg. "Widows like Cinderella shouldn't be wearing glass slippers at night."

Polly Reid looked at her strangely. "You don't know who Cinderella is, do you?"

Marianne lifted her lips in what she hoped looked like an *of course I do* smile.

Ezekiel settled in the buggy on the other side of the child. "Everyone knows who Cinderella is," he said in his usual lighthearted manner. He flicked the reins, and the horse and buggy started up the mountain.

"Mrs. Plum doesn't know."

Marianne kept her gaze on the road as he turned his head to look at her.

"You don't?"

She maintained her easy smile because that was all the answer she was going to give. Yet in her peripheral view, she could see his eyes were wide with shock.

"Marianne, have you ever read *The Renowned Tales of Mother Goose?*"

She sighed. If she didn't answer, he would nag her until she did. "No."

She could have explained more—like how her parents had never read to her or how she never attended school or even how she hadn't learned to read or write until her husband had taught her after they'd married. Besides the Bible, the only books she'd read on her own were *Gulliver's Travels*, *The Scarlet Letter*, and *Oliver Twist*, and only then after Henry had left for war. Not that there weren't other books in her husband's library. Reading was something they had done together. When she buried him, she had buried her interest in journeying to a literary world.

She could have explained that to them. Clearly Henry hadn't shared everything about her past with Ezekiel. Some inexplicable part of her wanted to be open and vulnerable with the staring-intently-at-her pair, but she let her "no" be the end of it.

She could not have them think less of her.

"Ma used to read it to me," the girl said, with sadness in her tone. The buggy hit a bump in the road, and she bounced on the bench. "The only book we were allowed to read in the orphanage was the Bible. After I arrived, they took all the books I had brought with me. Even *Mother Goose*. It wasn't fair. So when they tried to take my father's glengarry—I screamed and fought until they gave up." Her lips pinched together.

Marianne listened to the *clip-clop* of the horse's hooves on the hard road. Someone who'd had a good mother would speak encouraging words during a moment like this.

Do what your mother did.

Never. Never that.

Suddenly, the girl—Polly—reached over and took Marianne's hand in hers. Marianne flinched, but Polly squeezed her hand.

Hold tight, Marianne remembered her father saying the last day they'd been together. She fought the tears in her eyes. It wasn't fair. None of it! Children should grow up happy and blessed, in a house full of love with parents, where they could read *Mother Goose* and *Gulliver's Travels*, not to escape life, but for the sense of adventure.

Even with the upbringing she had, Marianne knew that. Somehow in the two days she had with Polly, she was going to help her remember that life doesn't have to continue to be how it has been. Life can change.

I can change. I can be fun like Ezekiel. I can love others as freely and easily as he does.

She wrapped her other hand around Polly's and held it snugly in her lap.

They continued in an easy silence to Marianne's home.

Once they arrived, even though she didn't ask him, Ezekiel saw that they were safe and secure inside the house. Marianne and Polly waited at the front window and watched him drive the buggy to Mrs. Decker's.

With Ezekiel out of sight, Marianne turned to Polly. "I know it's too late to still be up, but would you like—"

"Yes!"

"You don't even know what I am offering."

"Will I be with you?"

"Yes."

"I'm not tired. Really." The sleepiness in her eyes belied her energetic tone.

Marianne looked to the grandfather clock. The hour was late, but what could staying up a little longer hurt? Polly could sleep until noon. In fact, they both could.

Content with her decision, Marianne grabbed a crystal lamp and led Polly to the library. Together they searched the shelves, laughing at the obscure titles, until Marianne challenged Polly to find a book written by a woman. By the time the grandfather clock struck one, Polly found *The Wide, Wide World* by Elizabeth Wetherell. Having read the book with Henry, Marianne agreed it would make a fine choice.

She took Polly upstairs to the bedroom wallpapered with tiny yellow flowers. She tucked Polly in bed, sat next to her, and they took turns reading until Polly fell asleep.

Smiling, Marianne placed the book on the bedside table. She carried the lamp to her bedroom. She *could* be a temporary caregiver.

It didn't seem that difficult at all.

Chapter 6

"G ood morning, Mrs. Plum."

Marianne opened her eyes. By the amount of sunlight streaming into the room, she must have slept later than her usual sunrise waking. Polly, in a green-and-red plaid dress, set a wooden tray on the side of the bed. Instead of pink ribbons, today her cap had green ribbons pinned to the red ones hanging in back. In a room with white and ivory curtains, bedding, and window-coverings, Polly's colorful attire made her stand out.

"Good morning, Polly." Marianne pulled to a sitting position, her dark hair hanging in a loose braid over her shoulder. She smiled. "You look lovely and festive. Did you sleep well?"

"Absolutely! I made you breakfast all by myself." Polly placed the tray on Marianne's lap. "Mrs. Graff said you wouldn't mind."

"She spoke truthfully."

"I used to cook for Ma before she. . ." She shrugged, an action Marianne had realized last night was her way of answering when she became emotional.

"Polly, while you are with me, I want you to feel at home, all right?" She nodded.

"Now what do we have here?" Marianne said, turning her attention to the breakfast tray.

On a dinner plate of Marianne's best china sat three toasted biscuits next to a glob of strawberry preserves, pats of butter, and five slices of bacon—all looking as delicious as they smelled. And more than she could eat. Next to a goblet of goat's milk, the aroma of the steaming black coffee in the teacup chased away what little tiredness she felt.

"This looks wonderful. Thank you."

Polly grinned broadly. "I'm glad you're pleased."

"Have you eaten?"

"Ma says a hostess should see that her company is served first."

"You are *my* company." The adoration in Polly's blue eyes warmed Marianne's heart. She patted the spot next to her. "Come enjoy this bounty with me."

"Really?"

"Really."

In a flash, Polly was snuggled under the covers and next to Marianne, who immediately handed her a napkin to catch her crumbs.

As they ate, they talked about *The Wide, Wide World* and what Polly thought might happen next.

Marianne eased the breakfast plate closer for Polly to reach her second biscuit. "Many in the township donated items to the adopting families, but since you were unexpected, I thought we could go shopping. Would you enjoy that?"

Polly nodded vigorously. "Mrs. Plum, do you like Christmas?"

"Why do you ask?"

"You don't have any decorations."

Marianne sipped the last of her coffee as she pondered what to answer. The lack of decorations wasn't a result of any disfavor toward Christmas. When Henry had been alive, he relished all festivities. The twelve days of Christmas could have been twenty-four for him, and they had been the year before the war began. He always said the grander a holiday party the better. A ball held at the Belmont? They were there, at every one, because he wished it. At the Heath House? They were there, too. She pretended to have fun, for Henry's sake. Most of the time, she had felt as alone in a room of four hundred as she did in a room of two. Until after the war.

What began as gratitude toward Ezekiel for becoming her husband's closest friend changed this last year into something more than she'd ever thought possible. There at the Schroeders' wedding, sitting next to him, she'd realized she no longer felt alone. Polly didn't need to know that, though.

What had they been talking about? Oh yes, decorations.

"After my husband died, I had no cause to adorn the house for the season."

"Did you love him?"

She cradled the empty teacup in her hands. What she'd felt for Henry had been a gentle, steadfast, committed love, and he had loved her, too. With more passion than she deserved. Henry had rescued and redeemed her from the life set before her because of her parents.

She released a heart-heavy breath. "Henry Plum was a good man, Polly. Yes, I loved him, but not as much as he deserved, and my regret haunts me. If he were alive, I would make it up to him."

Polly nibbled on the biscuit. "Where did you first meet Mr. Plum?"

"In Central Park." Seeing a blank look on Polly's face, Marianne clarified. "New York City. It was windy, and my bonnet was loose because I had sold my hair so Father and I would have money to pay our rent. Henry caught my hat in the breeze, and then he rescued me. Love makes a man do peculiar things." She blinked away her tears. "Alas, that is more than you needed to know."

"My ma said she had to give me up because she loved me." Polly put the half-eaten biscuit back on the plate. "But I know she really didn't want me anymore."

On the tip of Marianne's tongue was the insistence that Polly's mother *had* wanted her. But was it fair or kind to say something she didn't know was truthful or not?

"Polly, if your mother knew she could not provide for your well-being, then giving you to a family who could *is* loving of her. She wants the best for you." Marianne wanted to add that all mothers desire the best for their children, but she knew that wasn't true.

"Ma's dead."

"Oh. I am sorry."

Polly shrugged. She sniffed then wiped her nose with the back of her hand instead of the napkin on the breakfast tray.

Marianne cringed yet kept herself from correcting Polly. Her task was to be Polly's temporary caregiver. For today and tomorrow. The child's future mother would teach her manners. The child's future mother would also remind her every day that she was wanted.

Hoping for that, Marianne slid off the bed, attended to her toiletries, then hurried into her dressing room to find a suitable day dress. She had a grand day planned. No sense dawdling in bed feeling morose over the past.

To fit the anticipation she felt for the day's events, she chose a purple and white horizontal-striped taffeta gown. Upon seeing the silky fabric at the New York City modiste's shop, Henry had ordered a day dress made out of it, even though he had already ordered seven other day dresses and three ballgowns. Henry did everything extravagantly.

Making money had been a joy to him, as had spending it on those he loved.

Without him to spend the returns on his investments, in the last four years since his death, the fortune he had made off his inheritance had doubled. Once a quarter, Marianne traveled to New York City to discuss her financial situation with Henry's older brother and listen to her in-laws beg her to move back. Not only had God blessed her with a godly husband, but his family's continued acceptance and generosity meant a great deal. They would say extravagance on an orphan was fitting.

After all, it was Christmastime.

"Mrs. Plum," Polly said as Marianne exited the dressing room, "if you were my mother, I would make breakfast for you every day."

"That would be—" Marianne stopped buttoning the side of her gloves.

Polly stood beside the opened door to the hallway, breakfast tray in hand. Yet where she had been sitting, biscuit and bacon crumbs spotted the white sheets. The grease from the bacon alone— Marianne pinched her lips together to stay calm, yet, unable to stop herself, she could feel her eyes widen in mortification and her heart pounding.

Child, you will clean up this mess immediately!

Her mother's voice. . .in her head. . .had to make it stop.

I am not her, I am not her. I have been made new in Jesus. I am redeemed and righteous and changed.

Marianne took several deep breaths then, as unaffected as possible, continued on the path to the door. Accidents happened. The sheets could be washed. All would be well.

"Now wasn't that a delightful breakfast?" she said, following Polly into the hall. "Tell me, what is your favorite color?"

As they made small talk, they walked to the kitchen to return the tray. Charlotte would say they should have left the tray in the bedroom for her to collect, but Marianne hated adding an additional task to the younger woman's daily list. Sadly, with the bedding being as it was. . .

Marianne sighed.

"Is something wrong?" Polly asked.

"No, no." She opened the door to the kitchen and allowed Polly to enter first. "I was merely thinking of something I needed to ask my housekeeper to—" Her mouth dropped open in a most unladylike manner. "Oh, my dear child," she said with measured calmness, "what have you done to my kitchen?"

⚜

Zeke checked the mare's saddle one last time before leading her out of the carriage house. Thankfully the above-seasonal warmth was continuing, but knowing how much cooler the temperature was on the mountain, he elected to wear the gray frock coat he had left at his mother's when he'd last stayed with her at Thanksgiving. He should have been on the road already to Pleasant Grove. He would have left earlier, if he'd been able to fall asleep upon climbing in bed. Thoughts of Marianne had kept him up half the night.

He'd almost kissed her.

She would have kissed him if Polly hadn't interrupted.

He knew it. Felt it, and had no idea what to do about it.

A ride across the mountain would help him sort this out. Zeke grabbed the saddle horn and prepared to mount. That is, until he heard a door slam shut. He looked to see Polly racing across the yard separating the two houses. Marianne stood on her back steps wearing a purple and white dress he hadn't seen before. It only accentuated her beauty.

"Polly, please come back here," Marianne called out in a composed-yet-firm manner.

Polly kept running until she reached the back steps of the Decker House. Instead of knocking on the back door, she sat on the bottom step. Marianne didn't follow, likely because she didn't want to risk a confrontation with her neighbor. Not that Zeke blamed her. When his mother was convinced she was right, *nothing* could change her mind.

She turned and walked back inside her house. Unlike Polly, she didn't slam the door.

Zeke checked his pocket watch. He could spare time talking to the pair.

After tying the mare to a hitching post, he jogged over to where Polly sat with her knees drawn up to her chest and her arms around her legs. Her glengarry had slid down near her eyes. Zeke sat next to her, setting his bowler on the top step. In a dandified manner, he stretched out his legs before him then crossed one booted foot over the other. He rested his elbows on the step behind him.

"Rough morning?"

With her gaze focused on the ground in front of her, Polly nodded.

He gave her back a gentle pat. "Care to talk about it?"

"Mrs. Plum is angry."

Zeke blinked twice in shock. Anger wasn't an emotion he could ever remember seeing in Marianne Plum. But in Polly's perspective, Marianne was angry, so saying otherwise wouldn't help the situation.

"What happened?" he asked instead.

Still not looking at him, Polly shrugged.

"Did you do something that upset Mrs. Plum?"

Polly shrugged again.

Zeke took that shrug as a yes. He tugged on the back of her glengarry until the front tip was back in the middle of her forehead. "Do you think she had a right to be upset?"

Polly nodded. As she looked to the side, her eyelids blinked rapidly against the growing tears. "I want her to love me." A tear slid down her cheek.

Zeke cradled her against him. He knew the feeling. "We can't make people love us, but we can do and say things to show them how much we care. Then we put our hope in that one day they will receive our love, and return it. Does that make sense?"

Polly nodded. "Mrs. Plum read me a book and tucked me in bed and said she would take me shopping." She sniffed then wiped her nose with the long sleeve of a different calico dress than she had on yesterday. "Why can't she be my mother?"

When Reverend Cottrell mentioned choosing a temporary caregiver who would not become emotionally involved, they should have taken into consideration Polly attaching to the caregiver. He should have seen it. He should have cautioned Polly last night.

Zeke didn't enjoy saying the words, but he had to. "Sweetheart, God has a new mother for you, and I hope to talk to her today. I need you to let go of that desire you have"—he tapped her chest—"in here of Mrs. Plum being your mother. A temporary caregiver is all she agreed to be."

Polly didn't respond.

He continued to hold her as, he hoped, she thought about what he said.

Several minutes later, she pointed and asked, "What's that?"

Zeke looked to the lean-to glass building. After he'd graduated from Rutgers, he and his mother celebrated with their first summer holiday at Schooley's Mountain since his father's death four years earlier. Before they got to Heath House, his mother had noticed a lush garden beside a glasshouse built against a lengthy brick wall. She'd insisted on investigating. Mr. Theodore Decker, widower, had spent the rest of the afternoon explaining to the enchanted woman how he borrowed the technology from a greenhouse in Massachusetts to create a one-hundred-foot-long wall with flues built into it where warm air could pass through from a wood stove.

"That is my mother's greatest treasure, her greenhouse. On the side is the door, if you would like to go in and look at her plants."

Polly perked up. "Really?"

"Really."

She took off running, the ribbons of her glengarry flapping in the wind.

Zeke stood. He brushed off the back of his black trousers then grabbed his hat, plopped it on his head, and gave the brim a smooth swipe. With a smug grin, he walked to the Plum house. He had successfully fixed one half of the relationship.

Now to fix the other.

Chapter 7

While she hadn't responded to the chaos in her kitchen in the best manner, things could have been worse. The mess only seemed as messy as it did because the room was small.

Marianne piled the last of the dirty utensils and cookware on the worktable in the middle of the kitchen and tried to retain a smidgeon of optimism. How Polly managed to coat the stove, dry sink, worktable, and mantel above the hearth with flour, well, she wasn't sure she wanted to know. Or why Polly had to rearrange the formerly alphabetized and neatly stacked canned goods in the pantry. And the bacon grease— At least it had stayed in the cast-iron skillet.

She could clean the mess herself. Or have Charlotte do it, since she had repeatedly volunteered. Sending her housekeeper upstairs to attend to her usual duties and to clean the crumbs Polly had left on the bed seemed the wiser course of action.

Maybe she ought to go over to her neighbor's and bring Polly home.

No. For all her orneriness to Marianne, Mrs. Decker had a soft spot for children. She would cheer Polly up and help her see the situation from an adult's perspective. Then Polly would return home. That's when Marianne would have a gentle talk with her about tidying up after oneself, and then they would clean the kitchen together so they could go shopping.

She rested against the edge of the dry sink and released a stream of breath between her lips, the action relaxing the tension in her shoulders. Yes, she could still make this work.

She wasn't the worst caregiver.

Even though she didn't like the crumbs on the bed or the disorder brought to her kitchen, she had not responded to Polly like her mother had to her—with screams and condemnation. And Ezekiel wasn't anything like her father. After three years of being his friend, she could trust him to help her, like she had trusted Henry.

How could she convince him to let go of whatever was holding him back from pursuing her? How could she tell Ezekiel she needed his strength? His joy? Him. They could have a wonderful life together even without the children he yearned to have. Because if being a father was that important to Ezekiel, he would have already married, right?

Surely a life with her alone would be enough for him.

Be brave, darling.

Had Henry told her that because he didn't think she had it in her? Or because he did, and he wanted her to see what he saw?

Staring absently at the flour-sprinkled wooden floor, Marianne ran the tip of her thumb along her bottom lip. Could she be brave?

The back door to her kitchen opened. She looked up.

Ezekiel walked inside wearing a gray frock coat over a cranberry-and floral-striped waistcoat that would look garish on any other man. On him it emphasized how, without a doubt, he was a prime specimen of the male sort. Then again, much could be said for how he confidently yet humbly wore the badge on his lapel and the holstered pistol at his hip.

As he closed the door behind him, his gaze moved across the kitchen. He nodded in a most approving manner. "Disorder to your order. No wonder Polly thinks you are angry."

"Oh, I am not angry."

"I never thought you were."

With a coy smile, she raised her brows. "Yet you seem rather pleased at the mess made to my kitchen."

"Woman, you seem rather pleased that I am pleased," he said in what she took as his attempt to sound accusatory but came out—dare she presume—as flirtatious.

Maybe that's what she needed to be to convince him she desired to be more than friends. And even if he refused her, at least she took a risk.

I can change, Lord. I want to be free to love even if love brings disappointment. I am weary of being alone.

Marianne grabbed an unused towel off the dry sink. The kitchen being the size it was meant that in five steps she was standing in front of him. "Deputy, since you insist on cleaning this disorder," she said, hearing a smile in her words, "then please do."

"I never offered to clean anything."

"You are so kind to insist." She placed the towel in his hand and wrapped his fingers around it. "I accept."

His nose scrunched up; the right corner of his mouth lifted. He looked so charming and kissable that her heart skipped a beat, and in an act of self-preservation, she pressed her lips together to hold back the brimming laughter. What was it about him that brought out merriment in her? Somehow around him, she felt her burdens lifted.

She felt free to rest and to have fun.

Around Henry she'd felt like she needed to meet his needs. She had to be the ideal wife to keep his favor. Not that he'd *ever* demanded that of her. Henry was too gracious and sincere for that. Why couldn't she have accepted his love without feeling like she had to do something to prove she was worthy of it?

Her heartbeat increased. She had to speak, had to be more than flirtatious, had to be vulnerable and confesss her darkest secrets. Now. While she felt brave and free. While she had nothing to lose but her pride.

"Ezekiel," she whispered, "I need you."

"To clean the kitchen?"

"In my life."

He gazed at her and didn't speak, didn't move, didn't even acknowledge he had heard her confession.

Marianne didn't look away. "I am not cold or heartless."

"I never said you were."

"My mother did. Essie Hasenclever did. Even your mother thinks I am."

"They are wrong," he said in a firm tone that would allow no argument from her. "In many things."

"When I was twelve, my mother ran off with another man. I never attended school. Henry taught me to read and write, and the day after my wedding, I put my father in an asylum."

"Your father's illness made him violent, Henry was an honorable man, and your mother was—wasn't a good person."

Knowing that did not lessen the shame she felt. Her decision to put Father in the asylum, like her mother's in deserting them, had been selfish. Someday she would atone for what she did. But that was not what she wished to discuss.

"Ezekiel Norcross," she said, gathering her remaining courage, "I love you with a passion that I never thought I was capable of experiencing. Even if you do not return my feelings, I praise God for falling in love with you because doing so showed me that being reserved does not make me cold or heartless."

"Even if I don't—?"

Before Marianne could be shocked or offended by the oath he uttered, he had wrapped the towel behind her back, and holding both ends, he pulled her to him.

Then he kissed her with an intensity she had never experienced before.

But soon reality captivated her thoughts, and Marianne forced herself to draw back. "About children—"

He groaned.

Marianne understood. A discussion was not what she wanted either at this moment.

"Later," he whispered. "I've waited too long. . ." and then found her lips again.

"But I. . .don't," she said between kisses, "and. . .you. . .do."

"Shh." He pulled her even closer, until she could feel his heart beating against hers. His lips slid from her mouth to her cheek and then back to her lips, kissing her as if she were his everything—his all.

And then, abruptly, he let her go.

"I have parents," he said, breathing hard, "to find. . .for Polly."

He looked as dazed as she felt.

"By order of the court," he muttered.

"Yes, you should go," she said, wishing her voice were a bit steadier.

He handed her the towel. "I will return."

"But about your mother—"

"Later."

Before she could form a reply, his lips were against hers again, kissing and whispering words she was too distracted to comprehend.

And then he was gone.

If it weren't for the tingle on her lips or the lingering woodsy scent of his cologne, she wouldn't have known he had been in her kitchen.

Breathless, Marianne absently walked to a stool near the unlit hearth. She sat, intending to patiently wait for Polly to return so they could have a day of adventure. Her heart had never felt so full. Even though Ezekiel had not specifically said he loved her or asked her to marry him or agreed to her desire not to have children, her smile grew.

This was truly the best time of the year.

She wouldn't even mind a little snow. After all, it was Christmas. *Christmas!*

With a gasp, Marianne stood. She couldn't let Polly leave without experiencing an extravagant Henry Plum–style Christmas.

❧

While Jacob took the wagon in search of a tree, mistletoe, and other greenery to liven up the mantels and tables throughout the house, Marianne enlisted Charlotte to help bring down the Christmas decorations from the attic. This had not been a simple task, because of the old trunks and hatboxes the former owners had left. They unpacked stockings, colored paper and crystal bells, cards from previous Christmases, gold-plated and tin Saint Nicholas figurines, pinecones surprisingly still holding a cinnamon scent, ornaments and feathers, three hand-carved nativities, and yards and yards of red ribbon.

"Mrs. Plum!"

Hearing Polly calling out, Marianne said, "We are in the front parlor."

Polly came running down the hall and into the room, her cheeks rosy, her smile broad, her hands behind her back. She stopped abruptly. Her eyes widened. "What happened in here?"

"What does it look like?"

"Like you spit Christmas all over the room."

Marianne couldn't help but laugh. "I suppose we did."

Charlotte closed the last emptied trunk with a thud. "Ma'am, would you like me to make a list of food supplies we need?"

"Please."

The petite housekeeper stepped to the secretary and withdrew a sheet of stationery and a pencil. "If you don't mind, I will work in the kitchen."

Marianne nodded. Like her, Charlotte married at age nineteen. Six weeks later, President Lincoln made his second call for enlisted men. After the war ended, Jacob returned alive yet no longer able to give his bride a child. The Graffs adored children. The young couple loved delivering clothes and food to the boarding school and to the orphanages in Chester and Pleasant Grove. Judge Fancer would have chosen them as an adoptive family. . .if they'd had their own home and the financial means.

Instead of faulting Charlotte for her brisk action and tone, Marianne ached for her. Life had dealt the Graffs an unfair lot.

After Charlotte left the room, Polly whispered, "Did I do something wrong?"

"No."

Polly stepped around the settee then wove around the trunks to reach Marianne. "I am sorry about the mess I made in the kitchen. Here." She offered a bouquet of pink camellias.

Marianne paused. Only one person had flora growing abundantly in December, and fanatical was the gentlest word that could be used to describe how the woman viewed her plants.

Even though she knew—and dreaded—the answer, she asked, "Where did you find such beautiful flowers?"

"Mrs. Decker has a greenhouse. It's warm and smells like heaven." The wonderment in Polly's tone matched that in her eyes.

"Did you have permission?"

"Yes."

Marianne realized she'd been holding her breath. Pleased that Polly hadn't trespassed, she went to the kitchen and found a vase. She took the list Charlotte had compiled. Until Jacob arrived with the tree and the greenery, decorating would have to wait. Shopping for toys, clothes, and a Christmas feast could not.

But first, Polly had to clean the kitchen.

❧

By sunset the house was bedecked in evergreen and mistletoe. To Marianne's delight, Jacob had also brought a bushel of pinecones and cuttings of bayberry, inkberry, and ivy, and the house smelled like Schooley's Mountain. Minus the fauna.

The only thing left to finish decorating was the tree.

With the twigs of holly berries now inserted and ribbon and strings of popcorn wrapped around the branches, Marianne and Polly wedged in old Christmas cards and dried sugared fruit wherever there was space. Later Marianne would place the gifts under the tree, including a hatbox for Polly's precious last memento of her father and the gifts Polly had chosen for Ezekiel. She glanced at Polly, who was so like Ezekiel, with her blue eyes and sandy-blond hair. Not to mention their affinity for keeping a hat on their heads.

Perhaps she could convince Judge Fancer to allow her to keep Polly for the remainder of the week. That way they could celebrate Christmas Day together, instead of Polly leaving tomorrow on Christmas Eve. Ezekiel would certainly spend part of the holiday with them, too. They could be Polly's temporary family.

"Mrs. Plum, look!" Polly raised to her nose a card with a gilded picture of Saint Nicholas's face. In a deep voice, she said, "Young lady, have you been good this year?"

Marianne curtsied. "Every day, sir."

"Every day!" Polly groaned. "All this goodness is too much! I am sure to run out of gifts." With the hand not holding up the card, she reached up and patted Marianne's shoulder. "I insist you no longer be good on Fridays. Can you do that for me?"

"I shall try my best."

"No, child. Try your worst."

Chuckling, Marianne lowered the card covering Polly's face. "You would *not* make a good Saint Nicholas."

Polly merely smiled. And Marianne smiled, too. The girl could be Ezekiel's child for all her natural ability to make Marianne feel happy.

Joyful.

Like every day was Christmas.

"Mrs. Plum, can I put the angel on top?"

Marianne glanced from the seven-foot tree to the folding ladder next to it. Polly had already stood on the ladder to decorate the top half of the tree. Putting the angel on would certainly be safer for the child to do instead of Marianne in heels and a full crinoline. Or they could wait for Ezekiel to arrive. She looked to the grandfather clock near the front door of the house. Almost six o'clock. Why wasn't he back yet?

With a smile to keep the worry out of her eyes, she turned to Polly. "Yes, but I will have to hold the ladder."

Polly squealed, handed Marianne the Saint Nicholas card, and then ran to the settee where she had placed the angel earlier.

At the pounding of her door knocker, Marianne's heart flipped against her ribs. Ezekiel! She laid the last three Christmas cards on a step near the ladder's middle. Then, brushing the pine needles off the front of her striped dress, she walked to the door.

She opened it, letting in a crisp breeze.

Mrs. Decker stood on the front steps, looking as irritated as when Marianne had given her pickled radishes and blueberry preserves for her birthday last week.

"Isn't this a pleasant surprise," Marianne said graciously. "Do come—"

"Polly, stop!" Mrs. Decker yelled, pushing Marianne to the side as she rushed past.

"But I can do it."

Marianne turned in time to see Polly's foot slip on the Christmas cards, causing her knee to jam into the step above and her chest to lunge forward. The ladder wobbled. Polly scrambled to hold on to the rails. Her grip on the angel loosened, and it fell to the wooden floor, the porcelain head shattering upon impact. Polly screamed. Mrs. Decker screamed. The ladder continued to wobble until Polly's weight sent it—and Polly—careening into the tree. Within seconds all three lay on the ground, the ladder in a bed of pine, Polly on the Persian rug.

Marianne ran to her and knelt, her hands shaking and pulse racing. *What do I do?*

Polly drew in a sudden gasp of air, the breath having been knocked from her lungs.

With a confidence and calmness Marianne admired, Mrs. Decker examined Polly's legs, muttering "everything is all right" as she worked. Yet she never muttered to Marianne that everything was all right. Why would she? Polly's fall was Marianne's fault. If she hadn't turned her attention away from Polly. . . If she hadn't left the Christmas cards on the ladder's step. . . If she hadn't already given Polly leave to climb the ladder. . .

Marianne awkwardly patted Polly's shoulder. "There, there."

Polly continued to lay motionless, her gaze on Marianne, her eyes filling with tears. "I'm sorry."

"Polly, where does it hurt?" Mrs. Decker asked.

She grimaced. "Nowhere."

Mrs. Decker helped Polly stand. "Now does anything hurt?"

"No." Polly's gaze shifted to the downed tree. "I should clean up—"

"Nonsense," Marianne interjected. She forced a smile. "Mrs. Decker, would you be so kind as to take Polly to your house?"

"Of course."

"But I want to stay with you!"

"I appreciate that, Polly." Unable to stand the condemnation on Mrs. Decker's face, Marianne focused on Polly. She kept her voice emotionless despite the wellspring in her heart. "However, Mrs. Decker will know what to look for if you have injuries we cannot see. Deputy Norcross will be bringing news of your new family. That you are at his mother's home will spare him the walk here. I fear the weather is turning for the worse."

Polly's chin trembled. "But—"

"I insist."

After a shake of her head, Mrs. Decker wrapped her arm over Polly's shoulder. "Let's go, sweetheart. I have chicken and dumplings on the stove." She nudged her to the front door and outside. "Ezekiel will be delighted to see you. He will have wonderful news about your new parents and how. . ."

Marianne stood in the parlor listening to Mrs. Decker's words until she couldn't hear them anymore.

Charlotte crossed the foyer and closed the front door. "Why did you send Polly away?"

Looking away from her housekeeper, Marianne eyed the crushed tree and ruined decorations strewn about the parlor floor. All their hard work in tatters. She hadn't wanted an extravagant Christmas for herself. She'd wanted it for Polly. She enjoyed giving. She enjoyed saying yes at the mercantile to anything Polly liked. She enjoyed making Polly feel loved and cherished and wanted.

Why *did* she send Polly away?

Marianne placed a hand on her chest, right where her heart beat strongest and hurt the deepest. Where existed a truth she could no longer ignore. How was it possible in such little time to have developed an attachment so rich, so beautiful, and so unmerited?

"Because she knows how to take care of a child."

⚜

Zeke exited the home of a lawyer he knew who lived on Schooley's Mountain and resumed riding south to Marianne's house. Despite the setting sun and dropping temperature, he saw no need to push the mare hard. He needed the travel time to sort out what he'd been advised, and then after the sorting, he needed to decide what to say to Judge Fancer tomorrow in Morristown. Tonight he needed to prepare his report.

In the eyes of the court, the best place for a child was with family.

Zeke, though, wasn't the court.

How much you going to pay me to take her? Victor Ralston had said upon learning his dead wife's cousin had given up her child to the Soldiers' Orphanage in Richmond before dying of consumption.

The question still grated on Zeke's every nerve. How much would he *pay* him?

"Nothing," he grumbled, even though no one was on the tree-lined road to hear. Polly came with no more than the clothes on her back and what little there was in her carpetbag.

To his shock, the lack of financial inducement failed to hinder Mr. Ralston from agreeing to take Polly. *A Christmas blessing,* Ralston eventually claimed she was. His three sons and the babe his wife had died birthing "could use a new ma." With Ralston's job at the granite quarry being what it was, Polly would be in charge of all the cooking, cleaning, and child-raising, leaving her no time to attend school. Not that a girl needed schooling anyway, according to Ralston.

"I will not put Polly in a home like that. I can't."

Ask Marianne.

That's what his legal advice had come down to—a marriage proposal.

Judge Fancer had already granted Marianne temporary custody. If she and Zeke married, they could petition the orphans' court for the right to adopt her and then hope Fancer would be merciful and choose their home for Polly's emotional, spiritual, educational, and physical well-being.

A drop-in-temperature breeze blew against his face, yet he felt warm. Hopeful.

It could work.

He loved Marianne, and she loved him. She seemed to genuinely like Polly. Once she knew of the life awaiting Polly with the Ralstons, her compassionate heart would help her move past not wanting to be a mother.

Proposing to Marianne had only been a matter of time, not a *"Should he?"* No sense spending weeks or months courting. They had known each other since the end of the war, had been friends the last year.

After kissing—

What they shared in her kitchen was going to haunt him until they wed.

Best marry her tonight.

Reverend Cottrell would be willing to officiate. The man had been encouraging Zeke since summer to find a wife and settle down.

He looked heavenward. "Lord, unless in the next five minutes You direct me otherwise, this is the best solution." With a broad grin, he kicked the mare into a run.

He couldn't think of anything he'd like better for Christmas.

❧

By the time Zeke reached the Plum house, he knew his plan would work.

Thus he rode up to the front door, dismounted, gave the lapels of his coat a tug, tipped his hat at a jaunty angle, then walked to the half-built covered porch and gave the front door a resounding knock. Come spring, he would add a paved walk. Maybe even replace a second-floor window with stained glass. Or add on a room in the back to enlarge the kitchen.

Before he could continue his architectural additions, Charlotte opened the door. She ushered him past the parlor. He took curious note of the downed yule-tree. They stopped at the dimly lit library. The Christmas-decorated room smelled of pine, cinnamon, and *home*. Marianne sat in a chair near the hearth, a diminishing fire inside. Although she held a book in her lap, she stared absently out the window.

Charlotte said nothing as she walked away.

He entered the library and knelt before Marianne, covering her hands with his. "Will you marry me?"

She met his gaze. "Why?"

Of all the answers he had imagined her saying (*Yes, Yes! Absolutely yes!* and—his least favorite—*What took you so long?*), *Why?* had never crossed his mind.

He kept his hands atop hers. "The cousins I investigated as a possible home for Polly are unacceptable to me. I won't allow her to be put back in an orphanage. What makes sense is you and me marrying and petitioning Judge Fancer to adopt Polly. She loves you. I know you will make a great mother."

"No."

Zeke stared at her, flummoxed. He had never claimed to understand the female mind, but what had he done wrong? He should have kissed her, wouldn't have minded, certainly wanted to, but after this morning, he knew better than to kiss her again before they were married.

"No?" he echoed.

"I knew a man once who proposed for the sake of rescuing a girl from an unacceptable-to-him situation. That is not the right reason to marry. Polly needs a mother and a father who both want to be parents. I do not. It would be selfish of me to ask you to settle for a life without children." She withdrew her hands from under his, placed her book on the floor, and stood.

Zeke stood, too. Still unsure how to process her refusal, he followed her to the front door, asking, "Where's Polly?"

She gripped the door handle. "You will find acceptable parents for Polly. Be patient. Please tell Mrs. Decker that in the morning I will send over the gifts I purchased for Polly. Merry Christmas."

"Wait, why is Polly next door?"

"Because Mrs. Decker is a mother."

She opened the door and gave his arm a nudge to make him walk outside. Zeke stopped on the second step then turned to face her.

"I will see you tomorrow," he muttered, since that seemed most fitting.

She nodded and closed the door.

Chapter 8

The next morning as she stood at the kitchen's dry sink, staring out the window, Marianne watched the snowflakes fluttering to the ground. Outside, Ezekiel chased Polly on the acreage behind Mrs. Decker's house. She suspected the snow was delaying his trip back to Morristown to discuss Polly with Judge Fancer.

Despite the ache in her heart, she looked down at the crate of tropical orchid bulbs she'd ordered from England because Mrs. Decker loved orchids yet grew none due to the extravagant prices the bulbs fetched on the European market. This gift would be Marianne's last attempt to make peace with her neighbor. Once Christmas was over, she would accept her in-laws' request she move back to New York City.

"They are the only family I have."

At a sudden pounding, Marianne hurried from the kitchen to the foyer where Charlotte had already opened the door. White flakes blew across the wooden floor. The wind chilled the house.

A snow-covered Azariah Sharpenstein, the father chosen to adopt Irena Barimore, stood on the front step holding a crying child wrapped in a quilt. "Here," he said, giving the bundle to her housekeeper, "I need you to take Irena."

As Charlotte whispered soothing words to the child, Marianne stepped forward. "Why are you giving her to us?"

"The mess, the crying. . . Eunice can't—" His voice broke, and he rubbed his reddened eyes with the back of his gloved hands. "I love my wife and the child. Being a mother. . .it's. . . Irena is too much for Eunice. I have to choose. With you having the other orphan and all— here. Give her to the judge."

Before she could question him more, he tossed a carpetbag into the foyer then pulled the door closed.

Charlotte drew the blanket off Irena's head.

Tears welled in Irena's gray-green eyes, but her crying stopped.

She clung to Charlotte, who looked pleadingly at Marianne.

"You should take her," Charlotte said with a tremble in her voice, yet she clung to Irena.

Marianne gripped the box of orchids tighter. What was she to do with a four-year-old? The child needed a mother and a father and a home where she could feel cherished and wanted and loved, something the Graffs could give her if they had their own home.

And it all became clear.

Is this what I should do, Lord?

A sudden peace in her spirit chased away all doubts.

"Charlotte Graff, I am giving you and Jacob this house." Ignoring the confusion on her housekeeper's face, she continued, "You will provide a home for children like Irena." *And Polly.* "Henry would want me to spend his fortune wisely, and I can think of no better way. I will set up a trust—"

"No trust. Please," Charlotte begged as her chin trembled. "Jacob's pride suffers enough from living off your charity. We can make a go of this, given the chance."

Marianne wrapped her arms around the two. Once she heard her housekeeper's tearful "thank you," she claimed her woolen cloak.

Time to be brave and face down her neighbor.

⁂

"So you think you can buy my affections?" Mrs. Decker's face held as much suspicion as her tone.

Marianne twisted the button on her cloak. Sitting down in the parlor would be more pleasant than having a conversation in the foyer, but at least her neighbor had invited her inside. Still, unsure what to answer, she looked into the parlor, where a yule-tree stood opposite the fire-filled hearth. She wouldn't mind curling up beside the fire with some eggnog and roasted chestnuts. Not that Henry had ever permitted roasting chestnuts in the stove. *What fun is that?* he'd say. *A man never misses a chance to build a fire and cook over it.* She suspected Ezekiel never roasted chestnuts in the stove either.

She turned back to her neighbor. "I am sorry for the things I have done to offend you. For the last twelve years, I have tried to cultivate a relationship with you because Henry believed God had provided us with a neighbor old enough to be my mother. He knew how I yearned to have one."

Her voice caught, and she fought against the pressure building in her chest.

"I thought maybe you would..." *love me.* Marianne wiped her eyes, humiliated at her outburst. "I am sorry. I should go." Turning away, she reached for the door.

"Stop." Mrs. Decker's voice softened. "Please."

Marianne looked into the older woman's blue eyes, so like her son's.

Mrs. Decker released a ragged breath. "Before you and Henry moved to Schooley's Mountain, my pickles won blue ribbons at the county fair. Then you arrived, and my pickles stopped winning. I have resented you and resisted your overtures of friendship because of your pickles."

"My pickles?" Marianne repeated with a nervous chuckle because the absurdity of it wasn't the easiest thing to comprehend. Her preserves had won more ribbons than her pickles.

"I daresay it must be the silliest reason for contention between two women." Blinking at her own brimming tears, Mrs. Decker pinched her lips together as if to stifle a laugh. Her shoulders shook, and she snorted. Her hand immediately covered her mouth, but then her gaze resettled on Marianne and the tension clearly building inside her burst.

Marianne felt her own lips twitch. Before she could hold onto any semblance of dignity, she was laughing alongside her neighbor.

And then she was in her arms, crying again and listening to Sarah Norcross Decker apologize for all the wounds her pride and jealousy had unfairly inflicted over the last twelve years. She led Marianne to the settee where they talked gardening, Christmas, Azariah Sharpenstein's return of Irena, and the reasons why Marianne was giving her home to the Graffs.

"Polly's fall was not your fault," Mrs. Decker said abruptly.

"How can you say that? You disapproved of my care."

"Disapproved?"

"You scowled at me."

"Oh, sweetheart." Mrs. Decker held Marianne's hand between her own. "I was stunned that you were sending her away over a little accident. Polly told me all you have done for and with her. You would make—no, you *are* a wonderful mother."

Marianne flinched.

Unsure what to say in response, she stood. "It's almost noon. I should go." She pulled on her cloak.

Mrs. Decker walked with her to the front door. "I shall send Polly over after she has warmed up and had something to eat. She would like to spend a little more time with you before she goes to her new family."

She didn't know? "What did Ezekiel share with you about yesterday?"

"He said he met with the child's cousins and needed to prepare his recommendation to Judge Fancer. Why? Is there something else?"

"I cannot imagine Ezekiel withholding any pertinent information from you." Unless he had a reason.

Marianne gave Mrs. Decker a hug then hurried outside and ran back to her house. The snow had finally accumulated enough to blanket the grass since it had started falling early that morning. Although the sky was still white, who knew how much snow they would have—if any—by tomorrow. She wasn't too sure she wanted to go to the War Memorial Dedication. But she had to relinquish Polly and Irena to Judge Fancer's custody. She had to do her duty.

No matter how much her heart hurt.

⁂

As his mother turned a bulb around, examining each side, she shared about how different orchids smelled like rose, hyacinth, citrus, and even chocolate. Zeke couldn't imagine what she was looking for. Each of the dozen bulbs looked the same to him.

He paused in eating his stew long enough to ask, "Who are those from?"

Polly stopped eating as well.

"Marianne," Mother answered, "and I will not listen to you say one critical word about my friend's extravagant generosity."

Zeke felt his eyes widen. "When did she become your friend?"

She rested the bulb next to the others on the table then stared at him for what felt like forever. "Earlier. When she came over to share that she was gifting her home to the Graffs and returning to New York."

Zeke dropped his spoon next to his half-filled bowl. Schooley's Mountain wouldn't be home to him if Marianne wasn't here. He should leave. Travel to the frontier. Once he found parents for Polly, he would leave New Jersey. As long as Marianne believed her actions were for his benefit, she wouldn't change her mind about marrying him.

"Let's move to Colorado," he blurted, "like we discussed before you married Theodore Decker." He picked up his spoon, but his lost appetite caused him to drop it again. "I'll build you a greenhouse there."

"I'd like to move to Colorado," Polly offered.

Mother kissed the top of Polly's head. "My precious child." She then looked to Zeke, who couldn't tear his gaze away from the orchid bulbs. "Son, why mention moving now?"

He shrugged. "Change is good. You'd like the Rocky Mountains."

"Probably, but why move from this mountain where—" She gasped. "Oh, Ezekiel. I was so focused on my own feelings that I never noticed yours."

"For Mrs. Plum?" Polly grinned. "I did."

Zeke shifted on the wooden seat.

With a softening gaze, his mother stood and walked to his end of the table. She sat in the chair next to his. "How long have you been in love with Marianne?"

"Long enough." He reached out and took her hand in his, clinging tight. "Mother, I don't know what else to do to convince her to marry me."

She sighed. "Marianne will do what she thinks is best for others, even at a cost to herself."

"Mr. Norcross," Polly said, "what you need is a Christmas miracle."

"That's it!" Mother stood. "You two finish your soup. Ezekiel, if you've been good this year, and I think you have, I know exactly who to talk to."

❧

Since it was Christmas Day, Marianne decided it fitting to ride to the War Memorial Dedication in the fifty-year-old red barouche that came with the house when Henry'd purchased it.

With a spring in his step that she hadn't seen since his wedding day four years earlier, Jacob removed the barouche from its eight-year slumber then dusted and dressed it in mistletoe and ivy for the drive. Charlotte had even searched through the old trunks in the attic to find her husband a bottle-green velvet cutaway coat, tan breeches, and high boots that looked like they were last worn in the early 1800s. Looking ever the dandy with a black top hat, he sat in the front seat and drove the barouche down the center of the village for all to see.

Each wearing a dress in a shade of green, Marianne and Polly enjoyed the ride with Charlotte, Irena, and Mrs. Decker facing them backward in the carriage. They passed snow-dusted buildings draped in holly, red ribbons, and American flags.

By the time they arrived at the memorial site, the orchestra was playing and most of the two hundred wooden seats were filled. On the stage with other dignitaries, Ezekiel, in a black wool suit, wore an embroidered damask vest every bit as bold and green as Jacob Graff's coat. While his bowler hat was cocked to the side, he didn't look the least bit at ease.

Hand in hand, Marianne and Polly searched through the crowd and located three seats near the front, on the side of the podium where Ezekiel sat, seats he had promised to save for them. Yet when Marianne stepped back to allow Mrs. Decker to take her seat first, the older woman wasn't there. Instead, she stood on the steps to the left of the stage, talking to Judge Fancer, before he nodded and stepped back on the podium.

⚜

Zeke shifted in his chair for what had to be the twentieth time since the program started. How many war veterans in the audience deserved this honor more than him? All.

After Judge Fancer's introduction of him and as the crowd applauded, Zeke stepped to the podium. Whatever Fancer thought about the report on Polly's cousins that Zeke had given him upon arriving at the dedication, he had given no indication. Now he merely patted Zeke's back then walked off the stage and sat in the empty seat next to Marianne.

The judge leaned close, whispering in her ear. Marianne listened intently.

Then something he said caused her to immediately look to Zeke. Her beautiful face held no expression he could read.

She nodded, and Fancer patted her hand.

Now was not the time to wonder what the man had said, or asked of her.

Zeke focused on his notes, on words he could recite from memory. "On July 24, 1861, President Lincoln made his second call for three-years' men. Captain James M. Brown raised Company K of the 7th New Jersey, the first distinctively Morris County company."

Noticing the tremble in his voice, he breathed deep to still his nerves.

"In the first week," he read, "sixty-four men were enlisted, and the company soon had its full complement. We were together as a company at the First Presbyterian Church, Morristown, on the evening of October 1, when Captain Brown was presented with sword, sash, and pistol."

Zeke paused long enough to gauge the audience. Though most in the crowd remembered the events, they listened with rapt attention.

"Reverend David Irving presented each of us with a copy of the New Testament and Psalms, on behalf of the Morris County Bible Society." From his inner coat pocket, he withdrew the copy he had been given. He held it up. "This book never stopped a bullet, but it told me why I needed God's mercy, led me to His grace, and gave me new life."

As the audience applauded and cheered, he rested the Bible on the podium. With little emotion, he listed the various engagements in which the 7th had taken part: Gettysburg, Manassas Gap, Bull Run, and Mine Run—before taking winter quarters in 1863 at Brandy Station, Virginia. By then, the New Jersey volunteer brigade was in the 2nd Army Corps. And by then, Henry Plum had become more than a brother to Zeke.

Somehow God used a man only three years older to mentor and father him. To show him that God was a warrior, mighty and terrible in battle, and that He intended for man to fight with Him. Henry had taught Zeke what things were worth fighting for.

Henry should be giving this speech.

Unable to continue speaking, Zeke looked up to see Silas Cutler standing in salute. During that winter at Brandy Station, Private Cutler's leg had been amputated the day after his seventeenth birthday. Gangrene.

Near the back of the audience, Jacob Graff stood.

Lemuel Schroeder stood.

One by one, men from Schooley's Mountain whom he'd served beside in Company K stood. *With him.* As if they could tell he was losing heart.

"On May 4, 1864," Zeke recited from memory, "we broke camp. By May 8 we concentrated around Spotsylvania Courthouse. After a day under heavy fire, at dawn on the twelfth of May, the 2nd Army Corps charged the enemy, capturing thirty cannons and Johnson's rebel division. In this battle—the severest of the war—the 7th New Jersey endured brutal losses in officers and men."

Sunlight glinted off the granite memorial in front of the stage. His enemy was no longer a man in gray. It was his own unworthiness to be alive when a godly warrior like Henry Plum should be standing in his place.

⚜

Marianne held onto Polly's hand, waiting anxiously for what Ezekiel would say next.

His gaze settled on her. "I'd been sent on a scouting mission and did not return until the battle was over. Good men died that day. Men better than I could ever be."

"Mrs. Plum," Polly whispered, "what does he mean by that?"

"I am not sure."

Ezekiel stepped to the side of the podium. "I am not the only man standing before you today who does not know why God was merciful and rescued us from an unacceptable-to-God situation. That day at Spotsylvania and the days after—"

Marianne did not hear the rest of his words because her own words came flooding back to her.

I knew a man once who proposed for the sake of rescuing a girl from an unacceptable-to-him situation.

God had been merciful and used Henry to rescue her from an

unacceptable-to-God situation. Henry had then introduced her to Jesus. Without Henry—

Would she be who she was today?

"I have repeatedly asked," Ezekiel was saying, "would I be the man I am today were it not for Staff Sergeant Henry Plum? I choose to believe that God in His great mercy would have brought someone else into my life to teach me what it is to be a man of God, but I am thankful it was Henry."

The light squeeze on her hand drew Marianne's attention away from Ezekiel's speech and onto Polly. According to Judge Fancer, Ezekiel's recommendation had been to place Polly in the Chester orphanage until a home—not with her cousins—could be found suitable for her educational, spiritual, emotional, and physical well-being. Yet because Judge Fancer had appointed Marianne as guardian to Polly until Ezekiel secured permanent guardianship, if she were to marry before he found a suitable family, then Judge Fancer, as he was granting custody of Irena to the Graffs, would be inclined to grant Marianne permanent custody of Polly. *If* she wanted to be a mother.

Her? She had no desire to be a mother.

She had *had* no desire.

Until Polly.

Overcome by the truth, Marianne made herself breathe. This was her opportunity to do for Polly what Henry had mercifully done for her. Yet, she had already turned down Ezekiel's proposal. How was she to go about accepting it?

Be brave, darling.

At that, all the passion, fear, and insecurity she had been fighting just. . .disappeared. She'd never been able to do enough to feel worthy of Henry's love because she had never been able to earn her parents' love. Her life's focus had been to give and to serve others to prove she was worthy of love, mercy, and forgiveness, but she could never do enough. God knew that.

That was why she needed His mercy new every day.

"Sweetheart," she whispered, drawing Polly's attention, "I would like to choose you to be my child, if that is all right with you."

Polly's gaze shifted to Judge Fancer, sitting on the other side of Marianne. "Really?"

"The court approves of Mrs. Plum," he answered. "She will, however, need a husband."

"Mr. Norcross loves her."

"Does he now?"

Marianne felt her cheeks warm at the amusement in the judge's tone.

"Yes sir. I heard him tell his mother yesterday."

"Then what she told me this morning must be true."

Marianne searched the crowd to spot Sarah Norcross Decker standing to the right of the stage, next to the Graffs and Irena.

"Mrs. Plum," Polly whispered, "you promised Saint Nicholas you wouldn't be good on Fridays, and today is Friday. I think that means you don't have to be proper like you always are either."

Not be proper? Could she?

Polly smiled. And Marianne smiled, too.

Today, after all, was Christmas, the perfect day for surprises.

⁂

Zeke returned his well-worn Bible to his coat pocket. He'd never wanted his speech to be about him. The War Memorial was for the community, to honor those who lost their lives in service. God had reasons for keeping him alive and allowing Henry to die.

I trust Your purposes, Lord, and I will fight whenever You call me to battle, but...

Leaving the rest of the service to Reverend Cottrell, Zeke grabbed his notes off the podium and walked across the stage, fully aware of the growing ache in his chest. He wanted more than another battle. He wanted more than protecting widows and orphans. Even if his mother didn't come with him, he was moving to Colorado.

He stepped onto the first stair.

"Deputy, where are you going?"

Startled out of his reverie, he looked to Marianne and Polly standing on the bottom step.

"Home," he offered with a cheeky grin, "before the clock strikes midnight."

He took a step down, and Marianne took one up.

"Fearing you will turn back into a pumpkin?" she asked, moving past him to the top step where their eyes were level. Before he could answer, she grabbed his lapel, keeping him from moving off the stairs. "I thought *at midnight* was the time the prince chased after the woman he loved."

"I. . ."

"Yes?"

The green-on-green print of her gown accentuated the brown of her hair, her eyes, and that kissable mole on the side of her mouth. He should speak. He should. Yet chasing after the woman he loved was the last thing on his mind when she was standing before him.

"I know," Marianne whispered.

"What?"

"I know why God kept you alive, Ezekiel. So that I could love you. So that you could love me. So that we could give a beautiful, clever, and funny little girl a home." She stepped closer to him. "If you will have me, know you gain an immediate child, too, and I know that's asking much—"

"Woman, *if* I will have—"

Zeke would have liked to have been the one who began the kiss, but he was man enough to admit Marianne pulled him against her and did the initiating, and that he gallantly held her close to keep them from toppling down the stairs. Like a true gentleman would.

Even though they were never in any danger of toppling.

Ignoring the whistles and applause, the sudden musical outburst from the orchestra, and Polly clinging to them, Zeke drew his lips from Marianne's to whisper, "Would you like to live in Colorado?"

Marianne released the front of his coat, wrapped her arms around his neck, and wove her fingers through his hair. "I will go wherever you take me."

Zeke raised a brow. "Even if my mother comes with us?"

"I would insist upon it."

"Really?"

Her grin took on a mischievous slant. "Really."

"Really!" Polly yelled.

Once again, Marianne began the kissing. Zeke didn't mind. His goal from the moment he arrived at Schooley's Mountain on Tuesday had been to find Polly a home. Not only did he do that, but three days later, he found a home for himself, too.

And he couldn't think of ever receiving a better Christmas gift.

ECPA-bestselling author **Gina Welborn** worked for a news radio station until she fell in love with writing romances. She serves on the American Christian Fiction Writers Foundation Board. Sharing her husband's love for the premier American sports car, she is a founding member of the Southwest Oklahoma Corvette Club and a lifetime member of the National Corvette Museum. Gina lives with her husband, three of their five Okie-Hokie children, two rabbits, two guinea pigs, and a dog that doesn't realize rabbits and pigs are edible. Find her online at www.ginawelborn.com.